the
GOOD ONES

JENN McKINLAY

JOVE
New York

A JOVE BOOK
Published by Berkley
An imprint of Penguin Random House LLC
1745 Broadway, New York, NY 10019

ISBN: 9780451492432

First Edition: February 2019

Printed in the United States of America
1   3   5   7   9   10   8   6   4   2

Cover art: *Cowboy* by Rob Lang / GettyImages; *Kitten* by Peter Wollinga / Shutterstock
Cover design by Katie Anderson
Book design by George Towne

ACKNOWLEDGMENTS

Big gushy thanks to my men: Chris, Beckett, and Wyatt. The three of you are my pillars of support, the voices of encouragement I need when in doubt, and the best huggers on the planet. I could never write these books without you. Love you forever.

More thanks to my extended families, the McKinlays and the Orfs, as well as my close friends—your unwavering encouragement and patience are invaluable. Thanks for understanding my struggle with dates and plans and get-togethers. I really do try, I swear.

What can I say about the amazing team of people who help me with the books? Such talent! Such enthusiasm! I am so lucky to have you all—Sarah Blumenstock, Fareeda Bullert, Jessica Mangicaro, Ryanne Probst, Katie Anderson, and Stacy Edwards. It is always a magical adventure to watch a book go from an idea to a fully realized work, and I am just thrilled to have you all with me.

Lastly, for Bea and Leah Koch, the amazing owners of The Ripped Bodice. Your genius helped to inspire this series! Thank you so much!

Chapter One

When Jake took off his cowboy hat and pulled her close, Clare wrapped her arms around him and the two became one. When they kissed she knew they were making each other a promise for today, tomorrow, and forever. Clare sighed. For the first time in her life, she knew that no matter what happened, this man, who was her partner and her best friend, would be by her side. For all time.

MAISY Kelly closed the book, *One Last Chance*, pressed it to her chest, and sighed. Jake Sinclair, the perfect man—why did he reside only in the pages of a book? It wasn't fair. She was twenty-nine and none of the men she'd ever dated had been even remotely as caring or charming as author Destiny Swann's swoon-worthy hero Jake Sinclair.

Knock knock knock.

Maisy blinked. Someone was at the door. No, no, no. She had a book hangover and she didn't want to deal with the world right now. If forced to, she might curl up in a fetal position right there on the floor and never move.

Knock knock knock.

They weren't going away. Maisy rose from where she'd been seated on the bottom step of the stairs. In theory, she was supposed to be cleaning out her great-aunt Eloise's house; in reality she was binge-reading Auntie El's hoarder's trove of romance novels. It wasn't making the task, which was heartbreaking to begin with, any easier.

Knock knock knock.

"All right, all right," Maisy grumbled. "I'm coming."

She strode to the door and yanked it open. Probably, if she had bothered to glance through the peephole or one of the long windows beside the door, she would have been prepared, but she hadn't and she wasn't.

Standing on her front step, looking impossibly handsome and imposing, was a cowboy. Maisy glanced down at her book. On the cover was the artist's rendering of Jake Sinclair, in jeans and a white T-shirt, sitting on a picnic table in the middle of a pasture, with a cowboy hat tipped carelessly over his brow. Maisy could practically hear the cattle mooing in the background.

She glanced back up. Jeans, white shirt, and a cowboy hat. This guy had it all going on, except where the artist had left Jake's face in shadow and not clearly defined, this guy was a full-on 3-D HD of hotness, with full lips, faint stubble on his chin, and quite possibly the bluest eyes Maisy had ever seen this side of the sky. She had a sudden urge to poke him with her pointer finger to see if he was real.

"Mornin', miss," the man drawled—*drawled!*

Miss? Huh, she hadn't been called *miss* since she'd started teaching at Fairdale University. Why would he . . . ? She glanced down.

She was wearing her favorite floral Converse All Stars, ripped-up denim shorts, and her old Fairdale University sweatshirt, the one with the sleeves that hung down past her hands, oh, and she had on no makeup and her hair was held back by an enormous pink headband. She probably looked like one of her college students, possibly a freshman.

In that brief shining moment, she was certain if it were possible to die of embarrassment, she would expire in three . . . two . . . one. She gave it a second. Nope, still standing. Damn it.

"Listen, I'm sorry, sir, but whatever you're selling, I'm not interested—" she began but he cut her off.

"Oh, I'm not selling anything," he said. He looked bewildered. "This is 323 Willow Lane, right?"

"Yes, it is. Now, if you'll excuse me, I need to get back—" She let her voice trail off, hoping he'd get the hint. He didn't.

"I have an appointment with a Ms. Kelly," he said. "Or Mrs. Kelly, I'm not sure."

Maisy closed one eye and squinted at him. She usually reserved this trick for her English 101 students when they asked if they could make up the final exam because they'd had a more pressing engagement, like recovering from their hangover, but she was more than willing to use it on tall, dark, and good-looking here.

She knew she didn't have any appointments today. That was why she'd indulged herself in a good long reading sesh. This guy was probably a hustler, trying to con her into buying some property insurance or new windows. Ever since she'd inherited this monster of a house from Auntie El she'd had all sorts of scammers climbing out of the cracks in the sidewalk, trying to get her to refinance or buy a security system. It was exhausting.

The man met her squinty stare with one of his own. He shrinkled up one eye and mimicked her look of disbelief right down to the small lip curl. The nerve! Then she saw the twinkle in his one open eye, and she burst out laughing.

He grinned at her and her ire diminished as she noted the cowboy had a sense of humor. Okay, that was a bonus point for him. She decided to give him a break and at least take his name and number. She could call him later and decline whatever it was he was hawking.

"I'm sorry," she said. "What was your appointment with Ms. Kelly about?"

"It's about the house, actually," he said.

Uh-huh. Maisy would bet her front teeth he was going to pitch all the reasons why she should take out a line of credit now.

"My name's Ryder Copeland," he said. "I'm a restoration architect, and you are?"

"Ryder Copeland?" Maisy's eyes went wide. So much for keeping her teeth. "But our appointment isn't until tomorrow, you know, Tuesday."

"Today is Tuesday," he said.

"No, it isn't," she said. "It's Monday."

"Sorry, it really is Tuesday. Wait," he said. "*Our* appointment? You're Maisy Kelly?"

"Uh." Maisy stalled. What to do. What to do. She pulled her phone out of her pocket and gave it a quick glance. There was a notification waiting. It said she had an appointment. Right now, in fact, with a Ryder Copeland. She checked the date. Today was Tuesday.

She glanced back up at him. He was looking at her in surprise, as if he didn't believe she was the owner of this house. She supposed she could fib and say Ms. Kelly was out but he'd figure that out the next time they met. Plus, she was a horrible liar. She blushed and stammered whenever she tried to prevaricate. Truly, it was just embarrassing. Finally, she nodded and whispered, "I'm Ms. Kelly."

"Pardon?" The man pushed back his hat and leaned in, although he didn't step any closer, probably knowing that at his height, she guessed him to be about six feet tall, he would tower over her and might scare her back inside the house like a rabbit jumping back into its hole.

Maisy cleared her throat and pushed her square-framed glasses up on her nose. Then she repeated, "I'm Ms. Kelly."

There. She used her professor voice. That'd tell him who was boss. Sure, that was why he looked perplexed as he studied her. She tipped her chin up, daring him to say anything about her youthful appearance or general slovenliness.

"It's nice to meet you." His smile was slow but when it came, it was wide and warm and genuine. He didn't look put out that she'd tried to give him the bum's rush. He also did not look like an architect. He looked like a man who'd be more at home on a horse, herding cattle, than drawing up designs for her old home.

Maisy felt her face get warm under his steady regard. She ignored it. Maybe she could redirect him.

"You aren't what I expected," she said.

Mr. Copeland's eyes moved from the pink headband in her short, curly dark hair to her bright floral sneakers, and he nodded. "I'd say we have that in common."

His tone was as dry as a hot summer breeze and it made Maisy laugh out loud, in a full-hearted chuckle. He grinned at her as if her laughter had been his aim all along.

"I'm Ryder," he said. He held out a hand that looked like a big old bear paw.

"Maisy," she returned.

She slid her slighter hand into his, feeling the callused warmth of his palm surround her more delicate fingers. His grip was firm, yet gentle, not trying to prove anything but not treating her like spun glass, either. It let Maisy know without words that he viewed her as an equal. Huh. She liked that.

"Sorry about mixing up the dates," she said. "Clearly, I wasn't prepared for our meeting and I apologize for that. I know your time is valuable."

"No harm done," he said. His voice was kind, and Maisy glanced up and noticed that his eyes were kind, too. "Your message said you were looking to restore your house." He stepped back to where he could see all three stories and tipped his head back to take it all in. "I'm assuming this is it?"

"Yes, in all its Queen Anne glory," she said. She forced her gaze away from his square jaw and the wide set to his shoulders, cleared her throat, and stuffed her fascination with him down deep, squashing it flat by talking in her teacher's voice. Calm, assured, capable, yes, that was better.

"Built in 1880 by my great-great-great—you get the idea—grandfather Stuart Kelly for his very well-to-do bride Margaret Hanover. Margaret is actually my given name, except it never fit, sort of like pants that are too long, you know?"

Ryder glanced from the house to her. He looked momentarily confused and then smiled and nodded. "In my experience pants are usually too short, but I get where you're going, Maisy."

She liked the way he said her name. It sounded as if he was trying it on for size and liked the fit. Be still her heart.

The last date she'd had was with a geology professor at the university, and while he'd been friendly enough, she'd lost her enthusiasm for the date when he'd gone into great detail about an article he'd just read called "Pedotransfer Functions of Soil Thermal Conductivity for the Textural Classes Sand, Silt, and Loam." She was certain it had made sense to him, but she'd spent the meal overeating to compensate for not having one word, not even a syllable, really, to add to the conversation.

She had a brief fantasy, truly no longer than a peripheral glimpse into a crystal ball, of having dinner with Ryder Copeland and talking about books, houses, and whether she could wrap both hands around his muscle-hardened bicep or not.

Ryder pushed his hat back and a swath of dark hair fell across his forehead. His eyes really were the purest blue she'd ever seen, like a midmorning sky after a night of rain, surrounded by long dark lashes that curled up at the tips. Again, he smiled at her and Maisy lost her train of thought for a moment.

House! They were talking about the house.

"Yes, well, my great-great—let's just call him Stuart— was smitten with Miss Margaret, but her father didn't like him, detested him actually, so Stuart built this house to prove that he could provide for her," Maisy babbled. She knew she should stop, but like a runaway train without its engineer she was incapable of putting the brakes on the spray of words spewing forth from her lips. "Finally, after Margaret threatened to run away and elope, her father gave in and approved the marriage. The house is almost one hundred and forty years old, and I'm afraid it's beginning to show its age, like gray hair, crow's-feet, and a double chin, only it's manifesting in leaky pipes, faulty wiring, and chipped plaster."

Ryder lifted his eyebrows. "That bad?"

Maisy shrugged. "Auntie El lived here alone until the last

few months of her life and then it was me and a crew of nurses looking after her. She was a tiny little thing and didn't take up much room. Her collection, on the other hand . . ."

"Collection?" Ryder tipped his head to the side. "Now I'm intrigued."

Maisy thought she should warn him, but really how could she? Seeing was believing.

"Did you want to tour the place?" she asked. "I can show you around and give you an idea of what I'm hoping to accomplish and what needs to be done."

"Absolutely," he said.

Maisy pulled the door open and gestured for him to come in. Ryder followed her, his gaze fixed on the house as if he couldn't wait to see inside.

Maisy would have laughed, because, boy, was he in for a surprise, but his arm brushed against hers, just the lightest contact, as he walked by and she felt a jolt of awareness. A zip zap of electricity and the intense feeling that this man could alter her life course with a snap of his fingers. It shook her to the core.

He stepped fully into the house and lifted his arm to take off his hat. The contact was broken and Maisy felt her common sense fall back into place like sand on a beach after being rolled by a wave. Seriously, she had to get out more.

"Can I get you anything? Water? Sweet tea? Lemonade?" she asked as she closed the door behind them.

Ryder didn't answer. Small wonder. He stood in the foyer, slack-jawed and boggled, looking at the sitting room to the left. Maisy couldn't blame him. Although she had begun to sort and arrange the titles, the room was still packed to bursting with books. Only a narrow three-foot pathway plowing through the center of the room to the settee and matching wing chairs on the opposite end made the room accessible.

"Books," Ryder said. "Your great-aunt collected books."

"Uh-huh." Maisy squeezed past him. "Romance novels, specifically."

Ryder said nothing. His eyes moved slowly over the room, the hallway, and the stacks on the stairs as if his brain could not comprehend the piles and piles and piles of paperbacks.

"Did she read them all?" he asked.

"Every one," she said.

"So, you have some decluttering to do," he said. "Before you get the house ready to sell?"

"Yes, sell," she said. The words stuck in her throat but if Ryder noticed he didn't say anything. She hated the idea of parting with Auntie El's house. It had been in the family for generations. "The rest of the house is equally crammed full to bursting and what's worse is I can't seem to find anyone who wants the books. The fact that they'll likely end up in a landfill would have broken Auntie El's heart."

"Is that the only option?" he asked. "Maybe a library would—"

Maisy shook her head.

"Senior center?"

"Nope."

"Prison?" he asked with a grimace.

A laugh bubbled up, surprising Maisy. "I actually hadn't thought of that, but I have to do something with them all, don't I?"

She knew her voice sounded forlorn when Ryder gave her a sympathetic close-lipped smile.

He put his hand on the back of his neck and said, "Maisy, when I meet with clients about renovating their property, the one thing I ask them, so that we're both clear about the project from the start, is how they want their space to function after the renovation. So, what is it that you really want to do with this house and these books? I saw your face when you said 'sell.' It wasn't the expression of a person who wants to part with something."

A little flicker of hope, or possibly agita, fluttered in her chest. Ryder was right. For the past few months, she'd been dithering about the house and its contents while she grieved for her aunt. But now she had to make a decision. What did she *want* to do with the house? She liked that he put it that way. He wasn't like her two older brothers, telling her what she had to do or what she should do, or what they would do in her place. No, he was asking what she *wanted* to do.

Completely disarmed, Maisy said, "Well, I think I know, maybe, what I *want* to do, possibly . . . perhaps."

"And?" He tipped his head to the side, his blue eyes regarding her with infinite patience.

She took a deep breath and said, "I want to turn this house into a bookstore, a romance bookstore."

Chapter Two

OH, *my God. Oh, my God. Oh, my God.*
  Maisy bolted up the stairs to the third floor. She burst through the door of her makeshift apartment and thumbed through the contacts on her phone until she found the voice of reason listed under *Bestie.* She pressed the number and put the phone on speaker.

"Maisy, my favorite Southern belle, what's up?" Savannah Wilson answered on the second ring.

"Rescue one," Maisy said. She waited a beat and then pulled the pink bandanna out of her hair, fluffing her dark, chin-length curls with her fingers.

"Uh-oh," Savannah said. "If you're deploying 'rescue one' this is serious. Are you on a date? Do you need me to text you a bogus emergency to get you out of there?"

"No."

"Have you been arrested? I'd love to help with bail but I'm kind of strapped right now. Think they'd take a promissory note? Or is it really bad and I need to show up with a shovel, no questions asked?"

Maisy started to laugh. This was why she'd called her former college roommate.

"No, it's nothing like that."

"I'm relieved and yet oddly disappointed. Go ahead. I'm all ears. What's happening?"

"I think I may have just scared off the only restoration architect in all of Fairdale, North Carolina," Maisy said.

"Whoa," Savannah said. "What happened? Did you two have a breakdown in the old form-versus-function debate?"

"No, first, I got the date wrong for our appointment, so rude, and then I let him into the house, and I think the sheer number of books Auntie El tucked into every available space may have freaked him out," Maisy said. She glanced in the mirror and drew in a breath at the sight of her reflection. In disgust, she yanked off the sweatshirt and stuffed it into the hamper.

"Why would you think that?" Savannah asked.

"Because his jaw hit the ground when he entered the house and I don't think it ever went back up," Maisy said. She smoothed the tank top she had on under the sweatshirt. "Can I really blame him?"

Savannah started laughing. "No, I haven't been in that house in seven years and even I remember feeling claustrophobic from all the books, and I am not what one would call an exacting housekeeper."

"You're a slob, Savy," Maisy said. "Your laundry used to be knee-deep in our apartment. I had to wade through your sweaters to get to the bathroom."

"Your point?" Savannah asked.

"Some people find messes off-putting," Maisy said. "And I'm betting an architect is one of them."

She kicked off her Chucks and slid out of her shorts. Over the back of a chair, she found her black flared skirt with tiny roses on it, which matched the shade of her tank top. She located one black flat under the couch and another behind a chair. She hopped on alternate feet while putting the shoes on.

"Um," Savannah said. "Where is he now?"

Maisy crossed the small apartment, which at one time had

been her great-great-something-or-other's rooms for the domestic staff, and glanced out the long window to the driveway below.

"He's getting a briefcase out of his truck or making a run for it. Hard to say," she said. She paused to watch him for a moment. Despite their awkward introduction, she had not forgotten that he was a fine-looking man. Yeah, a man who thought she was a college student. "He called me 'miss.'"

"Why would he do that?" Savannah sounded mystified.

"Probably because I was wearing my old Fairdale U sweatshirt, had no makeup on, and looked like I should be peddling Girl Scout cookies from a flowered basket on my bicycle," Maisy said.

She grabbed the phone and darted across the room to the small bathroom and retrieved her makeup bag from the vanity.

"I hope you corrected him," Savannah said. Her voice sounded tight, like she was trying not to laugh. Maisy couldn't blame her.

"Not right away. I was too embarrassed to have forgotten our appointment," Maisy said. "I thought about pretending 'Ms. Kelly' wasn't home."

"Stop!" Savannah roared. "That's classic. I bet he felt like a dope when you introduced yourself."

"He was very decent about it, actually." Maisy lined her eyes and fumbled with her mascara. Lastly she put a little color on her lips, a deeper rose than her top. "He seems very nice."

"You sound weird, like you're putting on lipstick." Now Savannah was full-on laughing. "Let me guess. Right now you're frantically trying to slam on makeup and a grown-up outfit before you go back out and face him."

"Precisely," Maisy said. She adjusted her top and skirt, grabbed the phone from the shelf in her bathroom, and headed for the door. "The question is—"

"Is it too late?" Savannah asked. "Has he already decided you're as crazy as a soup sandwich and is even now escaping down the driveway planning to change his phone number?"

"Well, if he can't handle a little originality then he isn't the architect for me," Maisy said. She left the third floor and wound her way down the stairs through the maze of books.

"Exactly," Savannah agreed.

"Ugh, who am I kidding? Maybe he's right to drive off. What am I going to do with all of the books in this house?" Maisy asked. "I mean, I am completely overwhelmed."

"What do you want to do?"

"Sell them, donate them, burn them, I guess."

"Yes, maybe, absolutely not. You're not a savage," Savannah said. "You know you don't have to figure it out this second. After that horrible breakup with your ex, who now has the full-time professorship that should be yours, you're out of work, right?"

"Yeah, I handed in my notice." Maisy thought about her ex, Dean Berry, and her stomach churned. The dingleberry, as she liked to call him, had romanced a promotion right out from under her. She closed her eyes. She refused to think about what an idiot she had been.

"So, why not take this opportunity to do the thing you've always talked about?" Savannah asked.

"Skydive?" Maisy asked. "I hardly think now is the right time."

"No, you know that's not what I'm talking about."

"I know. You mean the go-to-Paris daydream, the one where I live in a loft apartment with a sliver view of the Eiffel Tower and exist on cheese and crackers and red wine while I pen my first novel."

"You are being deliberately thick," Savy chided her. "I'm talking about what you suggested doing after you lost out on the promotion to that loser Berry. Your brilliant plan—come on, it's still in there, I know it is."

"You mean the crazy idea—"

"Yes, that's it. The one where you take the substantial trust fund Auntie El left you and remodel her house into a romance bookstore, like that supercool shop, The Ripped Bodice, we visited on vacation in California last summer, and shake off that miserable career at the university and become your own boss at last," Savannah said.

"Funny you should mention that. I did run the idea of turning the place into a bookstore by the architect."

"And what did he say?"

Maisy smiled. "He said, 'Let's get to work.'"

"Well, there you go," Savy said. "And in a weird circumstance of planets aligning, I have some free time. I can help you set up an online presence for your bookshop. Who knows, maybe there is a huge market for vintage romance novels."

"You'd do that?" Maisy asked. She paused on the landing as Savannah's words kicked in. "That's so nice of . . . wait. What aren't you telling me?"

"Nothing."

"Savy." Maisy used her friend's nickname to remind her that she knew all of Savy's deep, dark, warty secrets and now was not the time to withhold. Maisy twirled one of her chin-length curls around her index finger and then pushed it out of her face. "You are a publicity powerhouse for a top publisher, you don't have time to sneeze much less help me unless—"

"All right, all right, you don't have to badger me," Savannah said. "I am temporarily out of work."

"The merger?"

"Something like that. Publicists are always the first to go," she said, sighing.

"Damn, I'm sorry," Maisy said. She was indignant on her friend's behalf. No one was as clever as Savy at promotion. "It's their loss."

"Yes, let's hope they realize that and soon. Rent in New York City is positively unreasonable."

"Then, come here," Maisy said. As soon as the words left her mouth she knew it was the perfect solution for both of their situations.

"Come back to Fairdale, the itty-bitty city full of all-you-can-eat pie, horseback riding, and watching the grass grow?" Savannah asked. "Lawd, I haven't been back there to live since we graduated from Fairdale University seven years ago."

"I know the town's a bit tame compared to life in the Big Apple—"

"Sweetie, when watching fireflies light up the sky is your

idea of a big night out then you have been living in the Smoky Mountains of North Carolina way too long," Savannah said.

"Aw, come on, you're not as immune to the charms of Fairdale as you sound—"

"Ack! I forgot you're a native and therefore required to be a lover of all things Fairdale."

"It's not that I'm a lover. Okay, I totally am," Maisy said. "Fairdale is home, and you haven't been home in forever. Don't tell me you don't miss all-you-can-eat night at Pie in the Sky bakery. They still make your favorite coconut cream. Come on, Savy, you know you want to come home."

Savannah's sigh was so long and so loud, Maisy was pretty sure she was going to pass out before she inhaled again.

"Or not."

"Fine, I admit it. I love Fairdale, I do," Savy said. "I loved going to school there. I loved having you as my roommate and best friend. I loved the old Victorian mansions in the center of town, and I loved the wild beauty of the surrounding mountains and rivers and streams, but I love it more in my rearview mirror than in my windshield. You know what I'm saying?"

"You don't want to come back," Maisy said. She lowered her voice just to give it that little zing of pitiful and added, "Not even for me."

There were several beats of silence and Maisy knew that Savannah was wrestling with her desire to help her versus her desire not to drag her butt all the way down to North Carolina.

"I cannot believe I'm going to say this," Savy said, sounding genuinely surprised at herself. Then she laughed. "I have to be out of my apartment in a few days and I was planning to put all of my stuff in storage and crash at my parents' place on Long Island until I find a new job, which, given the dysfunction that is my parents' and my relationship, will be miserable for everyone involved. I suppose I can job hunt from Fairdale as easily as I can here."

"Yay!" Maisy cheered. "You won't regret it. We're going

to have the best time and you can help me convince Ryder to take the job if he balks."

"Ryder, huh? Is he cute?" Savannah asked.

Maisy stepped around several towering piles of books to get to the window by the front door. She moved the lace curtain aside and covertly studied the man now standing at the front door. He hadn't run away. Bless his heart.

"Honestly, he looks like he stepped off the cover of one of Auntie El's cowboy romances," she said. She felt her pulse pick up and she swallowed audibly. Oh, dear.

"Well, there you go. It's a sign," Savy said. "I guess I'll go pack my elastic waistband pants. All-you-can-eat pie, here I come."

Chapter Three

A BOOKSTORE. A romance bookstore. Ryder pushed back his hat and scratched his head. Of all the things Maisy Kelly had said she wanted to do with the house, even after seeing all of the books, that was probably the last thing he would have guessed. A bed-and-breakfast? Sure. A restaurant? Doable. A coffee shop? Predictable. But a romance bookstore? No, he hadn't seen that coming, which was really shortsighted of him given that she already had the inventory. It was actually a genius solution to her problem. He found himself admiring her resourcefulness as he knew all about making do with what you had.

Ryder had grown up poor, poorer than poor, in fact, and he never passed up an opportunity to work, to use his skills, to make some money, because he remembered all too clearly what it had felt like to go to bed hungry. When there had been only one can of soup in the house, he'd always made sure his baby brother, Sawyer, was fed, saving just the watered-down broth for himself. He never ever wanted to be that broke-ass poor again. And so here he was, taking on a summer project to fill the days and make some money before he moved down to Charleston for a high-paying administrative job.

He tipped his head back and studied the house, its delicate gingerbread scrollwork, with the chipped and peeling paint, that decorated the eaves and the stained-glass window sashes that accented the beautifully arched windows. He felt his fingers itch. He wanted this job. Not just because it would look fantastic on his résumé, but because he knew he could really make this Victorian into something special.

Ryder had been in Fairdale, North Carolina, for the past three years, working on several projects at Fairdale University. As a restoration architect, he'd been brought in to restore some of the oldest buildings on campus to save the university the cost of rebuilding but also to save the core structures that gave the school its historic significance. Fixing up this old Victorian would be his last chance to get his hands dirty and it might just keep his mind off the big life changes headed his way. Not that he was in denial or anything.

He'd worked on a variety of restoration projects all over the country. Traveling to jobs was the nature of his business. Some were straightforward, *bring the old building back to its former glory* types of jobs and others were the *take something old and repurpose it to be something new while maintaining the integrity of its original structure* types. Those were his favorite.

He stood back and stared at the Queen Anne looming over him and tried to picture it as a bookstore. The wraparound porch lent itself to potted ferns and comfy chairs, maybe some built-in display racks that could be opened during the day and shuttered at night. The front door was a big, old, thick oak door. ADA regulations would require it be automated for easy entry for all customers. In fact, a ramp off to the side for customers with mobility issues could be built to blend in with the existing structure.

The interior was more of a concern. He wanted to do a quick check of the plumbing and the electrical to make sure everything was up to code. If not, the restoration project might prove to be more expensive than Maisy was planning on, which brought another concern. Did she have any idea about what she was planning to do here? Turning this place into a bookstore, a romance bookstore, wasn't as easy as putting on some fresh plaster and paint, adding a few more bookshelves, opening the door, and waving people in to buy books.

How many people the building could realistically hold was a consideration. Heck, a structural engineer needed to come out and figure out if a house like this was meant to hold this many books. He remembered one of his professors telling his class about a university library that had to be closed because in the remodel of the new building, the architects hadn't taken into account the weight of the books, and the building was sinking into the ground. It had proven to be an urban legend used to scare young architects, but he'd never forgotten the importance of having a good structural engineer on his team.

Ryder shrugged into his utility vest, which held all of his tools, such as his flashlight and electrical testers, to help him inspect the building and gauge what sort of shape it was in. He'd have a professional building inspector come in and do a more thorough examination, but since he had started his architecture career as a carpenter, he liked to be as hands-on as possible. Clearly, he had no problem embracing his inner control freak.

He strode back up onto the porch, pulling on his leather work gloves, and knocked on the door. Maisy answered on the second knock and he wondered if she'd been waiting for him. He did a double take when she opened the door. Gone was the grungy college student and in her place was a pretty young professional woman in a skirt and tank top, with her loose curls dancing about her head as if they couldn't contain their exuberance.

Her black-framed glasses perched on her upturned nose and she appeared to have put on eye makeup and lipstick. Ryder would have to be half-dead, blind, and playing for a different team not to notice that she was all woman in a delicate package that provoked equal feelings of protectiveness and desire in him. He tried to ignore both, but dang, she was cute.

With one hand, she played with the curls at the nape of her neck as she waved him into the house. It was such a decidedly feminine gesture that Ryder was immediately beguiled by it. This was the first clang of the alarm bell in his head. He had a hard-and-fast rule that he didn't get involved with clients. Heck, he still wore his wedding ring, even though it was now a symbol of what had been as opposed to what was, to ward off any women who might get the wrong idea. He glanced down at his left hand and noted he'd put on his work gloves. Shoot.

When he glanced up, she was watching him as if she found him to be a curiosity. Sort of like the way people stared at the caged lions at the zoo. Good, that was good, he told himself. It would help him shut down any stray thoughts of romantic shenanigans on his part.

Despite the new look she was sporting, Ryder had a feeling Maisy was closer in age to his teenage daughter than she was to him, which made her even more hands-off than just being his client. He was thirty-five and he had rules about getting involved with anyone who did not have the same pop culture reference points as he did, because while some men might find that charming, it just made him feel as old as dirt. Dating anyone who didn't remember life before smartphones and the World Wide Web was a hard pass for him.

"Can I get you some lemonade?" she asked. "It's going to be a hot one today."

Ryder felt a trickle of sweat slide down the side of his face. He was pretty sure it wasn't the temperature that was making him perspire but he wasn't stupid enough to admit that.

"Sure," he said. "That'd be great. Thanks."

Maisy turned and led the way to the kitchen. Unsurprisingly, there were stacks of books lining the hallway that led to the back of the house. Ryder wondered if they were covering heat convectors and electrical outlets and he was amazed the house hadn't burned down with so much potential for fire. Staring at the books lining the walls kept his focus on something other than the swish and sway of Maisy's skirt as she walked ahead of him, and this redirected focus was good, very good. This was a short-term job meant just to fill the summer. He didn't want any complications. Period.

He moved around the old-fashioned kitchen while she poured two glasses of lemonade from a glass pitcher she pulled out of the refrigerator. The appliances were all black, the section of counter that he could see between piles of books was an old style of laminate, and the sink was a big steel double basin. If he had to guess, the last time the kitchen had been overhauled was in the late '80s, early '90s.

"This room seems functional," he said. "Were you planning to use it when you turn this place into a bookstore?"

Maisy glanced around the room. Ryder took a sip of the lemonade. It was tart and sweet and bits of pulp let him know it was real lemons he was drinking. He liked that. He supposed it was ridiculous but he liked that the lemonade wasn't made from a mix. He guessed it was the architect in him, or maybe the Texan. Either way, he liked authenticity in his beverages.

"I hadn't really thought about it," she said. "Mostly, I use it to make my lunch while I'm sorting books. I suppose if the bookstore is successful, it could become a break room for any staff I might hire."

Her eyes went round when she talked about hiring staff, and Ryder got the feeling she was nervous about taking on such a big challenge. That was good. She'd take it seriously if she was nervous.

Knock. Knock. Knock.

She looked surprised at the sound of someone at the front door. She put down her glass of lemonade without drinking and said, "Excuse me. I'll be right back."

"Sure," he said. "Okay if I check the plumbing and fixtures in here?" He pointed to the sink and the ancient dome light in the center of the ceiling and she nodded.

"Of course, thanks," she said.

He watched her disappear with a twirl of her skirt. He liked that skirt. Then he scowled and put down his lemonade. He decided to start with the kitchen sink to see how old the plumbing was. He could hear the murmur of voices and paused to make sure everything sounded okay before he bent down to check on the pipes.

He was halfway under the sink, pleased to see that the pipes were copper, when the voices grew louder and he realized that Maisy and whoever had been knocking on the door were headed his way. He thought about getting up, but he just wanted to see how modern the connection to the sink was. He figured if this was good the rest of the house might be, too. He wedged himself into the cabinet a little bit more.

"I don't want to discuss it anymore, Dean," Maisy said. "You can show yourself out."

"I still don't understand why you're not coming back to the university in the fall." It was a man's voice. Ryder froze. Was he about to land in a relationship drama? He hated relationship drama.

"Why?" Maisy's voice rose in pitch. Uh-oh. Ryder knew this higher register in a woman's voice. This was the *things are about to get thrown because this guy is an idiot* decibel. "Why am I not returning? Gee, Professor Berry, let me think about it. Hmm, maybe it's because you used me, betrayed my trust, and stole my job!"

Oh, man, he did not want to get in the middle of this. Ryder rose up quickly, too quickly, and cracked his head on the underside of the sink. *Smack!*

"What was that?"

"Ryder?" Maisy dropped down beside the open cabinet and peered in. "Are you okay?"

"Yup, sure, I'm fine," he said. She was pressed up beside him as she tried to see and he could smell the scent of her perfume or maybe it was her shampoo. It reminded him of sweet pea blossoms on a summer day, faintly floral and rather intoxicating.

"Who is that?" the man asked.

"Ryder Copeland," Maisy said.

"What is he doing under your sink?" This sounded ridiculously pervy to Ryder and he wondered if his head injury was more serious than he'd thought. "Are you seeing him?"

Maisy turned away from Ryder and glared at Dean.

"What if I am?" she asked. "I can't see how it's any

business of yours, given that you're married and all. What I do is none of your concern."

Ryder felt his head. He was pretty sure a lump was forming just above the temple. He pushed out of the cabinet and rose to his feet. He wobbled a bit, not so much from the knock to the head but from standing up too fast.

"Oh, let me help you." Maisy fluttered around him. She put her arm around his waist and led him to a chair at the large table in the center of the room. Her head fit right up against his shoulder and he was distracted by the surprising bursts of copper that were mixed in among her dark curls. Pretty.

It took him a second to register the tall, skinny man who was scowling at him. He wore glasses like Maisy's but while hers made her look cute his specs made him look anal. No, that was probably his haircut. The thinning blond hair was so precisely trimmed that Ryder would have bet money he went to the barber every week. Even if the hair and glasses didn't make him look so knotted up, the pressed slacks, glossy loafers, and tailored blazer over a crisp dress shirt definitely did. The ensemble screamed that the guy had a stick firmly wedged up his behind.

The professor was scowling at Maisy, and Ryder found himself leaning a bit more heavily on her just to piss the guy off. He let go of her only when she had maneuvered him into the chair and he couldn't think of a reason to hang on to her.

"Let me see," she said. Her hands were so gentle. He felt like he was getting assaulted by a butterfly, and wasn't that just lovely. "It needs some ice."

"Hmm," Ryder hummed. "Ice."

She spun away from him and crossed the room to the freezer.

"Maisy, I know you're angry—" The professor cast him a furious look, but Ryder just sat there feeling bemused by the way Maisy's fingers had brushed the hair off his forehead.

"Dean, just stop," Maisy said. "I am angry. In fact, I'm furious." She dropped some ice into a dish towel and used a rolling pin to smash the cubes into bits. If Ryder were the professor, he would have read the body language and beaten a hasty retreat. This guy did not seem to be quick on the uptake however. "I told you, Dean, I'm done with the university and you. I am not coming back next semester, next year, or ever."

"But what are you going to do?" Dean protested. "You can't live in this broken-down monstrosity with all of these . . . books. My God, it'll fall down around you and crush you."

"This 'monstrosity' is my home, and these books are mine, too," Maisy snapped. She came at Ryder with the cloth full of ice and he wondered if he should take charge of it in case she applied it to his head with the same force she'd used whacking the ice with the rolling pin. He needn't have worried. She was as gentle as before and he felt himself relax. "Besides, Ryder is going to fix it for me. Aren't you?"

He found himself nodding. Of course he would. He would do anything she asked when she stroked his hair and clucked at him with such tender concern. It had been a long time since a woman had tended to him with such gentleness and it was rendering him positively stupid.

"Ryder? What is he, a carpenter or a plumber?" Dean scoffed. "How is he going to fix this whole house?"

Maisy drew herself up straight at that. She stared at the professor and her lip curled just the slightest bit as she said, "I'll have you know—"

"I am a carpenter," Ryder interrupted. For some inexplicable reason, he felt compelled to needle this guy. He decided not to mention that he'd worked his way through architecture school as a day laborer. "It was an unfortunate choice because plumbers have a better union and make more money, but what can you do?"

The professor blinked at him and then he turned to Maisy. "You can't be serious."

"Like a heart attack," she said. She threw an arm around Ryder and ruffled his hair. He practically thumped the floor with his foot like a big old dog getting his ears scratched.

"You have made a horrible mistake, Maisy," Dean said. "Do not come crawling back to me when this whole house comes down around your ears because of that." He waved his hand dismissively at Ryder. Ryder was not bothered in the least. "You had so much potential. It's tragic to see you squander it. What would your aunt El say?"

In a flash, Maisy's eyes filled with tears and the tip of her nose turned pink. It was a low blow, and Ryder felt a white-hot ire rise up inside of him burning his sense of boundaries to ash. He removed Maisy's hand holding the ice to his head and stood. He was pleased to see that he had a few inches on the skinny man. He took two steps toward him, just enough to loom over the weakling, and said, "Leave."

Dean scooted backward toward the door, never taking his eyes off Ryder. So, he wasn't completely stupid. Then he looked at Maisy, who sniffed once and seemed to pull herself together.

"When you come to your senses, call me," he said.

"Not a chance, dingleberry," she said.

The professor's eyebrows shot up in shock and then he glowered. "Fine, you're giving me no choice but to hire your replacement. Don't say I didn't warn you. Whatever happens is on your—"

Ryder took another quick step toward him and the man jumped and then fled. The door slammed shut behind him. Ryder turned and found Maisy staring up at him as if he was her hero. He felt his chest puff up like he had actually done something worthy of her admiration, which was ridiculous. He shook it off.

"Dingleberry?" he asked. "As in not a very bright person?"

"Yeah, because he's Dean Berry, aka Dean-gle Berry." Maisy shrugged. "It does mean 'slow-witted,' but it's more commonly known in these parts as the bit of poop clinging to the fur on an animal's backside."

Ryder stared at her for a moment and then a laugh bubbled up, surprising him, making him laugh even harder. Maisy blinked at him and then she laughed, too. It had been a long time since Ryder had laughed with a woman. It felt good, too good.

"So, what's the story with that guy?" he asked. "Is he going to be a problem for you?"

"Nah. He's just my ex," she said. "In the simplest of terms, he turned out not to be the man I thought he was."

Ryder had a million questions. But this was a business relationship, despite the delicious memory of her wicked fingers ruffling his hair, and he wasn't going to cross that line.

"Are you still up for giving me a tour of the house?" he asked.

She nodded. "Absolutely."

He gestured for her to lead the way out of the room. "Onward."

She beamed at him and with a swish of her skirt she headed out of the kitchen. Ryder followed, feeling as if something in his world had irrevocably changed. But that was crazy. This was a job. He'd do his work and he'd move on like he always did. Right? Right.

Chapter Four

"DAD, you have that weird look on your face," Perry said. Ryder glanced in the truck's rearview mirror to see his fourteen-year-old daughter studying him from the backseat of his pickup truck.

"What weird look is that?" he asked.

"The one that says, *She's the one*," Perry said. She made her voice overly dramatic and he chuckled. The kid knew him too well. And weren't teenagers really awesome for checking the old ego, letting a guy know when he was being completely uncool?

"I do not have a look like that," he protested. He felt the need to defend himself even though he suspected what she said was true.

"Yes, you do," she argued. She leaned over the seat back and studied the large house in front of them through her rectangular-framed glasses. "And this ginormous house is totally the sort of building that gives you that sappy *She's the one* look. Every single time."

"It's a Queen Anne," Ryder explained. "Built sometime in the 1880s—"

"I know, I know," Perry cut him off. "The Victorian age, the height of creative residential architecture in your not-so-humble opinion. Go give the owner your bid already so at least you'll be in the game for the restoration job."

"Aren't you coming with me?" he asked. "You used to love checking out old houses with me."

"Not today," Perry said. She held up a well-worn biology textbook. "I'm studying for my final."

"Right," Ryder said. "Good choice. Very responsible of you."

"Well, I have to have top grades if I'm going to keep my coveted spot at Saint Mary's Prep, don't I?"

Ryder turned his head and narrowed his gaze on his daughter's face. Was there some sarcasm or snark in there? He couldn't tell. She blinked at him innocently from behind her glasses. She looked so much like her mother for a moment that it took his breath away. He shook his head. There was no point going there.

"Did you have something to say about Saint Mary's?" he asked. "You've worked your whole academic life to be considered for their nationally recognized science program. Have you changed your mind?"

"No." Her voice was curt, shutting him down and out. It set Ryder's teeth on edge. Why had no one ever warned him how mercurial teenagers could be? One minute they adored you and the next minute you were public enemy number one. It was exhausting.

"Okay, then," he said. "Be a champ, and if you hear me whistle, come and be my backup."

"In case the owner lady is crazy and you need an exit strategy or a chaperone?" Perry asked. She looked bored. "Sure, no prob."

"That's my girl," he said.

Of course, he didn't mention that the owner lady more than likely needed a chaperone from him, figuring it was more than his teenage daughter needed to know. It had been a few days since his first meeting with Maisy Kelly, but he hadn't been able to get her out of his mind. He wasn't sure if it was because he wanted the job to restore her old house so much or because she intrigued him so much. He could still feel her gentle touch as she tended to the knot on his head. During the rest of the tour, it had been strictly business, but she'd proven to be smart, funny, and kind. There was no denying he'd taken an immediate liking to the petite bibliophile.

Still, Perry knew the drill. If he whistled she'd come run interference and hopefully distract him if he was about to say or do something stupid like ask Maisy out. That way, when things went wrong with the job, because something always went wrong on a job, it didn't turn ugly—well, uglier.

He'd learned this lesson while working with a particularly aggressive real estate agent who had formed an unnatural attachment to Ryder, even going so far as to show up at his home, wearing nothing but a for sale sign over her listings, so to speak. He shuddered. Never again.

He snatched his cowboy hat off the seat beside him and stepped out of his big green truck. He studied the house and then slapped the hat on his head, blocking the sun and taking time with his appraisal of the outside of the house. Yep, she was as magnificent as he remembered. It was the perfect job to lose himself in while he dreaded the changes coming his way.

Perry was going to be leaving him soon. From the time she'd been born, he'd planned to send her to the same elite private high school in Connecticut that her mother had attended. Growing up on the poorer side of broke with an alcoholic father who hadn't been able to hang on to a job for longer than the first paycheck, Ryder had promised himself that when he had kids he would be nothing like that. He would provide. He would give them everything he'd never had.

On the day Perry was born, when the doctor put that red-faced, puffy-eyed squaller into his arms, he knew. He knew he would make sure she had every advantage, from the best care to the best education, that she would never know what it was like to feel hungry or unsafe, and, most of all, she would know how much he loved her. He would provide and protect with everything he had.

The plan was that when Perry left for school, he'd be leaving Fairdale, too, to take the high-paying position of resident restoration architect for the city of Charleston, South Carolina. It was a plum job and it would pay for Perry's education and solidify his reputation as one of the top restoration architects in the country. He had negotiated to take the job in a few months, wanting to be able to spend this last summer with Perry in the town they had both come to consider home.

He stepped onto the porch and glanced down at his hand where the bid was supposed to be. He rolled his eyes. He had so many emotions broiling inside him, he'd forgotten the paperwork in the truck. He turned around and stomped back to the green behemoth, hoping this was not indicative of how his day was going to go.

He opened the passenger-side door of his truck and grabbed his briefcase. He glanced at the backseat, expecting a wisecrack from the kid. A soft snore was the only sound. Perry was dead asleep across the seat, her phone clutched in one hand and her biology textbook open facedown across her belly.

She had wound her pale-brown hair into a thick braid and it draped down across the upholstery, strands twisting themselves free. Her glasses had dropped down on her upturned nose, which boasted a faint spray of freckles. For a moment, Ryder could see the wild young girl she had once been. The one who wore an old football jersey of his over her princess dress, who collected tree frogs and fireflies, and ate her body weight in chocolate ice cream. The same one who greeted him at the door in the evening with sticky hugs and kisses and *I love you, Daddy*s.

It made his heart hurt to know that little girl was gone. Oh, he loved his wisenheimer, practical-joke-playing middle schooler just as much, but every day he felt like she was taking one more step away from him as she forged her own life, and it took everything he had to let her go.

He slung his bag over his shoulder and quietly closed the door to the truck. The day was cool, the windows were down, and it wouldn't hurt his busy, busy teenage girl to catch a power nap while he talked with Maisy.

He had hoped the two would meet today, but if he got the job, there would be plenty of time for that. Heck, they'd have an entire summer to get to know each other before Perry left. He felt a twinge of anxiety at the thought of Perry out in the world on her own, but he pushed it aside.

There wasn't any point in thinking about that just yet. First, he had to get this job and make sure he could keep himself busy over the summer or else he might turn into one of those clingy helicopter sort of parents, which he knew for a fact both he and Perry would loathe. He glanced up at the house again. It called to him, but even if it didn't, he wouldn't care. He just wanted a project, something that would soothe the never-ending restlessness in his soul, also called "denial."

Now he just had to convince Maisy to hire him. He smoothed the wrinkles on his shirt and made sure he was properly tucked in before he crossed the porch to the front door. He had this—really, he did.

Ryder knocked on the door and waited. He forced himself not to shift from foot to foot. When no one answered right away, he tried to tell himself that she was likely upstairs and it would take her a moment. He thought about his first sight of her in her oversized sweatshirt. He'd thought she was just a college student. Clearly, she was a bit older. Possibly a grad student? He wondered what job the dingleberry had taken of hers. Teacher's assistant, maybe? Then he reminded himself it was none of his business.

He knocked one more time just in case she hadn't heard him and hoped that she hadn't mixed up the day again. Not that he had anything better to do, but he didn't want to interrupt her during a nap or, heaven forbid, a shower.

The door swung open, and he felt relief that she'd answered, followed by the swift realization that he had to keep his eyes on her face at all times.

"Ryder, hello," she said. "Sorry. I was packing boxes and didn't hear you right away."

Maisy was disheveled with her dark curls in a cloud around her head. Her skin was covered with a light sheen of sweat—and, man, was there a lot of skin showing—and a smudge of dirt was on her chin. He tried to keep his eyes on her face, really he did, but they drifted down to confirm what he thought he'd seen at a glance. She was wearing Lycra yoga pants with a hot-pink racing stripe up the side and a matching pink sports bra. Have mercy!

Chapter Five

"HI," he said. Ryder cleared his throat and his gaze jumped from her to the doorframe to the hall behind her and back to her eyes, where it stayed. He looked just as handsome as he had the other day, in jeans and a form-fitting gray T-shirt, topped by his cowboy hat. He also appeared a little stressed. Maisy hoped the bump on his head from the other morning hadn't given him a concussion. "One second," he said. "I need to call in my team."

"Team?"

Ryder didn't explain but turned away and parted his lips with his index finger and thumb and let loose a piercing whistle. Maisy stood up straight, not knowing what to expect, but half anticipated a crew of people to drop out of one of the two enormous oak trees in the front yard like an elite squad of house fixers.

Instead a head popped up from the backseat of the extended cab of the truck and just like that a young, lithe body was climbing over the front seat and sliding out of the open window of the passenger side of the truck. It was a girl who looked to be a young teen, wearing glasses much like

Maisy's. The girl had on jeans and a T-shirt that were rumpled as if she'd just woken from a nap, which would explain why Maisy hadn't seen her in the truck.

"Perry, nice of you to join us," Ryder said.

The young girl stretched and her mouth opened wide in a smile. "Happy to take a break from the rigorous studying."

"Studying, napping, yeah, I can understand the strain." Ryder smiled and shook his head.

When the girl stepped up beside him, he wrapped an arm around her shoulders and pulled her up against his side, planting a kiss on her head. They shared the same bright-blue eyes, full lips, and square jaw, making the resemblance between them impossible to miss.

"Perry, this is Ms. Kelly," he said. "This is her house that I'm putting a bid on." He glanced at Maisy and said, "My daughter, Perry."

"Nice to meet you, Ms. Kelly," Perry said.

"You, too, but please call me Maisy."

She felt a disappointed sigh slide out of her. Of course the cowboy architect had a kid, probably a bushel of them and with some sweet adorable prairie wife, too. It just proved the theory that the good ones were always taken. Ah, well, for a moment her heart had beaten a smidgen faster, but now she could just work with him without any of that pesky attraction getting in the way. Probably, it was for the best—really.

"Well, come on in," she said. "I'm glad you're here as I have some news."

She pulled open the old wooden front door, moving aside to let them pass before closing it. Perry walked cautiously inside as if she felt uncomfortable being the first one to enter but didn't know how to avoid it.

As Ryder removed his hat, Maisy noted that on the ring finger of his left hand he wore a plain gold band. Marriage confirmed. She wondered how she'd missed it and then remembered he'd been wearing work gloves when he toured the house before. She supposed it was just as well. After all, Ryder Copeland was so far out of her league he might as well be across the state line. Despite the flutter of awareness she felt when he was near, it was clear he was unavailable, and

Maisy wasn't the sort of woman who took a man's status lightly. Ever.

"Oh, wow," Perry said. She took in all of the books at a glance. "This is lit. I don't think I've ever seen so many books in one place before." She reached out to touch one but paused and asked, "May I?"

"Sure." Maisy nodded.

Perry reached for a novel on the top of the pile Maisy had already sorted. It was a Destiny Swann stack. Being one of the most prolific authors who had ever put pen to paper or fingers to keyboard, Maisy had already decided that Destiny Swann would have her own floor-to-ceiling bookcase in the shop when she opened it. On top of being a local author, Destiny Swann was also notoriously reclusive as she hadn't done a public appearance in over ten years. But, hey, maybe one day Destiny would visit for a book signing or a reading. Maisy felt a small swoon happen and she put her hand over her heart.

"Are you all right?" Ryder asked. His gaze took in her hand over her heart and then flew back up to meet hers.

"Yes," she said. "Just having a fan girl moment. You know, because Destiny." He looked bewildered and she didn't know how to explain so she changed the subject. "How's your head?"

A small smile lifted the corners of his lips. "No worries. The bump is pretty much gone so I don't think the damage was permanent."

His blue eyes were teasing and Maisy felt her face grow warm under his regard. Why did he have to be married? Why?

Ryder pulled one of the books off the stack. He flipped it over and studied the back and then replaced the book, moving his hand down the spines as he took in the variety of titles.

"Your aunt must have read a couple of books every day," he said.

"At least," Maisy said. "Sometimes more. When she became less mobile in her later years, she was plowing through five books per day."

"Five? A day?" That seemed to jolt Perry out of her stupor. "I'm lucky if I can read five in a year."

Ryder gave her an indulgent look. "Don't be too hard on yourself. You have all that Snapchat to keep up with. It likely interferes with your reading time."

"Dad." Perry rolled her eyes and then turned to Maisy and asked, "Is the whole house like this?"

"Yes . . . mostly," she said. "Auntie El didn't put as many books in the bathrooms."

Perry blinked and her dad nodded. "It's true."

"Or the kitchen, well, not the cooking part anyway. I did once find a boxed set of novels in her freezer."

"Maybe the books were too hot to handle," Perry said. Her eyes went wide behind her glasses when she realized she'd spoken out loud, and she blushed.

"Could be." Maisy laughed. Perry ducked her head and Maisy got the feeling that Perry was on the shy side or maybe she was just at an awkward stage. Either way, she was as cute as a button and clever, too. Maisy warmed to her.

With a hint of a smile on his lips Ryder glanced at his daughter. Then he turned to Maisy and she found herself flustered to be on the receiving end of his attention. Without his hat, she noted that his thick, wavy hair was in need of a trim as it had started to curl over the tips of his ears. The memory of its softness beneath her fingers made her fingers tingle. She clasped her hands together and forced her gaze away from him and back to the room.

"Naturally, I'm working on boxing and sorting the collection until we have the shop ready to hold it," she said.

"So, you've decided to keep all of the books?" Ryder asked.

"About that," Maisy said. "I had an *Idea!* and that's idea with a capital *I* and an exclamation point."

They both looked at Maisy and then Perry leaned close to her dad and whispered, "So, crazy?"

"Shh," he hushed her but the look in his eyes was full of worry as if he, too, was concerned.

Maisy pretended she hadn't heard them. Did Ryder think she was crazy? Oh, boy, she couldn't wait until he heard her *Idea!*

"Follow me," she said. "I want to show you something."

She gestured for them to follow her as she headed up the

stairs. The old wooden banister gave her a nice feeling of
support as she picked her way carefully up the carpeted steps
in between more knee-high stacks of books.

Ryder dropped his hat on the balustrade at the bottom of
the steps. His fingers brushed the exposed part of the balus-
ters not blocked by books. "Solid walnut and in excellent
condition. That's as good as a pie dinner."

"You're not from around here, are you?" Maisy asked.

"Grew up in Austin, Texas, in fact," he said. He placed
one big work boot on the step behind her, leaving Perry to
follow them. "What gave it away?"

"Your accent is a little harder on the *l*'s and the *r*'s than a
North Carolinian one," Maisy said. "And we tend to use *d*'s
for *t*'s but you don't, even though you definitely have a slow-
talking, syrupy drawl just like the rest of us Southerners."

"Syrupy?" Ryder asked. His forehead wrinkled as if he
was debating whether to be insulted or not.

"She's right, Dad, you do talk funny," Perry said. She
glanced over her father's shoulder at Maisy and grinned and
then quickly glanced away. It was an impish smile and it gave
Maisy an idea of what the young woman had looked like as
a toddler.

"Oh, what do you know?" Ryder asked his daughter.
"You're only fourteen and have lived in ten different states."

"That's how I know," she said.

Maisy glanced between them. The affection was obvious.
Not for the first time, she wondered what it would be like to
have this. She was almost thirty. She'd always assumed that
somewhere in her twenties she'd meet the right guy, a good
one, and settle down. Unfortunately, when she thought she'd
met the right one, he'd turned out to be a scheming, no-
good—dingleberry. She shook her head. She was not going
to let the past ruin her present. Not anymore.

She watched Ryder grab the end of his daughter's braid
and give it a gentle tug. Perry laughed and swatted at his
hand and he laughed, too. Maisy knew she hadn't known him
long enough to make a truly informed decision, but she decided she liked Ryder Copeland. She liked the way he paid

attention to his daughter and the way he listened to her, Maisy, when she spoke.

She got the feeling he saw beneath the surface of things, of people. Maybe that was what made him a good preservationist. He looked through the slapped-on layers of paint and paper all the way to the original structure.

"So, about this *Idea!*" he began but Maisy moved down the landing to the first door. She flung it open so they could see inside. He did a small stagger step. "Dang."

Perry peered around her father's back. Her eyes were huge.

This had been Auntie El's primary dumping room. It was the first bedroom at the top of the stairs, so it made sense. While the other bedrooms were stuffed with books as well, this was the one that looked as if it might heave its guts out at any moment.

The first day that Ryder had been here, he had mostly been checking the house's foundation—its wiring, furnace, radiators, and such. Maisy hadn't shown him what she was dealing with inside the upstairs bedrooms.

Ryder leaned out of the room and glanced down the book-lined hallway. Then he popped back in, held up four fingers, and squinted at Maisy.

"Safe to assume there are four more rooms like this one?" he asked.

"Not quite as full, but, yeah, pretty much the same and then there's the former domestic's apartment on the top floor, which is also crammed with books. I've been clearing that space out first since I plan to live above the bookstore," she said. "But my thought was to take all of these books and house them in an addition, you know, like a turret." She gave him side eye to see if he picked up on her *Idea!*

"Whoa," Ryder said. His drawl was thicker and Maisy watched his eyebrows rise up on his forehead. "You want to build a turret?"

"Isn't it a great idea?" she asked. She hugged her arms to her chest. A romance bookstore in an old Victorian house simply had to have a turret.

Ryder opened his mouth and then closed it. He cupped his

chin with one hand and pursed his lips. He looked as if he
was struggling to find the words. Finally, he said, "Adding on
a turret is going to be a huge expense."

"So?" Maisy asked. "I have a budget."

"I'm sure you do," he said. "And I'm sure at your age,
building an addition before you have the business up and
running—"

"What do you mean 'at your age'?" Maisy asked.

"Nothing," Ryder said. "It's just that you're pretty young yet."

Maisy leaned back and put a hand on her hip. "I'm not
that young."

"Sure, you're not." The amused smile that parted his lips
looked like one he'd give his daughter if she did something
adorable.

Maisy bristled. She knew she was a little sensitive, given
the recent events in her life—loss of a promotion to an un-
derqualified man being number one—and she knew Ryder's
first impression of her had been, well, unimpressive and her
petite size and round face made her look much younger than
she was, but she had never tolerated being talked down to
because of it and she wasn't going to put up with it now. Plus,
she was a little disappointed in him. She'd thought better of
Ryder Copeland. He hadn't seemed the sort of guy who
would mansplain.

"I'll have you know, I'm twenty-nine," she said. "I have
two master's degrees, I've been published in *Tin House* and
Room magazine, and I don't take crap from anyone."

Ryder blinked in surprise. Maisy felt a surge of satisfaction and she pushed her glasses up onto her nose while she
waited for his reply.

"Well," he said.

"Exactly." She gave him a curt nod and strode out of the
room, leaving him and Perry to follow or not.

Chapter Six

"NOT to be all Captain Obvious about it, but you really blew that," Perry said. She gave him a roll of the eyes with the sort of utter disdain only a teenager could execute and stepped around him to follow Maisy down the hall, leaving Ryder to mull over his own stupidity, because wasn't that always a good time?

He wanted to call Maisy back and apologize. He'd been a complete tool in assuming she was barely out of college, but in his defense, with her enormous brown eyes, and head of impish curls, she looked like she was barely out of high school, never mind college. And on their first meeting, with her in her oversized sweatshirt he'd been sure she was an undergrad.

Maybe he should pass on the job. What he'd thought would be a great work distraction for the summer was becoming an emotional complication. He hated emotional complications. He was an architect. He met with clients. He listened to their visions. He drafted plans to execute their visions and made sure the plans came to fruition. End of story.

Sure, he'd had some strange requests over the years, usually from people who had more money than sense. He hadn't thought Maisy fell into that category. He did not want to be the architect who took her money for a bit of whimsy that left her with no operating capital.

But how did he have this frank of a conversation with her, especially now that she was pissed at him? It was clear she wasn't his usual client. She was a dreamer. A person who thought adding a turret to an existing structure was perfectly reasonable. It wasn't. She had an irrepressible spark of life about her that he found more beguiling than he should. Dang it, he did not want to have to spend the next three months trying to squash his attraction to her. Still, the house was hard to resist.

Ryder glanced at the windows on the far wall and his gaze was captured by the stained glass window sashes on the upper part of the windows. Multicolored panes of ruby red and sapphire blue winked at him. This house, full of books as it was, was also a treasure trove of original Victorian architecture. The thought of walking away from the opportunity to help refurbish and preserve this dignified old lady to her former debutante glory was unthinkable.

Despite his better judgment, he wanted to help Maisy Kelly create her bookshop, and he wanted to see the great beauty hidden beneath the clutter and disorder of the house's present state fully revealed. He wanted it bad. Without overthinking it, Ryder charged after Maisy and Perry. He found them in the last bedroom. Maisy was handing Perry a book.

"You'll like this one," she said. "Trust me."

"That's what the school librarian told me when she handed me the latest young adult bestseller," Perry said. "All the characters died at the end. All of them. Seriously, why would I want to read that? I cried for four days."

Maisy smiled and patted the cover of the book. "No one dies. In fact, in this entire house the only endings are happy ones, because truly, isn't life hard enough?"

"I'll say." Perry nodded.

Ryder glanced at the book. Scrolled across the front cover

was the title *Pride and Prejudice*. He glanced in question at Maisy.

"Great-aunt El gave me that very book when I was Perry's age," she said. "It's a classic."

"Really?" he asked.

Maisy studied his face as if she was trying to decide if he was teasing her or not. "You have heard of Jane Austen, haven't you?"

"Um . . . yeah, the name sounds familiar," he hedged. "She's the heroine of the book, right?"

"More accurately, the author." Maisy crossed her arms over her chest. "The heroine is Elizabeth Bennet."

"Oh, yeah, that's right," he said. He was bluffing. While he'd heard of Jane Austen, he had no idea what she'd written, and Perry was no help as she flipped open the book and began to read, completely ignoring him.

Maisy shook her head at him. She was not fooled by him, not even a little. Of course, this perversely made him want to tease her all the more.

"You've never read it," she said.

"Sure, I have," he said. "Bennet works in an office, helping . . . er . . . spies on their missions. She's in love with one of the spies and when he goes missing, she jumps into the spy game to save him."

Maisy stood staring at him with her mouth hanging open. It took everything Ryder had not to laugh.

"Oh, my God, you just described a Melissa McCarthy movie. So not only have you not read it, you haven't seen the movie, either," she said.

"There's a movie? Chick flick, am I right?"

"Date movie," she countered. She looked outraged. "How have you missed one of the greatest love stories of all time?"

He shrugged.

"Dad, pro tip, it's set in Regency England. There are no spies," Perry said. She didn't glance up from the book.

"Pity," he said.

But his daughter was absorbed in reading and ignored him. It was a bit jarring to see Perry holding a book that wasn't required reading instead of her phone, so he said nothing, not wanting to express an opinion on the chance it would cause his daughter to set the book down. Teenagers being contrary and all.

Perry stepped around him, still reading, and threw herself, as loose limbed as a rag doll, onto the one chair in the room and continued reading. Her eyes darted across the page and Ryder felt his mouth curve up. He almost felt like taking a picture; it had been so long since he'd seen his daughter read for pleasure. Maybe he was a bad father for not making her read more, but he'd never wanted her to view reading as a chore. He'd hoped that she'd find her way back to books on her own and maybe, just maybe, this was her first step.

He put a finger to his lips and gestured for Maisy to lead the way out the door. Perry never even noticed their departure.

Maisy waited for him in the hallway. He gestured with a thumb back at the room.

"Small miracle there," he said.

"She's not a reader?" Maisy asked.

"She was," Ryder said. "Her mother and I read to her every single night, starting when she was still in the womb, and our weekends were spent at the library checking out stacks of books, beginning with picture books all the way through young adult mysteries and anime, but at some point in the past few years, she just stopped. I blame her phone."

"A lot of kids read on their phones," Maisy said. "I'm a fan of paper and ink myself, but many of my students carry their entire personal library on their devices."

"Students?"

"I'm an adjunct professor of English literature at Fairdale University, or I was."

"Professor," he said. "Is that how you got my name? From my work at the university?"

"Yep."

"You don't look like a professor."

"What do I look like?" she asked.

"Really, hadn't thought about it," he lied. He gazed into her brown eyes and realized he would go to his grave never admitting to her that he'd pictured her as a student and not a professor.

"Adjunct professor," he said. "Does that mean that dingleberry maneuvered his way into a full-time position that should have been yours?"

"Excellent powers of deduction there." She heaved a sigh. "He used his relationship with me to cozy up to the head of the department. Turns out dingleberry is a scratch golfer and our department head was in need of a fourth at his club. Never mind that I have two years' seniority, have been published, and am the better teacher. Ugh, it still makes me furious."

"If you ask me, it's dingleberry's and the university's loss," he said. "You're too good for the both of them."

She studied him as if trying to see if he was just giving her lip service or if he really meant it. He did. Very much so. Ryder knew he was about to give himself away, so he spoke, quickly, hoping to distract her. "So, that's why Austen is so near and dear to you. You're a serious book lover."

"Book nerd of the first order," she said. She gave him a mock salute. "And while I appreciate the classics, it's genre fiction that is my guilty pleasure and my first love."

He felt like he had just learned something significant about her, but he wasn't sure what to do with it. Her big brown eyes sparkled behind her glasses, and he noticed a spray of faint freckles on the bridge of her nose. She was ridiculously cute, an observation he was certain would get him a knuckle sandwich, or at the very least a severe frown of disapproval if he was stupid enough to utter it, which he wasn't. She was adorable, though, of that there was no question.

He thought back to the girls who'd been book nerds when he was at school. Sallie Jane Hewitt popped to mind. She'd always had her nose in a book and a scowl of disapproval on her face. Maybe she should have read more books with happy endings. She certainly hadn't turned his head like Maisy Kelly, warming him up from the inside out with her generous smile.

"Well, you're not like any other book nerd I've ever met," he said.

Maisy tipped her head to the side and one of her eyebrows lifted as if she was trying to decide if this was a compliment.

"It is," he said. "That's what you're wondering, right? If it was a compliment?"

She looked surprised and then a grin split her lips and hit him like a blast of sunshine right in the solar plexus.

"I was," she said. She glanced away. "Thank you."

She looked flustered by his ability to read her mind. A very delicate pink stained her cheeks and Ryder found himself fascinated by the embarrassed blush as he watched it bloom across her face. For a woman of twenty-nine, she had an authenticity that was rare and special. It lured him in.

He forced his gaze away before he said or did something truly stupid, like blather on about how refreshingly unexpected she was. He stepped toward the wall and ran a hand over the, dear God, burnt orange, floral damask wallpaper that was visible above the books.

"Keeping?" he asked. Please say no, he thought.

"No," she said. She gave a mock shudder. "That travesty is from the 1970s when brown, yellow, and orange were all the rage. I have no idea what Auntie El was thinking. *Bleck*."

And now he liked her even more.

"No idea," he said. "It's the stuff of nightmares. This isn't even that bad. I once worked on a house that was decorated in shades of avocado green, aqua, and gold, and to make it even more appalling, they papered right over the original wainscoting and put avocado shag carpeting over the hardwood floors."

Maisy put her hand over her mouth and made a fake retching noise that made him laugh.

"And I thought faux–dark wood paneling was bad," she said.

"She didn't," he said. He gave her a pained look.

"'Fraid so."

"Show me." He buried his smile behind a woebegone look, but by the way her eyes twinkled and her lips twitched he knew she'd caught on that he was joking—mostly. She spun on her heel and led him back down the stairs to the rooms below.

Ryder kept his gaze on the thick dark curls where they bounced at the nape of her neck. He refused to let his gaze stray to her very womanly figure. Okay, it slid down once, following the delicate line of her back—okay, maybe twice—but he yanked it back up before it could linger on the nip of her waist or the sweet curve of her—

"What are you going to name the bookstore?" The question flew out of him, derailing the trajectory of his thoughts. He wanted to pat himself on the back for the save, but he needed to remain vigilant and not let his focus stray.

Maisy glanced at him over her shoulder as she stepped onto the floor and turned to lead him down a narrow hallway, in the opposite direction of the rooms he'd seen before, also crammed with books.

"I don't want to say," she said.

"Why not?" he asked.

"You'll think it's dumb."

"How do you know? Maybe I'll love it."

She said nothing. Instead she flung open a door to the right and stepped inside. Ryder followed. Amazingly, the room was empty. It was also covered floor to ceiling in dark wood paneling. He felt his heart sink at what had likely been beneath the paneling: vintage wallpaper, plaster moldings—it could have been anything, really. Anything but paneling. He glanced down. Faux redbrick linoleum from the Dark Ages, or so it appeared, likely glued to the wood floor below. It was enough to make a grown man cry.

"I did warn you," she said. "This was the first room I cleared out, figuring I could use it as an office to oversee the bookshop. I thought whoever took on the reconstruction job could use it, too."

Ryder had a brief vision of working here in this room alongside her. It was a more inviting daydream than it ought to have been, given that she was a potential client and, ugh, the paneling and linoleum. He tried to picture her with the human equivalent of faux paneling, conjuring up an image of her with warts, halitosis, and body odor. He almost had a lock on it when she walked past him and the subtle scent of sweet peas wafted his way, curling around him in a hug of feminine warmth. Damn it.

He moved away from her, walking fast, not running, at least he hoped he wasn't running. He peered out the middle of the three arch-shaped windows that overlooked the far end of the porch. He checked the frames. They were solid. As was the glass. No chips or cracks. He felt a tingle of excitement as he noted the intricate glasswork at the top of the arches.

He wanted this job. He really did. The raw details were all here. Depending upon what she envisioned for the bookstore, he could do the restoration work and still be out of here before the end of the summer. As for his attraction to her, he could totally handle it. He'd just bury himself in his work like he always did. No big deal.

"Between the Covers," he said.

"What?" She froze.

The look of alarm on her face was comical. It was on the tip of his tongue to ask her what covers she had in mind, but that would be flirting and he wasn't going to do that.

"The name of your bookstore," he clarified. "Between the Covers?"

"Oh, ha! Funny," she said. She looked so relieved that he wasn't hitting on her that he was surprised she didn't melt into a puddle on the horrible linoleum floor. He wasn't sure whether to be offended or not.

"No? How about The Open Book?"

"No."

"Turn the Page?"

"I'm sensing a punny theme here," she said. She tried to look prim by pushing her glasses up, but the dimple in her right cheek gave her away.

"Wait!" he said. He spread his arms wide for dramatic effect. "I have it. Once Upon a Book."

Her eyebrows lifted and she tipped her head to the side, as if considering. "That's not it, but I really like it."

"Aw, come on, tell me," he said. "Otherwise, I'll just keep guessing and, believe me, they'll only get worse."

She pursed her lips. She had a nice pout. He glanced away, up at the ceiling, in fact. There were no cracks or stains. It was in remarkably good shape for a house this age. He found that encouraging.

"Fine, but you have to promise not to laugh," she said. She

laced her fingers in front of her chest as if putting up a shield to ward off any insults.

"I promise," he said.

"All right." She cleared her throat and blew out a breath, as if she were dusting off the words before saying them aloud. "I'm calling it the Happily Ever After Bookstore."

She covered her face with her hands, clearly afraid to see his reaction. Again, Ryder was charmed by her ability to let her vulnerability be witnessed. She peeked at him from between her fingers and he wanted to laugh.

"It's too corny, isn't it?" she asked. "You can tell me the truth. I can take it."

Ryder glanced out the door into the hall, to the stacks of books illustrated with women and men on the covers, sometimes alone but frequently together, holding hands or embracing, clothed, and occasionally not so much. He turned back and met her gaze and said, with complete honesty, "Nope, I think that's perfect."

Maisy lowered her hands. "Really?"

"Yes."

Her shoulders dropped, releasing her tension. "Thank you. You're the first person I've told and if you'd hated it, it would have been tainted and completely unusable."

Ryder sighed in relief. He would have felt like a real bastard if he'd ruined the name for her. It was perfectly charming, much like Maisy herself.

"And now"—she rolled her hand at him—"I'm thirsty. We should take a sweet tea break; don't you think? Because we still need to discuss the turret."

So, she wasn't letting that go. Okay, then. Ryder followed her to the kitchen. She pulled a pitcher of tea out of the refrigerator and poured three glasses. She led the way upstairs to Perry, who was sitting exactly where they'd left her, still reading in the upstairs bedroom.

Ryder silently toasted Maisy when Perry took the tea, barely glancing up from the book enough to say, "Thank you."

"Come on, I want to show you something," Maisy said.

Ryder followed her downstairs and outside onto the porch.

He took a sip of the tea and felt the cool bite of fresh mint on his tongue. Perfection. The May sun was warm, but the breeze was cool and he could hear the birds chirping in the trees. It was impossible not to feel optimistic while leaning against the porch rail as a pretty woman bounced on her toes beside him, enthusiasm in her eyes.

"Right here." Maisy spread her arms wide. The tea sloshed out of her glass and onto the floor, but she paid it no mind.

Ryder considered her over the rim of his glass. "Right here, what?"

"Right here is where my *Idea!* comes in. This is where I want the turret."

Chapter Seven

RYDER stared at her hard, and Maisy got the feeling that he wasn't as jazzed about her *Idea!* as she was.

"You can't have a turret," he said.

"Why not?"

"I thought you wanted to restore the house to its original state."

Maisy watched as he put his glass down on a closed box of books and then stood, closing the distance between them to stand beside her at the corner of the house. He studied the walls and the ceiling of the porch as if considering her idea even though he'd already said no.

"I do." She began her sales pitch. "But I also want a turret, and it wouldn't ruin the architectural integrity of the house because turrets were very popular on Queen Anne houses. While sorting through Auntie El's papers, I found the plans for this house in my great-great-whatever Stuart's library and it was supposed to have a turret, but he scrapped it at the last minute so he could hurry up the construction on the house and marry Margaret. He was getting worried someone else would snatch her up."

Ryder studied the house, then Maisy, then the house again. He paced the area. He peered over the railing toward the ground. He then leaned on the railing and glanced up at the side of the house. Maisy pressed her lips together to keep from begging. This was nonnegotiable for her.

"Why do you want a turret so badly?"

"Because who doesn't want a turret?" she countered.

"Fair point."

"They're romantic and whimsical, and I just feel that a place called the Happily Ever After Bookstore requires a turret," she said.

Maisy studied his face to see if her argument swayed him at all. If he refused, she'd have to find a new architect. The thought made her weary.

"The roof on the corner here does look like it was built to bear a heavier load. Turrets usually start on the second floor, so you'd still have this section of the porch with the add-on room above. The cost will be prohibitive," he said.

"I don't care," she said. "I'm going all in on this venture. Sink or swim. Fly or fall. Win or lose."

His gaze met hers. She didn't know what he was looking for. Resolve? Determination? Stubbornness? She had it all going on, and she met his bright-blue eyes with what she hoped was an unyielding stare of her own. Ryder blew out a breath. He raised his hands in a gesture of resignation. "I'll rework the bid and include it."

"Yay!" Maisy clapped.

"Oh, jeez, she got you to add in the turret, didn't she?"

Maisy spun around to see Jeri Lancaster striding across the porch toward them. Jeri was the epitome of poise, from the thick mass of black braids on her head all the way down to her purple-painted toenails.

Her skin was dark brown, her figure willowy, and her smile like a beacon of light in a storm. The happily married mother of three teen boys was one of Maisy's favorite people. Jeri had been Maisy's babysitter when Maisy was a child and they had remained close ever since, even when Jeri met and married Davis Lancaster, the love of her life. The couple lived in a house around the corner, which thankfully gave Maisy easy access to Jeri's formidable accounting skills.

"I'm only putting it in the bid," Ryder said. "I make no promises until I see the old plans and do some calculations of my own."

"Proceeding with caution," Jeri said. "Wise man."

Maisy glanced between the two of them. "You know, I think it's bad form to gang up on me before you've been properly introduced."

Jeri put her hand over her heart. "Oh, you're right. Where are my manners?" She held out her hand to Ryder. "Jeri Lancaster, accountant by trade and former babysitter, also known as the voice of reason to the dreamer here."

Ryder laughed. "Ryder Copeland, transplanted Texan, restoration architect, and facilitator or crusher of dreams, depending upon your point of view."

Jeri grinned and glanced at Maisy. "A pragmatist. I like him."

"You would," Maisy said. "Are you here to torture me with more paperwork?"

"Always," Jeri said. She glanced at the delicate gold watch on her wrist. "I only have about thirty minutes before my next appointment. I can come back later if that would work better for you."

Maisy crossed the porch and grabbed an old yellowed roll of papers. She handed them to Ryder. "These are copies of the original house blueprints. Do you want to look them over while I meet with Jeri?"

"Sounds like a plan." He made a face and said, "Sorry. That was a dad pun. I like to annoy Perry with those. She'd kill me if she was here."

Jeri burst out laughing. "You sound like my Davis with our boys. That was a good one."

Maisy smiled. She liked that Ryder and Jeri had formed an instant rapport. It boded well for hiring Ryder if the two of them got along.

"I'll find you if I have any questions," Ryder said. "Is it all right if I wander the house on my own as needed?"

"Absolutely, have at it," Maisy said. She waved her hands at him in a polite shooing gesture.

"Thanks," he said. He turned to Jeri. "It was nice to meet you."

"You, too," she said.

The two women were silent as he crossed the porch toward the house. When he paused by the front door and tipped his head in their direction, Maisy and Jeri gave him identical tiny finger waves. As soon as the door closed, Jeri's head swiveled to Maisy.

"Wherever did you find that man?" she asked. She fanned herself with her hand. "He looks like he walked right off the cover of one of Auntie El's romances."

"I know, right? Is it objectifying him if I observe that he is totally hot?" Maisy asked.

"Yes," Jeri said. "But it's also speaking the truth. So long as we don't pinch his butt when he walks by, I think we're okay."

"He showed up wearing a cowboy hat," Maisy said. "I almost fainted."

"Oh, man, like one of the cowboy hotties. I have to see that," Jeri said. "Think he'd put it on for me if I asked nicely?"

"Which wouldn't sound creepy and unprofessional at all," Maisy said.

"Hmm." Jeri seemed to consider this. "Maybe you could just take a picture of him for me."

"Jeri, what would Davis say?" Maisy moved toward the two padded wicker chairs, wedged among the boxes that she had hauled out of the house that morning. She gestured for Jeri to sit.

"I don't see why you're dragging my husband into this," Jeri said. "I just want a peek at the cowboy. Did you notice his accent? He has a real Texas twang."

"I thought it was more of a drawl," Maisy said.

"It's too bad," Jeri sighed.

"What is?"

"That he's so good-looking," Jeri said. "I mean, he seems nice, too, which is a shame."

"You have totally lost me," Maisy said.

"I don't think you should hire him."

"What? Why not?"

Jeri opened her bag and pulled out a sheaf of papers. "That man is so good-looking, and you haven't had a real date since the breakup. You'd be like a ticking time bomb with him around. It could be the equivalent of a natural disaster."

"No, it won't," Maisy protested. She reached for her sweet tea and took a long sip, trying to cool down from the thought of Ryder as anything more than the guy in charge of renovating her house. "Besides, he's married."

"Even more reason to keep your distance. You don't want to spend your days pining for something you can't have."

"With a kid," Maisy added.

"Oh, well, that is a game changer. It's easy to behave yourself when there are kids involved," Jeri said. Then she perked up. "Hey, this means a picture of him wouldn't be completely out of the question, then."

"Yes, it would. Stop ogling my architect," Maisy said. "You can't just take pictures of men because they're hot. How would we feel if a man did that to random women he found attractive?"

Jeri was silent.

"Well?" Maisy prodded.

"I'm trying to think of a man I know who wouldn't do that, given half a chance," Jeri said. Then she laughed and waved a hand. "Relax. I'm just teasing you. Of course I wouldn't take his picture like he's just some man candy."

"Thank you," Maisy said. "Now, what papers do you have for me?"

"*All* the paperwork. I have the forms for applying for your business license, your employer identification number, your trade name, and I brought your balance sheet, which breaks down the trust money Auntie El left you and separates out your operating capital, yada yada yada," Jeri said. Then she glanced back at the house. "Just one picture?"

"Stop," Maisy said. But she laughed. "Having seen him in the hat, though, all I can say is he is totally book cover worthy."

"I knew it," Jeri said. "I may have to cancel my next appointment, you know, and see if he needs help with his hat."

"Because that wouldn't be obvious," Maisy said. She took the papers Jeri handed her and scanned them. Accounting was not her gift, so she was ever grateful that her former babysitter had felt a pull to the mathematical arts.

Jeri watched her as if she was waiting for something. When Maisy sifted through the papers for the second time, Jeri chuckled.

"You have no idea what you're looking at, do you?" she asked.

"Sure I do," Maisy said. "It's just lacking a compelling narrative or character arc."

"Let me break it down for you. Here's your story line," Jeri said. She pointed to the figure at the bottom of the page. "That is your available capital to fix this place up. You'll want to be familiar with that number when cowboy-architect man gives you his bid, especially with the turret."

"Uh-huh," Maisy said. It was more money than she'd ever seen in her bank account before but she knew that renovating the place was not going to be cheap and the money would disappear pretty quickly. "What about working capital for the bookstore?"

"That's at the bottom of the next page," Jeri said. "Also, I set up meetings with booksellers for you for next week. You're going to want to be carrying the latest bestsellers if you're going to keep your customer base happy. As one of your customers, let me just say I will be expecting first dibs on the latest J.R. Ward books as soon as they come in."

Maisy flipped the page and looked at the number. She wasn't sure how long she could operate on that amount. She'd been hoping for a year, but it looked like Jeri had estimated it as more like six months. She glanced up at Jeri. "Can I afford you?"

"Of course you can," she said. "I'm giving you the friends and family, *hook me up with books and we'll call it even* discount."

"You can have any books you want," Maisy said. "Seriously, help yourself."

"Good to know," Jeri said. "Suddenly, I feel the need to have a cowboy romance at the ready."

Maisy rolled her eyes, but, yeah, she totally got it.

"Perry!" Ryder's voice sounded from inside the house.

Maisy and Jeri both turned toward the sound. He hadn't struck Maisy as a yeller, so she was surprised when he called his daughter's name again, even more loudly.

"Perry!"

Jeri hopped out of her seat. She strode toward the front door, calling over her shoulder, "I know that tone of voice. That's a worried parent."

Maisy stuffed the papers back into Jeri's bag and hurried after her.

They arrived in the foyer to see Ryder hurrying down the stairs. His mouth was set in a line, like he was trying to keep the concern on lockdown.

"What's wrong?" Maisy asked.

"It's Perry," he said. "She's not reading in the room where we left her, and I can't find her anywhere. She's not answering when I call her name, and she left her phone behind in the chair where she was reading. She's never without her phone. I'm a little worried that she might have toppled a pile of books and gotten hurt. Did she come outside?"

"No," Maisy said. "It was just us."

"Probably she just went looking for a bathroom," Jeri suggested. Her voice was perfectly calm and reasonable. "If we split up, we can cover more ground."

"Good idea," Ryder said. His brow furrowed with worry, and Maisy felt a pang as if this was somehow her fault because it was her house.

"I'll look on the third floor," Jeri said.

"I'll check the basement," Ryder said.

"I'll search the first floor," Maisy said.

"If you find her, give a shout. Otherwise, we'll meet back on the second floor where we left her," Ryder said.

The three of them separated, and Maisy hurried from room to room on the first floor, looking for a sign of Perry.

"Perry!" she cried. "Perry, hello! Are you here?"

There was no answer. With each room, she felt a growing

sense of unease. What if Ryder was right and a pile of books had fallen on her and knocked her out? What if someone had snuck into the house while Perry was reading and abducted her? Okay, that was from watching too many crime shows. She shook her head. Perry was here somewhere. She was sure of it.

"Perry!" she cried. She could hear the panic in her voice and she forced herself to calm down. "Perry, do you want more tea? How about chocolate? Ice cream? Anything?"

Still, there was no answer.

"Any sign of her?" Ryder popped into the last room Maisy was searching, and she let out a yelp. "Sorry."

"No, it's all right," she said. "I can't imagine where she's gone. I mean, there is a back door out of the kitchen but it just leads to the yard and the detached garage in the back and I can't imagine that she went out there. There's the side door out of the study but it was locked, so she couldn't have left that way. And if she went through the front, Jeri and I would have seen her leave, right?"

"This isn't like her, but lately, well, she's been different," Ryder said. He ran a hand through his hair as if trying to stimulate an idea. "I feel like she's keeping something from me, but I can't get her to talk to me."

Maisy wished she could offer him more than platitudes, but the teen years were notoriously difficult.

"Don't worry. We'll find her. Let's go back up to the room where she was reading," Maisy said. "Maybe we'll get a sense of where she went from there."

He nodded. With Maisy in the lead they climbed the stairs up to the second level. She was hyperaware of Ryder right behind her and she tried not to think about the view he was getting. She wasn't well endowed either upstairs or downstairs. As if he even cared if her butt was skinny or not when his daughter was missing. Ugh, she felt like a jerk.

They arrived in the room but there was no sign of Perry. With no idea what to do, Maisy worked her way around the piles of books. Ryder did the same.

"Perry!" he called.

"Perry!" Maisy echoed.

A faint knocking noise sounded.

Maisy jerked upright and looked at Ryder with wide eyes. "Did you hear that?"

He nodded and put one finger to his lips, listening. Three thumps sounded.

"Oh, my God!" Jeri called from the doorway. "Did you hear that? That sounded like knocking from the beyond! What if a ghost got her?"

Chapter Eight

"JERI, there are no such things as ghosts," Maisy said. She grabbed her friend's hand and gave it a squeeze.

Jeri was still for a second before she erupted. "How do you know? Auntie El died in this very house. Maybe she doesn't want you to turn the place into a bookstore. Maybe this is her way of saying no."

Maisy shook her head. "That's it. I'm telling Davis you're not allowed to watch scary movies anymore."

The knocking sounded again—*rap rap rap*—and Jeri's eyes went wide. Maisy shook her head at her and Jeri pressed her lips together.

Ryder crossed the room to a wide bench seat built into the wall beneath the large window. It looked as if the books that had been stacked on top of it had been moved. He yanked on the top. It didn't budge. He ran his fingers over the frame, feeling for something.

"Perry?" he called to the bench. "Don't worry, I'll get you out."

Maisy let go of Jeri's hand and crossed the room to join him. He moved his fingers over the front of the frame. He crouched down and worked his way up one side and then across the top and down the other side. There was nothing. "Damn it."

He rocked back on his heels. He studied the floor around it.

"What are you looking for?" Maisy asked. She crouched down, eager to help.

"Perry. She must have found a hidden room with the entrance built into the bench seat and now it's shut behind her and she can't open it."

"Hidden room?" Maisy asked. "That's impossible. I would know it."

She stopped. Would she know? Maybe no one knew. Maybe Auntie El had kept it a secret from everyone. Maybe Auntie El didn't even know. Intrigued, she started to search the bench and the floor.

"What are we looking for?" she asked.

"I do not like this," Jeri said. Her voice sounded shaky.

"Picture of calm, that one is," Ryder said. His eyes were twinkling, and Maisy couldn't believe he could be this amused while his daughter was trapped behind a wall. He reached over and squeezed her shoulder. "Don't look so worried. Now that I know where she is I just have to figure out how to get her out. These old houses are notorious for having secret rooms and little hideaways. The Victorians were a wily bunch. We need to find a latch or a lever of some kind. It will blend in but once we find it, it'll be obvious."

They ran their hands over the bench and the wall surrounding it. Maisy didn't see anything resembling a latch and she was beginning to feel frantic not knowing what sort of place Perry had landed in. Maybe there were rats trying to eat her or spiders the size of dinner plates. She shuddered.

"Wait," Ryder said. "I think I found it."

A floorboard on the side of the bench was loose. He pressed on it and nothing happened. He tried again in the middle. Nothing. And one more time on the opposite edge. The board came up with a *pop*. Maisy blinked. The board was on a hinge and it opened to reveal a latch. Ryder didn't hesitate; he reached in and yanked on the small metal handle.

The front of the bench fell open and as it did, the top of the bench was pushed up by an arm from inside.

Maisy felt her eyes widen. In the opening, a young face with dust on it peeked out at them. "You found me!"

"Ah!" Jeri cried from behind them.

"Oh, hello," Perry said. She smiled at Jeri.

"Are you all right?" Ryder asked.

"I'm great," Perry said. "Can you believe it? I, Perry Copeland, found a secret room. Seriously, this is the coolest thing that's ever happened to me."

Ryder beamed at his daughter. "I could not be more proud."

"Secret room?" Maisy asked. "Really?"

"Come on," Perry said. "I'll show you."

Maisy looked past Perry and noted that the young woman was standing on a narrow stairwell that twisted down into another room.

Ryder propped the top of the bench up and Perry moved down the stairs to give them room to follow her. Maisy watched Ryder in wonder as he gingerly stepped onto the small staircase. He grinned at her from his perch and Maisy felt herself smile in response.

"This is so cool," she said.

"Now you know why I love restoration so much." He ran a hand over the edge of the opening. "These old houses are full of secrets."

He began to walk down and Maisy peered over the edge, watching him. Perry stood below, smiling up at her as her father joined her in the room below. "Come on! It's amazing down here."

"All right," she said. Maisy maneuvered her body into the opening and stepped onto the top step. "Jeri, are you coming?"

"No, I do not do small cramped spaces," she said. "I'll wait right here, thanks. If you scream, I am calling 911 pronto."

Maisy moved down the steps. She could hear Ryder and Perry below, talking in hushed voices. She wondered why Auntie El had never told her about the secret room. The wooden step creaked and for a second, she hesitated. What if she didn't want to see what was below? What if it was intensely private and had contained some peculiar proclivities of Auntie El that she would rather not know about?

Maisy stepped onto the floor and glanced around her, prepared for the worst. Instead, she felt her heart clutch. The room smelled like honey and lemon, a scent she always associated with Auntie El. In the corner, two comfy armchairs were placed beside a small oak table with a Tiffany lamp, which was turned on and cast the room in a warm ambient light.

On the table, propped on a lace doily, was a framed picture of Auntie El in her wedding dress, standing next to her groom, Edwin Kelly. Maisy traced the photograph with the tip of her finger. She had seen this portrait a million times as its twin was framed and resided on Auntie El's nightstand, but somehow finding it in her secret room made Maisy look at it anew.

The look of love Auntie El bestowed upon her groom made Maisy's throat grow tight. Before she could stop it a tear spilled over her cheek and splashed onto the picture frame.

"Are you all right, Maisy?" Perry asked. Her voice was soft as if she was afraid she'd upset Maisy by finding the room.

"I'm fine," she said. She pointed to the picture. "This was my auntie El. She's the one who left me this house. She passed away several months ago, and I . . . well, I miss her."

Perry picked up the picture and studied the couple. She glanced up at Maisy and said, "She was beautiful."

"She was—inside and out." Maisy felt another tear spill. She wiped her cheeks and glanced at Ryder and Perry. "I'm sorry. I really am okay. It's just sometimes I miss her so much. You know, I think I'm fine and then *wham*, I'm a mess."

"That's why they call it *ambush grief*," Ryder said. His look was full of sympathy as if he understood how she was feeling. "It gets you when you least expect it."

"Ambush grief. Well, that's apt," Maisy said.

She gave them a small smile to let them know she was okay. She glanced around the room. It was surprisingly empty of books, and it was dusty as if no one had been down here in a long time. A fancy Oriental rug covered the floor and a large wooden hope chest sat off to the side.

Maisy approached the trunk, wondering what Auntie El could possibly have kept inside. Was it her wedding dress? Or mementos from her marriage? Maisy knelt in front of the trunk and popped the lid. She blinked.

"What is it?" Perry asked.

"Files," Maisy said. "Tons of them."

The hope chest had been turned into a filing cabinet. Maisy sifted through the folders closest to the top. Each one had the name of a charity and inside was a receipt for how much Auntie El had given to the cause. Maisy glanced at the chest. It was stuffed with folders, and the dates on the receipts she was looking at were from several years ago.

"Judging by this, Auntie El was quite the philanthropist," Maisy said.

"You didn't know?" Ryder asked. He looked at the chest with raised eyebrows, no doubt surprised by the number of folders inside.

"What on earth?"

They all turned to find Jeri on the steps, half-crouched as she peered into the room.

"Come on down, Jeri," Maisy said. "It's all right."

"There really is a secret room," Jeri said. She was giving them the side eye. "And no ghost?"

"No ghost," Maisy said. She pressed her lips together to keep from smiling.

"I knew that," Jeri said. She stiffened her spine, looking like she was trying to smooth out what was left of her dignity. She stepped into the room and glanced around the small space. "Well, doesn't this beat all?"

"I have to ask my grandfather if he knew about this room," Maisy said. She rose from her kneeling position and closed the chest. She would study those folders more fully at another time. "Or my dad. I can't believe they knew and didn't tell me."

"Maybe they forgot," Jeri said. "It doesn't look like anyone's been in here in a long time."

Maisy glanced at Perry, who was looking out the very small window tucked in behind the staircase. The girl looked like she was trying to figure out where the room was so that she could find it from the outside.

"Perry, how did you know to look for a secret opening beside the bench?" she asked. Perry started, as if feeling guilty. Maisy reassured her immediately, "I'm not upset. I think you're brilliant. But how did you know?"

"I remembered a house that Dad restored in New York. It belonged to the Vanderbilts and it had three secret rooms," she said.

"I remember that one," Ryder said. He looked at Maisy and Jeri. "Gilded Age stuff, really crazy with the extras."

"It was huge," Perry said. "I got lost once for an hour, and Mom and Dad completely freaked out."

She glanced at her father and he gave her a closed-lip smile that didn't quite reach his eyes. Perry cringed as if she hadn't meant to share personal family stuff. Ryder gave her a one-armed hug and a kiss on the head, letting her know it was okay. Huh.

"Well, you were only four," Ryder said. He let her go and ran a hand through his hair. "I can still feel the gray hair sprouting just thinking about it."

Perry laughed and the awkward moment passed. She looked at Maisy and continued, "To answer your question, one of the secret rooms was built into a window seat just like this one." She pointed above them. "When I was reading today, I glanced over, and it struck me that the bench looked the same. So I had to see if it led to a secret room and it did!"

Perry's eyes sparkled behind her glasses, and Maisy laughed, as Perry's delight was contagious.

"Well, I'm impressed that you found in an hour what I never even knew was here for decades."

"Question," Ryder said to Perry. "Why did you shut the door behind you?"

"I thought it would be hilarious to hide on you," Perry said. "But then the door got stuck. I panicked for second because I'd left my phone up in my chair, but I knew you'd find me."

She gave her father a charming smile and Maisy saw him

try to resist the lure. He failed. He tugged on her braid and said, "Always. But be more careful next time. This house is very old and you never know when a step or a railing might give way."

"I promise." Perry swatted his hand away.

"You also owe Maisy an apology," he said. "You can't just go tromping through people's private spaces. What if this room had been, well, private?"

"You mean like full of sex toys or bondage equipment?" Perry asked.

"Oh, my God," Ryder said. "How did you even . . . ? Never mind . . . we'll talk about it at home."

"Dad, I'm fourteen," Perry said. "I know about all of that stuff!"

"What? Who? How? You're right, you're fourteen," he retorted. "Entirely too young to even think about any of that stuff." The tips of his ears had turned bright red and he looked completely discomfited. Maisy found this ridiculously charming.

Jeri snorted, and said as an aside to Maisy, "Fourteen? Do you remember when you were fourteen? You got busted for letting Trevor Jones get to second base and wasn't he rounding for third when you got caught?"

Maisy closed her eyes. She loved Jeri, she did, but the woman had not been built with a whisper. Even when she tried to speak quietly, people across the room could hear what Jeri was saying whether they wanted to or not.

Maisy didn't need to check to know that both Ryder and Perry were looking at her. Maisy felt her face heat up like a bad reaction to a jalapeño. "Jeri, that is not . . . I didn't . . . don't you have an appointment?"

Jeri glanced at her phone. "Oh, shoot, I do. I have to go." She wagged her finger at Maisy. "Do not go into any more secret rooms without me." She turned to Ryder and Perry. "It was very nice to meet you."

"You, too," they said together. Ryder looked like he was trying not to laugh and, for that matter, so did Perry.

Jeri went to climb up the stairs and then looked back. "You know, just in case we have upset Auntie El by finding this room, I really think we should stick to the buddy system."

"You're afraid to go up there alone," Maisy said.

"No, I'm not," Jeri protested. She put one hand on her hip and, yet, she still didn't move toward the stairs.

Ryder nudged Perry and said, "Please walk Jeri out."

Perry nodded. With a reassuring smile at Jeri, she said, "It's all right—follow me."

She dashed up the steps with the speed of a squirrel climbing a tree, and Jeri shook her head as she followed. Maisy could just see her feet when Jeri called back, "I'll leave the papers for you to go over."

"Okay," Maisy said. "Thanks for coming by."

"Don't forget to sign them!"

"I won't!" Maisy could feel Ryder watching her and she felt like an idiot yelling up the stairs, but really, after Jeri blabbed about her misspent youth, could it really get any worse?

They heard the footsteps move across the floor above them.

"I think I should probably check the latch on the inside so that no one gets stuck again," Ryder said. "Would you mind holding the light for me?"

"No, not at all, and thank you," she said. "You don't have to, I mean, you haven't agreed to take the job yet."

"Well, I haven't finished my official bid, no," he said. "But after seeing this room and hearing what you want to do with the place, I have to say I'm all in."

Maisy felt her heart thump hard in her chest. *All in.* Then she shook her head. These words did not mean what she thought they meant. She knew that. He was talking about the job not about her. She was being an infatuated idiot, but as her gaze met his and his bright-blue eyes studied her face, how could she not wish he was talking about her?

Oh, boy, this was bad. She couldn't be crushing on a married man she hardly knew, whom she would likely be working very closely with over the summer. She had to shut this down.

She pushed her glasses up on her nose and tried for her most dignified professorial expression. When she met

Ryder's gaze again, he was grinning at her. No man should be that handsome when he smiled. It straight up wasn't fair.

"What?" she asked, losing her composure.

"Second base with Trevor Jones at fourteen," he said. He made a *tsk* noise and handed her his phone, on which he had opened the flashlight app. "Maisy Kelly, I am shocked."

Maisy put her hand over her face. "I'm going to strangle Jeri. No, even worse, I'm going to lock her down here and make scary ghost noises."

"You couldn't be that cruel," he said. He started up the stairs, motioning for Maisy to follow.

"Couldn't I?" she asked. She raised her hands in the air. "I mean, how can I hire you now? It's completely tainted. You think I was a fourteen-year-old floozy."

"Who caught you?" he asked.

"My dad," she said. "It was summer. We were on the front porch swing. I don't know who was more mortified."

"Not Trevor Jones, I'm betting," Ryder said.

"No, he wasn't." Maisy frowned. "How did you know?"

"Because I was caught at fourteen doing the same thing, and I didn't feel one bit bad about it," Ryder said. "Quite the opposite."

Maisy barked out a laugh and then clapped a hand over her mouth as it echoed in the small room. Ryder gestured for her to move closer. They were pressed together on the steps and he checked the edges of the opening, much as he had before. He pointed and Maisy shined the light in that spot. He reached up with a pocket knife and began to tighten the screws that held the inside latch in place.

"What was her name?" she asked.

Ryder glanced down at her and she realized they were close enough to be breathing the same air. It was oddly intimate and she wasn't sure if she wanted to press herself closer or jump back. She opted to stop breathing. Because that seemed a reasonable choice.

"Amanda Cook," he said. "I've never forgotten her."

"Oh, jeez, I'm hoping Trevor has forgotten me."

"Guys never forget. I know I'd never forget you," he said. Maisy wasn't sure if it was the heat in his gaze or the lack of oxygen from not breathing but she was pretty sure she was going to pass out. Ryder looked like he wanted to say something more but instead he pointed to a spot just above their heads and said, "Light, please."

Maisy shined the bright light on it and watched as he shut the doors and then pulled the latch and the doors popped open.

"Good," he said. "I don't think it was broken so much as Perry couldn't find it."

He led the way out of the secret room and then turned around and offered her a hand out of the crawl space. Again, Maisy was struck by how small her hand felt in his. When she stood beside him, she handed him his phone and tilted her head up to glance at his face.

"Well, I can honestly say everything about this day was unexpected," she said.

Ryder nodded, his gaze holding hers. "Agreed."

They met Perry in the hallway, and Maisy walked them out. Ryder said he'd have a new estimate for her within a matter of days. Maisy figured that gave her three to four days to get her reaction to him under control. She did not want to spend her summer, as Jeri said, pining for someone she couldn't have.

Still, even if Ryder Copeland refused this job, or it didn't work out, she was glad she had met him and his daughter. It reminded her that she wanted more out of life and maybe, just maybe, opening the Happily Ever After Bookshop was her first step.

Chapter Nine

"JAYNE Ann Krentz," Savannah said. "Are we shelving her with her alter ego Amanda Quick or keeping them separate?"

"Separate," Maisy said. "Quick is her historical pen name while Krentz is contemporary. Besides, any true fan will know that she's both."

"And Jayne Castle, too," Savannah added.

"Right," Maisy said. She glanced around at the piles and piles of books that didn't seem to be moving so much as being reshuffled. She tried not to be discouraged. Surely, they were making some sort of progress. Right? She glanced at Savannah and asked, "Is it wine o'clock yet?"

Savannah, who had arrived a few days ago, tossed back her long red hair and glanced at her wrist, the one that did not have a watch on it. "Well, hey, look at that! It is!"

She dropped the pile she was sorting back onto the floor and dusted off her hands. Then she rolled to her feet and held out her hand to Maisy.

"Right on." Maisy grabbed her hand and let her pull her to her feet.

They both stepped back and surveyed the room. To Maisy, it looked as if they were never going to get it sorted, but she refused to give up. She had quit her job. There was no going back to teaching for her.

When the announcement had come that Dean Berry was going to get the position of full-time professor instead of her, she had been stunned at first. Denial had followed swiftly after that. Surely, there must have been some mistake. Then, as the truth sank in, the rage came. He had one less master's degree and two years' less experience than she did. What he did have, however, was insider information from Maisy about the interview panel and what they were looking for—a scratch golfer, apparently—in a new hire. Oh, and he had a wife!

The humiliation still burned in her gut like a lava pit of rage. Maisy had met Dean Berry online. They were both English professors and even though he lived in Raleigh and taught at North Carolina State, she had thought they could make their long-distance relationship work because they had so much in common.

They had dated for a year. He coached her for her application for the full-time professor position at Fairdale University, all the while planning to nab it for himself, and Maisy had thought he was the most wonderful man she'd ever met. Right up until she came out of her interview and found him *waiting to be interviewed and sitting next to him was his wife!* She would never forget the feeling of ultimate betrayal. When he got the job, she had almost quit on the spot. Sheer pride had made her finish the semester.

She was determined to make a success of this shop or go down in flames. She had enjoyed her students and loved her job, but now she had the freedom of being her own boss. She could make her own hours and be in charge of her days. If she had to work sixteen-hour days seven days a week, so be it. Still, the books.

"Hey, don't stress. We got this," Savy said.

She was taller than Maisy by a lot and when she looped an arm around Maisy's shoulders and pulled her close, Maisy felt like a little kid being consoled by her big sister. The feeling should have chafed but it didn't. She was so glad her friend had come. In the time Savy had been here they'd managed to organize and sort two of the upstairs bedrooms, and whenever Maisy felt like she was going to collapse, Savy picked her up and brushed her off and made her keep on moving.

"So, when do I get to meet cowboy-architect guy?" Savy asked.

"Soon," Maisy said. She brushed off her hands, trying to look calm and composed. "I have to give Ryder an answer on the revised bid he dropped off by tomorrow."

"Oh, man, you've got it bad," Savannah said. "You can't even say his name without a dreamy look in your eyes."

"Pretty sure it's just dust," Maisy argued. She rubbed her eyes as if to prove her point. "He's just a nice guy. Is it so wrong to appreciate a nice guy? I mean, they're super rare, like Unicorn Frappuccinos."

"Which are disgusting."

"I kind of dig them."

"That's because you like anything with glitter on it," Savy said. "You're the only person I know who thinks everything is better if you add a little glitter."

"I'm not wrong," Maisy said.

"You've got that stubborn look on your face. I can see there is no point in debating you."

"About Ryder or glitter?"

"Both. Now, let's go. I can hear our wine calling my name."

Together they made their way up the two flights of stairs to the third floor, where they were sharing the former domestic's apartment, which mercifully had two bedrooms. The evening was warm so they'd left all the windows open and a beautiful cross breeze blew through the rooms, clearing out the dust and stale air, making everything seem fresh and new.

"So, what was the total of Ryder's estimate?" Savannah asked. Maisy opened the folder that contained the bid and handed it to her.

Savy let loose a low whistle. "That's a lot of money."

"I know," Maisy said. "When I cashed out the annuity Auntie El left me, I knew it was going to have to be put right back into the house whether I want to sell it or turn it into a bookstore."

"Is Ryder in line with the other estimates you've gotten?"

Maisy felt her face get warm. She fibbed anyway. "Yeah, totally."

Savannah stared at her. "Don't. Do not. For the love of Spanx, do not tell me that you haven't gotten any other bids."

"Okay, I won't tell you."

"M, you have got to check this infatuation right now," Savannah said.

"I am not infatuated," she protested.

"Girl, I have known you for eleven years. You are so crushing on the cowboy architect."

"I'm not," Maisy tried fibbing again. She was totally crushing, but she didn't feel the need to dwell on it. "I mean, he's married and with a kid. It would be stupid to get all fixated on a man who is taken."

"You're kidding, right? Your whole modus operandi is to find the most emotionally unavailable man in a fifty-mile radius and make him the focus of your interest for months. The more unavailable, the better."

"No, I don't."

"Yes, you do," Savy said. "The best relationship of your life was with dingleberry and he was just out to steal your job and was already married!"

Maisy winced. She hated even thinking about that job-stealing troll.

"I'm sorry," Savy said. "But I think you like the idea of a boyfriend more than the reality of one."

"That's ridiculous," Maisy said.

"Really? Name one guy you've been involved with that wasn't defective in some way."

"That's not relevant to this discussion," Maisy insisted. "Listen, I didn't get many bids because it's not as if there are a ton of restoration architects in Fairdale, North Carolina. As for liking Ryder, it doesn't matter, because he's married."

"Exactly. Which is why Ryder is even more dangerous for you. You'll give him the job and then pine for him for months for no good reason."

"It's not my fault he's unavailable."

"No, but it is your fault that you are obviously smitten and you haven't even tried to get bids from other architects, even if they're not in Fairdale." She gave Maisy a sympathetic look. "I don't mean to be a hard-ass but if you don't get at least two more bids, I'm going to do it myself."

"Fine," Maisy said. She tried to sound as if she actually was fine with this option. She wasn't. She couldn't even imagine anyone but Ryder working on the house. He loved the house as much as she did. It was kismet. She was sure of it.

"One of my missions while I'm here is going to be to get you into circulation," Savannah said. "I'm thinking we'll sign up for speed dating, maybe do some singles' happy hours, and there's a fun run we can do, too. A five-K just for singles."

"Fun run? That's an oxymoron, you know."

Savannah laughed and said, "It'll be great. You'll see."

"Oh, man, what have I done?" Maisy asked. "You're going to commandeer my life, aren't you?"

"Just the parts that need it," Savy said. She pointed to the folder with the bid. "Now, put that away. I declare tonight to be movie night. You know what that means."

"Yes, and it's glorious!" Maisy said. "Pajamas, cookies, ice cream, potato chips, and wine. Am I missing anything?"

"What movie are we watching?" Savannah said. "Has to be a chick flick. That's a rule."

"Okay, but nothing that will make me cry," Maisy said. "I'm battling enough tears over Auntie El as it is on a daily basis."

"Okay, then," Savannah said. She walked over to the small kitchenette and opened the pantry. "*Love Actually*?"

"Too Christmassy," Maisy answered. She ducked into her bedroom and changed into her pajamas, which consisted of a pink Bazooka gum tank top and matching pink plaid cotton bottoms. "How about *10 Things I Hate About You*?"

"I can't," Savannah said. "I'm still grieving for Heath Ledger. I'll cry."

"Understandable," Maisy agreed. She returned to the

kitchen and took over pouring the wine while Savannah ducked into her room to change.

"*Four Weddings and a Funeral*?" Savannah returned in pajamas much like Maisy's except they were green and sported a vintage 7 Up logo.

"No, I always cry at the funeral part, plus I feel bad for Duckface," Maisy said.

"She does look like a duck, though," Savannah said.

"Which is why I feel bad for her."

"I'm running out of ideas."

"We must look to the Cusack. He's the go to romcom guy."

"*Must Love Dogs* or *Say Anything* . . . ?"

"No, even better," Maisy said. "*The Sure Thing*."

"Oh, yes! A Rob Reiner film for the win. Daphne Zuniga and John Cusack, two broke college kids crossing the country in search of a 'sure thing.' Fabulous!" Savy held up her hand for a high five, and Maisy complied.

Agreed on their film, they set to work dishing ice cream and putting the chips into big bowls while cuing up the movie. The cramped living quarters consisted of two small bedrooms, the kitchenette, and one main room that was a shared common area. The room was sparsely decorated with the couch and television Maisy'd had in her old apartment.

She had taken the opportunity when she moved to declutter most of her belongings, realizing she really didn't need to keep her arts and crafts projects from the third grade or the volcano from her middle school science fair, which never worked when it was supposed to, opting to go off in the middle of someone else's presentation and spraying Maisy's science teacher right in the face. The D she got in that class had not been a big surprise.

The move had been cathartic, although she supposed it could be argued that she had just traded her own stuff for Auntie El's. Whatever. Auntie El had cooler stuff.

Savannah had just started the movie when the sound of banging ruptured the quiet and Maisy's pre-movie anticipation.

Savy raised one eyebrow. "Are we expecting anyone?"

"No," she said. "The only person likely would be Jeri, but she has a PTO meeting."

"We're in our pajamas," Savy said. "Maybe if we ignore them, they'll go away."

"It might be important."

"Then go answer it."

"But it's two flights down and then back up."

Savannah drooped her head on the back of the couch. "Fine, we'll RPS for it. One, two, three, shoot."

They shook their fists three times. Maisy went with paper, knowing that Savannah always played rock. Except for when she didn't, which was right now. Savannah's split-fingered scissors cut Maisy's paper.

"Two out of three," Maisy said.

"No."

Maisy made a face and rolled off the couch. "Don't eat all of the chips."

"Then don't take too long or I'll only leave you the crumbs."

Maisy picked up her pace. Savannah was tall, which meant she was able to pack away more chow than a vertically challenged gal like Maisy. Besides, Maisy hated the potato chip crumbs and Savy knew it.

She ducked and weaved between stacks of books as she jogged lightly down the first flight of steps, crossed the landing, and began down the second flight. She ran her fingers lightly over the banister, keeping it in reach in case one of the books tripped her up. *Note to self: get the books off the stairs.* They were a hazard.

Since she was in just her pajamas and it was getting dark outside, she flipped on the porch light and peered through the peephole before she opened the door. To her surprise, Perry was standing there. She was holding the book Maisy had given her and looking forlorn. Maisy moved her gaze from side to side. Perry appeared to be alone. Maisy let out a sigh of relief, as she was in her pajamas, refusing to acknowledge the twinge of disappointment that came with it.

"Perry, is everything all right?" she asked as she opened the door.

Chapter Ten

PERRY shifted from foot to foot. She looked nervous so Maisy smiled at her, hoping to put the girl at ease. Perry looked more alarmed than comforted and Maisy wondered if she had something stuck in her teeth. She surreptitiously tried to check with her tongue while she waited for Perry to say something.

"I finished the book!" Perry said. She thrust the copy of *Pride and Prejudice* at Maisy as if it were hot.

"Oh, great!" Maisy took the book. "What did you think?"

"I loved it," Perry gushed. "It was sweet and charming and Elizabeth Bennet is the best heroine ever, like how she doesn't let Darcy get away with his rudeness and how she stands by her family even though they are horribly embarrassing."

Maisy grinned. "She is wonderful, isn't she?"

Perry nodded. She twisted her fingers together in front of her waist. She looked as if she wanted to say something but she didn't know what.

"I'm going to take a wild guess here," Maisy said. She wagged the book at Perry. "This was your gateway drug, wasn't it? And now you're looking for another hit."

Perry glanced over each shoulder and then pushed her glasses up her nose. She leaned in close and in a low voice, she said, "So, can you hook me up? No one has to know."

It took Maisy a second to realize Perry was teasing her, and when she did, a surprised laugh barked out of her. Perry gave her a shy smile and Maisy decided she liked this kid—a lot. With her free hand she grabbed the teen by the arm and hauled her into the house.

"Take anything you want," Maisy said. "Take a bagful or a truckload, whatever will get you through the day."

Perry danced on her toes. "Thank you." Then she glanced around at the piles and piles and piles of books. "Um, I'm not sure where to start."

Maisy sighed. "That makes two of us."

They stood together, taking it all in, when a voice called from above, "John Cusack is on deck, what is the holdup?"

"Keep your pants on," Maisy yelled back. "I'm doing my very first reader advisory here."

"Ooooh, aren't you fancy with the booksy terms," Savy said. Then she noticed Perry and said, "Hi."

Perry's eyes went wide. Small wonder. Standing on the landing above them, with her fiery hair now in a ball on the top of her head, and wearing a tank top that showed off her muscular physique, Savannah looked like an Amazon.

"Hi," Perry chirped.

Savannah tipped her head to the side and then glanced at Maisy with a curious look. There was no dodging it—all she could hope was that Savannah didn't say anything mortifying.

"This is Perry Copeland. She's Ryder's daughter," Maisy said. "Perry, this is my roommate and social media strategist, Savannah Wilson."

"Hang on. I don't do intros from a floor away." And with that Savannah sat on the banister and slid her way down to them. She wobbled once, making Maisy yelp, and she kicked over two piles of books, making a mess, but she landed on her feet on the floor beside them, looking so pleased with herself that Maisy didn't have the heart to yell at her.

Savannah held out a hand to Perry. "Nice to meet you."

Perry looked even more owl eyed, but she took Savy's hand and said, "That was so cool."

"Thanks, I've been wanting to try it forever."

"Please tell me you've gotten it out of your system," Maisy said.

"Absolutely," Savy said. "For now. Plus, I think I got a splinter in my butt."

Maisy rolled her eyes. "Perry is here returning a book she borrowed and now she's looking for a new one."

"Well, this is the place. What are you looking for? Contemporary comedy? Historical? Suspenseful? Paranormal?"

"Para-what-al?" Perry asked.

"You know, with vampires and stuff," Savannah said.

"Can I have one of each?"

"Done," Maisy said.

She perused the titles. She didn't want to give the teen anything too erotic so she went with *The Hating Game*, *Venetia*, *The Other Daughter*, and *Born at Midnight*. She handed the pile to Perry.

"*Venetia* is a Regency by Georgette Heyer, the most Austen-like. If you want more, feel free to stop by anytime. We have all of hers."

"Thank you so much," Perry said. She cradled the books in her arms.

"Cool. Now come on upstairs and join us for junk food and a chick flick," Savy said.

"Oh, I should probably go," Perry said.

"Are your parents expecting you home?" Savy asked.

"No, Dad and Uncle Quino have soccer tonight," she said. "They won't be home until later."

"Uncle?" Maisy asked. "I didn't realize you had family here."

"I don't. Technically, Joaquin Solis is not my uncle," Perry said. "I've just called him that since I was born. He's my godfather, actually."

"Oh." Savy sent Maisy a look. Unfortunately, Maisy had no idea what it was supposed to mean, otherwise she would have waved her off or possibly tackled her to keep her from going where she went.

"So, does your mom play soccer, too?"

Perry shook her head. "Nah, at least, I don't think so. She doesn't live here."

"Really?" Savy asked. She made her green eyes round with curiosity. "Where does she live?'

"Well, when Dad and I moved here, she moved to Los Angeles," Perry said. "Then she went to Vancouver for a while for a show she was on. Now she's pretty much back and forth between Vancouver and L.A."

Savannah's eyes narrowed, but Perry was looking at the books in her hands and missed it. When she glanced up, Savannah was smiling. Maisy stood behind Perry, making slashing motions across her throat. This was not their business, not even a little.

Savannah looped her arm through Perry's and led her to the stairs. "Come on, then, text your dad and ask if you can join us for some movie time and ice cream."

"Okay, thanks," Perry said. She pulled out her phone and fired off a text to her father. In seconds, her phone chimed. "He wants to know what the movie is."

"Well, it was going to be *The Sure Thing* but to celebrate your finishing the book, we simply have to watch *Pride and Prejudice*," Maisy said.

"Firth or Macfadyen?" Savannah asked.

"Has to be Macfadyen," Maisy said. "The Firth one is six hours long. We'd be up all night."

Savannah and Perry both stared at her.

"No," Maisy said. She looked pointedly at Perry. "It's a school night."

"But the lake scene," Savannah protested.

"No," Maisy said.

Perry sighed and texted her father. Savannah smiled over the girl's head at Maisy and then wiggled her eyebrows. Maisy glowered. She was not discussing Ryder, not even in pantomime.

"Dad says it's okay, but to hold the movie for him," she said. "He's coming over and he's bringing pizza."

"Well, well, well," Savannah said.

Maisy shook her head, discouraging any rosy glow

Savannah was attaching to Ryder's motives. "That's because he's never seen it before."

"How do you know?"

"He told me when I lent Perry the book."

"It's true," Perry said. "He didn't even know who Jane Austen was."

"Horror," Savannah said.

"Right?" Perry asked.

The two of them turned and headed up the stairs, leaving Maisy to lock the front door and follow. They had just reached the first landing when Savy decided to clarify. "So even though your parents live in different states, they're still married? That takes a lot of work."

"Oh, no," Perry said. "They're divorced. They divorced three years ago when my mom went to Los Angeles for her career."

A book lurched off its pile and tripped Maisy. That was the only reason she could figure she was sprawled facedown on the steps.

"Are you all right?"

"Yup, just fine," Maisy lied. Nope, there was nothing to see here. Just that the earth had collapsed beneath her feet at the news that Ryder was single and she was having a complete freak-out. Otherwise, situation normal.

"Tomorrow we clean the stairs," Savy said as she reached down and hauled Maisy to her feet. "Priority one."

"Right," Maisy said. She wasn't listening. Savannah could have said they were going to get belly piercings the next day and she would have agreed, because she was consumed with this brand-new information *that changed everything*.

"But, Perry, your dad wears a wedding ring." The words flew out before Maisy had the presence of mind to stop them. Luckily, Perry didn't seem to think Maisy noticing her dad's ring was odd.

"Yeah, the women were chasing Dad pretty hard when he first got divorced. He said he wasn't interested in a relationship anytime soon," Perry said. "So he put his ring back on, hoping it would ward them off."

"Like garlic to a vampire," Savy said.

"Exactly," Perry said. "Only it doesn't seem to work on everyone."

"Imagine that," Savannah said. Her tone said she wasn't surprised at all.

"Yeah, turns out some women don't care that he's married. In fact, in some cases the women seem to chase him even more," Perry said. "That was a glimpse into human nature I did not need to see at my tender age."

"Preach it, sister," Savy said. "Thankfully, we have just the remedy for that. A little Elizabeth Bennet played by Keira Knightley will make everything all right."

Savannah broke into a jog and they trotted up the last flight of stairs, leaving Maisy to follow them with her heart thumping wildly in her chest and her pulse pounding in her ears. Ryder wasn't married. He was single. Available, but wearing a ring to ward off anyone who might be interested. Wait! Was he wearing it to keep her at arm's length?

Maisy wasn't sure how she felt about that. Had she been too aggressive? Did he think she was interested? She felt a hot flush color her face. This was just so embarrassing. She mentally reviewed all of her interactions with Ryder to see if there was anything she had done that was forward or pushy or inappropriate. She couldn't think of anything.

Still, he wore his ring, and he had never mentioned that he was divorced. Clearly, he was only interested in a professional relationship between them, which of course he was. Why was she even thinking that it could or should be anything else? Maisy slapped her forehead with her palm. She had to get it together.

Then again, he was coming over and bringing pizza. But only because his daughter was here! Ugh, Maisy felt like she was going to have a brain hemorrhage.

As soon as they got into the small apartment, she poured Perry a soda and then ducked into her room to change. She was not wearing her hang-out pajamas around the man. Savannah must have felt the same because she disappeared into her room, too. They both returned wearing jeans and T-shirts with all of the appropriate undergarments on.

A knock sounded downstairs and Perry jumped up from her seat on the floor and shouted, "I'll get it."

Maisy was more than happy to let her. The up-and-down of a three-story house had her in better shape than she'd been in years.

"So, he's coming over," Savy said.

"Don't," Maisy said. "Just don't."

"But it turns out he's apparently available. Why are you being weird?"

"I'm not being weird," Maisy insisted. "Obviously, he's not interested in anything other than a professional relationship or he'd have taken his ring off."

"Maybe he forgot."

"He didn't forget."

"Clearly, he's not oblivious to your charm."

Maisy barked out a laugh. "I have no charm."

"You have buckets of charm. You just waste them on the wrong guys."

"Savy, I love you like a sister, but I am telling you—"

"No man comes over to a woman's house to watch *Pride and Prejudice* with her, her bestie, and his teenage kid unless he's interested," she said.

"I'm sure he is interested," Maisy said. Savannah looked mollified until she added, "In having me accept his bid to work on the house."

It was Savannah's turn to roll her eyes. "You're impossible. And you're doing it again."

"Doing what?"

"When Ryder was unavailable, you were all gooey eyed about him, like he could be the one but, oh, shucks and darn it, he's married. But now that we know he's not and there's a chance that you could actually have your interest returned, you've wrapped yourself up in razor wire."

"I have not," Maisy protested. "But if we're going to work together I just think it would be prudent—"

"You got part of that word right," Savy said. "Prude—you."

Maisy gasped. "I am not."

"Yeah, you are," Savannah said. "I didn't want to be the

one to point it out to you, but there are critters in these Smoky Mountains that hibernate for half a year and they're getting more action than you."

"That is not—"

"Knock knock," a man's voice called from the doorway. "Are we interrupting anything?"

Maisy's head whipped in the direction of the open door. Ryder was standing there with Perry, holding two huge pizza boxes. Maisy couldn't move, quite certain the humiliation of being overheard might have turned her to stone.

"Not a thing!" Savannah cried. "We were just having a discussion about the mating habits of the local wildlife."

"Is that so?"

"Yeah, we're really into botany," Savy said.

"That's plants," Perry said.

"Bears, bushes, same difference," she said. She crossed the room and grabbed the pizza boxes from Ryder. "I'm Savannah. You must be Ryder. Come on in."

Ryder and Perry entered the apartment and Maisy forced herself to smile in welcome. It must have looked as forced as it felt because Ryder cast her a concerned look and asked, "Are you sure you're okay with me crashing the party? I just figured since I hadn't seen it and all, it would be a good time for me to expand my literary education."

"Absolutely. The more the merrier," she said. "Everyone should be familiar with Austen; she's one of the few literary authors who is actually widely read."

Savannah was standing behind Ryder. She gave Maisy a look of disbelief and then pretended to have fallen asleep standing up. Maisy knew she was telling her to stop being so boring, but Maisy was having a minor panic attack here, and she always tapped into her inner professor to ward off a bad case of nerves.

"See, Perry? I've been here for five minutes and I'm smarter already." Ryder smiled at Maisy and his gaze was kind, making her feel even more awkward, if that was even possible.

She wanted to go climb into her bed and pull the covers over her head. Why, oh, why couldn't do-overs happen in real life?

"How come you're not at soccer with Uncle Quino?" Perry asked her father.

"Because he took a cleat to the thigh and was so cut up and bloody we had to call the game," Ryder said.

"Daisy isn't going to like that," Perry said. She looked alarmed.

"Is Daisy his girlfriend?" Savannah asked.

Maisy would have told her to mind her own business, but she was so relieved to have everyone's attention off her, she was okay with having her friend's terminal nosiness spare her any more scrutiny.

"No, she's not," Perry said. Then she looked at her dad and laughed. "Or maybe she is."

Maisy and Savannah exchanged a confused glance, and Ryder explained, "Daisy is his horse."

"Quino owns Shadow Pine Stables," Ryder explained. "He's an old friend of mine from Texas. We rent the guesthouse on his property."

Savy looked at Perry. "You ride?"

"Every day," she said. "Uncle Quino has me teaching a few classes, too."

"You ladies should come out to the stables sometime," Ryder said. "We could go on a trail ride."

"That'd be great," Savy answered for them. "I haven't been on a horse in years."

Everyone turned to look at Maisy and she panicked. Seeing Ryder on a horse might end her, completely end her. "I don't know. We have a lot to do to get the bookstore open."

Savannah blinked as if she couldn't believe the stupidity she was being forced to witness. "M, I love you, but you know what they say about all work and no play." She turned back to Ryder and Perry with a determined look. "We'll figure it out, I promise."

Thankfully, Maisy's inability to articulate like a normal person disappeared as she got caught up in the movie. Occasionally, she'd glance at Perry to see how she was enjoying it. Once while looking at the teen, she caught Ryder looking at her. Their eyes met, only for a moment, but she felt it all the way down in the pit of her stomach. He sent her a small smile and she glanced away, back at the movie, before her expression revealed any of her feelings, which frankly were a hot mess of *holy banana*s and *oh, my God*s.

When George Wickham, the dashing and dastardly officer who elopes with one of Elizabeth's sisters, came on the screen, Ryder threw a piece of popcorn at him. His aim was true and the popcorn bopped Wickham on the nose.

"Dad!" Perry protested.

"What?" Ryder asked. "He's a bad guy."

"No, he isn't," Perry said. "He's just horribly misunderstood."

"Sorry, kiddo," Savy said. "I'm with cowboy-architect dad on this one."

"Me, too," Maisy chimed in. "Wickham is a scoundrel."

"I think he's handsome," Perry said. There was a mischievous twinkle in her eye.

"That's it," Ryder said. "You're never allowed to date. Your judgment is impaired. Why is it women always go for the rogue? They kick the decent, hardworking, nice guy to the curb and chase after the bad boy like a dog chasing a truck?"

"Is that what happened?" Perry asked.

"Huh?" Ryder glanced at his daughter, who was sitting on the floor beside him, leaving the couch for Maisy and Savy.

"Did Mom go chase a bad boy?" Perry asked. "Is that why she left us?"

Chapter Eleven

THE room went quiet. Even the sound of the movie seemed to fade to background noise. Maisy didn't know where to look, and yet she couldn't look away. She'd suffered a few awkward silences in her time, like when she ran into dingleberry and his *wife*. As appalling as that had been, at least it had involved her directly. This was a new level of awkward, like finding a mug shot of your boss online or bearing witness to the serving of a subpoena.

Maisy would have preferred either of those situations right now. No such luck. Instead, she was watching Ryder on the hot seat with his precocious daughter being the one to turn up the heat. To his credit, he pulled it together pretty quickly.

"No!" he stated emphatically. He glanced at Maisy and Savannah before looking back at his daughter. "You know she didn't, ladybug. Your mother was given a shot at her dream. She had to take it."

"You both said she left for her career," Perry said. "But she could have had a career and us, but she chose not to—why?"

Maisy felt her heart drop into her feet. Oh, boy, the man had been dumped and he was still wearing his wedding ring. No matter what Perry said about him wearing it to ward off aggressive women, Maisy wondered if that was true or if he really just couldn't let go of his wife. The warning bells were ringing so loudly in her head, she almost missed his next words.

"She got a major part on a TV show," he said. "She couldn't walk away from that, and I couldn't move to Los Angeles."

"Couldn't or didn't want to?" Perry asked.

Ryder looked at his daughter. His gaze was tender and his voice was gentle when he said, "Both."

Savannah gave Maisy a wild-eyed look. She knew Savy was thinking the same thing Maisy was. Primarily, that this was a conversation she didn't want to be in and she had no idea how to get out. Maisy gave her a tiny shrug, mostly with her eyebrows, to let her know she had no idea how to escape, either.

The disappointment on Perry's face was wrenching. She wrapped her arms around her knees, looking like she wanted to disappear right into the floor. Ryder sat beside her, looking like he wanted to hug her but was uncertain if it would be welcome. Maisy wanted to give him a hard shove to the back, but she didn't, because, really, this was none of her business.

"Hey, don't look so bummed," Ryder said. "Didn't you have a blast with her when you flew out to Disneyland and rode every ride at least one hundred times?"

"Yeah," she said. It was grudging, at best.

"Doesn't she call you every Sunday?"

"Yes, but it's not the same," Perry said. "I was eleven when she left and look at me now. I'm fourteen. I'm growing up and she's missing it. In a few more years, we'll be strangers."

"You won't," Ryder said. "Your mom and I will always be there for you. You know that."

"Sure, I guess," Perry said. She pushed up off the floor and stood. She glanced at Maisy. "Is it okay if I go look for more books?"

"Of course," Maisy said. "Help yourself."

Without another word, Perry spun on her heel and left the room.

Savannah stood, glanced between Maisy and Ryder, and said, "I'll go chaperone the selections."

"Thank you," Ryder said at the same time Maisy said, "Good idea."

Savannah darted out of the room after Perry.

Unsure of where to look, Maisy began to gather the popcorn bowls and pizza plates. Ryder moved to help her and she waved him off. "I've got it."

He ignored her and began gathering the dishes, too. He followed her to the little kitchen. Maisy could feel him studying the side of her face, but she didn't know if he wanted to talk or if he was trying to gauge her reaction to Perry's outburst.

They moved silently. Maisy filled up the sink and began to wash the dishes, as the small kitchenette didn't have a dishwasher. She cleaned the plates but before she could put them in the drying rack, Ryder took them and began to wipe them dry with a dishcloth. It was an oddly domestic situation to find herself in. Maisy had never lived with any of her boyfriends and she wondered if this was what married life had been like for Ryder. Had he and his wife done the dishes together while talking about their daughter? She didn't like the image of that in her brain.

"So, I'm not married," he said.

"I know," she said. "Perry actually told us earlier tonight."

"She did? Interesting. She's never outed me before."

"I suppose she felt Savannah and I were trustworthy."

"Huh." He looked embarrassed, but Maisy didn't feel bad about it.

She was too preoccupied with the news that Ryder's ex was an actress. Maisy found this fascinating. The likelihood of finding information about her online was high and she knew she would never be able to resist the impulse to do some online stalking. Still, more information would help. Only half hating herself, she went there.

"So, your wife is an actress?" she asked. "Was she in anything I would have seen?"

"Ex-wife and, yes, she was on a show," he said. "It was a network comedy called *Mother Knows Best*. Naturally, it was about a single mother bungling her way through raising two boys who are known for their mischief. The irony was not lost on Perry."

"Sounds familiar. It only lasted one season?" Maisy asked.

"Yeah, which I've never understood because the ratings were high," Ryder said. "I think something must have happened behind the scenes, but Whitney refused to talk about it."

Whitney! And now Maisy had her name and her show. The temptation to pull out her phone and see who this woman was who left Ryder and Perry for an acting career was almost more than she could stand. She stayed the course.

"It must have been hard for you and Perry to be on your own," Maisy said.

"No harder than it was for Whitney when I was working construction all day and going to school all night for my architecture degree. Our marriage didn't end because she wanted to pursue her career," he said. "It was her shot and I was happy for her to take it because she'd stood by me when I took mine."

Maisy studied his face. His expression looked 100 percent sincere. "Okay, this is totally none of my business. Let's just blame it on my lack of understanding of personal boundaries."

A small smile curved his lips. "Okay."

He draped the dish towel over his shoulder and propped a hip against the counter. He crossed his arms over his chest and studied her with his bright-blue gaze. For a second, he reminded Maisy of a bird, waiting on a picnicker to drop a crumb. Well, she had a whole fistful.

"Why do you still wear your wedding ring?" she asked.

"Because I am not interested in a relationship," he said.

Ouch! She hadn't been prepared for that level of honesty. It seemed there was a little more to it than Perry's belief that it was to ward off interested women.

"Because you're still in love with your wife?" she asked. She dropped the sponge and grabbed a towel to dry her hands. She mimicked his stance with her hip propped and her arms crossed and her gaze fastened right on the collar of his shirt.

"No, because I am lousy at relationships, any relationships," he said. "I will mess it up every time. Sharing feelings, intimacy, these are not my gifts." Maisy raised her eyebrows, and he looked chagrined. "Not physical intimacy—I've got that—it's emotional intimacy I'm not very good at it. In fact, I am really really bad at it."

"You could just tell people that," she said. She was feeling prickly and irritated with him for letting her think he was married when he wasn't. "It's not like every woman you meet is out to bag you like a trophy."

He blew out a sigh. "See? Look how annoyed you are. You've only known me for a few days, and I've already ticked you off, and I wasn't even trying. Just imagine if we were dating. Relationships are not my thing and wearing the ring is an easy way to let people know I'm unavailable and hopefully keep anyone from getting hurt."

"You know not every woman is looking for a relationship." Maisy tipped her chin up. "There are women who prefer their relationships to be fleeting."

"In all my thirty-five years, I have never met that woman," he said. He glanced at her from under his lashes. It was a charming look. Maisy refused to be charmed. She still had questions.

"If you supported your ex pursuing her career, then why did you divorce?" she asked.

He dropped his arms. He put his hand on the back of his neck and met her gaze. "You don't pull any punches, do you?"

"When you're as petite as I am," she said, "you can't afford to."

"All right," he said. "The truth is we were never really suited. She was studying drama at college in Austin, and I was working construction. We met tailgating at a football game and had some laughs. I was twenty-one and she was nineteen. She was easy on the eyes and I was young enough and dumb enough to like having a hot girl on the back of my motorcycle. We dated for about three months and it was already ending when she discovered she was pregnant."

"Oh."

"Yeah, oh," he said. "She told me the news and I asked her to marry me right then and there."

"Really?" Maisy wasn't really surprised. Ryder seemed the sort to take his responsibilities seriously.

"Amazingly enough she said yes," he said. "To this day I am not sure why, since she'd told me she never planned to marry or have kids, but I think the reality of her condition and my willingness to give it a try tipped the scale in that direction, and we were married in Vegas two weeks later."

"Wow," Maisy said. Of all the stories she had expected this was not a version she could have imagined. "That leap into maturity must have given you whiplash."

"Pretty much," he said. "From the moment the doctor put Perry in my arms, and she stared up at me from her puffy-eyed, red, wrinkled-up face, I knew it was the right decision."

Maisy sighed. Given that she lived her life riddled in self-doubt with a pinch of anxiety, she envied him the certainty of that moment in his life. Having seen him and Perry together, she had to agree. "You and Perry seem very close."

"We used to be, but lately—" He let the words hang. Maisy suspected there were volumes in the unfinished sentence. Maisy had a million questions but she didn't know how to articulate them without coming across as a busybody. She hoped if she was silent he might offer up more information. But he didn't. Instead, he turned it on her.

"What about you?" he asked.

"What about me?"

"What's your relationship status?" he asked. "Since I've spilled my guts, it's only fair to know a little bit about your life."

"You met my ex," she said. "He was the last in a string of losers."

Ryder studied her, his gaze moving over her features and her body. It was not the look of architect to client. It was man to woman, as if he was aware of her on the most elemental level and he was intrigued. It made Maisy's heart flutter and her skin heat up. She could feel the answering pull, the longing, the desire, bubble up inside of her, making her susceptible to his charm, lured by his masculinity. Frankly, she was warm for his form.

"Long or short?" he asked.

"I'm sorry?"

"The string of losers?" he clarified. His smile was a slash of white teeth in the dimly lit room. "Was it a long string or a short string?"

She smiled. She tipped her chin and arched her brows, staring him down through her glasses. "Wouldn't you like to know."

"Yes, I would," he said. He moved closer. Maisy didn't back away. This was flirting on a scale she'd never managed before. It made her giddy with her feminine power, a brand-new feeling for her. And she liked it.

"Why?" she asked.

"Well, if it's a long string, I'm guessing you haven't met the right guy yet," he said. He reached out with one hand and ran his fingers gently down her arm as if he couldn't resist touching her. Maisy shivered but she wasn't cold. He began to trace small patterns on the back of her hand with the pads of his fingers, watching her reaction to his touch as he spoke. "And if it's a short string, then I'm guessing someone broke your heart and you want to avoid that again."

"Is that what happened to you?" she asked. The words came out breathy. Given that she was barely breathing at the feel of his fingers on her skin, it was the best she could do.

"No." He shook his head. "You have to have a heart for it to be broken."

It was a warning shot. Maisy knew that. He was telling her he was damaged. He was giving her a chance to run, to shut this down, to save herself. Any man who said he didn't have a heart was not a man she should consider in a romantic light. She knew this. And yet, she couldn't back away. Not even if her heart depended upon it.

"It was a long string," she said. "But with only a few knots in it."

His smile when it appeared was wicked. Maisy had never been on the receiving end of such a smile. It made her feel drunk and bold and oh-so reckless.

"What sort of knots?" he asked.

"No marriages, if that's what you mean," she said.

"And?"

"No fiancés," she added. "No brushes with matrimony of any kind."

She studied his face. If he thought anything about this revelation, he was darn good at keeping it in check. Now she wished she hadn't shared quite so much.

"But if I had been married or engaged before," she began, pausing to take a breath before plowing forward into vulnerable territory, "I wouldn't keep wearing my wedding band, letting people think I am taken or that I am still emotionally involved with my past. And I wouldn't assume that every person I meet is interested in a long-term relationship because quite possibly they aren't."

"Really?"

"Really."

Ryder looked at her left hand. Then he looked at his own. Without saying a word, he slipped the wedding band off his ring finger and dropped it onto the counter.

Chapter Twelve

WHEN his gaze met hers, Maisy sucked in a breath. It was like being caught in a sudden storm when the sky turned dark and the lightning flashed blue and the wind whipped at her hair and clothes while the smell of rain on the air was a promise. Ryder was letting her know in no uncertain terms that he wasn't pining for anyone. Well, then.

Maisy wasn't sure who leaned into whom. One minute there was a reasonable space between them and the next his hand was on her hip, holding her in place while he moved in close. Maisy rose up on her toes to meet him, wanting him to know that she was 100 percent a participant and not a sidelined spectator.

His gaze was locked on hers as if making sure he was reading her right. Oh, he was. Maisy curled her fingers into her palms to keep from latching on to him like a stripper on a pole. A small smile tipped the corner of his mouth and there was a sexy twinkle in his eye. He was a mere breath away. With deliberate care, he reached up and took off her glasses, placing them on the counter beside his ring.

Maisy swallowed. It went down hard. Her heart was

thumping so hard in her chest she felt as if it were trying to punch through to reach his.

Then his mouth was on hers and it was everything. Like the strike of a match sparking a flame, the feel of his lips against hers lit a wick of desire in her belly. Maisy pressed herself closer and Ryder slid his hand to her back, holding her in place.

His lips were warm as they molded to hers, sipping, tasting, opening hers so that he could go deeper, taste more, drink her in as if she was something precious and rare. Maisy let him in without hesitation. She ran her hands up his chest and over his shoulders, latching on to him as if he was her safe spot in the storm instead of the one causing the chaos inside of her.

Ryder anchored her with one hand on the small of her back while the other cupped her head, her curls twining about his fingers as if to keep him there, while he eased out of the kiss so that he could run his lips along her jaw and down the column of her throat.

Something between a moan and a sigh slipped out of Maisy and she felt his mouth curve into a smile against her skin. The thought of kissing him had flitted through her mind for days but the reality, oh, dear God, she had simply not been prepared for this.

"Ryder." She whispered his name, uncertain if she was begging for more or pleading for mercy. She suspected it was one and the same.

"Maisy." His voice was husky and deep, muffled against the curve of her neck and shoulder, where he gently bit her skin, making her knees buckle. If he hadn't been holding her, she was sure she would have spilled onto the floor like a pot boiling over.

He lifted his head and pressed his forehead to hers. His blue gaze was molten when it met hers and he said, "You're driving me crazy—"

Beep beep beep!

Ryder's phone sounded in his pocket. And just like that they were thrust out of their passionate embrace and back into the reality of the moment. They stepped away from each other, wobbly and unsure, as if trying to get their bearings on land after months at sea. At least it felt like that to Maisy.

She snatched up her glasses and pushed them up onto her nose, then grabbed a dish towel and began to scrub at a non-existent stain on the old wooden counter. Ryder retrieved his ring and shoved it into his pocket while answering his phone.

"Copeland here," he barked.

"Rescue one," Savannah cried.

She was loud enough that Maisy could hear her. Savy didn't sound like she was kidding. Maisy snatched the phone from Ryder's hand.

"Savy, what's wrong? Why are you calling Ryder?"

"I'm on Perry's phone because I don't have mine and I don't know your number. We're downstairs on the front porch, and we have a situation," Savy said.

"What do you mean, 'a situation'?" Maisy looked at Ryder with wide eyes. He started moving toward the door and she followed.

"Just get down here," Savannah said, and she ended the call.

"They're on the front porch," she said.

Ryder broke into a run and Maisy fell in right behind him. They jogged around the piles of books, down one flight of stairs and then the next. They crossed the foyer but before Ryder could yank the door open, Maisy grabbed his arm and slowed him down.

"Whatever is going on, let's not make the situation worse by charging out there," she whispered.

"You're right," Ryder said.

He stealthily turned the knob and pulled the door open. Maisy peered around his side and saw Savannah and Perry crouched down behind a pile of boxes, looking at something on the other side. Maisy braced herself for a bear or a rabid raccoon. It was neither.

"What's going on?" Ryder whispered as he crept forward and knelt down behind his daughter.

"Look," Perry said. She lifted her phone, which had its flashlight feature on, and shined it on the floor of the porch on the other side of the boxes.

A little blob was on the porch. Maisy frowned. She had just swept the porch that afternoon. Was it a big leaf? A rogue sock? What? While she watched, a tiny face rolled up from the blob and blinked against the light. It was a teeny tiny kitten.

"Oh, my God." She shot to her feet and went to circle the boxes to grab the little baby. Ryder caught her by the elbow and gently held her still.

"If you pick it up and get your scent on it, its mother will reject it," he said. He let her go and scooted closer to his daughter. "Any sign of mama cat or other kittens?"

"No, we've been watching but it's just this little guy," Perry said. She moved the light off the kitten and its head drooped back down. "I think it's been abandoned. It looks cold and hungry."

"I think so, too," Savannah said. "I don't know much about cats, as I'm more of a non-animal person, but I don't think leaving the little one out in the open like this is normal. Wouldn't a mama cat hide her babies if she's going to go forage for food?"

"Agreed," Ryder said. "I'll take a walk around the property and see if I see the mother cat or any kittens in the area."

He slipped off the porch and out into the night.

The three women waited, huddled behind the boxes, watching the tiny kitten, who wasn't moving. Maisy started to get a bad feeling about the whole thing. What if the kitten died while they did nothing? What if he was injured or sick? She started to fret when Ryder reappeared.

"There's no sign of any other cats in the yard," he said.

"So we can take it inside?" Perry asked.

"I don't know. If she comes back, it would be a shame to take the kitten from its mother. Let's watch from inside for a little while. If she doesn't come back soon, we'll have to step in and help it."

"I don't want to leave it out here," Perry said. "What if an owl sees it and swoops down and snatches it?"

Ryder studied the porch roof. "There is no guarantee but I think it'll be okay for a little while."

They quietly left the porch, stationing themselves in the

foyer, where they could look out the long windows on each side of the front door and watch the kitten. It didn't move. It stayed curled up in a little ball of misery. Maisy felt her heart hurt a little bit more as each minute ticked by with no sign of its mother.

"How much longer, Daddy?" Perry asked after fifteen minutes.

Ryder patted his daughter on the shoulder. "Hang tough, kid."

"Supposing the mama doesn't come back," Savannah said. "What are we going to do with such a wee kitten?"

"I'll take care of it," Perry volunteered.

"You have school," Ryder said. "And I'll be working here. Pretty sure a kitten can't go that long without food."

"Does Hannah still work at the animal clinic here in town?" Savannah asked Maisy.

"No, she owns her own practice now," Maisy said. "In fact, she's in the gray house at the end of Willow Lane."

"Wow, good for her. We should call her." Savy held out her hand for Perry's phone and without hesitation the teen put it in her palm.

"You're right, she'll know what to do," Maisy said. "The name of her practice is the Fairdale Animal Center."

Savannah typed the name of the clinic into the browser on Perry's phone and then hit call when a match came up. She put the phone on speaker so they could all hear what Hannah said. Savy got the clinic's voice mail but when she pressed the number stating it was an emergency, she was patched through to Hannah's cell phone.

Hannah answered on the fourth ring. "Dr. Phillips—ah—what's your—uh—emergency?"

She sounded breathless, and Savannah's eyes went wide. She glanced at Maisy, who gestured for her to go on.

"Hey, Hannah, it's Savannah Wilson from Fairdale U. I don't know if you remember me—"

"Uh, yes, right there, ah—" Hannah grunted.

Savannah dropped the phone. Ryder clapped his hands over Perry's ears and Maisy scrambled to pick up the phone before they heard any more.

"Hi, Hannah, it's Maisy. Looks like we caught you at a bad time. We'll call back—"

She was about to hit end when Hannah's voice sounded, "Ugh, yes, good girl. That's how you do it. Take a break now."

Maisy frowned at the phone. "Hannah, just out of curiosity, what are you doing right now?"

Ryder made bug eyes at her, and Maisy almost laughed.

"At this exact moment, I am up to my elbows in a bovine's birth canal," she said. You're lucky I have John Michael here with me to answer the phone."

Ryder dropped his hands from Perry's ears and shook his head. His lips were screwed up tight as if he was trying not to laugh.

"Hi, John Michael," Maisy said. She glanced at Savannah, who was not even trying to hold in her snort laughs. "I hope your cow is going to be okay."

"Hi, Maisy," John Michael's deep voice came out of the phone. He was Hannah's younger brother and owned a local dairy farm. "She will be now. The little heifer wanted to come out feet first, but I think we've gotten him turned around."

"I only have a few seconds to spare," Hannah said. "What do you need? Oh, and hi, Savannah, sorry I can't talk long."

"No problem, we'll catch up another time," Savannah said. Her voice sounded strained as if she was still trying not to laugh.

"Listen, we found an abandoned kitten on our front porch," Maisy said. "There's no sign of the mother or any other kittens. It's looking weak and sickly. What should we do?"

"If you're sure the mother isn't coming back, you need to get it inside where it's safe from predators and get it warm. A heating pad on low wrapped in a towel will do it. Kittens can't regulate their own temperature for the first few weeks of life. How big is it?"

"It's tiny. Not much more than a handful," Maisy said.

"That is young, probably less than two weeks. It'll need to be bottle-fed every two hours with kitten replacement formula. Do not use cow's milk."

"Okay." Maisy looked at Ryder and he nodded as if this seemed doable.

"Oh, and this is important, you'll have to help it pee and poop."

"What, no, really?" Maisy asked.

"Yeah, their mom usually licks them to stimulate urination and defecation," Hannah said.

Ryder, Maisy, and Savannah all looked at one another. Maisy was hard pressed to decide which of them looked the most disgusted, but she was pretty sure Savannah edged her and Ryder out by a nose wrinkle.

"I can do that," Perry said. "I'll take really good care of it."

"Who are you?" Hannah asked.

"My name's Perry. I found it," she said.

"Well, it sounds like finders keepers, Perry." Hannah laughed, which was drowned out by a low mooing sound. "Sorry. I've got to go. Call me later if you have more questions."

"We will," Maisy said. "Thanks."

"Oh, one more thing," Hannah said. "Kittens that little don't generally thrive. It's going to be touch and go for a few weeks. Try not to get attached."

"We'll try," Maisy said. She knew when she glanced at Perry it was already too late.

"All right," Ryder said. "Let's go out and check one more time for Mom."

Perry did not bother to check for the mother. She went right to the kitten and gently scooped it up. It was so tiny, it barely filled her two palms.

"Let's get it inside," Maisy said. "I have a heating pad in the apartment."

"I'll set up a box," Ryder said. He went over to the stack of flattened boxes Maisy had been using to pack up Auntie El's collection.

"I'll go get some kitten formula," Savannah said.

"What should I do?" Perry asked.

"Follow Maisy upstairs and hold it close to your heart," Ryder said. "Your body heat and the sound of your heartbeat should keep it calm."

Maisy and Perry made their way upstairs. The young girl was careful, but still Maisy spotted her in case she tripped over some books. Back in the apartment, Maisy helped Perry to sit while she grabbed a towel and the heating pad. She plugged it in and wrapped it in a towel, then she set the temperature to low and put it in Perry's lap. Perry slowly lowered the kitten onto the towel.

It was the first time Maisy had seen the little one in good light and the only word that came to mind was *pitiful*. Its eyes were barely open and a cloudy blue, its ears were folded over, and its legs didn't look strong enough to support it, while its tail was just a sad little droop. It was mostly black fluff but its belly was pale gray and striped. Its face was white with dark-gray stripes that accentuated its eyes and mouth, and its nose was a tiny black dot. It was a thumbprint of a kitten and Hannah's warning not to get attached rang in Maisy's ears. Oh, boy.

Ryder, carrying the box, entered the room. He set the box beside the couch and, with something that looked like *aw*, he took in the sight of his daughter cradling the tiny kitten.

"How's it going?" he whispered.

"Not good." Perry looked up at her father with tears in her eyes. "It's going to die, isn't it?"

"I don't know, ladybug," he said. "I know that if you hadn't found it, it would have died for sure. So anything we can do for it now is more than it would have had if we'd left it on that porch. So, let's just try. We'll work really hard to save this little one, okay?"

Perry nodded. A tear slipped down her cheek and dropped from her chin onto the dark fuzz of the kitten. She gently brushed the tear away with her fingers and Maisy felt her heart clutch. She knew without being told that if this kitten died, Perry was going to take it hard. She glanced at Ryder and knew from the grim set of his features that he was thinking the same thing.

He sat beside his daughter on the couch and Maisy took a seat on the other side as if they could bookend her with the support she needed. Perry gave them both a tentative smile, letting them know that their presence was appreciated.

Maisy's phone chimed and she glanced at the lit-up display to see that it was a message from Hannah. She glanced at it and said, "Hannah sent us a website to look at for kitten care. She also sent us the name of a kitty nanny who might be able to take it."

"What?" Perry cried. "Give it up?"

"We want to give the kitten its best shot," Ryder said.

"I'm its best shot," Perry said.

She pulled the furball even closer and, as if sensing they were talking about it, the kitten let out a tiny little cry. It sounded like half of a meow. Maisy thought it was the cutest thing she'd ever heard.

"See? It's already bonding to me," Perry said.

"The veterinarian said that it's going to be touch and go," Ryder said. "Why don't we call the kitty nanny just to have her on deck?"

Perry looked like she would argue, but then she glanced down at the tiny face snuggling into her and nodded. "Okay."

Maisy made the call. The woman had two rescues already that were a few weeks older, but she was willing to take this one if need be. She sounded a bit overwhelmed and Maisy felt bad for trying to dump another baby on her when she already had her hands full. Maisy thanked her and told her that she'd be in touch.

They heard Savannah coming before she entered the apartment. She had several bags hanging off her arms and her wavy red hair was mussed as if she'd been caught in a strong wind and had to fight her way into the house.

"Sorry that took so long. I had to drive all the way to Asheville. And a storm's coming, which means everyone is panicking and no one can drive for beans."

She dropped the bags on the counter and then spun around and hurried back to the couch. "How is the little one?"

"Hanging in there," Maisy said. "But probably starving."

"I'll get the formula ready," Ryder said. "I have some experience."

"Wait until you see the baby bottle," Savy said. "It looks like it's made for a doll."

Ryder took it out of the bag. It looked tiny in his big callused hands. While he prepped the bottle, Maisy read from the webpage Hannah had referenced.

"It says to start with a tablespoon and you're supposed to

warm it to room temperature and test it on your wrist." Maisy glanced up to see Ryder shake the bottle and then dab some formula on his wrist.

"Perfect," he said. "Prepping a bottle is like riding a bicycle. You never forget."

He moved to the couch and sat beside Perry. He handed her the tiny bottle and she shook her head. "I can't. You do it. What if I hurt it?"

"You're feeding it," Ryder said. "That is the very definition of not hurting it."

"The website says to keep the kitten snuggled and on its belly, like it's feeding from its mom," Maisy said. "Oh, and keep the bottle at a forty-five-degree angle, so it doesn't suck up too much air." Perry gave her an exasperated look and Maisy said, "Sorry."

Perry gently tried to press the bottle into the kitten's mouth. Still nothing.

"It won't drink," Perry said. She looked at her father in alarm.

"Maybe it can't tell that there's milk in there," he said. "I'm betting the rubber smell of the nipple—"

"Dad!" Perry looked at Maisy and Savannah in alarm.

Ryder rolled his eyes. "That's what it is. I'm supposed to call it something else?"

"It's just, it's embarrassing," Perry said. Her face was bright pink.

"Don't worry about us," Savannah said. "We're hard to offend."

"Okay, just squeeze the bottle until there's a little formula on the rubber thingy," Ryder said. "Maybe the kitten will drink when it smells the milk."

Perry frowned. She handed her father the bottle and he squeezed it until some of the formula was on the tip. Then he handed it back to her. Perry held it to the kitten's mouth and this time there was a little interest.

She squeezed the bottle some more and the kitten opened its mouth. Perry looked at her dad in wonder and he smiled. "Keep going. See if you can get a tablespoon into it."

Perry talked softly to the little kitten, alternately rubbing its head with her thumb while squeezing formula into its mouth. It dribbled a little here and there, but then it latched on to the tip and started sucking.

"Aw, look at that," Savannah cried. "Its tiny ears move while it's drinking."

Maisy looked at the kitten. It was definitely the cutest thing she'd ever seen and when she saw the man hunkered over the little thing, patiently coaxing it to keep going, she was pretty sure she was going to have an ovary meltdown. Honestly, how was a woman supposed to resist such a sight?

When the kitten let go of the bottle it was almost empty. And the little one's eyes closed as if exhausted from the effort of drinking so much. Maisy glanced back down at her phone.

"You're supposed to burp it now."

Perry looked at her in confusion. "But it's so little."

"Here, let me," Ryder said. "I used to be able to get some solid burps out of you when you were a baby."

"Really, Dad," Perry protested. "Kind of an overshare."

"What? It's true," he said. He took the kitten from her and gently patted its back. "You used to screw up your little face and belch like a truck driver."

Perry closed her eyes as though if she couldn't see him then maybe he wasn't there. But he was and as Maisy watched him gently pat the tiny little critter in his hands, she didn't think she'd ever seen a more handsome man in her life. It should be a crime to be that good-looking and then tenderly hold a kitten. How was a woman supposed to block that image out of her mind?

Just when she thought she couldn't stand it anymore, a tiny little burp came out of the kitten and Ryder grinned. "I've still got it."

He handed the kitten back to his daughter. Perry snuggled it close, making sure it was warm. One look at her face and Maisy knew she was 100 percent kitten smitten.

"Aren't we supposed to help it go to the bathroom now?" Savannah asked. "And just so we're clear, by *we* I mean *you*."

Chapter Thirteen

"Oh, yeah," Maisy said. She glanced at Ryder. "How's your skill set there?"

"Tapped out," he said. "My only experience was with an eight-pound being that came fully functional in that area."

"Dad," Perry wailed. "Oh, my God. Stop talking, seriously."

"What? I was talking about my boyhood dog." She stared at him. Ryder feigned an innocent expression. "Oh, did you think I was talking about you? I would never."

"Uh-huh," she said.

"That is, until your first boyfriend comes around and I feel compelled to tell him about the time you shoved a Tic Tac up your nose, and I had to hold your other nostril so you could blow it out," he said. He started to laugh. "Do you remember? You pinged Dr. Campbell so hard, you cracked the lens in her glasses."

"And this is why I will die old and alone, untouched by a man, probably being devoured by my cats," Perry said.

Savannah and Maisy laughed while Ryder crossed his arms over his chest, and said, "My work here is done."

"Are we going to RPS this?" Savy asked.

"RPS?" Ryder asked.

"Rock, paper, scissors," Maisy explained. She turned back to Savannah. "No, you always win. I'll do it." She glanced back at her phone and read the directions. "Okay, I need some cotton balls and a towel, you know, in case it leaks all over."

"Got it," Savannah said. She went to their shared bathroom and Maisy watched while Perry rubbed the little fuzzball's head. Its eyes shut and it looked blissed out. Did they really have to do this now? She read the directions again. Yep, after feeding.

Savannah came back with a handful of warm wet cotton balls and an old towel. Maisy sat beside Perry, who gently handed off the kitten. Ryder sat on the floor beside Maisy. She suspected he was there in case she needed backup, which she appreciated.

"Okay, little one, this isn't going to hurt," Maisy said. "Just pretend I'm your mama."

Very gently she lifted the kitten up in her left hand and gently rubbed one of the warm wet cotton balls on the kitten's nether regions. The kitten's eyes popped open and it let out a high-pitched, ear-piercing cry. Maisy froze.

"What's wrong?" Perry cried. "Is it hurting it?"

"No," Ryder said. He glanced at Maisy and said, "I imagine it's just a bit of a shock. Keep going."

Maisy brushed the cotton over the kitten, trying to simulate how a mama cat would lick her baby. The kitten kept yelling.

"Well, at least we know there's nothing wrong with the lungs," Savannah said.

"It's not working," Maisy said over the feline wailing. "And I feel like I'm torturing it."

"You're not," Ryder said. "It's just not exactly like mom, so the kitten is probably freaking out a little."

The kitten kept crying and Maisy frowned at Ryder. "You think?"

"You're doing great, really," he said. His voice was so

confident and sure that Maisy believed him. She focused on
the kitten and tried to exude a calmness she didn't really feel
to help the kitten relax.

Just when she was about to give up, she felt the cotton ball
get warm. "It's working. It's peeing!"

"That's great!" Savannah cried. "And also, *ew.*"

The kitten dribbled on the towel but Maisy didn't care.
She'd gotten it to pee, even though it was still yowling.

"Should I keep going?" she asked.

Ryder looked at the kitten. "I'd give it a break. We have
to feed it again in two hours, so we can try to get it to go
again then."

"Okay," Maisy said.

"Wait here."

Ryder rose to his feet and grabbed an empty plastic gro-
cery sack from the counter. Maisy dropped the cotton ball
into it and he tied it off. Perry took the kitten back to the nest
in her lap while Maisy rinsed the towel and put it in the hamper and then washed up in the bathroom. When she returned,
they were all gathered around the kitten, who was fast asleep
in its fluffy towel.

"We have to set an alarm," Perry said. "We need to feed
it every two hours."

"Or," Savannah said, "we could call the kitty nanny and
have her come and take it." Maisy, Ryder, and Perry all
looked at her. "It was just a thought."

"It's ten o'clock," Maisy said. "It seems rude to call her
so late. We can do this tonight and then reevaluate in the
morning."

"We'll help," Perry said. Ryder glanced at her and she
stuck out her chin in a stubborn pose. "I found it. I'm not
leaving it."

"It's a school night," he said.

"Are you saying that school is more important than saving
a life?" she asked.

He opened his mouth and then looked helplessly at Maisy,
who was trying not to laugh. Perry was one smart cookie. No
doubt about it. Ryder looked stumped as to what to say so
Maisy figured she'd help him out.

"Of course he isn't saying that," she said. "Why don't you two stay here, and we'll each take a shift and then we can figure out what to do in the morning after Hannah has a chance to examine it?"

"Are you sure?" Ryder asked.

"Absolutely," Maisy fibbed. She absolutely was not. The thought of Ryder under her roof all night felt exciting, which had to be wrong. He was her architect. She had kissed him. This was bad, very very bad.

"I'll take the midnight shift," Savannah volunteered. "I'm pretty sure I can manage to stay awake for two more hours."

"I'll take the two a.m.," Maisy volunteered. She figured she wasn't going to sleep anyway.

"Okay, then, I'll take the four o'clock since I'm used to early mornings," Ryder volunteered.

"That leaves me with the six," Perry said.

"Just enough time to feed the kitten and get to school," Ryder said.

"Dad—" she protested.

"No," he said. "If you want to take care of this kitten, I support that but it can't interfere with school."

Perry heaved a sigh. "Fine."

"All right, it looks like we're having a sleepover." Savannah clapped her hands together and glanced at Maisy. "This couch folds out, doesn't it?"

Maisy nodded. "But it's pretty uncomfortable."

"It doesn't matter," Perry said. "I just need a blanket because I am sleeping on the floor next to the box."

Maisy looked at Ryder, and he shrugged. "She's a good floor sleeper. She used to sleep under her bed, convinced the monsters couldn't find her there."

Perry gave her dad a look but the kitten made a squeak and she was diverted.

"We'll get you kids some pillows and blankets," Savannah said. "Give a hand, M?"

"Sure."

Maisy studied Savannah's walk as she followed her to her room. It didn't look pissed off and stilted. Still, there had been something in her tone and words the subtext of which sounded like *I need to talk to you right now.* Uh-oh. Maisy hoped Savy wasn't put out about the kitten. She was not the world's biggest animal lover, but Maisy couldn't believe that Savannah would be okay with kicking a kitten out into the cold.

Savannah closed the door to her room after them. Then she turned on Maisy and said, "Spill it."

"Spill what?"

"Oh, don't you play innocent with me," Savy whispered.

Maisy blinked. "I sincerely have no idea what you're talking about."

"A man shows up here, wearing a wedding ring. The same man is left alone with you for ten minutes and the wedding ring is gone," Savy said. "Did you really think I wouldn't notice? So, tell me, what motivated him to take it off?"

Maisy shrugged. It was way overexaggerated and hampered by the fact that she could not meet her bestie's rather intense stare. She loved Savy like a sister, she did, but she wasn't prepared to say that there was something between her and Ryder when she didn't know what had happened right before they found the kitten. You know, minus her entire world imploding like a supernova of lust.

"Oh, come on," Savy said.

"I've got nothing," Maisy said. She walked past her friend to the closet. She opened the door and foraged on the top shelf until she found a set of sheets, two comforters, and matching pillows.

"I cannot believe you're holding out on me, M," Savy said. "I thought we were friends, best friends, top tier, no-secrets friends. I thought you were the one person I could share my deepest, darkest secrets with, the person who knew all of my flaws and misdeeds but loved me anyway." She paused and gave Maisy the side eye. When Maisy said nothing, she added in an injured tone, "I guess I was wrong."

"Oh, no, nuh-uh, you're not going to badger it out of me," Maisy said.

"*It!* You said 'it,' which implies that there is something to tell." Savannah's eyes flashed with triumph.

Maisy shook her head. "How is it that you didn't become a lawyer?"

"Because law is boring."

"Oh, right."

Maisy turned and headed for the door, thinking she might escape, but with her arms weighed down by blankets and pillows, she wasn't moving as fast as a getaway required. Savanah reached the door first and jumped in front of Maisy with her back to the door, blocking the exit.

"Did he kiss you?" Savannah asked. Her light-green eyes were narrowed on Maisy's face, which, traitor that it was, heated up as if it had a blowtorch on it. Savannah gasped. "He did!"

"Shh!" Maisy hissed. Her voice was too loud and she cringed and whispered, "Hush."

"He did, didn't he?" Savy pressed.

"There may have been a small shared moment where his mouth was pressed against mine, but then you two found the kitten and everything went sideways after that," she said.

Savannah jumped up and down and clapped her hands. "But this is so exciting. It's your first interested guy since—"

"Yeah, can we not go there?"

"You're right," Savy said. She glanced at Maisy. "You need to change into some sexy sleepwear, not that bubble gum thing you had going before."

"Are you insane?"

"No," Savy said. "More like logical—or were you trying to scare him off?"

"Hello? His kid is here. Nothing is going to happen and I'm pretty sure that bottle-feeding a kitten and then helping it pee in your hand is a mood killer."

"Details." Savy waved her hand in dismissal.

"Stop, just stop."

"Fine, but if you want to land hot cowboy-architect guy, this could be your best shot."

"He'll be working on the house all summer," Maisy said. "I think I have time."

Savy shook her head at Maisy. "We're going to be thirty. Time is the one thing we don't have."

"Stop."

"I have a better idea. We could offer to let Ryder sleep in your bed and Perry can bunk with me," Savannah said.

"You really did hit your head recently, didn't you?"

Savy grinned. "No, but I do love watching you blush. You're so cute."

"Go." Maisy waved her friend aside and opened the door. She called over her shoulder, "And behave yourself."

"Not really thinking it's me we have to worry about," Savy said. She grabbed the two pillows off the top of the pile and Maisy blew out an exasperated breath as she walked by her friend and returned to the living room.

Ryder had already opened up the couch, while Perry had moved to sit with the kitten in its towel bundle in the chair by the open window. The curtains wafted on the cool breeze and Perry tucked the kitten close as if afraid it might get a chill.

"I apologize in advance for the girliness of the linens," Maisy said to Ryder. "I don't have many men sleep over."

"Is that so?" he asked.

His grin let her know he was teasing her, and Maisy felt her face get fiery hot for the second time in as many minutes. She heard Savannah snort behind her but she refused to acknowledge her friend. Instead she lifted up the ruffled lavender-and-pink comforter and tossed it at Ryder. It covered his head, making him look like a girly ghost.

"Yes, that's so," she said.

With a laugh, Ryder pulled the comforter off his head. Maisy lowered her head to hide her smile and tossed a side of the sheet toward him and together they made the bed. It felt strangely intimate to be making a bed with a man, okay, a hot man, and she found she didn't know where to look. When she tucked a pillow under her chin and wrestled it into its case, she could feel him watching her as he did the same and it made her self-conscious in ways she hadn't been in forever. It made her want to launch herself at him and run away from him—at the same time.

She fluffed the pillow and dropped it in place. Then she hustled over to Savannah and Perry and helped settle the kitten into the box. It wiggled its way deeper into the towel and let out a small mewling cry that plucked Maisy's heartstrings. She wondered where its mama was and why it had been left on the front porch. She hoped mama cat was all right.

"Do you think he'll be warm enough?" Perry asked. She took the pillow her dad handed her and moved so he could spread her comforter on the floor. "What if he gets hungry? Or lonely?"

"We'll feed him again soon," Maisy said.

"You're right here if he gets lonely," Savy added.

"We'll keep an eye on him and the heating pad and make sure he's toasty," Ryder said. "We'll get him through tonight, for sure."

Maisy glanced at him in alarm and he shrugged. Was he crazy? Hearts were on the line here. This could be a disaster! She jerked her head toward the kitchenette, indicating that he should follow her. His eyes went wide, but he nodded in understanding.

Chapter Fourteen

RYDER felt like a kid being called out of the classroom for bad behavior. He supposed this should have bothered him, but if Maisy was the teach then he really didn't mind, especially if she let him kiss her again soon. He wondered if this was how all of her male students felt. He had a feeling it was.

"Did you need some help with cleanup?" he asked.

"Yes, thanks," Maisy said. Then under her breath, she whispered, "I was thinking more like damage control."

She turned and walked to the far end of the kitchenette and he followed. She walked with purpose. He liked that. He'd noticed that about her. She moved with direction and intent, sort of like an arrow shot out of a bow. She always seemed to have a target that she aimed herself at and then it was full speed ahead to her end point.

Once in the kitchen, Maisy opened the fridge, which was practically barren. Ryder got the feeling that neither she nor Savannah were big on the kitchen arts. He had only honed his culinary skills when his ex-wife left and he realized he needed to feed himself and Perry something besides canned soup. Over the past few years, he had actually come to enjoy prepping meals and looked forward to it as a stress reliever from his work days. He wondered how Maisy would react if he offered to cook her dinner.

"I think we can fit the boxes in here," she said. She gestured to the pizza boxes.

Ryder picked them up and slid them onto the empty upper shelf. Okay, that was definitely easier cleanup than when he was making homemade sauce or when he was feeling super-ambitious and baked bread. As much as she devoured whole loaves of his bread, even Perry complained that he got flour everywhere.

While they were hunkered in front of the open fridge, Maisy said, "I'm worried that something might happen to the kitten tonight, and it will be a crushing blow for Perry."

"It might, but it might not," he said.

"But—"

"Listen, Perry won't sleep at all if she thinks the kitten's in danger," he said. "And what good will that do? The kitten will either make it or not, but her worrying won't change a thing, so we might as well look at the situation in a positive light and do everything we can to keep the kitten alive."

Maisy knew he had a point. Worrying wouldn't change anything. But still.

"It's just so tiny and fragile," she said. She straightened up and closed the fridge. She grabbed the bags of chips and boxes of cookies, handing some to Ryder, and led the way into the walk-in pantry. It was a tight squeeze but it gave them a bit of privacy.

"Sometimes the tiniest are the mightiest," Ryder said. He leaned against the mostly empty shelves and regarded her under the light of the bare bulb overhead. "Did you know a leaf-cutter ant can lift up to fifty times its own weight?"

"Is that supposed to reassure me?" Maisy asked. "Because now all I can see is a muscle-laden ant making off with the kitten in the middle of the night while we're all sleeping."

Ryder laughed. It was as natural as breathing to loop an arm around her shoulders and pull her close. He placed a kiss on the top of her head, marveling at the softness of her curls. He twined one around his finger and gently tugged it straight and when he let go, it curled up tight. He was fascinated.

He felt her eyes on his face and he glanced down to see her watching him, studying his face as if trying to figure out what made him tick. His gaze drifted down to her mouth. He noticed her upper lip was just a little bit fuller than the lower one and he desperately wanted to kiss her again and see if it was as amazing the second time around. If only they hadn't been interrupted by the—

"Dad," Perry called him, and he dropped his arm from around Maisy and took a hasty step back into the kitchen.

"Yes, ladybug," he said as he walked back into the living room. Perry wasn't looking at him but rather into the box. Savannah, who was sitting on the floor beside her, was staring at him. Her eyes moved from him to Maisy and back. He had a feeling she suspected shenanigans were afoot. Totally worth it.

"Do you think it's a boy or a girl?" Perry asked.

"I'm not sure it's old enough for us to tell," he said. "If it's a boy, it's . . . um . . . man parts should be visible."

Perry looked at him. "You can say *testicles*."

"I can," he agreed. "But I was trying to be delicate. Besides, you freaked out when I said *nipple*."

"That's because it's one of those words that no one should say ever," Perry said.

"Yeah, like all those words that aren't pervy but sound it. For example, moist," Savy said.

"Right? Ew. Or caulk," Perry said.

"Ladybug!" Ryder said. He knew where this was headed and it wasn't good.

"Kumquat," Maisy said with a giggle. It rolled off her kissable lips and Ryder felt suddenly short of breath.

Savannah and Perry laughed and Ryder knew he was doomed. He gave Maisy his best stink eye. She laughed harder.

"Aw, come on cowboy architect," she taunted him. "Surely you can think of a word that isn't dirty but sounds it." She gave him a daring look. Ryder had a feeling he was going to see that arched eyebrow and twist of her lips in his dreams, his very sweaty dreams.

Ryder put his hand on the back of his neck and said, "Fine. Uvula."

He drew the word out and Maisy laughed while Savannah and Perry made pained expressions.

"Satisfied?" Ryder asked. He was enjoying watching this flirty version of Maisy. It was as if now that they'd gotten a taste they couldn't help but tease each other.

"I bet you can't say *testicles* in front of women," Maisy taunted him.

"Yes, I can," he said.

"Oh, really?" Savannah gave him a dubious look. "Can you say *vagina*?"

"You had to go there." Ryder looked pained.

"He can," Perry said. "He's always said that it was best to use the proper names for body parts, because it's just biology and there's no shame in biology. Right, Dad?"

"Yeah, but I was thinking of convos between you and your doctor not me and three women," he said.

"He can't do it," Maisy whispered, not really to Savannah.

"No? You really want to hear me say the biologically correct terms of the man parts and lady bits?"

All three women were grinning and nodding.

"Okay, then. Testiclevaginapenisbreasts. Boom." His voice cracked in the middle but he got it out.

Now Maisy laughed out loud, completely unrestrained. She put her hand on his arm as she doubled over to catch her breath. When she came back up, her glasses were askew and her grin was wide and framed by two deep dimples. Adorable.

"You made them one word," she said, still chuckling.

"I figured it was better that way. Commit and get it done, sort of like eating your vegetables," he said.

Savannah wagged a finger at him, but she was laughing, too, and said, "I like you."

"Most women do," Perry said. She said it as if she couldn't figure out why women liked him, but Ryder decided not to dwell on the implied insult and instead focused on the positive.

"Thanks, ladybug."

"On that note, I'm going to my room to rest up for the next shift," Savannah said. She looked at Maisy and the others. "You should do the same. I put some spare toothbrushes out in the bathroom, and I have some extra pajamas you can sleep in, Perry." She glanced at Ryder. "Sorry, nothing in your size."

"I'll try to contain my disappointment," he said. He turned to Perry. "She's right, ladybug, it's going to be a long night. You should sleep while you can."

"But what if the kitten needs me?" she said.

"It'll cry. Trust me. You'll hear it. It'll be perfectly safe in its box until it's time to feed him again," he said. "I promise. I'll stay up a bit and keep an eye." Perry looked like she would argue, but he shook his head and with a frown she nodded in agreement. She leaned into the box to kiss the kitten's head and then trudged to the bathroom.

"She looks exhausted," Maisy said. "I hope she can sleep. I hope you can, too. I'm not sure how comfortable that couch is."

"I used to sleep on the backseat of my car, which was a beat-up old Honda Civic, when I was working and going to school," he said. "Nothing can be worse than that and I slept like a baby."

Ryder grimaced when he remembered the catnaps he used to take in the back of the small sedan. It had been like trying to jam a whale into a tuna can. It was a wonder he wasn't permanently shaped like a question mark. Those had been relentlessly arduous days, one bleeding into another until he lost track of himself and his life.

"Was it worth it?" she asked. "Working that hard?"

Ryder had never really paused to think about it. It was just what he needed to do to provide for his family.

"Yes," he said. "It was worth it." He pointed at the bathroom door. "She was worth it."

"You're a good father, Ryder," Maisy said.

A shadow passed over his face and when he glanced up at her, his gaze was fierce. "I have to be. I won't fail her the way my father failed my younger brother, Sawyer, and me."

Maisy wanted to hear more but she didn't press, knowing that if he wanted to talk he would and if he didn't at least she'd gotten a glimpse into his personal pain, a random piece of the puzzle that was Ryder Copeland.

She tipped her head in what she hoped was an inquisitive way, encouraging his confidence but not badgering. Ryder ran a hand over his face and gave her a rueful glance. "Sorry, you don't want to hear this."

"Of course I do," she insisted. "I'll listen to anything you have to tell me."

Ryder gave her a small smile and she almost jumped with triumph when he began to speak.

"My mother passed away when I was seven and losing her broke my father," he said. "He crawled into a bottle and never came back out. We moved often because he couldn't hold a job. We were frequently homeless, occasionally on public assistance, and I learned very young that if Sawyer and I were going to eat, it was on me to provide. When I found out I was going to be a father, I vowed that my child would never ever know what it was like to be hungry or scared. Not ever."

"Oh, Ryder," Maisy said. "Perry is an amazing young woman. You've clearly done a great job raising her."

"Maybe," he said. "I wasn't around as much as I wanted to be when she was little because of work and school, but we've been on our own for a while and I feel like I might be doing okay. At least, the school principal doesn't have me on speed dial or anything."

"You're doing better than okay," Maisy said. "Look how she talks to you about everything and trusts you. There is real affection between you and she listens to you. I've worked with kids not much older than her and a lot of them do not have that with either parent and usually not with their dad. Trust me, you're doing good work here."

"Thanks," he said. He had tried so hard to be everything for Perry when her mother went to pursue her own dreams. It had been a rough adjustment, but he felt as if they'd hit their stride. He might have screwed it up somewhere along the way and maybe a big fail was looming, but it wasn't for lack of effort.

When Perry reappeared, Ryder had to resist the urge to tuck her in like she was five. It was one of the many things he'd had to let go of as she became a teenager. There were still days when he came home expecting to find his toddler daughter tottering around in her mother's heels and instead found a slender young woman painting her nails with a hoodie all but covering her face. Sometimes she was gregarious and chatty and other times she was sullen and withdrawn. He tried not to take it personally.

Perry climbed into her comforter on the floor. She pulled the covers up and glanced at him and Maisy with a look that was older than her fourteen years. "Wake me up if the kitten so much as hiccups," she said. "I will be distraught if I wake up in the morning and it's de . . . no longer with us."

"I promise," he said. He glanced at Maisy. "We promise."

Maisy nodded and Ryder felt a connection he hadn't felt since Whitney left. The feeling that he wasn't alone in raising this young woman. It was ridiculous, he knew that, but still, for a fleeting moment, it felt good to share the parenting worry.

"Well, good night," Maisy said. She gave them a small wave and disappeared into her room.

Ryder watched her go, wondering how it was that she was single. She was such a breath of fresh air; she was smart, lively, funny, and adorable. How had no man snapped her up by now?

Like a sucker punch to the jaw, it hit him then that he was assuming she was single. She'd said she had no marriage or fiancé in her past. But she could have a boyfriend. He shook his head. He hated the thought. Detested it. Despised it. In fact, his heretofore unknown inner caveman wanted to hammer the idea of her with another guy into the ground with his fist.

"Dad," Perry whispered.

"Yeah," he said. Who would know if Maisy was single? Wait, what was he thinking? If she accepted his bid, he was going to work for her. He couldn't think of her *that* way. It was one of his long-standing rules. Do not get involved with clients. But she wasn't a client yet. He shook his head. Obviously, kissing her had rattled something loose and he wasn't thinking clearly.

"Dad." Perry said his name, this time with a note of exasperation, sort of like when he made spaghetti and she wanted tacos.

"What?" he asked.

"Your pacing is making it very hard to sleep," she said.

"Pacing?" He glanced around and realized he was across the room and had been going back and forth the entire time he was thinking about Maisy's status. This was just more proof that he getting in way over his head. He glanced at his daughter. "Sorry, I was just thinking about . . . work."

"Well, do it from a stationary position, please," Perry said. Then she rolled over, tugged the covers up around her ears, and fell asleep.

Ryder made a face behind his daughter's back. He couldn't wait until some boy came along and dinged her radar, then she'd know how he felt. Whoa, hold on, there. Yes, he could wait. He could wait until she was thirty-five, at the earliest. Maybe then he'd be willing to let go a little bit. He sighed as he stretched out on the fold-out couch and stared up at the old plaster ceiling.

He could handle this, he told himself. Maisy Kelly was just one woman in a sea of women. There was absolutely no reason for him to get all tripped up over her *Ideas!* with capital *I*'s and exclamation points. In fact, judging by the turret she had her heart set on, she was probably going to be trouble with a capital *T*. His best line of defense would be to steer clear of the cute little bookseller.

Settled on his course of action, Ryder closed his eyes and tried to sleep. He couldn't help it if his carpenter's brain estimated that it was exactly twenty steps to her room from his spot on the couch. He wasn't going to do anything about it. Really, he wasn't.

But that didn't stop their kiss from replaying in his mind in a continuous loop that made a complete and utter mockery of any thought he had about staying away from her.

Chapter Fifteen

THE alarm on her phone flashed and beeped a high-pitched repetitive chime that was impossible to ignore. Maisy looked at it and blinked. That had to be wrong. Was she flying somewhere? Had she taken leave of her senses and decided to go for a run in the middle of the night with Savy? Was there a hot sale from some company on the other side of the world that she needed to catch online? No, no, no. Why the hell was her alarm ringing at two in the morning?

Oh, yeah, the kitten. She shut off the alarm and climbed out of bed. Her room was only half-unpacked so she switched on the light to avoid tripping on her boxes of stuff. She grabbed her robe as she slid out of her wrought iron bed. Her sheets were hydrangea blue with a matching comforter that was white with embroidered bunches of blue and violet hydrangea all over it. She loved this bedding. It always made her feel as if she were outside on a beautiful spring day and she was oh-so reluctant to leave it.

She stepped lightly as she opened her door, not wanting to wake Perry or Ryder if she could help it. It had been a long night already and if Ryder was taking the four o'clock feeding, he was going to need his sleep.

She stepped around Perry and peered into the cardboard box, hoping with everything she had that the little one was all right. She dreaded the thought of having to be the one to tell the others, especially Perry, that it hadn't made it.

In the dim glow coming from the night-light across the room, she could see that the fuzzy nugget had moved so its back was against the side of the box. Its feet looked tiny and thin as if they couldn't support the weight of its fluffy black fur never mind any milk weight it might gain. Maisy put the backs of her fingers on its chest to make sure it was breathing. It was. It was warm and its little chest was rising and falling. She sagged a bit in relief.

She tiptoed around the fold-out bed where Ryder was fast asleep. She took a moment to study the man and then his daughter. They both slept on their backs with their mouths slightly open and one arm was flung over their heads while the other was down at their side. With the softness of sleep, the similarity of their features was even more obvious. They each had a wide brow and a square jaw, high cheekbones and long dark eyelashes, hiding what Maisy already knew they shared, their bright-blue eyes.

She knew that Perry was in her awkward stage right now, but there was no doubt that she was going to grow up to be a heartbreaker. Ryder was going to have his hands full, no question.

She supposed he was lucky they lived in a community like Fairdale. It was a college town, but it was a small campus and despite the new crops of students that came and went every year, Fairdale was the sort of place where everyone knew everyone else and they kept an eye on one another. Raising a teen girl could be tricky, but he'd have a lot of help here.

She prepped the kitten's milk and then crept back to the box and scooped it up, taking it into the bathroom so as not to wake everyone. The kitten let out a soft meow, but settled into her hand as if trusting her. Maisy felt her heart go smoosh.

She sat on the tile floor of the bathroom with her back propped up against the tub. She grabbed a towel from the rack and put the kitten in the middle of it. She remembered to get some formula on the bottle's nipple and sure enough the kitten latched on, sucking with gusto and making its ears wiggle while it did so.

"You are wrecking me, kitten," she said. "Who knew a half pound of fuzz could crawl inside my heart in a matter of hours?"

The kitten spread its front paws and started to knead the blanket while it drank. Its little feet were so tiny as it extended its itty-bitty claws while padding the terry cloth. Maisy wanted to hug it close to her and promise nothing bad would ever happen to it again, but of course that would be a lie. She had no idea if it would survive the night, never mind the next week. She felt her anxiety spike.

As if risking everything she had by opening the bookstore wasn't stressful enough, now she had this little life looking to her, to all of them, to save it. The thrum of panic surged through Maisy. What if she failed? What if she lost everything? What if the kitten died? She'd already quit her job and lost Auntie El; she didn't think she could handle another crushing blow.

A sob bubbled up in her throat before she could stop it. Tears dropped onto the kitten's fur and she was sure she was going to make it wet and cold and it would croak, shivering from the dampness of her tears. She held her hand over its back, shielding it from the tears she could not seem to stop.

"You have to live," she said. She sniffed. She turned her head so she could wipe her face on her shoulder, first one side and then the other. "I don't want to pressure you or anything, but I will be overwrought if something happens to you."

The kitten finished the bottle and stretched. Maisy took it as a good sign. She sniffed again, relieved that her tears seemed to have stopped. She put the bottle down and lifted the kitten up so she could pat its back. When it burped, she held it so that they were face-to-face. Much to her surprise, the kitten licked her nose with its tiny pink tongue. Maisy sighed.

"You are a charmer. Just so you know, there is a little girl out there who will be devastated if you don't make it, and so will I," Maisy said. "So, even though I know you don't like this, you really need to make with the business. Deal?"

The kitten closed its eyes as if ignoring her. Maisy grabbed a cotton ball and wet it with warm water. As she expected, the kitten didn't like having its potty makers rubbed any more than Maisy like rubbing them. The kitten's eyes popped open and it wiggled and yowled but Maisy persevered until the cotton ball was flooded with warm wet. At least it seemed to have the peeing thing down. Still no sign of number two. Maisy wrapped the kitten in a towel while she cleaned up. Then she crept back into the living room, hoping that the kitty's caterwauling hadn't woken anyone.

She tucked it back into its box, checking that the heating pad was warm but not hot. The towels were fluffed and the box was safely up against the wall and out of any lines of traffic so it wouldn't get kicked.

She glanced down at Perry. She had rolled onto her side and was still asleep. She glanced at Ryder on the fold-out couch, expecting him to be asleep as well. He was still on his back, as he'd been before, but his eyes were open and he was watching her with a look of concern.

"How did the kitten do?" he whispered. He pushed the covers aside and rolled up to a sitting position and then got to his feet. Maisy felt her heart thump hard as she took in his bare chest. Thank goodness he'd opted to sleep in his jeans, otherwise she might have fainted. She watched as he pulled his T-shirt over his head. Even in the dim light, she could see the man was pure muscle. Lord-a-mercy!

She glanced away, trying to regroup. She shook her head. She cleared her throat. She studied the floor. Floors were good. Floors were boring. Floors didn't have muscles or big callused hands that she wanted to feel . . . ahem.

"The kitten ate like a champ," she whispered to the floor. Her voice sounded breathy and she cleared her throat. "Still working on number two."

She felt the heat of his body next to hers when he stepped close to peer into the box. She saw his slash of white teeth in the dark. His voice was soft in her ear when he said, "I'm up next. I'll see what I can do."

"Good luck," she said. It felt like a lame thing to say, and she was glad it was dark and he couldn't see her blush. She edged away from him, thinking it wasn't safe to be standing this close to temptation. The urge to lick him or bite him like he was a piece of chocolate cake found on a late-night refrigerator raid was too much. Complete and utter torture, in fact.

"I think we need to talk," Ryder said. His voice was so soft she had to lean in to hear him.

"About what?" she asked.

He didn't answer. Instead, he took her hand and led her into her room and shut the door. Before Maisy could gather her wits, he leaned against the door and crossed his arms over his chest.

"Why were you crying?" he asked. His eyes were worried. "And, no, I'm not leaving until you tell me."

"Does that strong-arm stuff work with Perry?" she asked. She needed to divert him. She didn't want to admit how scared and weak she felt about the bookstore or the kitten.

"Never," he admitted. "But she's a teen. Stubbornness is like their superpower."

Maisy laughed. He smiled but he didn't move. He stood leaning against the door, not crowding her, not pushing her, just a steady presence, sort of like a rock, patiently waiting for her to share.

"I'm fine," she said. She met his gaze with a steady one of her own so he wouldn't doubt her.

"Aha!" he said. "My friend Zach says that when a woman says she's 'fine' she is anything but."

"What does this Zach know about being a woman?" Maisy asked.

"Zachary Caine grew up in a house full of women and then married a woman with two daughters. He might be the most woke man I know," Ryder said. "Besides, he runs a brewery in Maine that I helped restore from an old factory, so I got to watch him up close and personal when he met his wife. The man knows what he is talking about. Fine is never fine."

"Be that as it may, I really am fine," she said.

He didn't move. In fact, if anything he relaxed into the door as if he was willing to wait all night for her to spill her guts. Talk about stubborn!

"All right," she said. "I got a little terrified about our kitten's mortality—it's just too tiny and frail—which then rolled into a freak-out about the house—what if we can't remodel it to be functional as a bookstore?—then I had a spike of anxiety about the bookstore—what if it fails and I'm left with nothing or even worse I have to crawl back to the university and beg for a job from the dingleberry, who has repeatedly told me I'm going to fail? Good grief, I'd rather sell insurance or cars or my soul. All of which twisted into a nice punch of ambush grief, as you so aptly named it, for my aunt just to top off the emotional cocktail. So, I leaked out my eyeballs a little bit and now I'm fine."

She didn't sound fine, even Maisy knew that. She sounded panicked or quite possibly deranged. The words had come out in a rush as if she might not choke on the fear attached to them if she said them fast enough. Now that her rant was over, her chest was heaving and she thought she might pass out.

Ryder nodded. "Okay."

Maisy stared at him. "That's it?"

"I think that's all very realistic fear. Frankly, I'm terrified now, too," he said.

She gaped at him. "What? You're supposed to be talking me off the ledge not giving me a push!"

"How can I?" he asked. "You are insisting on a frigging turret. Man, I had no idea you had so much riding on this. You really want to stick it to the old boyfriend, don't you?"

"Of course I'm insisting on a turret. The turret is critical," she said. "Besides, I gave you the original plans for the house. How hard can it be to add something that was supposed to be there all along? And, for your information, this shop isn't just a plot to stick it to dingleberry. That's a part of it, but it's a very small part. Mostly, I want to own the shop, so that I can be free. Free to make my own decisions about how I spend my time and my money. Free to do something I believe in, which is connecting readers to books they will love and promoting happy endings in a world that, quite frankly, tends to give women the short end of the stick, pun intended, on a daily basis by pushing us down and keeping their feet on our necks.

"I want to be free of that patriarchal garbage and read books about women who are empowered, who determine their own existence, who make their own decisions, in business and in relationships, and demand respect and love from a partner who values them and does an equal share of the heavy lifting and not just some jackass who sucks the emotional life out of them by expecting them to be his mommy and his wife and his whore."

Ryder blinked at her and Maisy sat, or more accurately fell, onto the wooden chest at the end of her bed. She was out of breath and a little dizzy from the lack of oxygen during her tirade.

"That!" he said. "That's what I was looking for." He pushed off the door and took four long strides until he was standing right in front of her. He reached down and cupped her face, tilting her chin, so that she was gazing up at him. His blue eyes were fierce and he said, "If you show that much purpose and passion while working toward your dream, you will not fail. I know it."

Then he kissed her. His fingers dug into her curls, holding her head in place and his mouth came down on hers in a kiss that felt like a celebration of all that she was and all that she could be. It was amazing.

If she'd thought their first kiss had been electric, this one was like a lightning strike. His mouth against hers was like a sparkler going off inside of her as a cascade of tingles and shivers rocketed around her insides. She arched her back and looped her arms around his neck, pulling him closer while she kissed him with all of the leftover worry and fear and angst still inside of her. But in the meeting of their mouths, all of the negative energy twisted in on itself, reemerging as something new, something hot, something wicked, and something unstoppable.

Ryder kissed her with a single-minded intensity that left her breathless. When she would have stood up to press herself against him, he released her and Maisy's arms slid from his shoulders as he took a quick step back.

Maisy sucked in a breath and had to force her spine to stay straight, so she didn't slide down the furniture and land in a heap at his feet.

"Um, sorry about that," he said. "In my head, I was supposed to kiss your forehead in comfort or something, but yours lips . . . I got distracted."

Maisy nodded. "I could see where that could happen. No problem."

"I told myself I wouldn't do that again, but you, we, this . . . er . . . I'm going to go before this gets awkward or weird," he said.

Too late.

He turned and opened the door. He stepped through it, but then glanced back at her over his shoulder. "Remember your purpose, Maisy. You've got this."

He shut the door after him, and Maisy sat there for a moment, feeling as if she were sitting in the aftermath of a small tornado. What the hell was that?

She'd kissed her share of men. None, not one, of those kisses had ever made her feel as cherished and desired as Ryder's kisses had. What did that mean? Was she just an overtired emotional wreck? Or was there something special happening here? She grinned. Of course, something special was happening here. After years of searching for her Mr. Right, she was pretty sure she'd found him.

She climbed up onto her bed, not even bothering to take off her robe, and rolled herself under her covers. She was certain that with the imprint of Ryder's mouth on her lips and the fact that he had just fractured every idea she'd ever had about what she should feel when she was being kissed that she'd never sleep. She was wrong. With a surge of optimism about the business and her love life, she fell asleep as if she'd taken a one-two punch to the noggin.

* * *

THE sound of voices woke her, and Maisy blinked at her ceiling. Her first thought was that it was awfully early for Savannah to have the television on. Her second thought was that the man's voice she heard sounded familiar. Ryder.

In a flash, she remembered their kiss. She remembered him in her room, making her share her fears even when she didn't want to and his absolute belief in her ability to make this bookstore happen. And the kiss. She was pretty sure she was never going to forget that moment. Not ever.

She rose from the bed, anxious to see Ryder. Had his dreams been punctuated by memories of their kisses? Had he thought about her like she'd thought about him all night long? She was sure he must have. What they'd shared, well, it was the stuff of romance novels, wasn't it?

She quickly changed into jeans and a T-shirt and ran a brush through her curls. Donning her glasses, she gave herself a quick check in the mirror. She looked casual but cleaned up. She debated putting on lipstick but she didn't want to appear too eager. She left her room and stepped into the living room to find everyone was up and gathered around Hannah Phillips, who was holding the kitten in one hand and covering a yawn with the other.

"Maisy, hi," she said when she caught sight of her in her doorway.

Maisy felt all eyes turn toward her, including Ryder's, but she kept her gaze on Hannah and turned her lips up in a smile. Be cool. Just be cool. Nothing to see here.

"Hannah, this is so great of you to come over and check on the kitten," she said. "You must be exhausted. What happened with the calf?"

"She got him out," Savy said. "Mama and baby are doing fine."

"Can I get you some coffee?" Maisy asked.

"No thanks," Hannah said. "I plan to go home and sleep all day." She looked at Perry. "Can I assume you are the in-case-of-emergency contact for this little one?"

Perry pushed her glasses up on her nose and glanced at her father as if in question. He nodded and she said, "Yes."

"All right, do we have a name?" Hannah asked.

"I was thinking Georgette," Perry said. "You know, after Georgette Heyer."

"The Regency novelist?" Hannah nodded in approval and her thick braid of blond hair, which had a few stray bits of hay in it, swung across her back. She was petite like Maisy, but the similarity ended there. When she wasn't tending sick animals, Hannah was a CrossFit junkie. Even her muscles had muscles, which only amped up her generous curves all the more.

"She looks like a Georgette, doesn't she?" Perry asked.

"Let's see." Hannah lifted up the kitten and checked its underside. "Well, you might want to shorten the name to George."

"The kitten's a dude?" Ryder asked. Maisy gave him a quick glance. He was in his T-shirt and jeans but his hair was mussed and he was barefoot. Why was that attractive? She'd never found a man's feet attractive before. They were feet. Feet were ugly. Except his. Oh, boy, she was totally besotted with this man.

"Yep," Hannah said. "He looks to be a little less than two weeks old. He's on the small side. His eyes are open, but they aren't dilating yet and his ears are folded. The next two weeks will be critical but if he thrives during those two, he should make it."

"Two weeks?" Savannah asked. "Of feeding him every two hours and helping him pee and poop?"

Hannah smiled. "You'll be able to start going longer between feedings soon and he'll take to the litter box pretty quickly. One thing to keep in mind. He's going to be sleeping about twenty hours a day. You'll want to keep him in a safe place where the light isn't too bright, since his eyes aren't fully developed yet."

She handed the kitten off to Perry, who held him close to her heart and whispered into his fur, "Hi, George, do you like the name George? It's very dignified. There's a prince named George and there was a character in the book I just read named George Wickham."

"I think he's more of a regal George than a rogue George," Ryder said. "Since he is the king of the castle, we should call him King George."

"Oh, I like that," Perry said. "King George, it is."

Savannah leaned over the back of the couch and rubbed George's head with her thumb. "I like it, too, so long as I don't have to curtsy every time he comes into the room."

"What about you, Maisy?" Ryder turned to her. She felt her heart thump hard in her chest as she forced her gaze to meet his and not move to his lips. Ack! Too late. She forced her eyes back up, met his gaze, and held it.

"I think King George is a perfect name," she said.

"All hail King George," Hannah said. "Great, now I have to go before I pass out on my feet. Call me if you need me, but barring anything unexpected, I'd say you've got this. If you plan to offer him up for adoption, you'll want to get him neutered and litter box trained first."

"I'll walk you out," Maisy volunteered.

"Thanks," Hannah said.

"I'll come, too," Ryder said. "I have some questions."

Maisy glanced at him. Was he using this as a ploy to get her alone? She went a little dizzy at the thought. Why hadn't she taken the time to shower or brush her teeth? Dang it.

As they made their way downstairs, Ryder asked Hannah all sorts of questions about feeding the kitten and what things they should look for in case he took a turn for the worse.

Hannah answered him with the calm patience of a woman who has had this conversation a million times before. "I can't give you a guarantee that he'll make it, but if you've got him eating and relieving himself, it's looking very promising. I'll come back and check on him in a few days."

"Thanks, Hannah," Maisy said. A yawn slipped out. She tried to stop it, but it was too powerful.

"Don't mention—" Hannah began but then she yawned, too. "Stop that."

With a wave, she strode down the steps and turned left, heading to her home at the end of the street for a long sleep.

Maisy turned back into the house. There. She and Ryder were alone. Would he make another move? Her pulse kicked up into high gear in anticipation. She glanced at him, trying to get a read on what he was thinking, but the man had his feelings on lockdown. She had her foot on the first step of the staircase, ready to jog back up, when she felt his fingers grasp hers, halting her progress.

"Hey," he said. "Before we're back in the thick of things, I think we should talk."

Talk? Was that code for "make out"? She certainly hoped so. Maisy forced herself not to overreact and instead politely asked, "Really? About what?"

"About those kisses," he said.

Chapter Sixteen

"KISSES?" she asked. Her voice went up higher than she would have liked and she cleared her throat, pretending there was something stuck in her larynx besides nerves.

He looked at her with one eyebrow lowered, and Maisy knew even fictional cowboy hero Jake Sinclair couldn't make a girl blush like Ryder did. He was clearly calling her on her bullshit with that look.

"Oh, yeah," she said. "Those kisses."

"I want to apologize," he said. "In the thick of all the chaos last night, I overstepped. It was incredibly unprofessional of me and it won't happen again."

It won't? Maisy felt her heart pop inside her chest like a balloon being pricked with a pin. So, he hadn't felt the same way about their moments together and was, in fact, rejecting her. The realization was a crusher. She wanted to protest. She wanted to insist he rethink his position. She wanted to kiss him senseless.

Praise be to all the stars in the sky that twinkled on high that the words did not actually slip from her lips. Instead, she swallowed her disappointment and tapped into her inner

Southern lady with a spine of steel hidden inside a peachy exterior, and said, "Don't you worry about it. I mean, it's not like those were real kisses. They were more like kissing-cousin sorts of kisses."

His right eyebrow lowered again, but Maisy didn't wait for his reply. She turned quickly and jogged up the stairs, tucking her disappointment way down deep. At the landing, she glanced at him over her shoulder, because she just had to get one more look at his wrinkly clothed, bewhiskered, and bed-headed, gloriously handsome person and caught him staring at her with a look of longing so sharp it cut away her defenses with surgical precision.

And that's when she knew Ryder Copeland was a big, fat liar. He was trying to pretend that their kisses meant nothing but she knew, absolutely knew, from the look on his face that he was just as drawn to her as she was to him. She paused until he was right behind her. The devil flew into her and she couldn't resist just one more poke at him.

"We'll just forget all about it, okay?" she said.

"I don't think—" he began but she interrupted.

"Oh, and I didn't get a chance to tell you, but I'm accepting your bid to renovate the house." She gazed at him through her lashes and lowered her voice in what she hoped sounded like an invitation and said, "I'm really looking forward to working with you."

Ryder looked like she'd sucker punched him. Maisy turned and strode into the apartment, hiding her smile. What had he said to her last night? "If you show that much purpose and passion while working toward your dream, you will not fail. I know it." Well, little did he know, Ryder had just become a part of her dream.

Savannah called a meeting about the kitten and they all agreed that the safest place for King George during the day when the house was under construction was in the hidden room, which was safe from all of the debris and dust of the renovation. With Ryder working on the house and Perry in school, it only made sense to keep the kitten here where there was always someone available to tend to him.

Maisy and Savannah agreed to take the nighttime and

early-morning feedings. Perry wanted the after-school and evening shifts, and Ryder volunteered to tuck King George in every night because, as he said, he was very good at reading bedtime stories. Maisy tried not to dwell on how ridiculously cute that was.

With a plan in motion, they tucked George into his box and Ryder left to take Perry home so she could get ready for school. Maisy shut the door after them and for the first time all morning she felt herself relax.

"You hired him, didn't you?" Savannah asked.

"Yes," Maisy said. "But just so you know I did get e-mails from two other architects and they were both way more expensive than Ryder, and they weren't local. He's local and already has a crew of men ready to get started."

"Listen, I like the guy," Savy said. "He and Perry seem like great people, but what do you know about him as relationship material?"

"It doesn't matter," Maisy said. "He and I talked and he was very clear that he felt he'd overstepped and it wouldn't happen again."

"So, how is that a good thing?"

"It's not, but it gives me the length of the restoration project to change his mind," Maisy said.

"No, no, no," Savy said. "This is such a bad idea. If a man tells you he's not interested, he usually means it. M, you're setting yourself up for a world of hurt."

"Nothing ventured, nothing gained."

"You're going to get heartbroken." Savy shook her head.

"Maybe, but I think it's worth the risk," she said. "I mean, I can't own the Happily Ever After Bookstore if I don't believe in HEAs for myself, can I? It might only be a summer fling and I'll be left with nothing but lovely memories, but I think that's better than nothing."

"Oh, please, the heart wants what the heart wants, and if you fall for him, you'll want more than a temporary fling."

"My heart wants a bookstore."

Savannah twisted her long red curls into a messy knot on the top of her head. "Well, your heart may want a bookstore, but your lady parts are probably hoping for something else entirely. You know what I'm saying?"

"Don't say it," Maisy said.

"Sexy time," Savannah sang. Then she smiled. "There. I didn't *say it*."

Maisy rolled her eyes. She refused to acknowledge how desperately her lady parts wanted a little sexy time, or a lot of sexy time, or, heck, any sexy time. Even the thought of doing any of that with Ryder practically made her cross-eyed, which was not her best look.

"Come on, we have packing and sorting to do," she said.

"Ugh, you did not mention the amount of manual labor involved in getting your bookstore up and running," Savy said. She flexed her arm, making her bicep pop. "I'm going to be in the best shape of my life after this."

"Good, maybe you'll find a Ryder of your own."

"No, I am merely passing through," Savy said. "And don't you forget it."

"We'll see," Maisy said as she led the way out of their apartment and down to the shop. "We'll see."

"WE'LL just forget all about it, okay?" Sure, no problem, Ryder thought. He could forget. It was just a couple of kisses. Yeah, right. He'd forget like he'd forget his own name or Perry's birthday or the number of yards his favorite wide receiver had run to make the game-winning touchdown in last year's playoff game. Sure, no big deal.

Huh. Who was he kidding? Kissing Maisy was a huge deal. First, because he had barely gotten his mouth on Maisy's when his good sense had kicked in and he knew he should let go of her, but the damage had been done—twice. Even now, he wanted to kiss her again and again and again.

But it wasn't fair to Maisy. He'd seen the way she looked at him. She had hearts in her eyes, clearly looking for more than he could give. He had an inability to sustain the romantic relationships in his life. In an effort to save his marriage, he'd read up on emotional detachment disorders as the adult child of an alcoholic. There'd been a checklist in the book. Control freak? Check. Conflict avoidance? Check. Inability to verbalize feelings? Check. On a scale of one to ten with ten being an emotional cripple, he was a solid eight, possibly a nine. Maisy deserved better than that.

"Dad!" Perry nudged his elbow. Lost in thought, Ryder had almost driven right by her school. He checked that the road was clear and cut the wheel sharply, bringing his green truck right up against the curb. They both lurched in their seats and Perry shook her head at him. "You need to get some sleep."

"Agreed," Ryder said. They had been moving at a clip since they left Maisy's, having stopped at their house for breakfast, showers, and a change of clothes. He was low on caffeine and not fully functional. He ran a hand over his face. "See you after school?"

"I'll go right to Maisy's to take care of King George," she said. "Text me about how he is during the day."

"Okay."

"Promise." Perry opened her door and perched on her seat, waiting for his answer.

"I promise."

"I love you, Dad." Perry glanced over her shoulder at him and Ryder was struck by how much he loved this kid. He raised his right hand and made the sign language sign for *I love you*, because he'd never managed to master those three little words even though he felt them all the way to his core, or maybe that was why he couldn't say them. Putting his emotions out there terrified his inner control freak, who was convinced the words invited tragedy. Perry flashed the sign back at him with a tired smile.

She hopped down, swinging her backpack onto her shoulder. Ryder watched her stride confidently into the building. He sure hoped she took all of that middle school swagger and confidence up to Connecticut with her.

His chest felt tight and he absently rubbed his fist over his sternum. Letting Perry go was going to be the greatest loss of his life, second only to watching his brother, Sawyer, pack up his motorcycle and head out for parts unknown when

Ryder married Whitney in preparation for Perry's arrival. Not a day went by that he didn't miss his brother and wish that they could have stayed close. He remembered how lost he'd felt without Sawyer, so he could only imagine how much worse letting Perry go was going to be. He really didn't know how he was going to survive it, but this wasn't about him. It was about her and giving her all of the opportunities he and his brother, Sawyer, had never had. So what if he cried himself to sleep every night after she left? He was man enough to handle it.

Ryder checked his mirrors and pulled out of the school drop-off lane. He had already called his foreman to rally his crew to meet up at Maisy's house and begin the renovation. He needed to get his head in the game. Lusting after his client was not the way to handle this project. Period. He had to shut that shit down.

Newly resolved, Ryder drove through Fairdale back to Maisy's house. Because of the university, the town had a population that surged from fifty thousand to over seventy-five during the school year. It was full of restaurants, bars, and quirky one-of-a-kind shops, the sort that appealed to a large student populace, and it all centered around the expansive town green that hosted a weekly farmer's market as well as festivals, art shows, and performances in the bandstand year-round. Fairdale had come into its own in the late 1800s, and the old redbrick buildings maintained the integrity of that time.

Ryder found a parking spot on the green across from the Perk Up, the local coffee shop. His timing was perfect as the morning rush had already passed. The smell of ground coffee greeted him as he opened the door. Heaven. The place was all dark wood and exposed brick. Businesspeople and students filled most of the tables, which was fine as he was taking his order to go.

The girl behind the counter wore large round glasses that gave her an owlish appearance. Her brown bib apron had a steaming coffee mug embroidered on it with the name *Kara*. She smiled at him.

"Hi, how can I help you?"

"I'd like three large coffees to go," he said. *Three?* Where had that come from? He realized that after the night they had all spent, sleep deprived because of George, he felt it was only polite to bring Maisy and Savannah some coffee. And maybe, just maybe, he was hoping any residual awkwardness between him and Maisy would be dissipated by a hot cup of joe.

He had Kara put the cream and sugar on the side and then he carried the three large cups in a cardboard holder out to his truck. It was going to be another spectacular day in the Smoky Mountains, with a clear-blue sky, warm sun, and cool breeze. It was the perfect day to start his new job; he just had to remember it was a job. Period.

He would treat Maisy like he did any other client. He'd never gotten personally involved with one before and he wasn't going to do so now. She was a nice lady. She deserved a nice guy who would be there for her. He was not that guy.

With this plan firmly set in his mind, he pulled up in front of the house to find his contractor, Seth Stolowicz, waiting for him. Maisy was standing on the porch, talking to Seth. Ryder could tell by the way she waved her arms at the corner of the house that she was explaining her *Idea!* for the turret. Judging by the grin on Seth's face, he thought it was a great *Idea!*

Seth was a good guy. He was married with four kids, he showed up early, and he worked late. He never complained and he took his work seriously. *Perfection* was his middle name and he expected the same out of the men he hired. Getting put on a job by Seth meant the work would be hard, but the rewards many, mostly because, in an uncertain economy like building, Seth's work ethic and quality of craftsmanship meant he was in high demand and his crew would always have a job.

Ryder liked Seth. He'd always liked Seth, but as he grabbed the coffee carrier off the passenger seat and strode across the front yard, a twisty feeling in his gut made him scowl at his right-hand man. Maisy was staring up at Seth—he stood about six-four in his work boots—and was laughing at something he said. For some inexplicable reason, this made Ryder cranky. He told himself it was the lack of caffeine running through his system.

"Mornin', Seth," he said. "You're early."

Seth shrugged. "I'm always early."

"Yeah, well." Ryder didn't have anything else to say. When Maisy smiled at Seth, Ryder's crankiness rolled into full-on grumpiness. He turned to Maisy, lifted his coffee out of the holder, and held out the remaining coffee to her. "Here, for you and Savannah."

She blinked at him from behind her glasses, then she smiled and said, "Thank you." Her smile was wide and warm and blew away his bad attitude like a brisk breeze blowing away a puff of smoke.

"No problem," he said. He stared at her a moment too long and then took a swig of his hot coffee, hoping the bitter brew would kick-start his common sense. It didn't. "How's George?"

"Sleeping," she said. "We put him in the secret room, so he'd be safely out of the way."

"Secret room, no kidding?" Seth asked. "I love those."

"I know, right?" Maisy asked. She danced on her toes and Ryder noticed she was in her flowery sneakers again but today she wore jeans and a blue tank top with a pink-and-blue-plaid shirt over it. Her curls were in wild disarray around her head and she had on a minimal amount of makeup. Adorable. "I didn't even know the house had a hidden room, and I've been coming here since I was born. It's crazy."

"Old houses have secrets," Seth said. He glanced up at the Queen Anne that loomed above them. "I bet we discover all sorts of things about this house."

"Well, we have our work cut out for us to get to those secrets," Ryder said.

"What do you mean?" Seth asked.

"Come on, I'll give you the tour," Ryder said. He glanced back at Maisy. "Is Savannah up in the apartment?"

"No, she's in the room we cleared out for an office, working on her laptop to develop our online profile," Maisy said. She glanced at Seth. "Has Ryder told you why we're renovating the place?"

"He said something about a bookshop," Seth said.

Maisy nodded. "A very specific type of bookshop."

Seth looked intrigued and Maisy cradled the coffee carrier and gestured for him to follow her into the house. She pushed open the door and they entered the foyer. Ryder noted that since he'd first come here, Maisy had done an amazing job sorting and boxing up what would become her inventory. There was actually room to move now, although stacks of books still lined the walls and it was to one of these stacks that Maisy led them.

She picked up a book with her free hand and held it out to Seth. The cover showed a cowboy sitting on a picnic table in a pasture. He was wearing jeans and white T-shirt and had a cowboy hat over his face. Seth glanced from the book to Maisy and back to the book.

"Remind you of anyone?" she asked. There was a wicked twinkle in her eye.

Seth looked confused and then he grinned. He held up the book next to Ryder's head and said, "Dude, I had no idea you were a romance novel cover model. Jade is going to freak out."

"What?" Ryder pulled back and looked at the cover. Dear God, he was dressed exactly like the man on the cover right down to the hat. "Great, now I'm going to have to burn all of my clothes."

Maisy and Seth burst out laughing. Then she sobered and said, "Don't do that. Jake Sinclair is one of my absolute favorite heroes. I like that you remind me of him." Then she turned back to Seth and gestured to all of the books and the boxes and said, "All of these are my great-aunt Eloise's romance novels, collected over the past fifty years. I'm going to open a shop and find them new homes."

"All of these?" Seth asked.

"And upstairs, too," Maisy said. "I haven't even been able to guestimate how many books there are."

"So, it'll be a romance bookstore," he said.

"Yep."

Ryder noticed that Maisy was watching Seth's reaction closely. To his surprise, he found that he was, too. He did not want Maisy's dream to get squashed or her feelings to get hurt if his foreman put his big boot in it. He needn't have worried.

"That is brilliant," Seth declared. "My wife, Jade, reads romance. I swear that woman goes through five books per week. I asked her why she reads so many and she said because when she is emotionally exhausted from giving me and the kids her all, the books fill her up again and give her what she needs to keep going."

"Aw, that's so well put," Maisy said. "So many people just don't get it. Feel free to take any books you'd like for her."

Seth glanced down at the book in his hand, but Maisy snatched it. "Except that one. Jake Sinclair is my book boyfriend."

Seth laughed. "Jade has a few of those." He leaned in close and said, "I appreciate them helping me out in the romance department, if you know what I mean."

Maisy laughed and Ryder frowned. Clearly, Seth was more up to speed on the whole romance novel genre than he was. Well, that was going to end today. How could he responsibly design the new space if he wasn't in the know? He grabbed the cowboy romance out of Maisy's hand. She looked at him in surprise.

"I have to find out if my doppelgänger is worthy or not," he said. He tried to sound all casual and he was pretty sure he had Maisy convinced, but one look at the shrewd glint in Seth's eyes and he knew he wasn't fooling him one bit. He shoved the novel into his back pocket. "Come on, Seth, I want to show you where we'll be starting before the rest of the crew gets here."

"Sure thing, boss," Seth said.

If there was a teasing note in his voice, Ryder refused to acknowledge it. Honestly, couldn't a man read a romance novel without people getting all judgy?

Chapter Seventeen

"WHO has King George?" Maisy asked as she hurried into the office. She was trying not to panic but she'd gone into the hidden room to feed him and he wasn't there.

Savannah looked up from her laptop and said, "Ryder heard him cry on the baby monitor so he went up to check on him. He probably took him up to our apartment to feed him."

"Oh, but it's my shift," Maisy said. The past thirty-six hours had been harried and messy, but they'd found a rhythm with caring for George. She had come to enjoy snuggling the tiny kitten as a nice break from the packing, sorting, and endless debates about the house and how Ryder and his crew were going to carry out her vision.

"I'm sure he won't mind if you take over," Savannah said. "The only reason he went was because we didn't know where you were."

"Sorry," Maisy said. "I was on the second floor measuring for shelving. I can't decide if I want to have shelving units like a library or display the books in shelves along the walls to make it easier to see where customers are."

"Go with half shelves for the new books, which will

separate them from the older volumes," Savannah said. "Best of both worlds and you can use the tops for displays."

"I was thinking the same thing," Maisy said. "Excellent. Will you write a note reminding me to ask Jeri how much we have in the budget for shelves?"

"Noted. Also, we could try to find some surplus shelves from bookstores or libraries that don't need them anymore."

"Good thought. Note that, too."

Savannah gave her a thumbs-up, which Maisy took as "you're dismissed."

She hurried upstairs to the apartment. Since neither she nor Savannah had anything of value in the apartment, they didn't keep it locked. She pushed the door open and sure enough, there was Ryder sitting on the couch feeding King George. The tiny kitten was eating like a champ and while he wasn't out of the woods yet, he was definitely putting up a heck of a fight. He'd even started pooping. A truly momentous occasion. So much so, that when it happened, Maisy was certain it was the single greatest achievement of her life to date.

Ryder had his back to the door and didn't hear her come in. Maisy paused on the threshold to observe the man and the kitten. It was dumb—she knew that. Since their talk yesterday morning, Ryder had treated her with nothing but friendly respect.

It was appropriate for the professional relationship they shared. Too bad Maisy had less than no interest in a strictly professional relationship with the man. She had told Savannah she was going to try and change Ryder's mind. She had no idea how to go about it other than to be ever present, not stalking him exactly, but rather weaving herself into the fabric of his days.

When Ryder's voice broke the silence, she thought he was talking to her and it took her a second to realize he was talking to George, reading to him, in fact. She didn't move, curious to know what he could be sharing with the kitten.

"*There certainly was some great mismanagement in the education of those two young men. One has got all the goodness, and the other all the appearance of it,*'" he read. He put the book down and adjusted the bottle George had latched on to. "That's your namesake they're talking about, George Wickham. He is a very, very bad man. Look how upset he made Elizabeth. Of course, she's been so mean to Mr. Darcy, I kind of feel like she deserves it. You're not going to turn out like Wickham, are you, Little G? I'm guessing no, since as soon as you're old enough, you'll be getting your boy parts snipped. Sorry about that, by the way. It's nothing personal."

Maisy tried to hold in her laugh, she really did, but when he started commiserating with the little guy about getting neutered, she lost it in one big undignified snort. Ryder's head whipped around at the noise and he smiled at her. It made his blue eyes brighten and she got the feeling he was happy to see her.

Maisy thought about pretending that she was coughing, but she knew it was useless. Instead, she let the laughter out and said, "Sorry. I didn't mean to interrupt. Were you actually reading *Pride and Prejudice* to him?"

"Yeah," he said. He held up the book Perry had returned to her. "We started reading it last night. Big fan of Austen, he is."

"Really?" she asked.

"Oh, yeah. I read a chapter or two to him during his feeding and he is out like a light," Ryder said.

Maisy gave him a horrified look. "Are you calling Austen boring?"

"Not for me," he said. "But I think it might be a bit over George's head."

"Maybe we should be reading him *Curious George* instead," Maisy said. She crossed the room and knelt down beside Ryder. Her face was level with the kitten's. If he knew she was there, he didn't show it. He kept working on his milk. His tiny paws were stretched out and his claws, the size of needles, were flexing as he kneaded the towel as if he were making kitty biscuits.

"He seems to be getting bigger," she said.

"He's getting a belly," he agreed. "His eyes seem clearer, but his ears are still tucked."

"Maybe he's a Scottish fold," Maisy said.

"A what?"

"It's a breed of cat whose ears stay folded down."

"Huh, I've never heard of that," he said.

"I hadn't, either, but Perry's been reading up on cats and educating me," she said.

Ryder smiled. "She is a bit attached. I'd discourage it, but it gives me hope."

"What do you mean?"

"When Dr. Phillips told us very clearly not to get attached because George likely won't survive, I saw the look on my daughter's face," he said. His gaze met Maisy's and she could see the pride shining through. "It was her ornery look, the one she gets when she digs in her heels and decides something needs to be done. An abandoned kitten, what to many would be a lost cause, a small inconsequential life of no importance, she decided was worth fighting for."

His voice was gruff and Maisy saw a glint of deep emotion in his eyes. She felt her own eyes get damp and her throat was tight.

"And in a world that can be pretty brutal, it made me realize that we're going to be okay."

Maisy swallowed, forcing the lump down. Ryder gave her a small smile and then looked down at the tiny kitten. He ran his thumb gently over the black and gray stripes on George's forehead. "You're going to make it, buddy, I promise."

Maisy sighed. For the first time since they'd found the kitten, her shoulders dropped from down around her ears and she felt like all of their efforts to save the little guy were going to pay off. She watched Ryder rub his eyes with the back of his hand. When he met her gaze, he looked chagrined.

"What? I'm not crying, you're crying," he teased.

Maisy laughed. She couldn't argue it. She rose and took a tissue from the box on the counter and blew her nose.

"Do you really think he'll survive?" she asked as she sat beside him.

"Yes," he said. "I really do. I don't know why he was on your front porch or how it was that we happened to find him, but I feel like he belongs to this house. Maisy, I think he was destined to be your bookstore cat."

George stopped drinking and fell backward off the bottle. He was still weak in the legs but he could scuttle around a bit. He seemed to know they were talking about him and he lurched toward Maisy with a soft cry. She held out her hands and scooped him up. She rubbed his soft fur against her cheek, kissed his tiny head, and marveled that this little guy had managed to find them.

"You're right," she said. "He belongs here."

"I'm glad you agree, because Seth and I were thinking we should build a cat tree for him," he said. "And I may have already made some sketches for it."

He gave her a wary look, but Maisy didn't have the heart to tease him by pretending to be put out. She gave him a side eye and said, "So, you had an *Idea!*"

It was Ryder's turn to laugh. "Okay, you got me there. It's not on as grand a scale as your turret, but I am going for optimum coolness with a hammock, scratching posts, swinging toys, and plenty of levels and cubbies. It's going to be amazing."

"Of course it will," she said.

They stared at each other for a second and Maisy wasn't sure what exactly changed between them, but there was a sudden charge to the air, exactly like before when he'd kissed her. The realization that only a few inches and one tiny little puff ball of fur sat between them seemed to occur to them at the same time.

Maisy knew that this was her moment. If she wanted to kiss Ryder again, this was her chance. She leaned in close so that the particular scent that she had come to know as his, coffee blended with sawdust and an old-fashioned bar soap, filled her senses. She was just a breath away when she saw him lean forward as well. Victory was so close.

"Where is my kitty?" A voice interrupted the moment and Maisy lurched back, still holding George cupped in her hands. "Oh, there he is! Gimme kitty."

Jeri came charging into the room with her hands outstretched and her fingers wiggling. Maisy loved Jeri like a sister, really she did, but at the moment she wasn't sure if she wanted to hug her or strangle her.

Jeri didn't give her a chance for either as she scooped George up and started kissing his tiny head. George let out half of a meow and then settled into Jeri's hands as if he knew it was useless to fight the loving she was putting on him. Maisy had seen similar expressions of resignation on all of Jeri's sons.

"You're just in time," she said. "He's finished eating and needs help going to the bathroom now."

"Ew." Jeri curled her lip. She held out the kitten to Maisy, who crossed her arms, and then to Ryder, who did the same. "Fine." She lifted George up so they were nose to nose. "You just let Auntie Jeri help you with your business, little man." She walked toward the bathroom with him. "We've got this."

Maisy and Ryder exchanged a grin. "Dodged a bullet there," he said.

"Totally," Maisy agreed.

"Well, I'd better get back," Ryder said. "Seth will sand the new woodwork too much if I don't keep an eye on him."

Maisy nodded and watched him leave. It didn't occur to her until after he left that the bullet he talked about dodging might have been their almost kiss as opposed to potty duty with George. She really hoped it was the latter.

THE next week was spent in a blur of shifting boxes as Maisy and Savannah tried to stay ahead of the restoration crew. Maisy also spent the week trying to get a read on Ryder and his feelings for her. The man gave nothing away. Maddening!

Maisy, Ryder, and Seth all agreed that the ground floor should be refurbished first, then the second floor and, lastly, the turret built, so that Maisy could open the bookshop as soon as possible and start a revenue stream, hopefully, even while the building was still under construction.

The care and feeding of King George became a refuge for Maisy. Somehow when she was tucked away in the secret room with the kitten all the problems with opening a bookstore fell away. Taking care of him and making sure he was thriving were her only purpose, plus she'd discovered he was a really good listener.

It was a particularly rough morning, after Maisy had

spent another sleepless night fretting about her bottom line, the bookstore's layout, the possibility of failure, and her terminal case of the hots for Ryder, that she spilled her guts while feeding the kitten. George, to his credit, didn't take much notice as Maisy was feeding him a bottle full of kitten formula.

"Can you keep a secret, Little G?" Maisy asked. He kept sucking on his bottle so she took that as a *yes*. "I'm feeling completely overwhelmed. I mean, I knew my aunt collected romance novels, but I didn't really appreciate how many until I started packing and moving them, trying to find some sort of order in the chaos. She had absolutely no system. I mean, the books aren't even grouped by author. Who does that?"

George blinked at her and Maisy felt like he understood.

"It's anarchy, I tell you. There are just too many books. I don't think I can clear out enough to even open the store and I think I might have a nervous breakdown," she said. She adjusted the bottle so it would flow better and George latched back on. "And then there's the fact that every book I touch reminds me of Auntie El. It's like she's here with me, but she's not and she never will be again."

Maisy took a shaky breath. She refused to cry all over the poor kitten. It'd likely scare the wee fella.

"I wish you could have met her, Georgie," she said. "Auntie El would have loved you. Even though her husband died young, she never stopped believing in true love. She always saw the best in people, even when they didn't see it themselves."

She sniffed. "I miss her so much, Georgie." The kitten finished his bottle and Maisy picked him up and patted his back. "She used to sing to me whenever I spent the night at her house, and it was always 'Over the Rainbow.' I felt so loved when she sang it to me."

Maisy took a deep breath and began to sing, which was not her gift, but she figured George wasn't that fussy and besides, it made her feel better, as if by sharing a piece of Auntie El she was keeping her memory alive. She sang softly and King George nestled into her palm, letting out a kitten yawn. Encouraged, she went all in, singing at top volume, drawing out every note. By the time she reached the end, the kitten was fast asleep.

"I hope you know how loved you are, Georgie," she whispered.

Maisy kissed his head and set him gently into his box. He was getting a round little belly and he looked stronger. Maybe Ryder was right and the little guy was going to make it after all. It gave Maisy hope.

Tiptoeing up the stairs, she closed the entrance to the hidden room and went back to her pile of books in the first room on the second floor. There she sat with her laptop, trying to create an inventory. She had decided to start a one hundred club for authors such as Anne Mather, Penny Jordan, and Charlotte Lamb, who'd each written over one hundred romances. She was just thinking she needed a five hundred club for Barbara Cartland, when Jeri and Savannah entered the room. She knew from the looks on their faces that they had come for more than chitchat. She felt her heart pound hard in her chest.

"What's wrong? Is everything all right? It's not King George, is it? I was just with him and he seemed fine."

"He is," Savy said. "He's great. Cutest cat ever and totally photogenic."

"For a woman who says she doesn't love animals, you're sounding awfully attached to Little G," Maisy said.

"That's different," Savy said. "Once you decided he was going to be the bookstore cat, I started to view him as a co-worker and not just a needy kitten. Besides, he is social media gold. I've put up pics and videos of him, linking him to the Happily Ever After Bookstore, and we already have several thousand followers. Genius, I know."

Jeri laughed. She pointed one well-manicured finger at Savannah and said, "Liar. It's not just promotion. You love him."

Savy tossed her hair and ignored her, most likely because they all knew what Jeri said was true.

"Okay, if you're not here about George then what is it?" Maisy asked. "You both look like you have something on your mind. Something not awesome."

"We were thinking," Jeri said. She pointed to herself and then Savannah. "That you have too many books."

Maisy nodded. This was not news, given that it was the reason for opening the bookstore, so the grand announcement left her a bit lost.

Savy jumped in, adding, "And we think you need to have a sidewalk sale to get rid of some stock, advertise the new business, and make some money."

And there it was. Maisy looked at Jeri. "Make some money? Is it that bad?"

"It's not bad, per se, but you know construction always costs twenty-five percent more than you think it will," she said. "Even with Ryder and Seth being as on top of costs as they are, there were the plumbing issues that cut into the budget and then all of that drywall had to be replaced because of mildew. This turret that you want is a major expense . . . unless you're rethinking the turret."

"I am not rethinking the turret," Maisy said. She narrowed her eyes. "Did Ryder send you in here to talk me out of it?"

"No," Savy said. "We came up with this on our own. And I, for one, think if you want a turret, you should have a turret, but you *are* going to need more money. And selling off some books in a one-time-only event, like a massive sidewalk sale, is a brilliant way to do a soft opening, get some foot traffic to the shop, generate a bit of online buzz, and, honestly, you need to lighten the load. There are just too many books."

Maisy glanced around the room she was in. She'd chosen to work in the most cluttered room, figuring if she could slay this beast, then the rest of the house wouldn't seem so overwhelming. She was still undone by the number of books Auntie El had. In the process of sorting, she had come to realize that Auntie El's love of books might have pushed her into the status of hoarder.

Maisy didn't know if her aunt's collection came out of trying to fill the hole in her heart caused by the death of her husband or if she would have become a collector of something else if he'd lived. Maybe it would have been cookie cutters, a yarn stash, or baby dolls. When she thought of it like that, Maisy felt better that it was books, but there were just so many. Earlier, when she'd been tending George, she'd confessed . . . wait a minute. Suddenly, it all came into focus.

"Did you hear me talking to George over the baby monitor?" she asked.

Savannah and Jeri exchanged a look. It was clear they were trying to telepathically come up with a lie.

"You did!" Maisy accused.

"Not just us," Jeri said. She pushed her long black braids over her shoulder and gave Maisy the same look she'd given her when she was her babysitter. "*Everyone* heard."

"Everyone?" Maisy felt her face get hot. "Define *everyone.*"

"Ryder, Seth, us, and a few of the crew," Savannah said.

"Oh, man, isn't there a confidentiality clause when a woman is unloading on her cat?"

"No," Jeri said.

"Nuh-uh," Savannah agreed.

She frantically scanned her brain, trying to remember if she'd overshared about her feelings for Ryder or, worse, how much she wanted to kiss him again. She was pretty sure she hadn't but—"Oh, no, I *sang* to him."

"Yeah, we heard," Savy said. She looked pained.

"Scale of one to ten, how embarrassed should I be?" Maisy asked.

"With ten being a walk through the center of town with the back of your skirt tucked into your underwear," Jeri said.

"And one being a false eyelash making a getaway down the side of your face during a hot date," Savanah added. "I'd go with a solid six."

"Seven," Jeri disagreed. "Those high notes were not good, really not good."

"That's it," Maisy said. "I am never leaving this room. Ever. Let's put a hole in the door and you can slide my meals in to me, because, yeah, I'm done."

"Now, now." Jeri sat on the floor beside her. "It's not that bad."

"Hmm, it was pretty bad," Savy said. "And I say that with love."

"I can't sing," Maisy said.

"We know," Jeri said, and patted her knee.

Maisy put her hands over her eyes and fell back among

the books. It was too much. The first man she'd thought was attractive in forever and he'd heard her sing. She'd rather he heard her snore, she'd be more on pitch. Ugh. How was she going to face him? She dropped her hands and looked at her friends.

"What did he say?" she asked. She dreaded the answer but had to know.

"Ryder? Well, he didn't vomit, if that's what you're asking," Savy said.

"Oh, I didn't make him physically ill," Maisy said. "Yay, me."

"Don't overthink it," Jeri said. "He's a man. He probably doesn't have 'ability to sing' on his list of criteria for women he's interested in."

"He is not interested in me," Maisy protested.

"Sure," Savy said. Then she rolled her eyes, letting Maisy know what she really thought about that.

"Hey, was there a meeting scheduled that I missed?" Ryder asked. He was leaning against the doorjamb, looking unreasonably handsome in jeans and a T-shirt.

His usual cowboy hat had been replaced with a hard hat, which made him even more attractive to Maisy. She liked that he was actually working with the crew and not just sitting on the sidelines. Good grief, if the man could cook and clean, she was done for.

"Nah, we were just selling Maisy on our idea to have a sidewalk sale," Savannah said. "And she agreed. Isn't that great?"

She slugged Ryder on the shoulder as she walked out and Jeri followed, calling over her shoulder, "I'll find some people to help us with the event. It could be a real community effort."

"What? Wait!" Maisy cried, but they blew her off.

Ryder glanced at them and then at Maisy. As soon as Savannah was far enough away, he mouthed the word *Ouch!* and rubbed his shoulder.

"Why is she not in the women's MMA?" he asked.

Maisy forced a laugh, relieved to have something else to

think about besides her own mortification. "She didn't hit you that hard, did she?"

"Nah," he said. "I don't need my left arm anyway."

He grinned at her. Darn, it only confirmed how much she liked his face. It was a good face. Square jawed with a nose that looked like it had been broken at least once, full lips, arching eyebrows over those bright blues, and a broad forehead that she liked to think indicated a big brainpan. He'd done nothing to disprove her theory so far.

He watched her in much the same way. As if she hadn't disproved his theory that she was an okay person so far, either, which was remarkable given that he'd heard her sing. Speaking of which, she supposed she'd better discuss the elephant in the room.

"I can't sing," she said. She felt her face get warm as she envisioned him listening to her butchering the classic tune with flats and sharps and cringeworthy enthusiasm. "And by 'can't sing,' I mean, I should never and, oh, my God, I can't believe you heard me. I'm dying. I'm dead."

There, it was out. The first of her personal truths, which included her dislike of pudding of any kind, opera, and amusement park rides with height requirements.

He stared at her for a moment. He looked as if he was trying to come to a decision. Maisy wondered if the no singing ability really was a thing for him. Maybe he had very strong views about a person's ability to carry a tune. It could be a total deal breaker for him and there went any plans she had for getting him to reconsider her romantically. Damn it. In that moment, she wasn't sure whether she should laugh or cry. She feared she was going to cry . . . again.

Chapter Eighteen

"You know I'm from Austin, right?" he asked. He took off his hard hat and set it on a pile of books.

She nodded.

"Well, pretty much anyone who is born in the Lone Star state arrives in this world with two things," he said. "The first is a pair of cowboy boots and the second is a sense of rhythm. It is a little-known fact that most Texans can two-step before they can walk."

"I'm not sure where you're going with this," she said.

He reached out a hand to her and Maisy took it. He pulled her up to her feet. He looked her square in the eye and said, "I can't dance."

Maisy sighed. "You don't have to make me feel better. It's very kind of you but really not necessary."

"Your singing wasn't that bad," he insisted. "At least, not as bad as my dancing."

Maisy looked at him and said, "I don't believe you."

"No?" he asked. He looked at her and then heaved a sigh of his own. "Okay, I hate to do this, but you're leaving me no choice."

He pulled his cell phone out of his pocket and thumbed through a few apps. Music filled the crowded room, and to Maisy's surprise, it was Pharrell Williams's "Happy." With an irresistible beat, Maisy started to bob her head. There wasn't much room to move in the tiny room, which was a mercy, because Ryder's style of dancing needed to be contained.

Maisy backed up as he was all swinging arms and bobbing up and down. He even did jazz hands, which made Maisy burst out laughing.

"What?" he cried over the music. "I warned you!"

At the clapping part, he hopelessly clapped on the downbeat and Maisy couldn't help but start singing to his terrible dancing, jumping around with him as the two of them stomped in between the books, singing at top volume, "Clap along if you feel like that's what you wanna do."

Laughing, Ryder grabbed Maisy's hand and spun her under his arm and then back out. It was awkward and they smashed into each other but she didn't care. Joining hands, they swung them back and forth, laughing when they knocked knees in the tiny space.

"What on earth?" Jeri appeared in the doorway with Savannah, Seth, and Perry behind her.

"Yay! Dance party!" Savy yelled, and began to dance in the hallway, dragging Perry with her. The two of them started busting out some solid hip-hop moves, grooving to the irrepressible song.

Jeri began to boogie and looked at Seth. He shook his head, but Jeri wasn't having it. "Come on, big boy, shake what your mama gave you!"

To Maisy's surprise, Seth busted out some robot moves that were spot-on. Not bad for such a big man. Then he turned the floor over to Ryder. He gamely stepped into the hallway with the others and began to groove. He was adorably, hilariously awful. So bad that Perry had to quit dancing to put her hand on her forehead as if she could not believe the horror she was being forced to watch. The song faded and Ryder ended with a move that looked like a chicken on an electric fence.

"Oh, my God, Dad, stop!" Perry pleaded, but she was

laughing. Ryder threw an arm around her and hugged her close, putting a smacking kiss on the top of her head.

"Stop? Who do you think you get your slick dance moves from?" he asked.

"Not you," she said.

"She's got you there, boss," Seth said. A mock glare from Ryder sent him trotting away with his hands raised in the air as he said, "Sorry."

"Water. I need water," Savy said. She fanned her face with her hands. "Anyone else?"

"Me," Perry said. "And then I'm on George duty."

Jeri took out her phone as she followed the other two. "Not me, I'm calling my man. I feel the need for a night out dancing."

Maisy watched them all leave. She supposed she should follow them, but she wanted to thank Ryder first. He didn't have to make an idiot of himself just to make her feel better but he had and that meant something to her. It meant a lot, in fact.

"Thank you," she said.

"For what?" he asked.

"You know," she said.

"No, I really don't," he said.

"Your dancing was terrible," she said. "You didn't have to do that to make me feel better about my singing."

"Are you saying I faked that travesty?" he asked. "I'll have you know I think I threw my back out, trying to legit groove."

Maisy laughed again. He couldn't be that bad. Really, he had to have been hamming it up for her, right?

"I was not making it worse than it is," he said. "Trust me, that was me in top form."

"Oh," she said. She looked at him in concern. "Oh, my."

"Exactly," he said. "You're lucky I didn't take out your eyeball with my elbow. Feel better now?"

"Is it bad if I say yes?"

He grinned. "No."

"Then, yes, I do feel a bit better."

"Good." He studied her face for a moment and then a noise downstairs drew his attention. "I'd better get back."

"Right. Me, too," she said.

"But, here's the thing," he said, standing in front of her as if reluctant to leave. "In the spirit of full disclosure, my inability to fast-dance is inversely proportional to my ability to slow-dance."

He winked at her and Maisy felt her insides flutter, as they always did when she was the center of his attention. Was he flirting with her? After a week of being the consummate professional, had her humiliation finally opened him up? She would sing like a freaking canary every day if that's what it took. In any case, she could not pass this opportunity up.

She strode forward until she was standing right in front of him. Then she glanced up at him, screwed up her courage, and said, "Prove it."

He looked surprised. Then he smiled. It started in one corner of his mouth and moved across his lips in a slow seductive slide. He reached forward and curved one hand around her hip as if it had been made just for him and then he pulled her in close. She could feel the heat coming off his body and she wanted to press herself up against the hard plane of his chest. So she did.

Ryder thumbed the face of his phone until a new song began to play, "Come Away with Me," by Norah Jones. Then he set the phone down on a box and slid his hand up Maisy's back until they were pressed together from thigh to thigh and chest to breast. Maisy couldn't breathe and she couldn't care less.

Ryder lowered his head. He whispered the lyrics against the shell of her ear while they swayed back and forth. Maisy clung to him as if he were the anchor, keeping her tethered to the ground while his very nearness made her feel as if she could float away. It was intoxicating and she slid her arms up and around his neck, holding on tight, wishing the song would never end.

He moved her in a slow, seductive box step. No frills, no spins, no dips, just two bodies entwined in a seductive embrace. Their eyes met and Maisy felt not lost but found. Was this what it felt like when you met your soul mate? The feeling of being complete.

Ryder took her hands in his and then pressed their palms together while still stepping in their small circle. It was lovely and perfect. Emotions bubbled up in Maisy as she felt cherished by this amazing man. He moved his hands to her hips and pulled her close, as if he could tuck her into himself and keep her there. Maisy would have let him.

His hands slid up her body slowly, as if memorizing her every curve. When he cupped her face and looked into her eyes, seeing *her* for all that she was, Maisy was undone. She parted her lips in silent invitation and Ryder answered, pressing his mouth to hers in the briefest, sweetest kiss she had ever received.

Then he was gone, whistling the tune they had just danced to as he made his way down the stairs. What the . . . what?

THREE days later, Maisy was having the mother of all melt-downs. It was the morning of the sidewalk sale, and even though Jeri and Savannah had put flyers up all over town, Maisy was worried that no one would show up, proving that her idea to open a romance bookstore was possibly the dumbest idea she'd ever had, second only to the time she'd bought a vintage Fiat because it looked cool and then had to walk everywhere for a year because it spent more time in her mechanic's garage than hers.

In a display of support Maisy wasn't sure was warranted, Ryder and Seth made an enormous vinyl sign that they suspended from the porch roof. It read HAPPILY EVER AFTER BOOKSHOP and when Maisy saw it, she burst into tears.

"Well, that's not the reaction I was expecting," Seth said to Ryder. "I thought we'd get hugs, not tears." He stepped back to examine their handiwork. "Please tell me we didn't spell something wrong. That would be mortifying."

"We didn't," Ryder said. He looked at Maisy with concern. "We can take it down if you hate it."

"No, no," she said. She fanned her face with her hands as

if she could dry up her tears with the wind propulsion from her fingers. "It's perfect." The words came out on a sob and the men exchanged a helpless look.

Savannah arrived and took the scene in at a glance. "Relax," she said. She threw an arm around Maisy and gave her a bolstering squeeze. "These are happy-dream-come-true tears. You did good."

Both men sagged in relief and then made hasty excuses to help Jeri set up the sale tables on the front lawn.

"Well, that was embarrassing," Maisy said. She wiped her eyes with her palms.

"Meh, you've done worse," Savy said. "Besides, this is your big day. It's natural that you'd be emotional."

Maisy stood on the front porch, looking out across the front lawn. "What if no one comes?"

"They'll come."

"But—"

"No." Savy held up her hand in a stop gesture. "No negativity."

"But that's my comfort zone."

Savy laughed and Maisy was reassured that she knew Maisy was kidding—mostly.

"It's going to be amazing," Savy said. "Look, we have a customer and we're not even open yet."

It was true. A woman, carrying her own bag, had slipped past Jeri, who was manning the cash register at the front of the yard, and was poring over the table of sweet romances. Maisy had a sudden memory of seventh-grade biology, where she read those same sweet romances tucked inside her lab book, with only her lab partner wise to her secret reading. She still had no idea what the purpose of learning the food chain was and was pretty sure she never would.

From that one customer, the activity in the yard grew and grew until as far as she could see there were readers crowding the tables, picking up the books, and reading the back cover copy. More and more people were wandering in from the street and in no time Maisy was hustling to refresh the coffee and lemonade and cookies, which they had put on the porch to entice people to linger.

Chairs had been placed all over the yard to encourage browsers to stay and read awhile. It seemed to be working, because every chair was full and some people had even sprawled on the lawn.

She glanced over at Jeri, who was happily managing the cash register. The line was five deep and Jeri was chatting and laughing with every person who bought books. Jeri met Maisy's eye over the heads of eager readers and her grin was huge. Their soft opening was a big success.

Excited, Maisy stepped into the house and did a fist pump, okay, two. Maybe the Happily Ever After Bookstore was going to get a running start after all. Feeling unstoppable, Maisy grabbed the food from the kitchen and headed back out into the bright sunny day to sell more books.

Savannah found her an hour later, hauling more paperbacks from the house as the table of historical romances had been practically wiped out. Without a word, Savy grabbed a box and followed Maisy outside. As they stacked the books on the table, a feeding frenzy of readers stood at the ready to snatch their favorites. One of the shoppers was a woman wearing scrubs; her blond hair was tied into a knot on the top of her head. Maisy did a double take.

"Hannah," Maisy said. "Aren't you here to check on King George?"

"I'm working my way there," she said. "But this sale is too good to miss. You know what a sucker I am for romances with dogs in them."

"Have you read the Bluff Point series?" Savy asked. "It's got them all: rescue dogs, old dogs, puppies, even a dog in a harness—a basset hound named Hot Wheels."

"Show me," Hannah ordered. She looked at Maisy and added, "I'll be up to check on George in a minute. A professional woman needs to have her downtime with books that make her smile, because life is hard, dang it."

"I hear that," Savy said.

"I'll let Perry know you're here," Maisy said. "Come up to the apartment when you're done."

"There in five," Hannah said. "I promise."

Maisy turned and headed back into the house. She hurried

upstairs to the hidden room to retrieve Perry and the kitten for the vet. She thought Hannah was going to be pretty impressed at how King George was doing. He had exceeded all of their expectations and while he was still a bit shaky and slept a lot he was also becoming playful and had even attempted a wobbly pounce or two.

The bench seat to the hidden room was open, so Maisy sat on the floor and swung her legs into the opening. She was halfway down the stairs when she heard a scuffle below.

"Perry, Hannah is here to look at Geor—oh, hello." Maisy stepped into the small room to find a boy about the same age as Perry, standing there with his hands in his pockets and an awkward look on his face.

"Hi," the boy said.

Maisy glanced around him to see Perry, standing there, holding the kitten, looking at her with wide eyes and a very red face. Maisy did a quick clothing check and noted that both teens seemed to be buttoned and tucked appropriately. A closer look at Perry's face and she noted that while she was blushing, she didn't look as if she'd been making out with the boy.

"Maisy, hi, this is Cooper," Perry said. "He's in my algebra class. We were studying. We have a test coming up. Very important."

Maisy glanced around the room. There was not a textbook in sight. She looked at Perry. "Really?"

"No," Cooper said. "What Perry meant was that we're trying to find some time to study together, and I asked to meet King George since he's all over her Snapchat and he looks like my kitten, Maverick." The teen held up an orange tabby, with a white belly and paws, about twice the size of George but still very young.

"We thought George could use a friend," Perry said. Her face was still bright pink.

"Ah," Maisy said. She scratched the orange kitten's head. It purred and then batted her hand, making her smile. She turned and held out her hands to Perry, who gave George to her. He gave a big kitty yawn and settled against her palm.

"Perry, are you down there?" Ryder's voice sounded from above and all three of them jumped.

Perry spun Maisy toward the stairs and whispered, "Please stall him. I will die, just die, if Dad finds Cooper down here and feels the need to grill him, and you know he will. Please, Maisy."

Maisy glanced at the desperate look on Perry's face. Oh, she remembered the pain of adolescence. "All right, but you both have exactly five minutes to get up there. I mean it."

"I promise," Perry said.

"Hey, there," Maisy called as she dashed up the stairs. "Can you help a girl out and grab this wiggly kitten?" She glanced at George, who was doing his best impression of a sedentary lump, and whispered, "Come on, buddy, help a sister out."

Ryder reached out and took the kitten from her. Maisy pushed forward so he was forced to back up from the hidden room's entrance. She took his arm as he cradled the cat and said, "Come on. Hannah is going to meet me upstairs in the apartment to check on George."

"Have you seen Perry? I thought she was watching George," he said.

"Yes," Maisy said. She pulled him out the door and up the stairs to her apartment, never breaking her stride. She didn't say any more, hoping that was the end of it because she didn't want to lie to him. Judging by the look on his face, he was expecting more of an explanation. She went for a diversionary tactic instead. "Did I thank you for the sign for the shop?"

"You were a little busy leaking out your eyeballs," he said. "But the thank-you came through loud and clear."

Maisy squeezed his arm. Wow, his bicep really did require more than one hand to wrap around it, possibly more than two.

"It was very thoughtful of you guys," she said.

They stopped in front of the apartment door and she let go of his arm and turned to look at him. Below, she heard a door open and shut and she knew that Perry had been as good as her word. Ryder turned at the sound as if he was going to go investigate and Maisy panicked and pulled him into a hug, being careful not to squash George as she laid her head on his chest.

"I really can't thank you enough," she said. The warm masculine scent of him made her head fuzzy and she pulled back to get some air and found him looking down at her with a raw longing that made her catch her breath. She wanted him and she knew he wanted her, too.

Before she could think it through, hesitate, or second-guess herself, Maisy rose up on her toes and kissed him.

Chapter Nineteen

A S impulse decisions went, this was definitely one of Maisy's better ones. It was supposed to last for only a moment, just the press of her lips against his, because, well, the bookstore sign, and his smile, the twinkle in his eye, and the way he was with George and Perry and everyone else.

But as soon as her mouth met his, Maisy lost control of the kiss. Using his free hand, Ryder cupped the back of Maisy's head and held her still while his mouth moved over hers in a surprise takeover of all her senses.

There was nothing tentative about the kiss. It was a statement, an acceptance of the awareness that had been snapping between them since they'd danced. Ryder kissed her as if it was an inevitability between them. That no matter what their intentions were, the pull between them, made stronger by every moment spent together, was just too potent to ignore.

Maisy felt the same way. She hadn't desired anyone like Ryder, well, ever. And she didn't want to pretend that she didn't. She slid her hands up his shirt front and pulled him in closer. Her mouth opened beneath his and she felt herself free-fall into a swirling crazy heat of want that she had never experienced before. She felt as if she could never get enough of him, of this, of them.

The heat, the connection, the instant burn that hit her low and deep, all of it made Maisy realize that of all the kisses she'd ever been on the receiving end of this one obliterated them all in its intensity and finesse. Gracious, this man knew how to kiss.

Yeow! The high-pitched cry broke through Maisy's lust-filled haze and she pulled away from Ryder and blinked. King George sat in Ryder's right hand in a football hold, held up against his side. With one tiny paw, he reached out and bopped Maisy on the nose.

She looked at Ryder, whose breathing was as irregular as hers, and burst out laughing.

"I think someone is jealous," she said.

Ryder lifted up the kitten and kissed his head and Maisy's heart went *squish*.

"Well, he is used to being the center of attention," Ryder said.

"Hey, kids," Hannah greeted them as she appeared on the landing. "How's our boy today?"

Maisy hopped back from Ryder and George. She felt her face get warm, but she hoped the dim lighting in the hallway would give her cover.

"Great!" she said with much more enthusiasm than the question warranted. She glanced at Ryder and he looked like he was trying to get it together and failing.

"Come on in," Maisy said. "Can I get you some sweet tea, water, coffee?"

"I'm good, but thanks," Hannah said. "I had lemonade downstairs. Speaking of which, did I tell you what a brilliant idea the bookstore is? I mean, truly, a romance bookstore! Genius!"

"Thanks," Maisy said. "It's still more an idea than a reality, but I appreciate the support."

"I can't believe there aren't more of them," Hannah said.

"Given that romance novels account for more sales than any other genre, it is surprising," Maisy said. "Then again, small businesses are always dicey, so it's a gamble. Failure is a distinct possibility." She felt her anxiety spike.

"Yours won't," Ryder said. His absolute confidence checked Maisy's fears and she almost kissed him again in gratitude.

"He's right," Hannah said. She reached out and took George out of Ryder's hand and sat on the couch. "It's going to be a phenomenal success. You'll see."

She popped open her medical bag with one hand and pulled out a stethoscope. She made kissy noises at George, who looked up at her with his green eyes as if she was the most interesting thing he'd ever seen.

"Hey there, kitty baby," Hannah cooed. "Look at you. Who's a big boy?"

Maisy sat on the couch beside Hannah while Ryder stood off to the side and, from beneath a furrowed brow, watched George's examination. Maisy had the odd thought that they were like anxious parents having their baby examined.

"He's been eating like a champ," Ryder said.

"And he's begun to use his litter box," Maisy said.

"His ears are popping up, too," he said.

"And his eyes are tracking really well," she added.

"Uh-huh," Hannah said. She ran her hands over the kitten. Checked his ears, his teeth, his privates, and his paws.

"Well?" Ryder asked as if he couldn't take it anymore. "Do you think he's thriving?"

Hannah didn't say anything and Maisy felt her heart constrict. What if there was something wrong with George? What if, after all this, they lost him because he wasn't strong enough to survive? What if his mama had abandoned him because she instinctively knew there was something wrong with him? Maisy looked at the sweet little face staring up at her and felt a fear she hadn't known was possible. How had this little guy wrapped her around his paw so tightly in just two weeks?

Hannah let go of George's front paw and checked his back ones. In response, he flopped down on the couch cushion and waved his feet in the air. Maisy rubbed his striped tummy, and he wrapped his paws around her hand as if he'd hold on to her forever. She felt her throat get tight and she glanced up at Hannah, afraid to hear bad news.

"I think it's safe to say that this little guy is going to be just fine," Hannah said. She rubbed his head and he purred. "He is more than thriving. He's exceeding all growth and wellness expectations. I mean, look at these feet. He's going to be huge."

Ryder let out an audible sigh and when Maisy looked at him in question, he struck a nonchalant pose and said, "I knew she was going to say that. My man George is a warrior."

"Yes, he is," she said.

"And now you'll be starting his gruel phase," Hannah said.

"Gruel? What's that?" Perry asked. She entered the apartment and joined them by the couch.

"Like grits but runnier," Ryder said.

"Ew." Perry made a face.

"Agreed," Hannah said. "You're going to want to mash up some canned kitten food and formula and feed it to him in a bottle to start. You'll need to cut the nipple wider, or if he takes to it you can try to get him to lap it up from a spoon."

"So, he's doing well?" Perry asked. Maisy glanced at the girl and saw the same concerned expression her father had had a few moments before.

"Thriving!" Ryder said. He held up his fist and Perry gave him a solid knuckle bump.

"We did it?" she asked. "He's going to make it?"

"Given his growth and alertness and the lack of health issues," Hannah said, "I'd give him a very optimistic prognosis."

Perry collapsed into her father's side. He wrapped an arm around her and kissed her head.

"We still need to get him eating solid food," Hannah said. "But given how he took to the kitten replacement formula and his substantial growth, I think he'll take to kibble and canned food, no problem."

"Did you hear that, King George? You're going to be all right, buddy." Perry crouched down by the couch to be nose to nose with the kitten. He reached out a paw and bopped her on the nose and she giggled. "I love you, silly boy." She bounced back up to her feet and said, "I'm going to go tell Co—Savannah. She'll want to know."

She glanced at Maisy, who knew she had been about to say *Cooper*. Maisy gave her the hairy eyeball and asked, "Is *Savannah* outside?"

"Yes, *she* is," Perry said. "Can I go?"

"Sure," Maisy and Ryder said together. Maisy looked at Ryder and said, "Sorry, I'm used to answering students when they ask."

"No worries."

"I'll be right back, Georgie." Perry kissed the kitten's head and dashed from the apartment.

Hannah put her things back into her bag and rose to her feet. "I need to go open the clinic. Call me if you have any questions."

"I will," Maisy said. She picked up George and followed Hannah to the door. "Thanks for coming by."

"Are you kidding?" Hannah asked. "Anything for King George."

She reached out and scratched his ears. George gave a sleepy purr. Maisy shut the door behind her, feeling gratitude for her friend and for the fact that George was doing so well.

"Do we have any canned kitten food?" Ryder asked.

"No," she said. "I didn't realize he'd be transitioning to big-boy food so soon."

"Well, that's no problem," he said. "We'll pick some up on our date tonight."

"Sure—wait—what?"

"Date," he said. He looked as if the idea had just popped into his head but he was going for it. "You, me, dinner, and a conversation. What do you say?"

"Yes," she said. The kiss! It had to have been today's kiss that broke through the reserve he'd been maintaining. Well, she was happy to keep on chipping away at it. She smiled. "I'd like that."

"Excellent," he said. "I'll pick you up at seven."

He stepped forward and kissed her quick and then he was out the door and headed down the stairs before she could fully process what had just happened.

*   *   *

"LET me get this straight, after weeks of *I can't get involved with my client*, you asked Maisy out, just like that," Joaquin Solis said. He was standing in the doorway to Ryder's bedroom with his arms crossed over his chest as he watched Ryder pick a shirt.

"I had to," Ryder said. He shuffled past the blue, paused on the pale yellow, nah, and then settled on a pale-gray dress shirt, yanking it off the hanger. "I . . . it's just . . . she's . . . I've never . . . the woman jacks my radar."

"Like an incoming missile?" Quino asked. Tall with dark hair, eyes, and skin, Quino was all lean strength and roped muscle. Ryder had met him years ago when they were both young men working on a construction crew in Texas. With a shared love of horses, hot women, beer, and brawling, the two men had forged an unbreakable friendship that had lasted through the sudden death of Quino's parents, the surprise arrival of Perry, and Ryder's recent divorce.

"No, she's more like a shooting star," Ryder said. He knew the ever-romantic Maisy would love that and it was true. Catching sight of her in the bookstore during the day when she was flitting from one crisis to the next, pausing to make everyone smile or laugh with a kind word or a bad joke or with one of her *Ideas!* made him feel like he was catching a glimpse of something purely magical.

"Oh, you should see your face. You've got it bad," Quino said.

"You have no idea," Ryder said. He ran his hands through his hair as if he could erase the impact of Maisy's kiss from his mind. He couldn't. Her mouth was shaped perfectly with that slightly larger upper lip that fascinated him until he was almost stupid with the longing to kiss her. Gah! "That's why at dinner tonight I'm going to lay it all out for her."

Quino shook his head like he was sure he'd misheard. "Lay what out, exactly?"

"That I'm not relationship material," Ryder said. He picked a black tie with gray flecks and began to shape it into a half-Windsor knot. "I'm not great at expressing my feelings, and by that I mean lousy, and Maisy is totally a word girl. She's the type who needs to hear the words. I can't do the words.

"Plus, I'm leaving soon and she's about to open a bookstore here. We're a terrible fit. I'm just not interested in getting involved with anyone right now, and I don't want any commitments. Perry is the only thing I care about, and as much as I like Maisy, this thing between us is doomed. It's got to stop."

"Which is why you shaved?" Quino said.

"What's that supposed to mean?"

"It means you're pathetic," Quino said. He pushed Ryder's fumbling fingers aside, taking over the tie. "A dude does not shave to give a woman the heave-ho, he doesn't put on a suit, and he definitely doesn't take her to dinner. He ignores her, hopes she goes away, and if forced, he shows interest in another woman to make it clear that he's not interested."

"Well, that's shitty," Ryder said. "I could never do that to her." He imagined the hurt he'd see in her big brown eyes and it gutted him.

"Which is why you're going to fold like a house of cards tonight," Quino said. "You'll make her your girlfriend tonight, bank on it."

"Because you know so much about relationships?" Ryder asked. "You haven't gotten serious with anyone since you moved back to Fairdale to take care of Desi."

Quino's face went dark and Ryder immediately regretted his words. Quino had left Texas ten years ago to race home to take care of his little sister, Desi, after their parents were killed in a car accident, because that was the sort of guy he was.

"Sorry, man, I didn't mean—"

Quino barked out a laugh and he tightened Ryder's tie until it almost choked him, then he tossed the ends up over his face. "It's cool. I know I haven't dated anyone seriously in a long time, but that doesn't mean I'm not looking. When I find her, and I will, that's it. I'm going all in."

"Good luck with that," Ryder said. He shook his head at

his friend's cockeyed optimism. Didn't he get that relationships weren't that easy? Love didn't just fall from a tree like an apple. It was messy and complicated and mostly disappointing.

"Not gonna need it," Quino said. He led the way into the kitchen, where he helped himself to a beer.

"Do me a solid and keep an eye on your goddaughter for me, would you?" Ryder asked. "She's been weird lately."

"Did you tell her about your hot date tonight?"

Ryder frowned. "No, because it's not going to amount to anything and you're not to say anything, either."

"If you say so," Quino said. "She and Desi made me promise to take them to see a movie in town."

He made a face and Ryder asked, "Chick flick?"

"Worse, it's some historical drama. *Bleck*." Quino took a big swig of beer as if it would help. "Just once I want to go to a movie where stuff gets blown up and people get beat up, but my sister and your daughter only want smart films. Shoot me."

Ryder hid his smile as he grabbed his keys and headed out the door. He knew tonight was going to be awkward between him and Maisy, but at least he didn't have to sit through an artsy movie.

"I CAN'T go," Maisy said. "I have nothing to wear. Nothing. I looked up his ex-wife, and because life is cruel and unfair, she's tall and thin and blond, with a perfectly upturned nose and enormous gray eyes. Honestly, how am I supposed to compete with that?"

"Well, given that they're divorced, I'm thinking you're not really competing," Savy said.

"I even watched her show," Maisy said. "She's good, really good, great comic timing and all that. She's a gourmet meal and by comparison I'm forgotten leftovers shoved to the back of the fridge. Ack! I can't do this."

"Yes, you can," Savy said. "Stop being an idiot. It's you he's interested in, not her. Now relax."

"How can I relax? All of my clothes are either workout

clothes or professor clothes. There is nothing in this sad closet that says *hot mama* or even *tepid mama*, for that matter."

"Well, I don't think *mama* of any sort is something you should be looking for in there," Savy said. "How about *sexy lady*? Do you own anything that says that?"

"Not unless neon green yoga pants and a matching sports bra count," Maisy said.

"Uh, no." Savy shook her head. She was reclined on Maisy's bed, watching her rip through her closet while George burrowed in the pile of discarded skirts, blouses, and jeans on the bed.

"I don't even know where we're going," Maisy said. "He said something about dinner and conversation."

"Fairdale is a foodie town," Savannah said. "With over fifty eateries, you could literally be in for anything. Here's what I want to know—what happened?"

"What do you mean?"

"When did you crack him?" Savy asked. "He went from being very hands-off for the past week to suddenly asking you out. What gives?"

Maisy shrugged. "N . . . no idea."

Savannah narrowed her eyes. "Worst liar ever."

"If you must know, we were taking care of George and I, well, I kissed him," Maisy said. "It was just supposed to be quick but then he . . . and we . . . and it was *not* quick. Honestly, I've never been kissed like that in my entire life. I need to text him. I don't think we should see each other. It could ruin everything."

Savy snorted. "Ruin what exactly? The way you two stare at each other when you think no one's looking?"

"We don't. Well, I do, he doesn't."

"Yeah, he does."

Maisy felt that fluttery feeling again. Oh, man, she was falling so hard. Suddenly, she knew that she had more on the line than she'd ever had before. This man had the ability to absolutely crush her. She didn't know if she was brave enough for that.

"I can't do this."

"Yes, you can," Savy said. "Here's where I get to be the

hard-nosed friend who calls you on your bullshit. Ryder is awesome. He's kind, funny, charming, smart, and fully invested in your dream, not to mention freaking adorable when he takes care of George."

"So, why don't *you* date him?" Maisy asked. A spurt of petty jealousy bubbled up inside of her, which made her even crankier. She hated feeling small.

"Because there's no spark between us, but, boy howdy, there is between you two," Savy said. "M, you can't let something this good pass you by. You may never find anything like this again. You have to give this a chance."

Knock knock.

They both glanced at the door.

"Maisy, it's Perry, are you in there?"

"Come on in," Maisy called. She was relieved to have the teenager interrupt the life lecture she was getting from Savanah. She knew her friend was right. She knew her track record was bad and that Ryder wasn't like any man she'd ever dated before. He made her feel so much more. Lord, it was terrifying.

"Hi," Perry said. She included both Savannah and Maisy in her greeting. "Is George in here?"

"Under the hideous black sweater with cherries on it," Savannah said.

"Hey!" Maisy protested.

"What's going on?" Perry asked. "Are you cleaning out your closet?"

"No, she's having a fashion meltdown, because she can't decide what to wear on a date with your da—" Savannah began, but Maisy interrupted.

"Perry, your dad asked me to dinner and I said yes," Maisy explained. She tried to sound casual while gauging the girl's feelings. "Does it bother you that your dad and I are going to dinner?"

Perry dug George out from beneath the sweater. She cuddled him close and he let out a happy squeak of recognition. Perry smiled and then her face crumbled and she looked so sad. She glanced up at Maisy with tears in her eyes.

"Why would it bother me when I'm going to be moving away in a few weeks and so is Dad?" she asked.

"You're moving?" Maisy asked. Thankfully, Perry was so preoccupied with George, she didn't notice the shocked look on Maisy's face.

"Yes, I'm going to a private high school for girls in Connecticut, and Dad is taking a job on the board of a historic preservation society in Charleston, South Carolina," she said.

"Boarding school in Connecticut?" Savy asked. She sounded horrified. "By choice?"

Perry shrugged. "They have a really strong science program, which is my thing. It's also where my mother went to school and her mother before her. It was always understood that I'd go, too. My dad says he wants the best for me, and he thinks Saint Mary's Prep is the best."

Maisy and Savy exchanged a glance. This was the first Maisy had heard of Perry's leaving. She and her dad were so close, Maisy had a hard time imagining Ryder letting her go. It was also the first time she'd heard of Ryder leaving, too. The thought made her stomach hurt.

"But is that where you want to go?" Savy asked.

"I thought I did," Perry said. She glanced quickly at Maisy and suddenly it was all coming into focus.

"Cooper," she said.

"Yeah," Perry muttered. She pressed her face against George's soft fur. "But not just him. There's King George, and all of my friends, my teachers, Uncle Quino, and the horses at Shadow Pine. I love my life here. I love Fairdale. I don't want to leave the place that's been my home for the past three years. This is the longest I've lived anywhere and it's . . . home."

Tears coursed down her cheeks, and Maisy felt her heart twist. She loved Fairdale, too. She had been born here and had never left. She couldn't imagine living anywhere else.

"I'm so sorry, Perry," Maisy said. "I know change is difficult."

Savannah gave her a bug-eyed look as if to say *What changes?*

"I've made changes," Maisy insisted. "I gave up a job to open a bookstore."

"Fine, I'll give you that one," Savy said. She turned her attention back to Perry. "Listen, I've moved around a lot, too. I know how you feel, I do. Have you considered talking to your dad?"

"I can't," she said. "This has been the plan for so long and he's worked so hard to make it happen. It would crush him if I told him I didn't want to go."

"But will it crush you to leave a place you love?" Maisy asked.

Perry shrugged. She looked sad but resigned. "Please don't tell him I said anything. I love my dad, and I don't want to hurt him." She walked toward the door with George. "I'm going to go feed him." She glanced at Maisy's closet. "Wear the teal-colored dress hanging there. Dad loves that color."

The door shut behind her and Maisy went to the closet and pulled out the teal dress. It had a halter top and a flared skirt. It was light and pretty and very feminine. Given that Ryder had seen her mostly in yoga pants and T-shirts, this might prove a refreshing change for him.

"So, how do you feel about Ryder leaving?" Savannah asked.

Maisy stopped examining her reflection with the dress held up in front of her and stepped into her walk-in closet to change.

"I feel okay, I guess." Which was a total lie. She was shocked. She'd thought he and Perry were established here. She'd had no inkling that they might leave. And she hated the idea. And now her pre-date freak-out seemed silly since her date was leaving the state in a few weeks. She peeked around the doorjamb and looked at Savy. "I guess it kind of takes the pressure off. I mean, how serious can we get if he's leaving?"

"Making him the perfect guy for you," Savannah said. "I take back everything I said about him being a good guy. I don't think you should go out with him."

"What? Why not?" Maisy stepped back in the closet, pulled the dress over her head, and smoothed the skirt down.

"Because you are going to get your heart broken," Savannah said.

"But I won't," Maisy insisted. Judging by the pain in her

chest, she was sure her heart was already breaking. "Because he's leaving."

"Which finally answers the question of what's wrong with him," Savannah said. "He's a tumbling tumbleweed, who is just going to show you a good time for the moment and then roll right on out of your life, ruining you for any other man. Damn it, Maisy. You deserve better than this."

Chapter Twenty

MAISY froze. She stared at her reflection in the mirror. Looking back from the glass was a woman who had her heart on her sleeve. Heck, she had her heart in her hands, offering it to Ryder like it was a cupcake.

It hit her then that she didn't want to play the fool again. The dingleberry had lied to her and conned her and made her feel gullible and dumb. Now, here was Ryder kissing her delirious and asking her out for a "conversation" just before he blew town. She had a good idea what that "conversation" was going to be about—him leaving. When exactly had he been planning to tell her he was leaving? Had he been planning to tell her at all? She didn't think her poor battered heart could take another tumble.

"You're right," she said. "I have to friend-zone him."

She hurried back into her closet and pulled out her favorite pair of overalls. She took off the teal dress and pulled on a bright-orange tank top and then the overalls. She then slid on her floral sneakers. Yep, she looked like she should be out wrestling hogs. She stepped out of the closet, looking prepared for battle rather than a date.

"Wait, what is *that*?" Savy asked. "You can friend-zone him and not give the poor man nightmares."

"I won't," Maisy said. "This is me dressing cute."

"Cute is for Frisbee in the park or a day at the carnival," Savy said. "Not for grown-up dates, where menus and moonlight and *honest* conversations are involved."

Maisy faced her. She had to come clean, if not with Savannah then with herself. "No, you're right. Ryder does have the potential to break my heart. I have to protect myself."

"And your go-to method is to dress like Farmer Ted instead of just being honest with him?"

"Well, that and this pretty much guarantees that no passes will be made tonight," Maisy said. She ran her thumbs under the suspenders and rocked back on her heels. "I mean, what sort of guy is going to fight his way through all of this?"

"You're an idiot," Savy said. But there was affection in her voice, so Maisy didn't take offense.

"Hello?" a male voice called from the apartment. Ryder's voice.

Maisy felt her insides clench. This was it. Her heart thumped hard in her chest. She was full-on panicking. And now she was in overalls. Savy was right. She looked like an idiot. Maybe she should change. No, no, there was no time. Oh, jeez, what a nightmare.

She was woefully unprepared to date. What had she been thinking? She should have said no. She should have made up an excuse. She should have . . . but then she remembered their kiss. That's what had gotten her into this mess. She was so starved for affection that she was going on a date. With her cowboy architect. This had bad *Idea!* written all over it.

"Do you want me to stall him so you can change?" Savannah asked hopefully.

"Nope." Maisy tipped up her chin. "What he sees is what he gets."

"Oh, brother," Savy muttered. She opened the door and led the way out. It took everything Maisy had not to retreat and hide in her closet.

"Hi, Ryder," Savy greeted him. She glanced back at

Maisy and mouthed the words, *Last chance*. Maisy shook her head, and Savannah said, "Okay, you kids have fun."

She disappeared into her room, giving Maisy her first full glance at her date.

Oh, crud. He was dressed in a suit with a tie and he was holding a huge bunch of pink peonies, her favorite. Maisy glanced down at her overalls. The urge to punch herself in the temple and knock herself out had never been so strong.

She shook her head, making her curls bounce around her face. She was just going to have to brazen it out. Her hair and makeup were on point so that was something. Besides, what did she care? Ryder was going to be leaving soon. It wasn't as if there was a relationship at stake here. With that thought lodged firmly at the front of her mind, she forced her lips into a smile and strode forward.

"Hi, Ryder," she said. To his credit, his face revealed nothing of what he thought about her outfit. Meanwhile, in a black jacket and pants, with a gray dress shirt and matching tie, the man looked positively edible. Ugh.

"Hi," he said. He held out the flowers. "These are for you."

"Thank you. Peonies are my favorite," she said. She took the bouquet and sighed. The blooms were about the size of her fist, pale pink with deep-pink edges, just beautiful.

"I know," he said. "Jeri told me."

Maisy led the way to the kitchen. "Can I get you a drink? Wine? Beer?"

"No, thanks," he said. He slid onto a stool at the counter while she put the flowers in water.

Maisy arranged the flowers and set them on the center of the small café table where she and Savannah ate their meals. The light from the window shone on the flowers, making them look translucent. Maisy smiled at Ryder.

"They really are lovely. Thank you," she said.

"Don't mention it," he said. "Are you ready to go?"

"Yes," she said. She waited for him to ask if she wanted to change. He didn't. Instead, he led the way to the door, leaving Maisy no choice but to grab her purse and follow. It occurred to her that her decision to wear overalls might be the worst idea she'd had since she'd gotten her first eyebrow wax and asked to having arching brows like Angelina Jolie. She'd spent the next month looking like she was in a constant state of surprise.

They walked side by side through the house, which now had actual hallways with no books in them, rooms with books on shelves only, as well as fresh paint and plasterwork. Under the old carpets, wood flooring had been discovered and was in the process of being sanded, varnished, and polished to a high sheen.

Thick plastic sheeting separated work areas from non-work areas, but Maisy had a good feeling about their progress and Ryder's ability to make her vision a reality. It distracted her from her outfit and put a spring in her step. The Happily Ever After Bookshop was on its way.

"Any word on final sales today?" Ryder asked. He stepped into the foyer and turned to look at her.

"Jeri is still tallying the credit card purchases, but she said it far exceeded expectations," she said.

"Congratulations."

"Thank you."

He opened the door for her and Maisy stepped out, waiting for him to follow so she could lock the door behind them. The books and tables had been cleared from the lawn and it was hard for her to reconcile the empty space with the bustling yard sale it had been just a few hours earlier.

Ryder's green truck was parked in the driveway and he opened the passenger door for Maisy, closing it behind her when she climbed inside. He circled around the front and again she noted that he was about the handsomest man she had ever seen. Her heart did a somersault in her chest and she knew that the overalls were a good choice. She had to maintain some buffer against him otherwise she'd be lost. With that thought firmly in mind, she kept her smile in place and tried her level best to think of Ryder as a brother or a neighbor or a cousin, anything but hot cowboy-architect guy.

He took off his jacket and his tie and tossed them both into the backseat, where he kept his hat. Maisy didn't say anything even though she was a bit sorry to see the snappy jacket and tie go.

"Where are we going?" she asked.

"It's a surprise," he said. He gave her a small smile and Maisy relaxed back against her seat. She trusted him.

WHERE were they going? Ryder had no freaking idea. He'd had reservations for a fancy French bistro in the heart of town but given Maisy's decidedly casual style of dress, he figured that was out. She clearly wasn't thinking of their date as the intimate one-on-one conversation he'd envisioned.

He tried to remember when he asked her out if he'd given her the idea that this was just a friendly outing between pals. No, he was pretty sure, after they'd shared that brain-melter of a kiss, that he'd asked her out for a real dinner date. Sure, he'd been planning to let her down easy sometime between the vichyssoise and the crème brûlée, but now he wondered why he'd even bothered. Clearly, their kiss hadn't rocked her world as much as his. The realization made him cranky.

He'd thought when he asked her out to dinner she would know he meant it was an *eating at a nice restaurant with cloth napkins and candlelight* experience, but maybe she thought a sack of burgers and a milkshake was a big night out. He wasn't sure what to make of the overalls, although she did look pretty cute in those. He wondered what that said about him that he thought a woman in overalls and sneakers was equally as hot as a woman in high heels and a dress. Hmm.

He drove through town with Maisy beside him, staring out the window as if she'd never seen Fairdale before. Maybe she didn't get out that much. He debated taking her back to his house, where he could cook dinner, but Perry, Joaquin, and Desi were there, having dinner before their movie, so that would be awkward. He didn't particularly want Perry with him on his outing with Maisy, because even though they'd clearly had mixed signals about tonight, he knew he still needed to hammer it home to Maisy that he was not a datable prospect.

He thought about picking up beer and a pizza and having a picnic in the bed of his pickup truck on Whiskey Mountain, but he was afraid they'd get cold, plus by the time the pizza was ready, they'd miss the sunset and just be sitting in the dark, which would be weird.

He had enough struggles with the whole sharing-his-feelings thing without starting off awkwardly. Who was he kidding? They were already at uncomfortable. What the heck had happened?

He felt as if someone, Maisy, had flipped the script on him. He'd delivered the *do not get attached to me* speech to every woman he'd dated since his divorce. He had it down. It worked like a charm, and after their kiss today, he'd been gearing up to deliver the talk to Maisy, but it looked like she didn't need it.

Ryder had the feeling Maisy had already decided he wasn't going to be more than a friend. He wasn't sure how he felt about that. He knew he should be relieved, but he wasn't, which made him feel as if everything he'd ever believed to be true was wrong.

There was no doubt that he was different with Maisy. She made him open up more than any person he'd ever known. Heck, he'd even gotten watered up while talking about Perry's determination to save George. He'd shown more emotion in that moment than he had in years.

There was something about Maisy, the way her eyes turned up in the corners when she smiled, the calming scent of her when she was nearby, the feeling of being safe that he felt with her, that he had never experienced with another person. Perhaps that was how she made everyone feel and to her it was no big deal. Ryder tried to ignore the twist in his gut at the probability that he meant no more to her than dingle-berry had. Even though he knew it was for the best, the thought did not sit well.

He turned onto an old postal route, locally known as the beeline highway, that ran to his favorite barbeque joint, Adam's Rib. It was named for the owner, Adam Jacobs, a big blustery black man who made a Carolina barbeque sauce so good, Ryder was pretty sure angels sang when he served it. Of course, being from Austin he had to insist that it didn't hold a candle to Texas barbeque, but in truth, between the barbeque and the cobbler, Adam's Rib was his favorite restaurant in Fairdale.

With a course set in mind, Ryder stepped on the gas and they wound their way along the serpentine route until they broke through the trees and parked beside the old converted barn that housed the restaurant.

"Adam's Rib," Maisy said. "I love this place."

"Glad to hear it." Ryder smiled. Okay, he could do this. If they were just going to be friends, he could totally hang with that. He parked in a row of pickup trucks and then jogged around the front of the truck to get Maisy's door for her. She had already popped it open, but he was there in time to give her a hand down.

He put his hand on the gentle curve of her lower back and walked her to the front door. The rolling doors on the front of the big barn were pulled back, and music spilled out of the building along with the overhead lights that cut a bright path in the dark. Peanut shells covered the floor and the room was filled with picnic tables with checkered cloths. Families filled the big tables and smaller ones were scattered around the room.

A teenage girl was stationed by the front door. She greeted them with a smile and asked, "Two?"

"Please," Ryder said.

She grabbed menus and gestured for them to follow her. She put them at a small table tucked into the corner of the massive room, far away from the band that was plucking a lively number in the corner of the big barn. Ryder was glad. The privacy would give him a chance to feel her out and try to figure out what was going on in that pretty head of hers, because suddenly he was consumed with the need to know what Maisy was thinking.

A daisy sat in a Coke bottle on their table, along with a wire basket full of barbeque sauces and wet wipes. Okay, it was going to be a messy interrogation, but he could live with that.

He held out Maisy's seat for her and was about to take his own when two arms grabbed him from behind and lifted him off his feet in a hug that felt like being mauled by a bear. He was dropped to his feet and hammered into the ground with a pat on his back that almost sent him reeling into the table. Okay, maybe Adam's place had not been his best plan. Not unless he wanted Maisy to see him being manhandled by the goliath that was Adam. The first time Adam had hugged him, Ryder had said he wasn't a hugger and Adam had put him in a headlock until he cried for mercy. From then on, if Adam hugged him, Ryder let him.

"Ryder Copeland, my man, where have you been?"

Ryder pushed himself up off the table and turned to face his friend. "Adam, how are you?"

"Good, but y'all wouldn't have to ask if you'd been around the last week or so," Adam said. He crossed his arms over his massive chest and frowned.

Ryder leaned in, and out of the corner of his mouth said, "Dude, I'm on a date here, can you not toss me around like a head of cabbage?"

"Date?" Adam leaned back and then peered around Ryder at Maisy. "Well, hello, Maisy Kelly, and aren't you looking— wait, I thought you said this was a date."

"Hi, Adam," Maisy said.

She hopped out of her chair and lifted her arms up for a hug. Ryder almost jumped in to keep Adam from squashing her, but he needn't have worried. Adam hunkered his six-foot-eight, three-hundred-pound frame down and very gently hugged Maisy as if she were made out of paper.

When Adam stepped back, he raised one eyebrow higher than the other and looked Maisy over from head to toe. "You know, you're as cute as a bug's ear but, sister, those are not date clothes."

"They are for me," Maisy insisted. "Besides, it's not a *date* date. As I recall, I was invited for dinner and a 'conversation,' not romance, so it's a non-date date."

"I'm confused," Adam said. He looked Ryder up and down and then Maisy, taking in their different attire as if it was evidence of their different intentions. "Looks like I'm not the only one. You better be careful, cowboy, this little lady will break your heart."

Ryder smiled but it was a tad forced as he had a feeling he was halfway there already. Maisy had known. Somehow, she'd known that in his world "dinner and conversation" meant him avoiding entanglement. She "got" him. He didn't need to spend the meal spelling out to her why they wouldn't work. He felt as if the floor shifted beneath his feet and he didn't know how to get his equilibrium back.

"Two Fairdale Ales coming up," Adam said. He picked up their menus. "And I'll put your order in for you. I know just what to serve." He gave them a huge grin that was actually rather terrifying. "Turning non-dates into dates is my specialty."

Maisy and Ryder sat back down. She propped her chin on her hand and studied him. "So, you're friends with Adam."

"We bonded over a love of barbeque and beer," Ryder said. "Are you okay with beer? He didn't really give us much say there."

"I like beer," she said. "It goes well with barbeque. Plus, I like to support the Fairdale Brewery."

She liked beer. One more thing to like about Maisy Kelly. Ryder tried to remember if there was anything on the negative side. At the moment he couldn't think of a one except maybe the fact that she saw him more clearly than he liked to be seen. He wasn't used to that.

"Non-date, huh?" he asked.

She met his gaze. Her brown gaze was bright, honest, and warm. They were the sort of eyes a man could lose his way inside of and not mind in the least.

"Isn't it?" she asked. Her voice was soft.

"No," he said. "It isn't." As soon as the words left his lips he knew it was true. Quino had been right. He was pathetic. He wanted Maisy. He wanted her in his arms, he wanted her in his life, and he wanted, with a desperation that he had never felt before, to be hers, to belong to her. God help him.

At that moment, the band kicked into a country-western song that made conversation nearly impossible. People crowded the dance floor and Maisy settled back to watch them while Ryder watched her.

With her dark curls and upturned nose, she had a look of innocence about her that he was willing to bet had gotten her out of trouble more than once in her life. She was whip smart and had a musical laugh that made him smile when he heard her laughing somewhere in the house while he was working. Usually, he found an excuse to seek her out after hearing her laugh, just to see her happy. He'd found that the sight of her lifted him up in ways he hadn't felt in a very long time. It occurred to him that he was completely infatuated with her and he had no clue as to what to do about it. Check that. He knew what he wanted to do about it, he just didn't know if he should.

The band broke into a slow song, and Ryder found himself up on his feet and holding out his hand to her before he'd really thought it through. Maisy gave him side eye and he smiled.

"Come on, it's a slow song," he said. "I promise I won't step on your toes."

"You forget," Maisy said. "I've seen you dance." But she stood and put her hand in his and allowed him to lead her to the dance floor, making Ryder think that maybe she was as desperate for an excuse to be close as he was. No, there was no way she could be that desperate.

He put his right hand on her hip and held her hand loosely in his left. As the band kicked it into a slow two-step, he led her around the floor, trying not to count out loud. He really couldn't dance for beans, but if this was the only way he could get her in his arms, he was willing to risk public humiliation just to have her there for a few minutes.

Maisy was graceful and light on her feet. In a matter of steps, she'd figured him out and matched her pace to his. They circled the floor in little more than a small well-metered shuffle. There was no flash, no twirls, no dips, no breathtaking moments, except he could smell her hair and it had that amazing scent of sun-warmed sweet peas that always wafted around her, as if she'd been plucked from a vine herself. And the softness of her skin beneath his callused fingers made him want to see if she was just as soft at the bend in her elbow or at the back of her neck or other more personal spaces.

His gaze met hers and he wondered if she knew the direction his thoughts were taking, because a faint pink flush was coloring her face. She opened her mouth to speak but then glanced away. Ryder waited, holding his breath—would she tell him what she was thinking? Should he ask, insist, cajole her into sharing? He didn't. He waited some more, wanting her to share with him because she wanted to.

The band stopped playing. Maisy stepped back but Ryder didn't let go of her hand. He had the feeling that if he let her go, he'd never get to hold her again. He waited, hoping she'd say something. Anything.

But the moment slipped by and he sensed he had missed something important. He kept her hand in his and turned to walk back to their table, but Maisy didn't move. As couples streamed around them, she pulled him back around to face her.

"Are you really leaving after you finish the bookstore restoration?" she asked. Her voice was soft and vulnerable and he had to lean in close to hear her. "Are you leaving Fairdale? Are you leaving me?"

Chapter Twenty-one

HER eyes looked enormous behind her glasses. And in their depths, Ryder saw a fragility he hadn't expected. It rocked him back on his heels, forcing him to admit that there was more happening between them than just attraction. They had a genuine connection, the real deal. If things moved forward between them, his potential for hurt was great, but even worse, Maisy stood to get hurt, too. He couldn't live with that.

And yet, unlike him, she was strong enough to be vulnerable. That wasn't him. That could never be him. Emotionally, he was in so far over his head, he felt like he was drowning.

"Yes," he said. "I've taken a job in Charleston, and I'll be leaving right after I get Perry settled at her new school in Connecticut." There, he said it. It had to be as clear to her as it was to him that anything between them was doomed.

"Oh." Maisy nodded but she didn't back away and she didn't leave him standing on the dance floor like a fool.

Instead, she dropped his hand. He wanted to snatch it back and hold on tight, but he didn't. Rather, he shoved his hands in his pockets while she crossed her arms over her chest. They were now a living example of a date gone wrong and even though he knew it was probably for the best, he hated it. Together they left the dance floor.

He glanced up and saw Adam and their waitress standing by their table. Adam looked decidedly pleased with himself. It was easy to see why. Their small table was groaning with food. Barbeque ribs, a half-smoked chicken, sweet potato fries, baked beans, potato salad, buttered corn, green beans with bacon, and fresh-baked biscuits. Have mercy.

"This is your idea of date food?" Ryder asked Adam.

"Yep."

"If I eat all of this, I'm going to be incapacitated," Ryder protested. "How is that a date?"

Adam's grin was as wide as the horizon. Then he winked at Maisy and said, "This should keep him from getting fresh."

With that, Adam tossed a red-and-white-checked dish towel over his shoulder and left them to their meal.

"Call me if you need anything," the waitress said before she skipped after him.

Ryder pulled Maisy's chair back for her. "A forklift—do you think they have one of those in back? Because we're going to need one to get us out of our chairs if we eat all of this."

To his relief, Maisy laughed and the awkwardness between them dissipated like rain on hot pavement.

"Adam does believe in generous helpings," she said.

With a pragmatism he found admirable, she grabbed a fistful of paper towels that sat in a spool in the center of the food and tucked them into the top of her overalls. They draped over the denim, protecting them from dripping sauce. She used her fork to grab up a rack of ribs and set to work.

Ryder loved her enthusiasm for her food and wanted to high-five her for having the wherewithal to dive right in. This was no lettuce-eating, slave-to-the-bathroom-scale woman in his midst. Maisy went after the food hard-core and ate with gusto. In fact, if he didn't get a move on, she was going to plow through the food without him.

Ryder tucked in. They ate without speaking. Ryder figured now that she knew he was leaving, there wasn't anything left for them to say. She'd told him before that she would never date long-distance again, and having met dingleberry, he couldn't blame her. Still, he didn't like the distance he felt between them now. He wanted to reinvent this night, maybe forge it into something new by talking about their common interest in the bookstore.

"There are so many interesting features to your house," he said, breaking the silence. "Like, on the first floor, the cast-iron tub with the claw feet. We can paint the ceramic and restore it, but do you want it on the first floor? We could shore up the third floor and put it in the bathroom up there."

Maisy considered him for a moment as if she knew what he was doing and wasn't sure if she was on board or not. Finally, she answered him.

"I like that idea," she said. "If I'm going to be an old spinster lady with a bookstore and cats, I think soaks in a vintage bathtub will be required."

This, unfortunately, brought an image of Maisy up to her neck in bubbles to the front of Ryder's brain. He took a long sip of his beer, willing the image away. With each second that ticked by, he knew this whole stupid plan of his had been ill advised. He never should have taken her out without the others. He needed the hustle and bustle of the bookstore and his crew, and even King George, around them to keep him from getting too caught up in her.

Maisy wasn't a fling, she wasn't a for-now, or a for-the-moment type of girl. She was a forever sort of woman. She was the kind of gal a man spent his whole life looking for, because she was as true as the tall trees on her property. She dug her roots in deep and withstood all the storms and droughts and bitter cold winters that life threw at her. If they got involved, Ryder couldn't live with himself if he was the lightning strike that split her spirit and left her burned and damaged.

"What are you thinking about?" Maisy asked. "Your frown line looks like it's been chiseled into your forehead."

Ryder blinked. "Sorry."

"Was it something about the house?" she asked. "Is there a problem, something you aren't telling me?"

"No, that's not it," he said. He shoved a biscuit into his mouth to keep himself from saying something he shouldn't, like how much he wanted to see her in those bubbles in that tub. Instead, he figured he'd better redirect their non-date, or what he was beginning to think of as an exercise in masochism. Since Maisy was a forever girl and he was a for-now boy, he had to stay the course and rebrand their outing into something innocuous.

"Listen," he said. "I'm really glad we decided to have this business dinner together."

Maisy tipped her head to the side. She was working on a sparerib, and the barbeque sauce was on her fingers and a small blob was on her upper lip, drawing his gaze to her mouth. Damn it.

"Business dinner?" she asked.

"Yeah," he bluffed. He wondered if she could hear the pounding of his heart in his chest. Even now, lying made his heart race just like it had when he was a kid and he'd hid his father's booze. He always knew there would be hell to pay, but he did it anyway just to have his dad sober for a little while. "You know, so we could talk without everyone around. I figured we needed to discuss what you want for the second floor, besides the turret, and how about the hidden room— are you wanting to block it off or keep it open?"

He took a bite of rib. Adam's sauce was the nectar of the gods, but it might as well have been made out of sewage and sludge, because Ryder couldn't taste anything but his own desperation.

"That's it," Maisy said. She dropped the rib onto her plate. "I can't do this anymore." She picked up a wet wipe and began to scrub her hands. Her gaze ran over the table. "As amazing as this spread is, there isn't enough food here for me to eat my feelings. Damn it."

Sensing she was getting ready to leave, Ryder dropped his rib and began to clean his fingers, too. It was for the best, really. This whole evening had been ill advised, as Quino had tried to warn him.

Maisy rose from her chair, but instead of storming out, she moved to stand beside him. She ran one hand up her bare arm, pausing at the strap of her overalls. With the flick of a thumb, she unclasped the suspender and let it fall down behind her back. She arched her back and her petite curves were thrust into his face. She dug one hand into her hair and tipped her head back, exposing her throat. Then she made a move that he was sure would replay in his brain for the rest of his life. She lowered her glasses and looked over the tops at him.

"The truth is, you want me as much as I want you, Ryder. Now, what are you going to do about it?" she asked.

Ryder didn't remember moving. In fact, he didn't remember dropping a wad of bills on the table or tossing his napkin onto his seat. He did remember sliding his arm around Maisy and hauling her up to his side while he strode out of the barn.

"Told you," Adam said as they passed him on their way out the sliding doors. "Date food."

Maisy's shorter legs could barely keep up with him, so Ryder hauled her half up in his arms as he strode toward his truck. They were only halfway there when Maisy put her head on his shoulder and pressed her lips against the rapid pulse at the base of his throat.

Ryder lost his footing at the feel of the soft butterfly kiss. He was a big, muscly man. How did such an achingly tender touch render him incoherent? He stopped right where he was and shifted her so his hands were full of her. Maisy obliged by sliding her legs around his waist and her arms around his neck. This time when she kissed him, she took no prisoners. It was a thorough plundering of his mouth beneath hers and it left him seeing stars and quite possibly a few planets.

When she pulled away, her lips were swollen and red and parted in a smile that felt like a blast of sunshine.

"Tell me again how this was a business dinner," she said. She had a teasing gleam in her eye. "That's so hot."

Ryder gripped her tighter and let loose something that sounded like a growl. How did this tiny little woman bring out the alpha in him? It was an embarrassment he refused to dwell on right now. Instead, he continued walking until he reached his truck. Then he leaned her up against it, so that she was wedged between him and the cab, and he kissed her.

It was the kiss he'd wanted to plant on her for days. It was a full-on, *getting to know each other in a most intimate way* sort of kiss. Ryder liked the feel of her soft mouth beneath his and how she gripped his shoulders as if she was hanging on while her mouth moved beneath his, inviting him in and savoring the taste of him.

He loved the feel of her curves pressed against him, as if her femininity tempered his masculinity, although when she dug her fingers into his hair and held him still while she took command of the kiss, he thought maybe it was the other way around. Maybe he was the one tempering her. She bit his lower lip gently between her teeth and he felt his knees buckle. Yep, he was definitely the only one exercising some restraint.

He pulled away from her and sucked in some cool night air, hoping it would ease the raging bonfire of need inside of him. It didn't. Not trusting himself to keep holding her, he eased away, letting her slide down his body, a wonderfully bad decision, until she was standing on her own. He reached around her and opened the passenger-side door to the truck.

Maisy climbed in, and with one shoulder strap still unfastened, she looked like a walking invitation to debauchery. As she settled back into the seat, Ryder reached forward and fastened her overall strap, setting it to rights as if it would remind him to keep his hands to himself. He almost laughed, the idea was so preposterous.

In fact, instead of walking away, he went back in. He kissed her just as he'd imagined doing over the past few weeks. Not the brief exchanges they'd shared before but the all-in, fully present, *kissing her like the world was about to end* sort of kiss. He kissed her lips, her cheek, the slender curve of her neck. He ran his lips along the scoop of her tank top, marveling that her skin was just as soft as he'd imagined.

When she dug her fingers into his hair and pulled his head up so that she could kiss him on the lips, he complied. When she gently took his lower lip between her teeth and gave it a tender tug, he felt a shock wave of lust rocket right through him. He pulled back, knowing that he was seconds away from having those overalls unsnapped and her tank top shoved aside so he could fully investigate the curves that had taunted him every day for weeks.

Instead, he locked his hands on her hips and stepped in between her legs so that he could feel her warmth against him. It was a delicious sort of torture. He wanted more, though. He wanted to hear her say what he had finally admitted to himself.

"Say it," he said.

"Say what?" she asked. She straightened her glasses and peered at him with glazed eyes. A faint blush of pink colored her cheeks, and her lips, especially that delightful top one, were swollen from being kissed. He'd done that.

"Admit that this was a *date* date," he said.

She licked her lips and he almost forgot what he was asking. The look she gave him was teasing and playful. "First, I need some clarification."

"Okay." He wondered if he should be nervous.

"Was this a *date* date for you?" she asked.

"At first, no," he said. "My plan was to take you out and convince you over a very expensive French dinner that the chemistry between us should just be ignored."

Her eyebrows lifted. Ryder wasn't sure if she was surprised by his candor or the realization that she'd missed out on a fancy-shmancy dinner.

"One problem, a big problem," he said. "I. Can't. Ignore. You."

For as long as he lived, Ryder would remember the smile that burst across her lips. Maisy beamed at him, positively beamed, and it made him feel like he was everything she'd ever been looking for in a man, which, of course, was ridiculous, but there it was.

"Then, yes, this is a *date* date," she said. And then she kissed him and Ryder forgot about not being dateable, and the fact that he was leaving soon, and that Maisy didn't do long-distance relationships. None of it mattered because she was in his arms, obliterating everything but the feel of her mouth beneath his.

"Hey, can a girl finagle some ice cream out of you on a

first date or is that second-date protocol?" Maisy asked when they finally came up for air.

At the moment, Ryder was sure she could talk him into pretty much anything. Turrets, ice cream, lassoing the moon. He almost said as much but good sense kicked in and he just nodded.

"Sure," he said. He stepped back, giving her room to buckle her seat belt. "I'm betting you want to hit Fat Daddy's in the center of town."

"Is there any other ice cream place?" she asked.

"Not that I've seen," he said. He closed her door and walked around the front of the truck. He slid into the driver's seat, started up the engine, and drove out of the dirt lot and headed back toward Fairdale. "Perry is addicted to their mint chocolate chip."

"You know, I took an online quiz once that tells you what your flavor choice says about you," she said. "Mint chocolate chip people were feisty."

"Well, they got that one right," he said. He glanced sideways at her. "Let me guess, your favorite flavor is . . ."

"You'll never guess," she said.

"Don't be a doubter." He shot her a reproving look. Then he tapped the steering wheel. "Not vanilla. People who like vanilla are subtle, persuasive types—you're much more direct."

"Interesting take," she said. "And you're right, it's not vanilla."

"Not chocolate," he said.

"What makes you say that?"

"Everyone likes chocolate. You're not like everyone."

Her lips curved up a little and he knew she was pleased that he found her unique. That was certainly accurate. He'd never met anyone like her before. She was so bighearted for being such a petite thing. He wondered how caring so deeply for so many people didn't leave her with nothing left for herself.

"Rocky road," he said. "That's your ice cream."

She laughed. "What made you choose that one?"

"Rocky road is for people who take the road less traveled," he said. "It's for treasure seekers and adventurers, forge-your-own-path types. You know, people who aren't afraid to color outside the lines or travel without a map."

Her eyes were enormous. "That's how you see me?"

"Um, you're having me build a turret for your bookstore," he said. "Hell, yeah, that's how I see you."

"That might be the most complimentary description of my character I've ever gotten," she said. "Thank you."

"So, is it?" he asked.

"Is what?"

"Is rocky road your favorite?"

"It is now," she said. Then she laughed in a way that made his heart lift up in his chest as if she were the wave that lifted his boat out of low tide and took him with her to destinations unknown. It was alarming to realize that if things were different, if he didn't have Perry to get through school and a job waiting for him, he'd follow Maisy anywhere or nowhere.

Chapter Twenty-two

THE ice cream was perfection. Maisy ordered the rocky road, because why wouldn't she? After that description, she didn't think she'd ever order another flavor ever again. She had never actually had a favorite flavor of ice cream because she liked to think of herself as an equal-opportunity eater of all frozen dairy goodness, but Ryder didn't need to know that.

She noted that Ryder ordered pistachio. She wondered what that said about him. She didn't remember it in the quiz, but it was definitely an outlier in the flavor field, which had to mean something, right? He was independent? Not a joiner? A tumbleweed?

Maisy took a huge bite of her cone to stop herself from saying anything out loud. This caused a solid case of brain freeze, which made her slap her palm onto her forehead with a wince.

"You all right over there?" Ryder asked.

"You'd think at twenty-nine with the amount of ice cream I've consumed—hundreds of gallons, I'm sure—I'd know how to eat it without giving myself a brain freeze."

"Put your tongue against the roof of your mouth for ten seconds," he said. "Seriously, it's the ice cream hitting the roof of your mouth that causes blood vessels to constrict and give you an ice cream headache."

Maisy did as she was told. Amazingly her headache eased much faster than it usually did.

She looked at him in surprise and he shrugged. "Dad 101. Perry did that every time she had ice cream as a kid, which, because she loved it, was a lot. I had to read up on how to cure it or we had big drama. You can also drink something warm and that helps, too."

Maisy took another bite of her ice cream, more carefully this time. "You're a good dad."

"Thanks," he said. "I could be better."

They sat side by side on a park bench on the Fairdale town green just outside the ice cream shop. Maisy said hi to just about everyone who passed. She introduced Ryder to a few people, but between living on Joaquin Solis's horse farm, playing in the town soccer league, and working on the historic buildings at the university, he already knew a lot of them.

When Hank Seagraves, the facilities manager from the university, stopped by and the two of them began to chat about the remodel and how it was going, Maisy felt like he was the resident and she was the visitor. It hit her then that Ryder could slip right into Fairdale and be woven into the fabric of town life as firmly as any of them. The thought made her giddy. She loved this. She loved sitting here with him, being a couple in town, doing couple things.

She'd never really had that. Much as she hated to admit it, Savannah was right. She always picked the low-hanging fruit, the ones that were usually bruised or had worms. It wasn't that she was lazy or lacking confidence, it was just that an English professor at a modest-sized university in a small city really didn't meet that many eligible men. And, yes, maybe she had always liked the idea of a boyfriend more than the reality, mostly because she had never met a man who made her feel the way Ryder did.

She wasn't sure what had come over her at Adam's Rib, but when Ryder looked at her and admitted he was leaving, she was hit with such a sense of panic that this fleeting moment in time was all she was going to get with him that suddenly the idea of friend-zoning him just seemed so stupid and wasteful. If this was all she got with Ryder, she was not going to let it slip through her fingers.

Ryder was so above and beyond any other man she had ever dated—she glanced down and noted her overalls—she had panicked. Yep, that's exactly what she had done. Straight-up panicked that she was going on a real date with a man who did not still live with his mom, who was employed, who didn't have an addiction to video games, women, drugs, drinking, what have you, but who was leaving in a matter of weeks.

She ate her ice cream in silence while she studied him talking to Hank. Ryder wasn't classically good-looking in the *stare at him with your mouth hanging open because you forgot how to close it while looking at this godlike man before you* sort of way. Nope. That actually would have been a turnoff for Maisy. Perfection made her uncomfortable.

Flaws were what interested her because the book lover inside of her knew that there was a story behind the calluses on Ryder's palms just like there was a tale to be told about the scar just below his left eyebrow and the subtle bend in his nose. It was the imperfections that told the stories of a person's life and that's what interested her.

"Sorry about that," he said. "Hank's a good guy. It was nice seeing him again."

"No worries," she said. She finished her ice cream and dropped the remaining soggy cone into a nearby trash can. Ryder did the same. As they walked back to the truck, it felt like the most natural thing in the world to take his hand. Ryder must have thought so, too, because they reached for each other at the same time.

Maisy liked having her hand folded into his as they strolled. She didn't feel like she had to make the evening special for him—it just was. She also didn't feel as if she was putting him out by being herself—he accepted her. And she didn't feel like he had an ulterior motive. Well, at least he didn't have one that was any different from her own.

She wanted to be with him. She realized that had pretty much been decided when he didn't say a word about her outfit but just rolled with it, accepting her exactly as she was. Honestly, she'd have to be made of stone to resist him.

"Ready to head back home?" he asked when they reached his truck.

"Sure," she said. "Or we could go for a drive."

"Sounds good." He gave her a boost into the passenger seat and circled the truck. He climbed in beside her and asked, "Where to?"

"Have you seen the old covered bridge on the outskirts of town?"

"Once, but I didn't get a very good look at it as Quino was driving and he barely slowed down," he said. "If I had blinked, I'd have missed it altogether."

"Well, let's go see it and make up for that," she said.

Ryder put the truck in gear and followed her directions through town. While they were driving, Maisy pointed out the historic sights of significance in Fairdale. She showed him the town cemetery where most of her relatives were buried, the town house where she and Savannah shared their first apartment, the preschool she'd attended, the old diner where her mom had been a waitress and her dad had sat there and eaten three whole pies while he tried to get the courage to ask her out.

Ryder laughed at that one and then laughed even harder when Maisy admitted that her father had never eaten another bite of apple pie after that. When they arrived at the bridge, the dirt parking lot to the side was empty. Ryder shut off his headlights and Maisy rolled down her window so they could hear the roar of the water in the Smoky River as it rushed under the old covered bridge.

"The bridge has been here since 1884," Maisy said. She was feeling nervous and her professor voice came out of her mouth even though she was trying to sound hip, as opposed to professorial. "It was washed out in the flood of '38 and then again in '72 but the town always rebuilds it."

"Where does it lead?" Ryder asked.

"Pardon?"

"Where does it lead?"

"To the other side." She smiled.

"I gathered that," he said. "It being a bridge and all, but what I meant was, where does this road go?"

"Nowhere," Maisy said. "At least nowhere important. There are some farmers on the other side but they all use the metal bridge down the river as it's wider and closer to town."

"So, why does the town keep rebuilding the bridge?" he asked. "Why not let it go?"

Maisy gasped. "Fairdale would never do that. This bridge is the most romantic spot in town. Everyone comes here. Why, I'll bet half the babies born in Fairdale were conceived around this bridge."

"And just how much time have you spent in cars parked around this bridge, young lady?" he asked.

Maisy laughed. He was using his dad voice on her. "Why would you care?"

"Because as galling as it is to admit, if you've been here with dingleberry, I'm going to have to find him and beat him up," he said.

"Are you jealous?"

"I'm not sure," he said. "I've never felt jealousy before, so it's unfamiliar. Is jealousy when the thought of you making out with someone else makes me want to punch him in the face?"

"Yeah, I'm pretty sure that's it."

"Then, yes, I'm jealous but only if it's been within the last year," he said. He looked at her expectantly.

"At the risk of losing my reputation as a player," she began, pausing to sigh, "then I have to be honest and say it's been about five years. Dingleberry and I never . . . we didn't . . . oh, this is embarrassing. In the year that we dated, it never went beyond a perfunctory kiss good night."

"Good," he said. He shook his whole body like a dog shaking water off its fur. "Jealousy managed, then."

"Good, because I'd never want you to feel that because of me," she said. "It's a lousy emotion."

"Agreed. So, let me make sure I understand. You knowingly took me to a notorious spot for parking?" he asked. Maisy nodded. The look he gave her was wicked and she shivered in the most delicious way. "Then I have a follow-up question. Maisy Kelly, did you bring me here so we could make out?"

She thought about lying; she did. But she really was the worst liar ever, she could already feel her face getting hot, and besides, she *had* brought him here for precisely this reason. Why not admit it?

"Yes, I did," she said. She tipped up her chin and arched a brow at him. "So, what are you going to do about it?"

"This." He reached for her and pulled her close and then he kissed her.

If the kisses between them had been hot before, this one was off the charts. Maisy met him halfway and dug her fingers into his thick dark hair so she could hold him still while she opened her mouth beneath his and kissed him with the same single-minded attention he was giving her. He put one hand on her waist and pulled her as close as the console in between them would allow. It wasn't close enough as far as Maisy was concerned, which was very frustrating.

His mouth left hers to trail down her neck. The sensation of his lips on her skin was everything she'd imagined and more. And she wanted more. So much more. She pushed the straps of her overalls off so that the bib sagged around her waist. She hoisted herself over the console and slid into his lap, so that she was straddling him. Ryder gave what sounded like a growl of approval, but Maisy was so caught up in feeling pure fevered desire that she really wasn't paying attention.

Instead her focus was on the pesky buttons of his shirt and the battle they were giving her fingers. She wanted to feel his skin and see if it was as warm as his hands, which had slid up under her tank top and were holding her sides so gently, barely stroking her with his thumbs, as if she were some wild creature he was trying to tame. She liked that. It made her feel bolder than she'd ever felt with a guy before.

She loosened three buttons, enough to pull back his collar and press her mouth against the skittish pulse at the base of his throat. It ticked faster when she ran her tongue across it. She smiled against his neck as she moved her mouth up to his ear. She gently bit his earlobe and then whispered, "I think I want to do more than make out."

Ryder pulled back from her and the look in his blue eyes was so hot, Maisy was surprised it didn't leave scorch marks on her skin. Then he pulled her up against him, and said, "So do I."

It was a relief. After all these days of working side by side, of seeing him and laughing with him, of taking care of King George together and getting to know the tender soul inside the burly man, it felt like the end of a long, lonely wait to finally feel his hands on her, moving up her body, cupping her curves and kissing her mouth as if he, too, had been desperate for this.

Maisy felt as if she was falling into a haze of heat and lust so thick that she could barely breathe. Who needed oxygen anyway? She was pretty sure she could live off the fire that was burning between them, at least until it consumed her completely. A flash of light blasted her right in the face and she was sure they were about to spontaneously combust.

"Maisy?" a deep voice called through the open window. "Maisy Kelly, is that you?"

Maisy rocked back from Ryder, yanking her tank top down as she did. She turned her head only to get blasted right through her glasses with what appeared to be a spotlight.

She put her hand over her face, and said, "Yes, it's me, going blind here."

"Oh, sorry."

The light was redirected to the ground and Maisy blinked, trying to see around the spots swimming in her vision. A big-jawed face, the sort that looked like it could withstand a punch with a hammer, appeared in the open window.

"Nice evening out, isn't it, Maisy?" Travis Wainwright, the Fairdale chief of police, grinned at her. "Unusually warm, I reckon."

Growing up, Travis had been best buddies with Maisy's older brother. She had no doubt he was going to set the cell phone towers on fire reporting this to Tucker.

"Yeah, we were just saying that, weren't we, Ryder?" she

asked. She sent him a pleading glance as she slid off his lap and back over to her side of the truck.

He shifted in his seat. He cleared his throat and smiled at Travis. Travis didn't smile back. Instead, he rested his arms on the edge of the window and said, "I got a call that there was a young couple going hot and heavy over by the bridge. Now, you two wouldn't have seen anything like that, now, would you?"

"*Young* couple?" Ryder asked. "Nope, I can't say that I've seen anything like that."

"Nice save." Travis chuckled.

Maisy was pretty sure she was going to collapse into her seat in relief. Travis had the wherewithal to humiliate her with this, but he was opting not to.

"Travis Wainwright, this is my . . . friend Ryder. He's the architect working on the bookstore for me. Ryder Copeland, this is Travis Wainwright, chief of police of Fairdale and longtime family friend," Maisy said. She carefully slid the straps up on her overalls, trying not to draw any attention to herself.

"Copeland?" Travis said. "Your daughter is Perry?"

"Yes, she's mine," Ryder said. He sat up straighter and his brows furrowed. "Is there a reason the chief of police knows her name?"

"Well, not as the chief of police," Travis said. "I'm Cooper's dad, you know, the boy she's dating. Coop. He's my kid."

"She's . . . I'm sorry . . . did you say *dating*?" Ryder asked.

"Yeah, or whatever 'going out with' means in eighth grade," he said. "My wife and I were hoping to have you over for dinner sometime."

Maisy watched as Ryder's furrowed brow lifted into a look of stunned surprise. Perry hadn't told him about her and Cooper at all, that was clear. Poor Ryder. His face turned a mottled shade of red and his gaze, when he turned to Travis, was so intense it looked like it was going to shoot laser beams.

"You know my daughter is only fourteen, right?" Ryder said. "How old is your boy?"

"Same as Perry. They're in algebra class together," Travis

said. He looked at Ryder's face and then his expression cleared. "Sorry. You didn't know?"

"No. How long have they been going out?"

"A few months, I guess," Travis said. He looked like he wanted to spare Ryder, but knew better than to try. "Listen, they're just kids. It's harmless. They mostly hang out at our house and watch YouTube videos or study, both under the supervision of my wife. I'm sure it's all very innocent."

"Are you?" Ryder asked. "Tell me, what sort of things were you thinking about when you were fourteen?"

"I . . . uh . . . oh."

"Exactly," Ryder said. "I'm sorry, but we have to go."

"I understand completely, but my offer for dinner still stands," Travis said.

"Great," Ryder said. "I'd love to get to know—Cooper, was it?—and his family."

"Terrific! And, Maisy, since you two are a thing, you should come, too," Travis said.

"Sounds lovely," Maisy said. Yeah, hanging out with her older brother's best friend and her new boy . . . whatever he was, while they squared off over their kids—not exactly her idea of a good time.

"I'll be in touch," Travis said.

Ryder nodded at him and switched on the truck and put it in gear.

Maisy pulled on her seat belt and waved out the window as they left, leaving a cloud of dirt and Travis behind them.

"Perry has a boyfriend," Ryder said.

"Cooper," Maisy confirmed. She remembered the boy she'd found with Perry in the hidden room. They were "going out." Perry hadn't told her that and now Maisy was an accomplice to her deceit because she hadn't said anything to Ryder about Perry and the boy. This was terrible. "What are you going to do?"

"Perry and I are going to have a conversation," he said.

That's what he said, but it sounded more like he was going to yell and Perry was going to listen. Uh-oh.

Chapter Twenty-three

RYDER made record time from the covered bridge back to the bookstore. Using an app on his phone, he had tracked Perry to the bookstore. Maisy had called Savannah to confirm Perry's whereabouts and discovered that Perry had just arrived to see George and planned to watch a chick flick with Savannah. Maisy hoped for Perry's sake that she had enjoyed her evening, because Maisy had a feeling the kid was about to be grounded until she was old enough to vote.

Ryder pulled into the driveway and braked hard. He popped out of his side and circled the truck to help Maisy out. She swung the door open and met him halfway. He took her hand in his and they strode toward the house with Maisy having to do double time to keep up with his longer stride. It seemed the closer they got, the more intense he became. She knew she needed to slow down the mad-dad train, because he was going to do more harm than good if he approached Perry like this.

She jumped in front of him and grabbed his other hand. "Hey, whoa there, cowboy architect."

Ryder looked at her but he didn't smile. He did, however,

stop walking. They were at the base of the steps in front of the bookshop and she took the opportunity to hop onto the first step so that they were more eye to eye.

"Can I offer a word of advice from a woman who was once a fourteen-year-old girl?" she asked. His back was so rigid he could have been one of the porch pillars. "Please?"

Ryder tipped his head back and looked up. Maisy followed his gaze. The stars were out and they twinkled in the sky, breaking up the unrelenting darkness with little pinpricks of hope. He must have seen something similar, because he sighed and lowered his head, looking a bit calmer.

"All right," he said.

"I know you want answers," she said.

"Damn straight. I hate lies and secrets," he said. "Do you know how many times my father stood in front of me and Sawyer, swearing to us that he wouldn't get drunk, wouldn't lose his job, that he'd be there at the ball game, or the teacher's conference? And every single time, he lied."

"Fair enough," Maisy said. "But Perry isn't your dad and I think you'll get more information if you let her do most of the talking, without being too aggressive."

"But she knows she's not allowed to date. We agreed a long time ago that that sort of thing would wait until high school," he said. "She's never lied to me before—and it's over a boy."

He made a face like he was sucking a lemon and Maisy had a hard time not smiling. The guy was trying really hard not to freak out. For the first time she saw how vulnerable he felt as a single dad. It wrecked her. If ever there was a guy who loved his kid, it was Ryder.

"Just be calm and try to hear her side of it first," Maisy said. She hugged him tight and was relieved when he hugged her back. "Okay?"

"I'll try," he said. He released her reluctantly, which made Maisy smile again.

She noted that his color had returned to normal and the crazy light in his eyes had diminished somewhat. She figured this was as good as it was going to get.

They walked up the three flights of stairs to the upper-level apartment. They could hear the sound of the television before they reached the door, and Maisy said a quick prayer that Perry was honest with her dad. She unlocked the door and pushed it open.

To her surprise, it was a full-on hen party happening. Savannah, Perry, Jeri, and Hannah were all in attendance, with King George sacked out in the middle of them on the couch.

"Hello," Savy greeted them. "You're just in time!"

Maisy walked into the room, flicking on the light switch, as the ladies had it turned down low for the movie.

"Ah, no lights!" Hannah cried. She was hugging a bowl of popcorn to her middle over her veterinarian scrubs.

Maisy snapped the light back off and Jeri said, "Thank you."

"We're in the final scene," Savy said in a stage whisper, which of course was no stage whisper at all.

"What's the movie?"

"*The Sure Thing*," Perry said.

"Oh, hell no," Ryder said. He snapped the lights back on and fumbled for the remote. Not finding it, he snapped the TV off on the console.

"Dad!" Perry cried. "What are you doing?"

"There are no sure things," he said to Perry. "Ever. Sure things are bad, very bad."

Savy looked at Maisy. "Good date?"

"I'll explain later," she said.

"Oh, I can't wait to hear this," Jeri said to Hannah. They both dug a hand into the popcorn bowl and watched Ryder and Maisy as if they were the feature film. Maisy gave them a discouraging scowl, but they didn't turn away.

Ryder was still staring at his daughter. "Who is Cooper Wainwright?"

Maisy cringed. This was not exactly the way she'd envisioned this going down.

Perry met her father's gaze. Maisy had to give her props for that. She was unflinching as she tipped up her chin and said, "He's my boyfriend."

"What?" Savannah cried.

"Hey, now," Jeri said. "That is not what you told us before."

"Honestly, Perry, I am shocked," Hannah said. "We asked you if you were seeing anyone and you said no."

"You even swore an oath on it," Savannah said. She held up a vintage paperback and looked at Maisy in chagrin. "She swore on Kathleen Woodiwiss's *The Flame and the Flower*."

"Oh, the betrayal," Jeri said.

"It cuts deep," Hannah said.

"I'm sorry," Perry addressed the women. "Truly, I was trying to keep it on the down-low, because it's really no big deal."

Maisy looked at Perry's face. There was a quiver to her chin and her eyes looked suspiciously watery. This was anything but "no big deal" to her. Maisy felt her heart clench in her chest. Perry was looking heartbreak full in the face and she was doing it unflinchingly. How incredibly brave she was.

"If it's no big deal then why didn't you tell me?" Ryder asked.

Perry shrugged in that dismissive *whatever* sort of way that teenagers had. Maisy wanted to stand behind Ryder in Perry's line of sight and wave her arms or make a slashing motion across her throat—anything to clue her in that this was the worst possible tack to take. Too late.

"What does *that* mean?" Ryder asked. He mimicked her shrug, which made Perry's face turn red. Maisy wasn't sure if it was embarrassment or anger, but she was pretty sure it didn't matter. Both were bad. "What else haven't you told me?"

Perry hopped to her feet. She grabbed her backpack off the floor and swung it over one shoulder. "What I do and who I see are none of your business."

Collectively, Savannah's, Hannah's, and Jeri's jaws dropped. They all looked at Ryder as if expecting his head to explode in three, two . . . Maisy knew what was coming. She tried to give him the hand sign to take it down, remain calm, breathe. Yeah, Ryder was having none of that.

"You listen here, young lady, as long as you are under my roof everything you do is my business," he said. He crossed his arms over his chest in stern-dad stance. Perry was not intimidated, not at all.

"Then, it's a good thing I'm not going to be under your roof much longer," she said.

Maisy heard one of the ladies suck in a breath.

"I say she's winning," Jeri said. "Three to one."

"No, no, he's coming back. You'll see," Hannah said.

"Nah, I'm with Jeri," Savy said. "I think Perry's got him at least two to one."

"Hush," Maisy shushed her friends.

Ryder looked gobsmacked, as if he couldn't believe Perry had just spoken to him like that. He stared at her as if he didn't recognize her, and Maisy had a feeling this was their first real father-daughter contest of wills. Even without the ladies keeping track, it was clear Perry wasn't holding back.

"How did you find out, anyway?" Perry asked. She glared at Maisy, and Maisy wanted to protest that she hadn't said a word, but then how would that look to Ryder? Ergh, this was a nightmare. Perry scowled at her father. "Did Maisy tell you?"

"Maisy?" Ryder asked. He looked bewildered and then looked at Maisy. "Did you know about this?"

"Not exactly," Maisy said.

"Meaning?" Ryder's jaw was tight. He looked pissed, and Maisy couldn't blame him.

"I ran into Perry in the hidden room with Cooper, but I didn't know they were a couple."

"But you saw them alone together?" he asked. "And you didn't tell me?"

"No, I didn't," Maisy said.

Ryder looked furious and hurt. Maisy wanted to explain, but Perry was not letting go of her advantage.

"If you didn't hear it from Maisy, who did you hear it from?"

"I happened to meet Cooper's father, Travis Wainwright, tonight," Ryder said. "Imagine my surprise when he said you were going out with his son."

"Where did you meet Mr. Wainwright?" Perry asked.

"That's not the point," Ryder said.

"Yes, it is," Perry insisted. "What were you doing that warranted a chat with the chief of police?"

"Did you get pulled over?" Hannah asked. "Travis tagged me for speeding, but I still say his radar gun was faulty. It added thirty miles onto my actual speed."

Maisy and Jeri exchanged a knowing look. Everyone in town knew that Hannah Phillips had a lead foot.

"No, I didn't get pulled over," Ryder said.

"Jaywalking?" Jeri asked. "Travis is a stickler for the rules. Remember when he was the hall monitor in school? I've never spent so much time in the principal's office."

"No."

"Maisy Kelly, did Travis catch you two, *you know*?" Savy asked.

"Uh . . . I . . . we . . . it's complicated." Maisy's inability to lie tripped her up.

Ryder snapped his head around to look at her and she shrugged.

"Oh, my God," Perry said. "I can never go out in public again. My dad was caught hooking up! This is humiliating. I am socially ruined."

"It was not that bad," Ryder said. "We were simply taking in the sights by the covered bridge—"

"You were by the bridge!" Perry's eyes were huge behind her glasses. "That's the town's make-out spot. *I've* never even been there! And that's where all the high school kids go. Did anyone see you? Did you see anyone? Did they recognize you?"

She whipped out her phone and began thumbing through screens.

"What are you doing?" Ryder asked.

"Checking to see how much damage you've done to my social standing," she said. "You know, most teen girls do not have to deal with their dad making out in public on dates. Jeez, it's like my life has become a Jennifer Crusie novel."

"Oh, horror," Savy deadpanned.

"Right?" Perry asked. "I mean, she's hilarious, but I don't want to live it, you know?"

Maisy's lips twitched. Having never had that much of a social life, she was amazed that she was now the cause of such an uproar.

"Ladybug, you need to settle down," Ryder said. He lowered one eyebrow at her and gave her a hard stare. "This is not about me and Maisy, it's about you having a boyfriend and not telling me, especially when we agreed you're too young to date."

"No, that *was* the issue, but now it's you and your girlfriend,"

Perry argued. "I mean, jeez, Dad, you're old. You can't be hooking up in public. What will people say?"

At least Maisy was pretty sure that's what she said, because honestly, after Perry threw out the G-word, she started to have heart palpitations, the kind where she could feel her heart beating hard in her chest, and the thumps were so strong and so loud she got only about every other word of what the girl was saying.

"I don't care what people say about me," Ryder said. "I care about you. Why didn't you tell me about Cooper? We have a pact to tell each other everything. When did that change?"

Perry shoved her phone in her pocket and faced her dad. "Really, Dad? And when exactly were you going to tell me about you and Maisy?"

Maisy could tell from his expression that he hadn't been planning to tell her anytime soon. Because of course he hadn't. He'd already admitted that he'd planned to take her out tonight and talk her out of a relationship with him. Ryder's jaw clenched and Maisy knew he wasn't going to say a word.

Perry knew it, too. She stormed to the door, saying over her shoulder, "You can't have it both ways. You can't keep things from me but expect me to tell you everything. I'm not a little kid anymore."

She opened the door to the apartment, stomped through it, and then gently shut it behind her. Maisy suspected she would have slammed it except for George, who was sound asleep on the couch. Perry wouldn't want to startle the little guy.

Ryder stared at the door as if she had slipped through a portal to another dimension. He glanced at all of them and then back at the door. He raised his hands in the air as if asking for some kind of divine intervention. Jeri patted him on the back.

"Come hold George," she said. "He'll remind you why babies are cute."

"I'll go after her," Maisy said, "and make sure she's okay."

"Thanks," Ryder said. He picked up the kitten and King George snuggled into him as if he'd just been waiting for Ryder to hold him. The frown on Ryder's face eased as the kitten worked his magic.

Maisy jogged down the stairs. Thankfully, the piles of books had been removed, otherwise she'd never have been able to catch up. She banged through the front door and found Perry sitting on the steps.

She had pulled her braid over her shoulder and was fidgeting with the end, and her posture was slumped as if in defeat.

Maisy sat down beside her. She didn't speak, mostly because she didn't know what to say. The evening had grown cool and Maisy shivered in her tank top. She rubbed her arms and rocked back and forth in an effort to warm up.

"You don't have to sit here with me," Perry said. "I can wait for Dad by myself."

"I know."

"You probably think I'm a jerk."

"No."

"I'm not that mad about you two," she said. She dropped her braid and twisted her fingers together, pausing to study her nails. She picked at a cuticle and then at her green polish.

"I'm glad," Maisy said. "Travis Wainwright is my older brother's best friend. I am going to suffer enough when he hears about it."

Perry turned to look at her. Her mouth formed an O. She understood completely. "In that case, I'm sorry."

Maisy shrugged. "It's fine. My brother will tease me, I'll get mad, he'll apologize, and we'll be fine. That's the thing about family. They make you crazy but you can always count on them. Even though you're at odds now, your dad loves you, Perry."

"Does he?" Perry met her stare. Her eyes looked forlorn. "Because he never says it."

Perry pushed off the steps and trudged to the truck, pulling the door open and climbing inside without another word.

Maisy watched her go. She had no idea what to say. Ryder didn't tell his daughter that he loved her. *Really?* In the time she'd known him, she'd learned that talking about his feelings was not his thing, but there had been a few moments, like when he told her about his childhood and when he talked about Perry, that he laid it all bare. Maybe Perry was being overly dramatic or perhaps Ryder needed a gentle reminder that his daughter needed to hear how he felt now more than ever. Maisy felt singularly unqualified for any of this.

But the summer was slipping by and if Perry and Ryder didn't talk soon, Perry would be hundreds of miles away in a school she didn't want to go to and Ryder would leave to take a job he might not even want just to pay for it. It was maddening watching the communication break down between two people who cared about each other so much.

Then, there were her own feelings to consider. She knew she had a decision to make. Was she in for as long as she had them here? Or should she protect herself and end things before she got crushed by their impending departure? She glanced up at the stars, looking for an answer, but saw nothing in their twinkling lights to indicate a path. She rose to her feet and turned to go into the house. On a small table by the front door was a book.

It was the paperback *One Last Chance*, featuring Jake Sinclair. It was the same book she'd been reading the day Ryder knocked on her door. The same book he had borrowed a week or so ago and returned. What was it doing out here? She was sure she'd put it on her favorites shelf in the main room. Maisy felt the hair on the back of her neck prickle.

"Auntie El?" she whispered. There was no answer, but she felt a cool breeze ripple across her skin almost like a caress. Whoa.

Chapter Twenty-four

"MAISY."

"Ah!" She jumped, dropping the book.

"Sorry, I didn't mean to startle you," Ryder said. He opened the door and stepped outside, pausing to pick up her book for her on the way. "Are you all right? You look pale."

"Um, yeah, I'm good," Maisy said. Her voice sounded unnaturally high so she cleared her throat and forced a smile while she took the book from him and clutched it to her chest.

"George is set for the night," he said. He glanced at the truck. "I guess I'd better go have a father-daughter talk."

He stepped close and kissed Maisy's temple. She tried not to think about how platonic that felt. He was almost at the steps when she grabbed his hand, stopping him. Ryder turned toward her and Maisy let his fingers slip through hers, knowing that they were likely being observed.

"Ryder, I think if you give Perry a chance to explain, you'll see—" Maisy began, but he interrupted.

"Oh, I see," he said. "She lied to me. About a boy. For months."

Maisy noted the stubborn set to his chin. This was what

she'd come to think of as Ryder's control freak face. When his vision about the restoration of the house—say, the exact shade of paint he wanted in the main room of the shop—was not what came out of the paint can, he spent the afternoon at the paint store modifying their process until the paint came out the exact shade he had envisioned. Oh, boy.

She wanted to tell him that Perry was not a can of paint, but she didn't think that would go over very well. Still, she had to try and help him see his daughter's side for both their sakes.

"Maybe she didn't tell you because she knew you wouldn't be happy about it and she values your opinion above all others," Maisy said.

"A lie is a lie is a lie," he said. "Speaking of which, why didn't you tell me you'd seen her with a boy?"

Maisy knew she could have ducked and weaved a direct answer but if what they had started tonight was going to be worth anything, even if it lasted only until he left, it demanded nothing less than the truth.

"Because she asked me not to," she said.

He gave her a sharp nod as if he had expected as much. "Don't do that again."

Maisy tilted her head to the side. His tone was bossy and it made her bristle. "In my defense, I didn't know they were dating or I would have said something. Also, just so we're clear, you're not the boss of me."

Ryder's gaze snapped to hers and narrowed. He didn't look away but let his gaze move over her, every inch of her from her head to her feet and back. Then, to her surprise, he smiled and he said, "Well, that was sassy."

Relief that he wasn't put off or miffed by her standing her ground made Maisy a bit weak in the knees. Well, it was that and the way he was staring at her mouth as if thinking up new and wicked things to do with her. Maisy resisted the urge to fan herself.

She put her hand on his forearm and said, "Just let her talk to you. I remember being fourteen and feeling like no one listened to me. Listen to her. You might be surprised by what she has to say."

She thought about telling him what she suspected Perry wouldn't tell him, that she didn't want to go away to private school, but she didn't. This was something for the two of them to figure out.

"I'll try," he said. This time when he kissed her it was right on the mouth and he lingered, making Maisy's insides liquefy. When he stepped away, she caught herself on the porch railing so she didn't slide onto the floor into a puddle of want at his feet.

"Good night, Maisy."

Ryder strode off toward his truck. Maisy glanced down at the book in her hands, remembering how Clare, the heroine of the novel, had gotten through to her man. As she recalled, Clare threatened Jake with a shotgun in chapter five. Yeah, being a pacifist, that didn't really translate for Maisy except it made for a heck of a scene to read. She turned and headed back into the house, relieved that a shotgun had not been required to make her point.

"ALL right, drum roll please," Savy said. She gave Maisy a pointed look and Maisy immediately began to tap her fingers on her desk, making what sounded sort of like a drum roll.

"Okay, why?" Maisy asked over the low rumbling beat of her fingers.

"We are live!" Savy announced. "Our website is up and running!"

"What?" Maisy jumped up from her seat at the desk opposite Savannah's and hurried around to look at her computer.

Their office space had been relieved of its horrid paneling and was now a sunny, airy room with plants hanging in the windows and King George playing in an empty box in the corner. The hardwood floor had been polished to a high sheen and the walls had been replastered and were now painted a lovely duck-egg blue, with the window and door frames, baseboards, and crown molding painted in Swiss coffee, which was a delicious creamy white color.

Ryder usually worked at a drafting table and desk in the corner, while another desk had been set up for Jeri, who came in every few days to go over the books.

Maisy watched as Savannah opened the webpage. Classical music played in the background as the screen filled with a video of the house. It was shot from an angle that hid the construction of the turret but focused on the steps, which were lined with pots of flowers. The video paused on the porch, where Seth had installed a porch swing, and moved past a tea set on a cart that also had a heaping plate of raspberry thumbprint cookies on it. And then the video centered on the front door, which slowly opened, revealing the shelves of books inside, while the words *Happily Ever After Bookstore* scrolled across the screen.

"That is awesome!" Maisy yelled. She leaned down and hugged Savannah, shaking her because she was still jumping up and down.

"So glad you like it—ulk—can't breathe," Savannah choked.

"Sorry!" Maisy jumped back and let her go. She clapped her hands. "It's just so perfect."

"It still needs fine-tuning, but it'll do for our opening," Savannah said. "I've dedicated pages to Shop, Contact Us, Events, and then I put in a page about Auntie El, with her wedding picture and a little bio about how her love of romance novels helped her through losing the love of her life."

"Savy, you have outdone yourself," Maisy said. She reached over and clicked on the Auntie El page and felt a lump form in her throat as a slide show of Auntie El through the years began, coupled with a brief history of her and her life. "This is so great. I can't thank you enough."

"Don't thank me until I get the rest of your social media tied in and we begin driving customers into the shop," Savy said.

"Do you think that will take very long?" Maisy asked.

"I hope not," Savannah said. "If we want this place to be successful, we've got to get the buzz going. In that regard, I have some ideas."

"Ideas or *Ideas!*? You know, with the capital *I* and an exclamation point," Maisy said.

"And here I thought it was going to be a quiet day at the office." Ryder entered the room. He looked tired and Maisy suspected things hadn't gone smoothly with Perry.

She shared a glance with Savannah and said, "I'll be right back."

"I'll go get more coffee. Want some?" Savy said.

"Yes, please."

"Yo, Ryder, you want some coffee?" Savannah asked.

"I'll be your best friend," he said.

"Not necessary," she answered. Then she walked out of the room, leaving Maisy and Ryder alone.

Ryder was unpacking his laptop and checking his phone. Maisy wasn't sure if she should say anything about last night or not. There were so many things she wanted to talk about, not the least of which was the fact that Perry had called her his girlfriend. And she desperately wanted to know if it was true that he'd never told Perry he loved her or whether it was just the overwrought complaint of an angry teen.

"So, how did it go last night?" Maisy asked.

Ryder glanced up from his phone. His lips tipped up in the corner as if pleased to see her. Then her question registered and he frowned.

"Perry isn't speaking to me," he said. "Apparently, I have humiliated her *to death* and she doesn't know how she'll face Cooper or any of her friends since her dad was caught hooking up. Apparently, we caused quite the scandal in her world."

"I'm pretty sure the only person who saw us is Travis, and I don't see him telling anyone who would care, at least anyone local," she said.

"I said the same thing, but she was so angry," he said. "It was positively glacial at our house. I'm surprised I don't have frostbite."

Maisy smiled. She appreciated that he was trying to make light of a situation that he obviously found hurtful and bewildering. She wondered if she should mention what she suspected was happening. She decided to go for it.

"Do you think maybe she's angry not about us and the 'scandal' but because of something else?"

"What else?" he asked. "She seemed pretty clear that it was humiliation making her hate me with every fiber of her being."

"She doesn't hate you," Maisy said. "But maybe she's angry because she feels powerless."

"About my dating?" he asked. He gestured between them and then looked down at his desk. "This is temporary; why would she be upset about it?"

Maisy felt her mouth drop open. The breath stalled in her lungs and she had to force herself to remember how to breathe before she could suck in some oxygen.

"Right," she said. Her voice sounded faint, but Ryder was still looking down, not at her. Clearly, he had no idea he had just knocked her to her knees. Maisy shook her head. Well, he had certainly answered her question about her status. *Temporary.* This shouldn't have been such a surprise. She'd been clear that she didn't do long-distance relationships and he'd been honest about not wanting to get involved with anyone. She supposed she should see it as a victory to get even *temporary* out of him and, yet, she felt a bit nauseous.

"You all right?" He glanced up.

"Me? Yeah, sure, I'm fine," she lied. He must have been preoccupied, because he didn't notice how terrible she was at fibbing. "About Perry, I was thinking maybe she's angry because she doesn't want to leave Fairdale now that she has a boyfriend and all. Perhaps she's angry about that but blaming it on the . . . er . . . incident."

"Incident? Is that what we're calling it?" he asked.

"For lack of a better word," she said.

"No boyfriend, or whatever this Cooper guy is, is going to change Perry's mind about going to Saint Mary's," he said. "She's wanted this all her life. It's been the plan since before she was born. Her mother went there, her grandmother went there. You know, when I first met the family, Whitney's father told me I wasn't good enough for his daughter, that I clearly couldn't provide for her and our child the way he had for his wife and daughter. I swore on that day that Perry would never want for anything."

"What if all she wants is to be with her father?" Maisy said.

Ryder reared back as if she'd slapped him. Maisy hadn't meant to be that blunt, but she remembered being fourteen, and she knew for a fact that she would have hated being separated from her family, even her pain-in-the-butt older brothers, and Perry didn't even have that. She had only Ryder. The prospect of leaving him must feel devastating for her, no matter how amazing the school was.

"You don't know what you're saying," he said. Maisy lifted her eyebrows at his tone and he raised his hands in a placating gesture. "Listen, I'm sorry, but I've had this plan in motion since before she was born and it isn't going to change because she has a crush on some boy."

"Did you hear what you said?" Maisy asked. "You said 'I've had this plan.' What about Perry? What about what she wants?"

"She wants to go to the new school," Ryder insisted. "That's why I'm leaving for Charleston to take an administrative position that's going to suck the soul right out of me. So I can pay for what isn't covered by the scholarship she's received."

"What if she's changed her mind?" Maisy persisted.

"She hasn't," he said. "She's just temporarily distracted." He gave her a meaningful look. "We both are. Now, I appreciate your input, really, I do, but none of this concerns you."

It was Maisy's turn to fall back a step. She had never heard Ryder speak in such a dismissive tone, not even when one of the crew installed one of the many built-in bookcases upside down. She had clearly hit a nerve. She supposed she could mind her own business and go back to where they'd been last night. She could just grab whatever joy she could find with him for the next few weeks. But now she wasn't so sure if that's what she wanted, mostly because she was so furious that he wouldn't listen to her or Perry. It was time for some self-preservation.

"If that's the way you feel, I can respect that," she said.

"Thank you." He looked surprised.

"I also think it's best if we go back to our former association as employer and employee," she said. The words came out short and tight and anyone who knew her at all would recognize she was angry, but Ryder didn't know her well. Did he? It was a good reminder to get out while the getting was good.

He stared at her. She saw the muscles bunch in his jaw. He looked like he was losing his temper, too. Good.

"I suppose you're right," he paused, "boss."

Maisy stiffened her spine. She wasn't going to let him rattle her. She met his gaze and said, "I think this will keep things from getting confused."

"Sweetheart, we're already there." His tone was as dry as dust. "But whatever you want."

"Thank you," she said.

With that she turned on her heel and strode from the room, half wishing he'd follow her and half wishing he'd fall into a big vat of slime to be justly rewarded for letting their newfound coupledom go without a blink or a sigh or an orgasm. Damn it!

RYDER thought about going after Maisy several times during the day. Wasn't that what the hero was supposed to do? Swoop in and throw the heroine over the back of his horse and ride off into the sunset with her? Yeah, there were a couple of problems with that. First, he didn't have a horse, he'd have to borrow one from Joaquin, who would likely not be down with his using it to kidnap a woman. Second, Maisy was the sort of woman who if she knew he'd even thought such a clichéd thing, she'd likely give him a black eye, which was one of the many reasons he lo—

He stopped the thought with a vigorous shake of his head. He was not in love with Maisy Kelly. He liked her—a lot—but that wasn't love. He had no room in his life for loving someone right now. The only person he loved with his whole heart was Perry. Giving her everything he hadn't had as a kid—unconditional love, a safe and happy home, opportunities—that was all he cared about.

Maisy stayed out in the bookshop all morning, probably avoiding him. Ryder tried to convince himself it was all for the best. It was good that Maisy had put a definitive end to whatever they'd been doing. It wasn't going anywhere and the potential to get hurt was high for both of them. No, he would go to Charleston and take the big-paying pencil jockey position he'd been offered, and Maisy would open her bookstore and meet some nice guy who'd marry her and make babies with her and they'd live in Fairdale for the rest of their lives.

"Hey, bro, what did that pencil do to you?"

Ryder glanced up to see Quino standing in the doorway. He looked down at his hand to find he'd snapped a number two between his fingers. He dropped the pencil onto the drawing table.

"Nothing," he said. "I guess I don't know my own strength."

He faked a laugh, but Quino wasn't buying it as he didn't return the smile. Instead he pushed his cowboy hat back on his head, letting his thick dark hair poke out under the crown, while his steady dark-brown eyes regarded Ryder with sympathy, as if he knew there was an inner turmoil chewing up Ryder's insides like one of his horses did with a bucket of oats.

Ryder scowled. "What brings you by?"

Joaquin tossed the book bag he was holding in his other hand at Ryder, who caught it before it hit him in the chest. It was Perry's. He recognized the *Stranger Things* sticker stuck on the front.

"She was at the stables this morning," Quino said. "She left that behind." He tipped his head to the side and studied Ryder's face. "She had that same look on her face."

"What look?"

"That stubborn thing you've got going on, where your eyebrows meet in the middle and your lower jaw sticks out," he said. "Are you two having a fight?"

"A difference of opinion," Ryder said. "We'll sort it out."

Quino nodded. He turned to leave, his limp from his soccer injury barely visible now, but he had to jump back as Savannah charged into the office. She saw him standing there but didn't slow down. She just plowed past him into the room. Ryder caught Quino's look of surprise and almost laughed.

"Hey, cowboy-architect guy," Savannah said. She planted her hands on her hips and glared at him. "What did you say to Maisy?"

"Nothing, why?" He tried to ignore how his pulse jumped at the sound of Maisy's name, coupled with the worry that she might be upset by their talk. It just proved that halting the budding relationship was a good thing, since he absolutely hated the idea that she might be sad and it would only be worse if they stayed together and then parted ways when he left.

"Liar," Savannah said. "She's with King George right now and she's—"

"Crying?" Ryder asked in alarm.

"Singing." Savannah gave him a dark look.

Oh, singing was bad, very bad, for a variety of reasons. " 'Over the Rainbow'?"

"Worse. 'Too-Ra-Loo-Ra-Loo-Ral,' " she said.

"The Irish lullaby?" Quino asked. "What's wrong with that?"

Savannah and Ryder shared a look and then Savannah said, "I'm sorry, this is your business why?"

"Because Ryder is my friend," he said.

"Well, Maisy is mine," she countered.

Ryder glanced between them. If ever there were two people who should not be in the same room together, it was these two. Both were fiercely independent, stubborn, and frankly, mouthy.

"Here's a thought. If you don't want me knowing your friend's business, maybe you shouldn't talk about it in front of me," Quino said. He crossed his arms over his chest, doing a fair imitation of a wall.

"If you had any manners, you wouldn't have listened in on what was obviously private information," Savannah said. She ended it with a hair toss, and Ryder saw his friend's pupils dilate. Quino had always had a thing for gingers.

"Steady, you two," Ryder said. "We're all friends here."

He cast a glance at Savannah. "At least, I hope we are. Joaquin Solis, this is Savannah Wilson. There, you've been introduced, now play nice."

Quino's eyes moved over Savannah's tall, curvy frame. She was dressed for success today in a skirt and blouse and spiky heels. Her long red curls were loose and framed her face becomingly while her green eyes blazed provocatively. Ryder would have felt sorry for his friend if he wasn't all consumed by his own female-based misery right now.

"You're a city girl, aren't you?" Quino asked.

"Woman. I am a woman, not a girl," Savannah said. "And, yes, I'm from Manhattan, or as we like to call it, *civilization.*"

A slow smile spread across Quino's lips. Ruh-roh. Ryder knew that look. It practically shouted *challenge accepted.*

"Well, *woman,* since we've established that I lack manners, I'm going to say exactly what I'm thinking," he said.

"That should be a short sentence," she retorted.

This time Quino laughed and it hit the room like a sonic boom of warmth. Ryder noticed that even Savannah responded to it by relaxing her posture a bit. She turned to face him, and Quino moved forward until they were an arm's length apart.

"I think you should go on a date with me," he said. Tall and muscular, with movie star good looks and a friendly personality, it had long been established that Quino could have any woman he wanted. In fact, in all the years Ryder had known him him no woman had ever refused a date with him.

"That is never going to happen," Savannah said. "But thanks for the offer."

Ryder was pretty sure his jaw hit the ground. He tried to cover it up by faking a yawn, but seriously—*holy shit!*—no one ever said no to Joaquin Solis. He thought his friend might be embarrassed to have crashed and burned in front of him.

Nope. Quite the opposite. Quino looked at him as if to say *Her. I'll take her.* Ryder had the abrupt epiphany that his world had just gotten infinitely more complicated. This had to be nipped. Immediately!

"Okay, then, this was fun," Ryder said. He threw an arm around Quino and half pushed, half dragged him to the door. "But we'd better get going since I need to deliver Perry's book bag to her before she has a meltdown and since she's not speaking to me, you'd better be the one to drop it off at the office at the school. Thanks, man, you're the best."

He kept up the steady stream of chatter until Savannah closed the door after them with a decisive bang. He shoved Quino into the passenger seat and got into his truck. As he fired up the engine and headed toward the school, he asked, "What was that?"

"That was history in the making," Quino said. There was a smile still on his lips and he turned to Ryder and winked. "That was the first meeting between me and my wife."

"Did Daisy throw you? Did you hit your head and sustain a brain injury that you haven't told me about?" Ryder asked. "Savannah is about as far removed from life in the Smoky Mountains as a woman can be. She is mani-pedis, lattes, and shopping until her credit card catches on fire."

"I'm not seeing your point," Quino said.

"You are horses, small-town life, and you buy your clothes at the feed and tack store," Ryder said.

Quino shrugged. "None of that matters."

"You really did concuss yourself, didn't you?"

Joaquin just grinned at him. It was the smile that had broken a hundred female hearts and probably a few male ones, too. "By Christmas, she'll be my wife, you'll see."

Ryder shook his head. He wanted to say that by Christmas, Fairdale, Maisy, and the Happily Ever After Bookstore would be a distant memory for him, but he didn't, because the thought hurt like pressing on a bruise. And he suspected that voicing it aloud would hurt even more, in the realm of taking a knee to the man junk, or a punch right in the sternum. He absently rubbed his knuckles over his ribs and forced himself to think about Perry. She was going to love her new school. She would have every opportunity. Maybe she'd even take up one of those scholarly sports like lacrosse or crew.

Yeah, that was the plan and Ryder was sticking to it. Perry

was going to pursue her dreams as far as they took her and Ryder would be there, always, the hand at her back, the leg up when she needed it, always.

Because that's what a good father did even if the thought of leaving Maisy behind in Fairdale killed him.

Chapter Twenty-five

LOST in thought, Ryder barely had time to hit the brakes when a stop sign sprung up out of nowhere.

"Ryder, dude, what is up?" Quino pushed himself off the dashboard and adjusted the seat belt that looked to be trying to strangle him.

Ryder fell back against his seat. He shook his head. "Sorry. I'm just . . . I have some stuff on my mind."

The driver behind him, clearly out of patience with Ryder's poor driving, began to lean on his horn. The sound was jarring, and Ryder stepped on the gas and moved through the intersection.

"Seriously, bro, are you okay?" Quino asked him. "You look upset."

Ryder met his stare and said, "I am."

"Explain."

"There's no point," he said. He turned back to the road and focused on his driving. "It is what it is."

"Want me to drive?"

"No, I'm good," he said.

This might have been the biggest lie Ryder had ever told.

He was not good. He could try and tell himself a million times that he was fine with walking away from whatever had been happening between him and Maisy, but he wasn't fine. It felt like for one brief shining moment, he'd managed to catch something magical in his hands and just like that it slipped between his fingers. Lost forever.

He supposed he shouldn't be surprised. His marriage had unraveled in much the same way. He and Whitney had never really fought during their marriage. Ryder had thought it was because things were okay between them—not great, but okay. He came to find out during their run at marriage counseling that it was mostly because neither one of them cared enough to fight it out. When they disagreed, they just avoided each other until the disagreement passed.

He thought about Maisy giving him what for about her turret and about Perry. Yeah, things would never just pass with Maisy. She dug her heels in, she called him on his bullshit, she cared. How long had it been since a woman cared like that about him? He couldn't even remember. Maybe when his mother had been alive. Maybe never. And wasn't that a sad statement on his life? What was even sadder was that he had no idea how to change it.

"YOU look like someone told you Jake Sinclair is fictional," Savy said.

"Huh?" Maisy looked up from her poke bowl.

The two women were sitting on the front porch of the bookstore, enjoying the last of the quiet before the bookstore's grand opening the next day. Savannah had picked up poké bowls from a new shop in town and they were enjoying salmon and ahi over brown rice and kale. It was a good, healthy, heart-smart choice for dinner and Maisy would have given anything to exchange it for half of a triple-layer chocolate fudge cake or a whole cake. She really wasn't picky at the moment.

"Jake Sinclair? The perfect man is fiction," Savannah said.

"I know," Maisy said. "The good ones are always either fictional or taken or gay."

"I see I'm going to have to be blunt. You look depressed, like *someone stole your truck, ran over your dog, lit your barn on fire, and knocked up your sister* depressed," Savannah said.

"So, I'm a bad country-western song?"

"Yes, which really sucks, given that we're about to achieve your dream by opening this bookstore. You just had to let a man get all up in your business."

"I didn't do it on purpose," Maisy said.

"Maybe not but you sure can't pick 'em in the man department," Savannah said. "I like Ryder, I do, but you can tell just by looking at him that he is not relationship material."

"You say that about every man," Maisy said.

"That doesn't mean it isn't true."

"In my defense, I didn't know Ryder was leaving at first," Maisy said. "And we didn't split up because of that so much as because things got complicated. Besides, you're one to talk. Jeri told me that Joaquin Solis got you all flustered."

"I was not flustered," Savy said. She used her chopsticks to stab a piece of tuna and chewed it as though it had done something to offend her. "He's way too sure of himself. Just because he's tall, built like a Jersey barrier, good-looking in that square-jawed, dark-eyed, smoldering way, and has a smile that makes reasonable women lose all of their self-esteem and throw themselves or their underwear at him, he thinks he can have whatever he wants. Well, he can't have it from me."

"Really? You saw all that within five minutes of meeting him?" Maisy asked. "You are good. And here Jeri was saying you were smitten with the cowboy who asked you out."

"Smitten?" Savy curled her lip. "Hardly."

"I only know Joaquin in passing but I had his younger sister, Desi, in my English 101 class," Maisy said. "From what she said about him, he seems like a good guy, the type who will step up and help you carry bags if you have too many, or open a door for you, or give you a lift if he finds you stranded on a road somewhere—without trying to make a move on you. You know, a good one, a keeper."

"You might want to raise the bar there. Good manners are

mandatory, but not indicative of relationship material. I don't care if he does help with bags or gives lifts to the stranded, that does not make Joaquin Solis worth dating," Savannah said. "That guy might seem nice, but I'm betting it's because he has an ulterior motive going the entire time."

"If you say so," Maisy said.

"I do," Savannah said. "Now, quit trying to change the subject. What are you going to do about you and Ryder?"

"Nothing," Maisy said.

Savy shook her head, clearly rejecting this response. "It's too late to do nothing. You blew that option the minute you kissed him. Now you have to figure out what is happening between you."

"Yeah, nothing is happening," Maisy said. "I made that pretty clear."

"Really?" Savy said. She turned to Maisy and stared her down. "So, when he strolls into a room with his hat on, you're not going to feel anything? When he smiles at you, you're not going to die a little inside? When he leaves, you're not going to be filled with regret?"

Maisy glanced away. She knew Savy was pushing her, but she wasn't saying anything that wasn't true and they both knew it.

"M, the only things we regret in life are the chances we don't take," Savy said. Her voice was soft and her eyes were kind. "Do you really want to live with that?"

"But—" Maisy wanted to argue but the words got stuck.

"But?" Savy pushed.

"But he's leaving, which makes the whole thing doomed. And besides, when I tried to point out that I didn't think Perry wanted to go away to school, he completely shut me down."

"That's no good," Savy said.

"No, it isn't," Maisy said. "I mean, how can we have a meaningful relationship if he just closes himself off if I say something he doesn't want to hear?"

"You can't," Savy said. "Unless you make yourself heard."

"Exactly," Maisy said. "I don't know if I'm up for that." She glanced at her friend and added, "I don't think Quino is like that, by the way."

"Doesn't matter, I'm not dating him," Savy said.

"Why not?" Maisy asked. "He's cute, he's here, and you're going to be here for . . ."

Savannah rolled her eyes. "It's not going to work. I'm onto you, Maisy Kelly. You're trying to figure out how long I'm going to be staying and you think if I start dating the hot stable owner guy maybe I'll stay longer."

"Me?" Maisy asked. She put her hand over her chest in a protestation of innocence. Savy shook her head, clearly not buying it.

"You," she said. "Listen, I haven't gotten any job offers worth taking but when I do, I will have to go. I'm a city girl, M. I love it here and all, but I'm subways and sushi not trail rides and barbeques."

"I know. I just like having you here," Maisy said. "Try to screw up all of your job interviews for at least a few more months?"

"I'll do my best," Savy said. "Not."

OPENING day was a blur of last-minute panic attacks and freak-outs. Maisy had planned to wear a cute summer dress, but then she thought it didn't look professional enough, so she put on one of her professor outfits but it was too uptight. She reached for jeans, but they seemed wrong. Finally, Savannah came in and picked out a skirt and blouse that were flirty and fun, but also demure and professional.

Jeri brought three boxes of donuts from Big Bottom Donuts, which was in the center of town right next to the Perk Up coffee shop. It was a place Maisy tried with little success to avoid. She popped open the first box and, wham, there was a cruller staring right back at her. Knowing it was a losing battle, she tucked in.

"Wipe that guilty look off your face," Jeri said. "You're going to be working it off today, so don't worry about it. Enjoy your life, Maisy, every bit of it."

Reassured, Maisy took a second donut and washed both down with coffee. Duly fortified, she had everyone gather in the main office for a quick meeting.

"Okay, does everyone know where they're stationed for the day?"

"Cash register by the front door," Jeri said.

"Outside, working the book display tables on the front porch, while maintaining the supply of coffee, tea, and lemonade," Savannah said.

Maisy looked for Perry, who had volunteered to be on the second floor to help people. She wasn't in the room.

"Jeri, would you mind monitoring the second floor, too?" Maisy asked. "Perry isn't here, and I don't want the second floor unsupervised on our first day."

"Roger that," Jeri said.

"It's almost time," Savy said.

"All right, people," Maisy said. "Man your stations. I'll be moving around the store all day, so call me if you need me and be sure to take breaks."

The three women scattered and Maisy took a deep breath. This was it. Her first day as a bookstore owner. She was the last one to leave the office. She had the keys in hand and went to the front door to do the official unlocking. Ryder and his crew had taken the day off, so as not to dissuade customers with a lot of banging. The framing of the turret was done, but it still had a ways to go before completion. Maisy refused to think about the fact that once it was done, Ryder would be gone, too.

Jeri took her spot at the vintage counter Maisy had repurposed from an old hotel to use as their primary purchase point. In a glass display case behind it were all of Auntie El's treasured signed books by her favorite authors. Those were not for sale. Savannah went to the kitchen, which they'd modernized a bit, on the first floor to grab the cart with beverages and cookies to wheel outside to the porch.

Maisy wiped her hands on her skirt. She glanced around the shop, disappointed not to have Ryder here to share the moment with her. He'd been such an integral part of the remodel, helping her choose the best flooring and colors for the walls, fixing up the windows and light fixtures while maintaining the integrity of the old house's origins.

Maisy turned the knob on the newly installed dead bolt

and unlocked the door. She glanced at Jeri, who smiled and nodded at her as she opened the door. Now, it wasn't that she expected a horde to be out on the lawn waiting to get in, but with the balloon arch they'd fastened over the walkway, the GRAND OPENING sign out on a sandwich board on the street, and the article that had run in the local paper a few days ago, she had hoped for at least a few people.

On this bright, beautiful Saturday morning in the Smoky Mountains of North Carolina, while the birds were singing and the sun was shining and the smell of freshly mown grass mingled with the scent of lilacs on the air, she had thought there might be a handful of people at the opening. There was just one.

Her braid was messy, her glasses were drooping off her nose, she wore a baggy cardigan sweater that hung off her shoulders as if it, too, were in despair. Perry.

"Hey, kiddo, are you all right?" Maisy asked.

Perry nodded but when she glanced up at Maisy, it was easy to see she'd been crying. "Oh, Maisy," she sobbed. "I just want to die." With that she threw herself into Maisy's arms and began to weep.

Chapter Twenty-six

"OH, no, what happened?" Maisy asked as she hugged the teen. She stepped back and studied Perry's face. "Are you all right? Is your father okay?"

"I'm f . . . fine," Perry cried.

"That is not fine," Jeri said. She twirled her finger to encompass the sobbing girl and said, "I've got things down here. Go ahead and take her upstairs to see King George. He'll perk her up."

"Are you sure?" Maisy asked.

Jeri nodded. "If we need you, we know where to find you."

"Thanks," Maisy said. She put her arm around Perry and led her upstairs. King George was in the hidden room, enjoying the insane cat tree that Ryder had built for him even though he was too small to do much more than swat at the soft pom-poms that swung from the lowest branch.

Maisy and Perry went upstairs, entered the last bedroom, and crossed over to the bench. Like a pro, Perry popped the seat open and scooted into the opening. Maisy followed a bit more carefully since she was in a skirt. The hidden room had been transformed in the weeks that they'd been working on the house. It was King George's daytime play area, so there was a soft carpet, food and water, a litter box, and the crazy cat tree with perches and cubbies and toys.

"Hey, George," Perry called.

A soft meow sounded. King George was curled up in his cat bed, which was actually a huge fish with a soft fleecy lining that he enjoyed kneading. Two front paws poked out of the fish's mouth and a small head with enormous ears followed.

Recognizing his favorite person's voice, King George bounded forward and jumped on Perry's foot. She bent over and scooped him up, nuzzling her face against his soft fur. Maisy reached over and rubbed George's head. A deep purr was her reward and she knew if anything could make Perry feel better, it was this little guy.

"Oh, Georgie, what would I do without you?" Perry asked him. As if he could sense her stress, the kitten licked her face, making her smile.

Maisy let out a pent-up breath and sank onto one of the chairs in the room. Perry took the one beside her, still holding George. The kitten rolled onto his back, letting her rub his tummy while he swiped at her fingers.

"So, what's going on?" Maisy asked.

"I broke up with Cooper," Perry said. Her voice wobbled a bit but she managed to get the words out without breaking down. "I'm leaving soon and it just didn't seem fair to him."

"Oh, that is rough," Maisy said. "Is it your first breakup?"

"First boyfriend, first breakup," Perry said. "It's brutal. And there's this girl, Taylor, she's just been waiting for us to break up so she could make her move. She's all busty and blond, and she laughs at everything Cooper says. It makes me want to vomit."

Maisy nodded. She'd known a few Taylors in her time.

"What did Cooper say when you ended things?"

"He was upset. He said he didn't care that I was leaving and that having this time together was better than nothing at all, but I don't think it is, because the more time I spend with him the more I like him and when I leave I'm going to be crushed and with Dad moving to Charleston and Mom in Los Angeles,

I'll never come back here to Fairdale, so seriously, what's the point when we'll *never* see each other again?" Perry collapsed against the seat back, out of words or air or both.

Hearing it put so bluntly that Maisy would never see either Ryder or Perry again was like getting hit with a bucket of ice water. It seemed so final and she hated it. She hated everything about it. But she said nothing. This wasn't about her.

"I hear what you're saying about not wanting to get hurt. But don't you want to know if what you feel is real? What if Cooper is right?" she asked. "What if the weeks before you leave are just fun? You don't want to miss that. And maybe you'll get to know each other well enough that when you leave it will be a relief because what you felt wasn't real after all. I mean, what if it turns out that he's a terrible boyfriend?"

"We're fourteen, how terrible can he be?"

"Maybe he never texts you or he blows you off to hang out with the guys. Maybe he forgets his deodorant all the time and he starts to smell like rancid bologna and it makes you sick. Maybe you find out he's a whiner or a complainer or a terrible tipper," Maisy said.

Perry looked at her as if she was crazy, but her tears had dried up and a shadow of a smile graced her lips. "Maybe."

"Just think about it, okay?"

Perry nodded. George wiggled out of her grasp, and she put him on the floor, where he scurried to his food bowl. Maisy and Perry watched him eat, and Maisy was pretty sure the crisis was averted, which was fabulous because she really needed to get back downstairs.

"Can I ask you something?" Perry said.

"Sure." Maisy relaxed back into her seat, hoping she didn't look like she was about to run.

"What about you and my dad? Do you love him?"

Oh, boy, what should she say? Maisy decided on the truth.

"I might have if things had worked out differently," Maisy said.

"He cares about you," Perry said. She gave her a sly look. "A lot. Maybe you need to spend time with him, so you can discover his bad habits."

"Nice try," Maisy said. "It's different when you're an adult.

You jump in a little bit deeper and tangle up a little bit tighter. Extricating yourself from a relationship can be brutal."

"You mean there's sex involved," Perry said.

"Uh—" Maisy stalled.

"How's everything going down here?" Savy asked. Her feet showed up on the stairs and the rest of her followed. Praise the Lord! She was carrying a tray with sweet tea and cookies. "I thought you might need some sugar to chase the blues away."

"Thanks," Maisy said. She wanted to ask how business was, but since Savy was here and not serving the shopping masses at their door, she figured she had her answer.

Perry took a glass of tea and a cookie and Maisy did the same. George pounced on Savannah's flouncy skirt and she laughed as she scooped him up and kissed his nose. He put his paw on her lips as if to say *Stop it*, and they all laughed.

"Are we having a party?" Jeri came down the steps, taking them all in. "I love parties."

Perry looked around the room. "I suppose we are. It's a breakup party."

"Who broke up?" Savy asked.

"Perry and Cooper," Maisy said. "First boyfriend, first breakup."

"Oh, that's a tough one," Jeri said. "But you know what you have to do."

"Eat copious amounts of ice cream?" Savy offered.

"Buy a new outfit or four?" Maisy suggested.

"No, no, no," Jeri said as she helped herself to a cookie. "You need a dance party."

"A what?" Perry looked equal parts intrigued and horrified.

"Tonight, here in the secret room, let's have a girls-only dance party," Jeri said. "Now, all of you get your butts back up there. I've got a carload of librarians, a new moms' group, and a professional women's club all here and I can't help them all by myself. I'm good, but I'm not that good. Let's move out, troops!"

"What?" Maisy jumped to her feet. "We have customers?"

"And more arriving," Jeri said. "Thank goodness the boys showed up to check on their turret, or I couldn't have left.

Ryder and Seth are down there by themselves. We'd better go before they make a mess of it."

Maisy turned to Perry. "Can you handle this? You're welcome to stay here with George if it's too much."

"No, I'm good," Perry said. "A dance party will be fun to look forward to. I'll feed George and play with him and then I'll be right down."

"Atta girl," Maisy said. She gave her a quick hug and then dashed up the stairs to return to the shop.

Jeri was not kidding. Every room had customers in it. Music was playing. When had that been arranged? People were talking and laughing and perusing Auntie El's old books as well as checking out the copies of the new ones Maisy had recently acquired from the local sales reps for the big publishers.

A few of the publishers had authors they were looking to push and had gladly paid Maisy to put up some sweet waterfall display racks with lots of promo materials. Considering the women flocking to the rack, it looked to be a solid investment.

"Congratulations."

Maisy turned around to find Ryder standing there. He was smiling at her but there was tension in his face, and she could tell that he was feeling as awkward as she was.

"Thanks," she said. "Perry is up in the hidden room with George."

He nodded. "I figured she'd be here. She's been upset about, well, honestly, I don't know because she's stopped talking to me."

"I'm sorry," Maisy said. "I know that must be hard. The ladies and I are trying to cheer her up. In fact, we're having a girls' night tonight."

"Another movie?" Ryder looked eager and Maisy shook her head.

"Tonight is girls only, but I promise we will do our best to lift her spirits, and if she says anything I think you should know, I will encourage her to talk to you," she said.

"Thanks, I—"

"Maisy, there you are." Kathy Tisdale sprang at them from behind a shelf of books, interrupting Ryder. "This is fantastic! A bookstore devoted to books by women, about women, for women. I love it."

"Well, men are welcome, too," Maisy said. She gave Ryder a side eye and decided to have some fun. "In fact, Ryder, here, was just reading some romances, weren't you, Ryder?"

Ryder's blue gaze met and held hers, letting her know that if she was going to challenge him, he was going to rise to it. "I was," he said.

"No, sir," Kathy said. Her eyes were wide in disbelief and then they narrowed, "Who is your favorite romance author?"

"Well, you can't go wrong with Jane Austen, she is the mother of the romantic novel, after all," he said.

Kathy blinked. "Go on."

"But there is a whole diverse world of romance novels nowadays," he said. "You've got your sweet romances, romantic comedies, historical romances—I'm partial to the ones with pirates myself—paranormal romances . . . do you like vampires?"

Kathy turned from Ryder to Maisy. "I love him. Does he work here?"

"Sort of," Maisy said. "He's my architect. He's building the turret addition for me."

"And he's an architect," Kathy said. She put her hand over her heart as if she couldn't take it all in.

"And he's from Texas and frequently wears a cowboy hat," Maisy added.

"Stop," Kathy said. "It's too much." She began to fan herself with one of the paperbacks in her hand.

"There's lemonade and sweet tea out on the porch," Maisy said.

"Good, that's good," Kathy said. She glanced at Ryder, who gave her a low bow. Kathy giggled and waved a hand at him. "Oh, you."

She walked outside and Maisy turned to Ryder and said, "Well, you have a fan for life. When did you get so savvy about romance novels?"

"I've been reading up," he said. He gave a careless shrug as if it weren't the single greatest thing any man had ever said to her.

Maisy tried to ignore the flutter in her chest that she was pretty sure was her heart springing to life in the eternal hope that something was going to happen between her and Ryder. She tried to mentally beat it down, but it was a persistent little bugger.

"Perry's been bringing home stacks of them," he said. "So, I figured I'd better get hip to what she was reading so we could have something in common."

At that, Maisy's heart simply would not be shut down. *This guy,* it said, *I want this guy.* She tried to hide it by putting on her professor facade.

"I've seen some of the books Perry's been borrowing," she said. "She seems partial to the historical ones. Some critics argue that romances give women unrealistic expectations in relationships. Aren't you worried about that?"

"Hell, no," Ryder said. Maisy blinked. "From what I've read the heroines are fierce and feisty and the heroes who are lucky enough to win their hearts treat them with respect and value them, or they learn to pretty darn quick. If my daughter grows up expecting a man to value her and cherish her, why would that bother me? It just means that every boy who isn't up to scratch will get kicked to the curb. Honestly, I think romance novels should be mandatory."

That did it. Maisy saw her fluttering heart explode into a million tiny hearts like a glitter bomb right over his head. Didn't he see it or feel it? She felt like her feelings were stuck all over him like confetti.

"What an interesting perspective," she said. Good grief, she sounded like she had a stick up her behind when she really just wanted to throw her arms around him and cry, *Yes, yes, yes!* in an orgasmlike way, which would likely terrify him and send him running into the street.

"Thanks," he said. "I've found I'm really partial to Beverly Jenkins."

Maisy was impressed but required proof. "Favorite title?"

"*Indigo*," he said. "I think I learned more about the underground railroad from that book than I ever did in history class."

"That's it!" Maisy raised her hands in the air. "I can't take it. You need to get away from me right now."

"What? Why? What did I say?"

They were standing in the main room and Maisy noticed that everyone had stopped browsing to watch them. She would have been embarrassed, but she was already at the breaking point and there was just no room in her emotional wheelbarrow to haul mortification around, too. She spun on her heel and stomped into the office.

Ryder followed her, clearly not appreciating her need to get away from him. The man had no sense of self-preservation. How was she supposed to deal with that?

"Maisy?" he asked as he shut the door behind them. "Are you all right? I didn't mean to—"

That was all he got out before she jumped him. She hadn't thought it through. He was taller than she was by a lot, and if he hadn't caught her around the waist, she likely would have splatted up against his chest and slid down to the ground in a pitiful heap.

But he did catch her, and when he was about to ask her what was up, she wrapped her arms around his neck and kissed him.

Chapter Twenty-seven

SHE didn't mean to, but he was right there and he'd read Bev Jenkins, for Fitzwilliam Darcy's sake. How was a romance novel loving woman supposed to resist this man? She couldn't. She didn't have the inner fortitude or the will.

Maisy dug her fingers into his thick hair and angled his head so that she could take full advantage. Ryder made a grunting sound and then moved his hands so that they cupped her bottom, holding her in place while she kissed him with all of the pent-up longing she'd been struggling to suppress.

The smell of him, of sawdust and soap with a splash of coffee, swirled in her head, making her dizzy. She felt as if she couldn't get close enough. She arched into him, wanting to feel his heat against her. Ryder must have felt the same because he moved one hand up her back and pulled her in.

The need to breathe made them break the kiss. But the drive to be joined remained and Ryder moved his mouth to her neck. Maisy tipped her head to the side, allowing him full access. His lips moved over her skin, pausing just below her ear to plant the softest of kisses. Maisy hissed air through her teeth as her insides turned into liquid heat.

It felt like a particular sort of madness, this crazed lust that made her vision fuzzy as all of her senses shut out everything but him. She couldn't get enough of the feel of him beneath her fingers, the sound of his raspy breath in her ear, the taste of him still on her lips, the hard press of his body against hers. When he turned and plopped her on top of an empty book cart, Maisy took a deep breath and tried to get her bearings as the cool air hit her hot skin. Ryder didn't give her a chance.

He stepped in between her legs, moving her skirt up so he could get as close as their clothing would allow. He cupped the back of her head and lowered his mouth to hers, kissing her as if he'd been thinking of doing this very thing every second of every day since their last kiss. When he moved his other hand to the front of her blouse, Maisy helped him out by yanking her top down and giving him full access to her breasts. It felt wicked and wanton and she loved every bit of it.

Ryder didn't hesitate. He moved his mouth over her exposed skin and then hooked her bra with one finger and tugged it down, revealing the rosy peaks that were puckered for his attention. When he put his mouth on one nipple, Maisy couldn't keep the soft moan from escaping her lips.

Knock. Knock. Knock. A fist pounded on the office door.

"Hey, boss, now is not the time to be watching porn in your office." Savannah's voice hit Maisy like a Taser. "These walls, while lovely with their fresh paint, are not exactly soundproof."

It took Maisy a moment for her friend's words to kick in. Ryder was right there with her. He lifted his head and, as if he couldn't help himself, he kissed her quickly on the mouth. Then he pulled her off the cart and adjusted her clothing, pulling up the cups of her bra and adjusting her blouse. If his fingers lingered, Maisy didn't call him on it, mostly because she had steadied herself by putting her hand on his side and had yet to remove it, even though she was clearly standing just fine on her own two feet.

"Okay to come in?" Savannah asked. She opened the door but had her hand over her eyes, which was a token gesture at best since she was peeking at them between her middle and ring fingers.

Maisy cleared her throat. "Yeah, we were just—"

"Acting out a scene from a book," Ryder said.

Maisy gave him an *Are you crazy* look and he shrugged.

"Yeah, well, there is a salesperson here from a romance publisher and she wants to talk to you," Savannah said. "I told her you were tied up for the moment. You weren't, were you?"

Maisy glowered at her friend, which was obviously terrifying as Savy laughed really hard, even slapping her knee when she doubled up.

"Please tell her I'll be right there," Maisy said.

"I'll have her wait on the porch," Savy said, still chuckling. She punched Ryder on the shoulder as she left. "Good going, cowboy-architect guy."

The door shut behind her and Maisy put her face in her hands. "I can never ever leave this room. If I cross the threshold, I'm sure I will go all human-torch-aflame in embarrassment."

"I'm sure it wasn't that bad," he said. "Probably only Savannah heard us because she was right outside the door when she came to get you. Really, you're fine."

"You think?"

"Yeah," he said. "But I think it's apparent that we can't ignore this." He pointed at himself and then at her. "There's something here, Maisy, that is just too potent to ignore."

Maisy stared at him. She knew it was fanciful, but she could still see the bits and pieces of her heart that had exploded all over him. But he didn't know. He couldn't see it, but she could. The fact was that she was in love with him and it wasn't going to go away or be diminished by time spent together. In fact, if anything, the more time she spent with him, the worse her heartbreak was going to be when he left, and he was going to leave, of that he had been very clear.

She supposed it was selfish of her, but she didn't want a long-distance relationship. She didn't want to have him just on weekends or, even worse, every other weekend. She wanted a best friend and a partner, someone she went to bed with every night and woke up with every morning, and if that made her demanding, so be it. Ryder's life was on a different course than hers and she knew that going forward with him would just ruin her for any other man, but the reality was, another man was exactly what she needed if she wanted her heart's desire. Damn it.

"I have to go," she said. She pushed her glasses up on her nose and ran her hands over her skirt, smoothing out the wrinkles. "As for this"—she mimicked his gesture of pointing between them—"it was an error in judgment. It won't happen again."

Ryder studied her face. He must have seen a resolve in her that she didn't know she possessed, because he gave a reluctant nod. With one hand he reached up and pushed a stray curl off her forehead. It took everything Maisy had not to lean into his touch, and when his hand dropped, she bolted from the room as if she was running for her life.

JERI made herself unofficial DJ of their dance party that night. They pushed the furniture back and rolled up the carpet. Savy had a small strobe light that she plugged in, while Jeri spun tunes off her phone through a small Bluetooth speaker.

King George watched all of the shenanigans from the safety of his fish-shaped bed, coming out only once to try and pounce on the lights that moved across the floor. Perry scooped him up and danced, holding him close to her chest while she bopped to Michael Franti's "The Sound of Sunshine."

The rest of them formed a circle around her and took turns going in and out of the center. Maisy's favorite part was when Jeri tried to teach her to twerk. They were both terrible and Savy forced them to sit down and watch a professional. The woman could most def shake what her mama gave her. Maisy laughed herself stupid and when she glanced at Perry, she saw the teen was hiccupping she was laughing so hard.

"Ice cream break!" Savy declared. The volume on the tunes was lowered and they all tucked into the chocolate ice cream Jeri had brought, swearing it was the only known cure for breakup blues. It made Maisy think of Ryder and his preference for pistachio. She shoved a huge bite into her mouth, not caring if she got a brain freeze.

"How are you doing, hon?" Maisy asked Perry. "Feeling any better?"

"A little," she said. She pushed the ice cream around her bowl while King George crawled up her shirt, trying to reach the bowl to see what was inside. "I just wish I didn't feel so crushed."

"Think of things that make you happy," Savy said. "Name one thing that brings you joy."

"King George," Perry said without hesitation. "Saving him is probably the greatest thing I've ever done with my life."

"Given that you're only fourteen, that's pretty good," Jeri said. "I've found that when I am feeling poorly about life it helps to think about someone else. If I put all of my energy into helping them, I forget about myself and I find joy in being an agent of change."

"A good deed doer, like Auntie El?" Savannah asked. She pointed to the trunk in the corner. Maisy had left it in the hidden room and was reading through all of the files, amazed that her aunt had managed to give so much to so many.

"Exactly," Maisy said.

"I could use some of that," Jeri said. "I love my family something fierce, but oh, they get me riled. I need to channel my energy into something positive instead of nagging them."

"We could form a secret society," Perry said. "We already have a secret room and a mascot. We could do things to help people anonymously like Auntie El did."

"I love it. It could be a sisterhood, but we need a name," Savy said. "The HEA club?"

"HEA?" Jeri asked.

"Happily Ever After," Savy said. "Like the shop."

"No, that would make it too easy to trace back to us," Maisy said. "Just like if we named it after Auntie El, it would out us before we even got going."

"How about . . ." Perry paused. She glanced at them and picked up George in her free hand, holding him next to her face. "The Royal Order of George? After all, he is our first good deed."

Maisy grinned. "I love it. All in favor, say *Aye*."

A chorus of *aye*s sounded and Maisy felt as if something unexpectedly cool had just happened. They finished their ice cream and hashed out some club rules. Perry was elected to be president, Maisy vice president, Savy secretary, and Jeri to be treasurer, natch.

Weekly meetings were scheduled for Sunday nights since that was the only night that the bookstore closed early and no one had any other standing Sunday commitments. They made a list of people who they would like to help in a variety of ways. After much discussion, Perry's nomination of Hannah the vet was approved since they all agreed that she had gone above and beyond in her care of King George, and they wanted to repay her commitment to all animals in some way. They had no ideas as yet, but planned to come up with something amazing. In the meantime, they all agreed that they would be on the lookout for ways to help their fellow residents and the community of Fairdale.

Savy had just finished writing it all down and storing it in Auntie El's trunk when a ruckus kicked up outside. Music was blaring and Maisy wasn't positive, but she thought someone was throwing rocks at the small window.

"What the hell?" She darted up the stairs and hurried through the room that housed most of the romantic suspense collection, with everything from Daphne du Maurier to Catherine Coulter, and out into the hallway. The noise was louder here and she realized someone was outside in front of the bookstore.

"It sounds like someone is having a dance party outside," Savy said. She caught up to Maisy and the two of them jogged down the stairs to the first floor.

Since they were closed, the lights in the shop were dim. Maisy snapped on the porch light and glanced through the side window to see Cooper Wainwright standing on the front porch, holding a bouquet of flowers in one hand and a small Bluetooth speaker in the other.

"Would you look at that," Savannah said from the other

window. "Give the boy a boom box and a trench coat and he's John Cusack from *Say Anything . . .*"

"Be still my heart," Maisy said. She turned around and glanced at the stairs. Perry was skipping down with Jeri right behind her. "I think this is for you, Perry."

"What do you mean?"

Maisy gestured to the window and Perry peeked outside. "Cooper!" She stepped back and looked at the group. "What do I do?"

"What do you mean, 'What do I do?' " Jeri asked. "That boy is putting himself on the line. You march yourself out there and find out what he wants."

"What if he wants to get back together?" Perry asked.

"Do you want to get back together?" Savy asked.

"I don't know," Perry wailed.

"Hush, child." Jeri stepped forward. She took her by the shoulders and looked her over. She then pinched her cheeks, fluffed her hair, and said, "Bite your lips and give them some color." Perry did as she was told. "Okay, now you're ready. Go see what he has to say, bless his heart, and then don't think about your answer, just listen to your heart. Now go."

Savannah opened the door, and Jeri gave Perry a shove outside. Maisy slid out behind her to monitor the situation in case it went weird or sad or awkward. As she slid into the shadows, she recognized the song playing as Christina Perri's "A Thousand Years." Not bad.

"Cooper, what's going on?" Perry asked.

He turned down the volume on the speaker and thrust the flowers at her. "These are for you."

Maisy noticed that they were roses, red ones, and she felt her heart go squish as she realized this was probably Perry's first bouquet from a boy.

"I know you said you didn't want to go out with me, because you're leaving and it's pointless," Cooper said. "But I disagree. I don't think it's pointless. I don't care where you go, I want to date you for as long as I can, and I don't care if my heart gets smashed to bits when you leave. I'd rather be miserable later because I got to spend the summer with the girl I love than be miserable now because you're here and I can't be with you. Perry, please, I know you care about me, too. Give us a chance."

He stood with his arms wide, offering himself to her completely. It was the most romantic thing Maisy had ever seen. She glanced at Perry. She couldn't imagine saying no to this boy, but Perry wasn't her and she'd already had a lot of loss in her life. Maisy held her breath, waiting to see what Perry would do.

The young woman stared down at her flowers and then glanced up at Cooper. He gave her a lopsided smile and that seemed to tip the scale in his favor. Perry took one step forward and then another and then she threw herself into his arms and Cooper hugged her, lifting her off her feet.

He kissed her quick on the lips and asked, "I take it that's a *yes*?"

Perry smiled. She nodded and said, "Yes, I'll go out with you."

Cooper made a fist and pulled it into his side. "What are you doing tomorrow, and the next day, and the day after?"

"Nothing," she laughed.

"Change of plans," he said. "How about we go on a horseback ride? I already asked Mr. Solis and he said we could take two of his horses for a trail ride, and then there's the county fair, we can ride the rides until we puke."

Perry tipped her chin up. "You were pretty sure of me."

"I was hopeful," Cooper said. His grin lit up the night. "Plus, I had an inside source who told me you might say yes if I made a big enough impression." He pointed behind him with his thumb, and Maisy saw Ryder standing in the driveway, leaning against his truck.

"Dad?" Perry asked.

"Hey, ladybug," he said.

"Did you tell Cooper to come here or are you waiting to tackle him to the ground?" she asked.

"I gave him a lift. I thought he should at least give it his best shot," he said. He looked past her at Maisy for just a moment and then back at his daughter. "You don't want to let go of something amazing just because the timing isn't right."

Maisy felt her willpower slip away like a shadow in the

dark as Perry ran down the steps, still holding her flowers, and hugged her father. Ryder held her tight and kissed the top of her head.

Cooper followed her. He and Ryder shook hands, then Ryder nodded. Maisy watched as Perry handed her father the flowers and then took Cooper's hand and walked down the driveway with him, obviously headed into town. Maisy wondered if they were going for ice cream and didn't that just make her heart melt.

Ryder walked up the steps and Maisy heard a scramble of footsteps behind her in the house, indicating that her friends were aware that something big was happening. Sure enough, the door flew open and Jeri trotted past as if someone had set her behind on fire.

"Look at the time," Jeri called. "Gotta go!"

The woman cackled as she climbed into her minivan, which was parked on the street in front of the house. With a honk and a squeal of tires she was gone. Maisy turned toward the open front door and saw Savannah standing there.

"What has gotten into her?" she asked.

Savy shrugged and opened her mouth in the fakest fake yawn Maisy had ever seen, contorting her face into all sorts of shapes while stretching her arms up over her head.

"Lord-a-mercy, I am tired," she said.

"You're from New York. Why do you suddenly sound like Scarlett O'Hara?" Maisy asked.

"Sorry, no time to chat, off to bed, where I'll be in my room, watching TV really loudly in case anyone needs the rest of the house to themselves," Savy said. She stepped into the house and shut the door behind her.

Maisy spread her arms wide and asked, "Was it something I said?"

Ryder snagged one of her hands in his and pulled her over to the newly installed porch swing. Maisy sat down on the padded seat and Ryder put Perry's flowers on the side table before he sat beside her. He pushed off the floor with his foot and they began to rock back and forth.

Ryder lifted his arm and said, "Come here."

Maisy knew it was useless to resist. She scooted over and

tucked herself under his arm, resting her head on his shoulder. It was fully dark now. The neighborhood was quiet. Against the night sky, Maisy could see bats swooping low to catch bugs while fireflies flickered against the thick hedges that separated her lawn from the neighbors'.

"So, do I need to stand on the front porch with music playing while holding a bouquet of flowers to get you to give us another shot?" he asked. "Because I can do that. I could also stand there with pie, or ice cream, or an entire sheet cake."

Maisy laughed at the thought of him holding an enormous sheet cake. He'd do it, too, she had no doubt. What was she supposed to do? Deny herself the time she had left with him to preserve her heart? Wasn't she pretty wrecked already? And that was just at the idea that he and Perry were leaving.

"What kind of sheet cake?" she asked. After all, she didn't want to appear to be easy.

"Vanilla cake with chocolate icing," he said. "With tons of frosting roses on it."

"What color are the roses?" She tipped her head up to see his face.

"Any color you want," he said. "Pink, purple, blue."

"How about orange roses, like a sunset?" she asked. "And let's flip the cake so it's chocolate cake and vanilla icing."

"Keep it up and I'm going to have to leave," he said. "Now all I can think about is cake."

"I think I can help with that," she said. She stopped the swing with her feet and stood, pulling Ryder up to his feet with one hand and grabbing Perry's roses with the other. She led him through the house to the first-floor kitchen. It had been their main food station as Savannah served up sweet tea, lemonade, and coffee all day.

In the middle of the afternoon, food had begun to arrive from several of the local eateries to celebrate the opening of the bookstore. Big Bottom Donuts sent a couple dozen of their finest, Pie in the Sky pie shop sent three pies, and Conniption Cakes, the local cake bakery, sent over an enormous sheet cake. Maisy had been too busy to eat any earlier but now it was like a worm in her head.

All of the food was in containers in the large refrigerator

and she opened it and gestured for Ryder to peek inside. Every shelf was full of food.

"It's like we hit the mother lode," he said. He gave a low whistle and Maisy nodded.

"What's your poison?" she asked. They stood side by side, staring at the contents of the fridge. "Coconut cream pie, red velvet donuts, or my personal fave, sheet cake, although the roses are purple instead of orange—"

That was as far as she got before he leaned down and kissed her. It wasn't a nice kiss. He backed her up into the open refrigerator and kissed her with a single-mindedness that took her breath away. The cold hit her back while his warmth engulfed her front. The kiss was hot and heavy, full of longing and ripe with want. And then he stepped back, letting go of her and raising his hands as if she held a gun on him.

"Sorry, sorry, sorry," he said. "I know you said that wasn't supposed to happen again. It's just . . . standing next to you . . . I can't . . . *you* are what I want."

The fierce light in his bright-blue eyes hit her with an intensity Maisy had never felt before. He wanted her. Him. This knuckle-dragging cowboy architect who was so full of heart, who loved his daughter so much he would sacrifice his own happiness for her, who read Austen to a stray kitten, who read romances just so he could communicate with his teenager who was shutting him out, and who was building her a freaking turret. Him, he was standing there, wanting her.

"I want you, too."

Maisy slammed the refrigerator door shut and grabbed the front of Ryder's shirt and pulled him close. She rose up on her toes and twined her arms about his neck. She wanted him, all of him, and she wanted him right now. She planted her mouth on his and he responded by looping his arm around her back and hauling her in close.

With one arm, Ryder swept everything off the kitchen counter. Plastic cups and paper plates and a basket full of plastic utensils landed with a crash and neither of them cared. Ryder hoisted her up onto the counter and moved to stand between her legs. They fit perfectly together and Maisy reached for his T-shirt. She grabbed the hem and helped pull it over his head.

He had a builder's body, lean but ripped with muscles, callused hands that rubbed deliciously against her skin as he moved his palms up her calves, to her thighs, nudging them apart so he could get even closer. He pulled her tight against him, and Maisy felt her head go fuzzy. She realized she had never known desire like this. Ryder was even more compelling than a piece of cake, and that was saying something.

It hit her then that this crazy ass-over-teakettle feeling of wanting to be with him all the time, to see him every day, to joke with him, to touch him and hug him and worry about his daughter with him, all of it, was what the romance authors wrote about. It was love, it was being in love. She could try and avoid it or deny it, but the truth was Maisy was a romantic all the way to the core, and she had loved Ryder Copeland from the first moment she'd opened the door to him and there was no taking it back or changing it. It just was.

And if she could have him only right now, for these brief few weeks that their lives would intersect, then wasn't it worth it to have it all? Just as she'd said to Perry about Cooper—wasn't it worth the risk to see if it was real or not? Could she really ask less of herself than she did of a fourteen-year-old? No, she couldn't.

Ryder must have felt the same way because his hands were everywhere while his mouth remembered all of the sensitive spots he'd found before. He lingered just below her ear. He moved his mouth down the side of her neck. He pulled her blouse and bra down, letting his mouth linger on her curves while Maisy arched into his touch, straining to get closer as if she couldn't get enough unless they were actually fused together.

"Are you sure?" Ryder asked. His voice was a rough growl that made the heat pool in between her legs.

"Yes," she whispered. "Positive."

He needed no more invitation. One hand moved up her leg, where his thumb brushed over her underwear in a soft circular motion over the hypersensitive spot nestled there. It felt as if he'd pulled a trigger as a crazy lust-filled Maisy wriggled out of her skirt and blouse while at the same time yanking at his clothes. In moments, they were both bare-assed naked and Maisy laughed, loving him and the freedom of being with him.

"This is crazy, right?" she asked.

"Utter madness," he agreed.

Maisy cupped his face and said, "I'm on birth control and have a clean bill of health. You?"

"Totally clean," he said. "Too busy doing the dad thing to get busy, if you know what I mean."

In answer Maisy licked her way from his collarbone up to his ear, where she whispered, "Well, then, what are you waiting for?"

"Now you've done it," he said.

He grabbed her hips, and in one slow, pointed thrust, they were joined. It was glorious, beautiful, and loving. Exquisite feelings of anticipation and joy throbbed through Maisy, robbing her of speech and thought. As they slid together and apart, ripples of sensation coursed through her and she touched and kissed and caressed every part of Ryder that she could reach until every single nerve inside of her drew taut and she arched her back as the delicious spasms rocked through her entire body from head to toe.

Ryder was right there with her. Just as she began to relax, he hauled her up close and tight and she felt him stiffen as his own orgasm poured into her. He didn't let her go. Instead, he kissed her hair and her face and nuzzled her neck as if he could stay here forever. She knew the feeling. She wrapped her arms around his shoulders and held him close as their skin cooled and their heart rates slowed.

"I need to tell you something," she said. He pulled back just enough to see her face. Maisy knew it was too soon, but she felt like she had to get it out now before she lost her nerve.

"I hope it's praise," he said. "Because, truly, that was the most singular sexual encounter of my life."

Maisy laughed. She cupped his face in her hands and stared into his eyes. "Me, too, and I just have to tell you that I love you."

He glanced away. He turned his head and kissed her

palm. His words were soft when he said, "Thank you. That means more than I can say."

"You don't have to say it back," she said. "I get it if you're not ready, but I want you to know how I feel. I love you, I'm in love with you, and nothing is going to change that."

"Maisy, I . . ." His voice trailed off as he leaned in and kissed her. It was the gentlest of kisses and it wrecked her, positively wrecked her.

He kissed her face, her nose, her cheeks, her ears. He ran his hands over her shoulders and down her arms until his fingers were laced with hers. He moved his mouth over every part of her body, worshipping her as she had imagined him doing during all of the lonely nights in her bed since she'd met him.

When Ryder nudged her back down on the counter, she surrendered to his loving assault upon her person and smiled. Maybe he wasn't ready to declare his feelings. That was okay. For this moment in time, he was hers, and she was going to make certain he knew it all the way down to his toes.

Chapter Twenty-eight

RYDER was destroyed. She had ruined him. Not just for to-night, but for the rest of his life and for any other woman ever. For as long as he lived, he would never forget the sight of Maisy, arching in front of him, lost in a swirl of erotic pleasure that he had given her. He had done that. To her. It straight up blew his mind, and he wanted to do it again and again and again.

And he would have if she hadn't turned the tables on him. She owned him and not just by how masterfully she'd wran-gled his rod. It was her pet now; he was pretty sure. His cock was going to sit, stay, or get hard on her command and her command alone. He was 100 percent fine with that. But his feelings for her were a separate issue, and he was not fine that he had just avoided telling her how he felt about her. She deserved to know how he felt. It was just three little words, but he couldn't choke them out. Damn it.

He knew he'd used sex to distract her and while she had seemingly appreciated his efforts, he couldn't assume that she could decipher his actions into words. Had he actually said "thank you" when she told him she loved him? What the fuck was wrong with him?

In the aftermath of their second go-round, Ryder had wrapped himself around Maisy like a bear hugging a tree and now he slowly untangled himself from her to find that they hadn't been magically transported to some other realm, even though it certainly felt like they had, but were in fact standing butt naked in her kitchen.

He grabbed his T-shirt off the floor and pulled it over her head. Her glasses got tangled and he gently righted them on her face while pulling her rebellious curls free of the collar. The shirt came to midthigh on her and if he had it his way, she'd wear just that forever. He searched around for his boxers but couldn't find them, so he hauled on his jeans instead, being extra careful with the zipper.

"I don't know about you but I am starved," Maisy said.

She dodged around him and opened the fridge. In the time it took him to run his hand over his face in an effort to get his wits about him, she had hauled cake, pie, and donuts over to the table for what looked like a marathon dessert session. She was returning with a glass pitcher of sweet tea and two glasses when he caught her around the waist. He gently took the stacked glasses and put them on the table and then the pitcher.

He spun her around so they were facing each other and said, "Whoa, steady there, sweetheart, are you all right?"

"You're kidding, right?" she asked. She waved her hand at the counter where they'd just been and said, "Do you even have to ask?"

"Yeah, I do," he said. "Because you're moving at the speed of light and I'm having a hard time tracking you."

"Sorry. I just really need to eat some cake right now."

"Understood," he said. He let her go and reached into a drawer and grabbed two forks. "Are we bothering with plates?"

"No." She wiggled her fingers and he put one of the forks in her hand.

Maisy slid onto one of the chairs and Ryder took the seat beside her. He grabbed her chair by the arm and pulled it across the floor so it was up against his. He found he didn't want her too far out of reach.

Then he glanced at the table in front of him. He didn't know where to start but suddenly he, too, was starving. Maisy glanced at him. It was a sly look just over the dark frame of her glasses.

Then she grinned.

"I'm going in," she said.

He watched as she went for the cake. It was a ridiculously girly confection. Pink icing with purple roses and a wide white banner that looked like it had said *Congratulations!* at one time but now just said *tions!* as all the other letters had been eaten.

The cake was a chocolate-vanilla swirl and he had to admit he was impressed when he saw how much cake Maisy could shove in her mouth in one go. A glob of frosting landed on her upper lip, but she must have felt it because she licked it off with her tongue. Guh.

Hunger made him stop staring at her and focus on the food. He could see that the pie was caramel apple, a weakness of his, so he tucked into the remaining quarter of pie, letting the tart apples, tangy cinnamon, and sweet caramel topping melt in his mouth. He was pretty sure this was the best pie he had ever had, and yeah, maybe it was the postcoital glow making it seem that way but it was still really good pie. It took him a moment to realize Maisy was staring at him.

Shoving one more bite into his mouth, he turned to face her. He did a quick three chews and swallowed it down. It went down hard.

"What?" he asked.

"You went for the pie first," she said. She shook her head as if in disbelief.

"Was that wrong?" he asked. "Is there some snack etiquette I don't know about in regards to what comes first, pie or cake or donuts?"

"Not precisely," she said. She bit her lip. Concern furrowed her brow. "I'm just afraid of what it might mean."

"I'm not following," he said. But then he caught the glint

in her eye. She was teasing him. He was swamped with a feeling of acute relief. If she was teasing him then surely she wasn't upset that he hadn't said *I love you* back.

She tossed her curls and closed her eyes for a moment as if bracing herself. Then she slowly opened her eyes and met his gaze. "I just think it's best if you tell me now."

"Tell you what?" he asked. He tucked his smile into his cheek at her overly dramatic tone. If she wanted to play, he was okay with that.

"That you are one of those people who does birthday pie instead of cake," she said. She waved her fork at him. "I can overlook a lot of stuff—chronic lateness, forgetting anniversaries, an inability to follow directions—but pie over cake on a birthday is not one of them. If you're going to be my boyfriend, you have to change your ways. This is not negotiable."

"Boyfriend, huh?" Ryder asked. He was pleased that he sounded so cool, because inside he was doing a fist bump and a high five and quite possibly a cartwheel.

"Yes," she said. "I simply cannot have a birthday pie–eating boyfriend."

There was a flash of vulnerability that made him want to scoop her up and hold her close. So even though he hadn't professed his love for her, she had invited him to be her guy. He would grab on to that and hold it tight with both hands until he figured out a way to let her know how he felt about her. There had to be a way.

"Well, I suppose it depends on what flavor the cake is," he said. He reached past her and scooped up a dollop of pink icing on the edge of the cake plate. Then he dabbed her on the end of her nose. Her eyes went wide behind her glasses and he laughed. Then he kissed her nose, catching all of the frosting.

"That's pretty good," he said. He licked his lips. Her eyes dilated while she watched him and he knew they were about to get pervy with the pink cake and he wanted to howl at the moon he was so ready.

She swabbed some icing with her fingers and slid them across his lips. He caught the frosting with his tongue and she shivered. She then leaned close to lick the remaining frosting off his lips and Ryder was pretty sure he was going to have a heart attack.

From there, it just got crazy. Frosting went everywhere, she was naked, again, and Ryder found her tickle spot, on her sides right above her hips, and he used it mercilessly against her, until she was thrashing and gasping, and pleading for mercy. But he wasn't done yet. He set her up on the table, hauling his T-shirt out of the way, then he parted her legs and put his mouth on her.

She fell back against the table, mercifully missing any of the food, and made pleasurable sounds in her throat that he was sure he would hear in his dreams for the rest of his life. Just before she came, he rose to his feet and loosened his jeans so he could thrust into her one more time. That was all it took. When she shouted his name, he felt a feeling of satisfaction he was pretty sure he'd never experienced before. It was everything.

He braced himself with an arm on either side of her. As he moved forward and back, he watched her fall back into herself, and he said, "Birthday cake. I am definitely a birthday cake sort of guy, which I suppose means I am also your boyfriend."

Maisy grinned and then reached for him, pulling him down so that they were pressed together. Then she looked him straight in the eye and whispered, "Best. Boyfriend. Ever."

Ryder lost himself then. He drove into her as if he could actually merge them into one if he tried hard enough. Maisy matched him thrust for thrust, until she let go, arching her back and convulsing around him so hard that with a shout, he released in a surge that felt like his soul had just poured itself right into her. He dropped onto his elbows on the table and rested his head beside hers.

"I'm pretty sure you got that wrong," he said.

"What?" she asked. Her voice was groggy and she was threading her fingers through his hair. He hoped she never stopped.

"It's not me, it's you," he said. He lifted up enough to kiss her. "Best. Girlfriend. Ever."

The smile she sent him was blinding and he knew for sure that he would never ever forget how she looked right here, right now. The words. They were right there. He could feel them, clambering to be said, to be whispered in her ear. But he couldn't do it. He couldn't get them out.

He pushed aside his frustration. He didn't want anything to taint the moment. He had time, a few weeks in fact, to say what needed to be said. He had things he needed to figure out, like how to get Perry up to Connecticut, where she could get the best education he could provide without feeling like he was ripping his heart out, and squaring things with Maisy so she knew exactly how he felt about her. He was determined that he'd do it, and in doing so would be able to convince her that a long-distance relationship could work. It had to, because he absolutely was not giving this woman up.

"WHAT happened to all of the cake?" Savannah asked. "And the pie? We had some left over after the opening, I know we did."

"Huh?" Maisy looked up from her computer, where she was reviewing the sales figures for yesterday's opening day. Reviewing figures. Ha, that was a laugh. Her brain was the consistency of pudding, she had bruises in places she didn't think it was possible to bruise, and she couldn't stop thinking about the hot cowboy architect, who was out working on her turret. In fact, she'd spent the past twenty minutes trying to come up with a plausible excuse to go see him.

"What happened to all the pie and cake?" Savannah asked. "The only thing left in the kitchen is a box of stale donuts."

"I had the midnight munchies," Maisy said. "Really bad. Went down there after checking on George and plowed all the food. It was crazy."

"It must have been, because the last time I checked you didn't wear men's underwear," Savy said. She pulled a pair of barbeque tongs from behind her back, in which were clamped a pair of plaid boxers. "These were in the pantry. Explain."

"The pantry?" Maisy asked. She knew they'd gotten carried away, but the pantry? "Well, that's unexpected."

"Uh-huh," Savy said. "So, how was it?"

She wiggled her eyebrows and Maisy felt her face get hot. Not just a little hot but *eating a habanero pepper, sweating and panting* kind of hot. Still, she tried to bluff her way out.

"I have no idea what you're talking about," she said.

"Really?" Savy asked. "Okay, I'll just trot these out among all of our muscle-bound, hard hat–wearing construction workers and see if anyone claims them."

She turned and headed for the door with a swish of her hips. Maisy knew she should let her go—it was the only way to save face and not get grilled with a million questions, like, *Why is Ryder's underwear in our pantry?* but she couldn't stand the thought of Ryder getting caught off guard, plus, he might claim them and then everyone would know. Ack! This was a nightmare.

"Stop!" Maisy jumped to her feet as Savy reached the door. "All right, I'll tell all, just give me the boxers."

Savannah turned back around and when Maisy reached for the boxers Savy extended the tongs only to snatch them away at the last moment. "Talk first."

"Aw, come on." Maisy tried to grab them but Savannah lifted them up and out of reach, like an Olympic torch except plaid cotton.

"No, I know you. If you get these shorts, I'll never hear a word," Savy said. "So spill it."

"Fine, but you're getting the abridged version and nothing more," Maisy said.

Savannah nodded and rolled her hand in a *go on* gesture and Maisy took a deep breath and said, "So, Ryder and I had a long talk—"

"Really? These beg to differ." Savy waved the shorts in the air like a flag.

"Did you want to the hear the story or did you want to torture me? Because you can't do both."

"Are you sure? Because I really feel like I'm having my cake and eating it, too. Oh, wait, is that what you were doing?" Savannah snorted.

Maisy did not smile, opting instead to assume her resting bitch face. "How long have you been holding that one in?"

"Pretty much since I found the boxers." Savy was still laughing. "And it serves you right. You two ate all the cake."

"I'm never going to hear the end of this, am I?" Maisy asked. "When we're one hundred and sitting in our rockers in the old age home, you're still going to tease me, aren't you?"

"M, if we make it to one hundred, we'll be off our rockers," Savy said. "But yes, I'll still be teasing you. So, after you 'ate all the cake'—and isn't that a fabulous euphemism?— then what happened?"

"Nothing much," she said.

"So, it was a *one and done, scratch the itch, and move on* sort of thing?" Savy sounded disappointed.

"Not exactly," Maisy said. "And it wasn't one."

"Whaaaaat?!" Savy stared at her in admiration. "Went back for more cake, did you? So, will there be more in your future?"

"Probably, given that we're dating and all," Maisy said.

At this, Savannah dropped the boxers. "You are? That's wonderful, despite all of the impending heartbreak when he moves away. I think he's a good guy, so if you're happy, I'm happy."

"Gee, thanks," Maisy said. She snatched the boxers off the tongs. "I don't know if he's told Perry yet, so do me a solid and keep it on the down-low."

"And here I was going to hire a billboard to announce to all of Fairdale that Maisy Kelly is finally getting a little something."

Maisy glowered and Savy laughed. "So, was it, you know?" She wiggled her eyebrows.

"I am not talking about this," Maisy said. She very primly tucked Ryder's boxers into her back pocket and started for the door. "If you'll excuse me, I need to go—"

"Find your man, yeah, yeah, I get it," Savy said. "I'll just be here, toiling away, trying to make your brand for you. Don't you worry about me; I can live without knowing all the deets."

"Good," Maisy said. She slipped out of the office, shutting

the door behind her. Then she dashed up the stairs to the area Ryder and Seth had cordoned off while they built out the turret on the second floor.

The scent of wood hit her nostrils. The aroma reminded her of Ryder. He always seemed to have that earthy smell about him. Much like she probably smelled of paper and books. It made her feel as if they were matched. Then she squashed the thought.

Savannah was right. He was still leaving. Just because they'd jumped each other and now they were a thing did not mean their outcome was going to change. Heartbreak loomed and she was kidding herself if she thought any different. Still, with his boxers in her pocket, she had a reason to see him and that would do for now.

The workers had framed the turret, installed the electrical and the outside boards. Now they were working on putting up the sheetrock on the interior around the windows. It was going to be the most spectacular room. Maisy was so excited. She wasn't sure if this was going to be her office—she was pretty sure it was—or a specialty room that could be used for book signings and events. Maybe it could be both. She didn't know yet. She just knew that she loved it already.

"Hello?" she called into the room.

Four men in hard hats turned at the sound of her voice, but only one made her heart thump hard in her chest. She grinned. She couldn't help it. Ryder grinned back and then muttered something to his crew as he stepped over tools to get to her. He removed his hard hat on the way and she could see where it had squashed his hair flat. She wanted to shove her fingers into it and mess it up, but she resisted as she noticed Seth was watching them with an amused look.

"Everything all right?" he asked.

"Yeah, but can I talk to you for sec?"

"Sure."

Maisy gestured for him to follow her into one of the adjoining rooms. It was devoted to sweet romances and women's fiction.

As Ryder walked behind her it was all she could do to keep images of him bracing her up against a bookshelf and having his way with her out of her head. She fanned her face with her hand. Good grief, she was becoming the naughty bookseller.

She glanced around the room, relieved that it was empty. She then dug into her pocket and pulled out his boxers. She held them out to him and he laughed.

"I wondered where those had gotten to last night," he said. "Where'd you find them?"

"Savannah discovered them in the pantry."

"The pantry?" He shoved them in his pocket and scratched his chin. "Huh."

Maisy studied his face. He didn't look even the littlest bit embarrassed. Maybe he didn't hear her. "Did you catch the part where *Savannah* found them?"

"Yeah, I caught that," he said. He glanced around the room. He seemed satisfied with what he saw and reached behind him to shut the door. "So, she knows we're a couple."

"We're a couple who got up to shenanigans in the kitchen."

He started to walk toward her and Maisy backed up. "Shenanigans? Is that what you call it?"

"Do you have a better word?" she asked. She backed up right into a bookcase and he took swift advantage, blocking her exit by putting an arm on each side of her. It was thrilling.

Chapter Twenty-nine

"I HAVE a whole dictionary of better words," he said. He then proceeded to lean close to her so that his mouth was just a breath from her ear and he whispered all of the words he would use to describe what they had done the night before. Some of the words were sweet and some were wicked and one was downright filthy and made her break into a light sweat.

"Intercourse." He planted a kiss on her. "Coupling." He moved his lips down her throat. "Fornicating."

"Oh, my," she whispered.

"Copulation." His hands slid up her sides, cupping her breasts. "Fucking." His thumbs slid over her nipples and Maisy thought she might faint.

She wanted to grab him but she didn't want to stop the wordy torment he was causing inside of her, so she gripped the bookshelf at her back, digging her fingers into the shelf so hard she was pretty sure she was going to leave claw marks while he continued to turn up the heat with his sexy words. Maisy suspected she was going to dissolve into a puddle at his feet but she held on, breathless and dizzy from the lust that had her temporarily blinded.

"Lovemaking," he said. Then he leaned into her, kissing her until she didn't know which way was up. Ryder was the only thing holding her together and she clung to him. And then he pulled back, stepping away from her as if he'd done nothing more than describe the weather. Maisy blinked twice and with a shaky hand pushed her glasses up on her nose.

"Tell me I get to see you tonight," he said.

Incapable of speech, mostly because she was afraid she'd beg him to strip off her clothes and have his way with her right then and there, Maisy nodded. She felt like a bobble-head, the sort they gave out at baseball games, but he smiled as if quite pleased with himself. Then he leaned in close and she was so sure he was going to kiss her, but he didn't. He just whispered in her ear, "Seven o'clock." And then he was gone.

"You okay?" Savannah asked when she returned to their office on the first floor.

"I could use a fan and a bucket of ice," Maisy said. Then she thunked her head onto her desk and tried not to fixate on the clock and how long it would be until seven o'clock.

RYDER was waiting for her at seven just like he promised. He had a picnic packed and he hustled her out of the bookstore and into his truck, where he kissed her and snapped her into the passenger seat as if she was the most precious cargo in the world.

He took a dusty winding road out of town, holding her hand for the entire ride. Maisy felt giddy. Being with Ryder, just the two of them, was everything falling for someone should be.

They spread a blanket on the banks of Crescent Lake, where they sat, talking about the bookstore and laughing, while the sun set in a blaze of tangerine and magenta, fading into a deep purple. When the first star winked at them from above, Maisy grabbed Ryder's hand in hers and cast her desperate wish up into the heavens, hoping that this time might never end, that maybe a happily ever after could be hers after all.

"What are you doing?" Ryder asked. She could feel him watching her as she focused on her star.

"Wishing," she said. She pointed to the sky and he glanced up. "You should make a wish, too."

Ryder looked at her. His blue gaze swept over her face as if he was trying to memorize every eyelash and freckle.

"I don't need to," he said. His voice was gruff when he added, "You're already here."

Oh. Maisy pounced, flattening him beneath her slight frame as she kissed him with all of the love and longing that beat in her fierce heart. This man. Her man. How she loved him.

THE next two weeks were the most singular of Maisy's life and it wasn't just the sex, or Ryder, or the sex with Ryder. That was the cherry on top of the awesome life sundae she had going on. The local news station out of Asheville had come out to do a story on her bookstore and her first two Saturdays, their busiest day of the week, had been full of customers from opening until closing.

Savannah had gotten the website fully functioning and they had begun taking online orders, and Maisy's system for inventory was almost finished. It felt as if all of Fairdale and the surrounding area had embraced her dream of a romance bookstore and she could not be more thrilled. She knew that the novelty would wear off and that she had to be ready to entice readers back to the shop. Savanah had started a mailing list, and they were sending out coupons in their first newsletter.

Maisy also scheduled their first official author book signing. The writer, Tara McDonough, was local, living just over the border in Tennessee, and her publisher had sent Maisy an advance reader copy of her latest book. It was a beautiful time travel, love story saga, spanning decades and generations, where a woman from the Smoky Mountains steps through a mystical portal and travels back in time to the highlands of her Scottish ancestors.

There were battle scenes, a hero wearing a kilt, an epic voyage across the North Sea, a hero wearing a kilt, a plague that ravages the population, a hero wearing a kilt . . . oh, my, that hero wearing a kilt. On the third night that Maisy picked up the book to read during a quiet night in with Ryder, he grabbed a plaid throw from the corner of her bedroom and wrapped it around his waist.

He then spoken in a Scottish brogue to her and Maisy tossed the book aside to jump on her man. Afterward when their skin cooled and their heart rates returned to normal, Maisy read to him from the book. She read about the heroine's love of the hero even as she tried desperately to find her way home to her own time and place, and then she read of the hero's reluctance to let the woman he loved leave his side, even if she didn't truly belong to him.

Maisy had never read to a man in bed and certainly not the poignant and at times deeply erotic scenes that she read to Ryder. When she yawned, he took the book and put it aside and then made love to her in the slowest, sweetest way imaginable, as if he was trying to draw out and savor every single second of their time together. Maisy knew exactly how he felt. When they were joined, she felt complete but all too soon, it ended, and despite the joy that filled her during their time together, she was left feeling bereft.

Still, she refused to waste a second of their time together being sad. She would fret about it when the moment came. For now, Ryder was hers. They found excuses to see each other during the day. At dinnertime they took care of George together and then Perry dashed out to be with Cooper while Maisy and Ryder spent their evening together at home or out.

They even double-dated with Perry and Cooper to the movies once and bowling another time. Maisy only caught Ryder giving Cooper the hairy eyeball three or four times, which she corrected with a neat elbow jab to the side. Perry positively glowed. She was clearly deeply infatuated with Cooper and he seemed to feel the same. Maisy felt as if she was watching a reflection of her own feelings in the young couple and every now and again, she got nervous about when the bottom would fall out as Ryder and Perry left Fairdale for good.

THE Royal Order of George met in the hidden room every Sunday night, and those were the only evenings Maisy and Perry didn't meet their fellas. The ladies, all four, each shared what good deeds they'd done during the week, always keeping it anonymous so that the recipient wouldn't know who bought their coffee for them in the morning, or who left a bouquet of flowers on their door, or who had dinner delivered from a local restaurant so that they didn't have to cook.

"It felt so good to see Bethany open the door to her son," Jeri said. "She has been missing him for weeks, but he just didn't have the bus fare to come up from school for the weekend. So, I sent him a round-trip ticket. My husband thought I was crazy as I pretended to water my rosebushes so I could watch her boy knock on the door and see Bethany answer. My goodness, it was as if ten years rolled back off of that woman. She beamed pure sunshine out of her smile, positively beamed."

They all laughed while they ate the strawberry rhubarb pie that Savannah had picked up at the Pie in the Sky pie shop for their meeting. They washed it down with ginger ale and despite not being with Ryder at the moment, Maisy felt a sense of completeness that she knew had been missing in her life before they started the good deed club.

King George, who was now mostly enamored with his own tail, romped around the room, chasing his toys, or his tail, while turning into a miniature cat. He batted at her shoelaces and when she reached down to pet him, he scurried away with his tail down, stalking like a little tiger in forests of Asia. Then he caught sight of Perry's shoelace and did the same thing.

"All right, who's next?" Savy asked. "You all know what I did already—I sacrificed myself in getting this pie."

"Pie?" Jeri asked.

"It was the last one," Savannah said. "I had to throw an elbow into Mr. Hudson's side to get him out of the way so I could grab it."

"I think that's the opposite of the point of the Royal Order of George," Perry said. She picked up the kitten and put her face next to his. So much cuteness in a girl and her cat, it was almost too much. Maisy felt her ovaries drop their eggs like ducks being hit in a shooting gallery. Even though she was using birth control, perhaps it was good that she wasn't seeing Ryder tonight.

"Besides, I have it on good authority that you did more than get pie this week," Jeri said. She tossed her black braids and gave Savy her best Tiffany Haddish, *Do not even try to mess with me* look.

"I don't know what you're talking about," Savannah said. Then she shoveled a huge bite of pie into her mouth as if that would be the end of the conversation.

Maisy shook her head and turned to Jeri. "What do you know?"

"Well," Jeri said as she huddled closer. "I heard from Wanda at the Food Lion that she saw Savy talking to Quino in the produce section and the next thing she knew they were taking pictures of the melons. She said it was kinky."

"Oh, my God!" Savy protested. She swallowed hard before continuing, "That's not at all what was happening. I was merely answering his question about photography."

"Uh-huh," Maisy said, making it sound as if she thought *photography* meant something else entirely.

"I was! He asked me to help him with the marketing for his stable, and I offered to teach him some free basic stuff about social media posts, like what sort of things are engaging. And the bright colors of the fruits under the skylight in the produce section make a nice shot. Oh, man, that does sound perverted."

They all looked at her and then Perry said, "It's all right, Uncle Quino does that to all the ladies."

Savy looked at the teen and opened her mouth and then shoved another bite of pie past her lips, chewing furiously as if she didn't like hearing about Quino and other women. Hmm.

"How about you, Perry?" Maisy asked. "What was your good deed?"

"Cooper and I started a pocket change campaign to buy Mrs. Bierman a new motorized scooter," she said. "She's our favorite substitute teacher."

"Mrs. Bierman is still teaching?" Maisy asked. "Bless her heart, she was there when I was your age. She was the sweetest of the sweet. I want to donate, too."

Perry smiled and said, "You don't have to."

"Sure I do. Isn't that the whole point of the Royal Order of George, to help out and pitch in?" Maisy asked.

The kitten flopped into the middle of the group and stretched his legs as far as he could. He let out a yawn and Maisy reached down to scratch his tummy. He hugged her hand with his front feet and mouthed her fingers as if looking for food or comfort. "Look what you started, Georgie. A whole wave of good deeds."

"I have to say," Jeri said, "I think Auntie El would be very proud of us for changing our corner of the world."

"I think you're right," Maisy said. She waited for the ambush grief to hit her, but it didn't. Instead, for the first time since losing Auntie El, she felt a sense of peace, of letting go. Maybe the good deeds and having Ryder in her life were exactly what she needed to pull her through her mourning. She glanced at her friends and was filled with gratitude. She couldn't help but hope that somehow everything was going to work out.

WHILE the days remained hot in the Smoky Mountains, the nights started to get cooler. Maisy knew that summer was almost over and she dreaded the day that Ryder and Perry packed up and left, leaving her lonely and heartbroken with only King George to comfort her.

Determined to enjoy the time they had, Maisy spent every moment she could with Ryder, trying to make as many memories as possible before he left. They were sitting on the porch swing after a particularly grueling day in the bookshop. New books had arrived that needed to be shelved and they'd had two reading clubs come in, as well as the plumber when the guest bathroom on the first floor had backed up due to excessive toilet paper being used.

Maisy had joined the ABA, American Booksellers Association, and was thrilled to see that indie bookstores were thriving. But then she and Jeri had a meeting over the bookstore's costs versus revenue, and Maisy had made the painful decision to tap into more of her reserves from the trust

Auntie El had left her. She would take out a bank loan if she had to, but she was going to make a success of this business even if it killed her.

At the moment, however, she just wanted to sit on the porch swing with her guy and watch the bats swoop, listen to the meadowlarks cry, and smell the scent of freshly mown grass and honeysuckle on the breeze. Ryder had his arm around her shoulders and their fingers were laced together and every few minutes he would kiss the top of her head. This moment right here was perfection. Maisy tried to imprint it in her mind, because she knew it would never get better than this.

When a police car pulled into the drive in front of the house, Maisy wondered if something had happened nearby. When Travis Wainwright stepped out of the car, she felt her heart pound a little bit faster. Perry had a date with Cooper tonight. Surely, Travis must know that.

"Hi, Trav," she called, hoping she sounded normal and not alarmed.

"Hi, Maisy, Ryder," Travis said.

Ryder rose to his feet and Maisy followed him as he crossed the porch. He looked at Travis and maybe it was fatherly intuition but he said, "You're not here on a social call, are you?"

"'Fraid not," Travis said. "The truth is, I've got Perry down at the station with Cooper. I'm sorry to say one of my officers took them and two of their friends in."

"In?" Maisy asked. "What does that mean—*in* like 'indoors'?"

"No, *in* as 'in jail,'" Travis clarified.

"What on earth for?" Maisy asked.

"Vandalism," Travis said. "My officer spotted them out on route twenty-seven. Apparently, they took it upon themselves to paint Mr. Hargraves's barn pink, and not just a light red sort of pink but a make-your-eyes-water, bubble gum pink."

Chapter Thirty

"SHE'S a minor, so I'm going to need you to be there when we talk about what happened," Travis said.

Ryder stood staring at him as if he couldn't quite comprehend what was being said. Then he shook his head and said, "Sure, right. I'll follow you to the station."

Both men turned to leave, and Maisy caught Ryder by the arm and said, "Wait. I'm coming with you."

She ducked into the bookstore and grabbed her purse then she hit the lights and locked the door. Ryder was already in his truck with the engine running when she ran down the steps and jumped up into the passenger seat.

It was a short ride to the station as it was located across the town green from the bookstore. It was in a squat little redbrick building that Maisy was sure was left over from the post-Depression era, built by the WPA.

They parked in the lot behind the station and Travis ushered them in through the back door. Sitting on a bench in the hallway, under the watchful eye of the desk officer, were Perry, Cooper, and two other teens, one Maisy recognized as Jasmine Long, Perry's best friend, who'd been a frequent visitor to the bookshop since they'd opened. The other she didn't know.

Perry jumped to her feet immediately and said, "Dad, I can explain."

"Vandalism?" Ryder asked. "Exactly how are you going to explain that?"

"Yes, that's what I'd like to know, too," a voice said from behind them. They turned around to see a short, squat man, charging forward. "Travis, what's this I hear about my kid being arrested?"

Billy Snyder stomped in like he was looking for a fight, ahead of another set of parents who arrived behind him. Maisy didn't know the second couple, but judging by the looks on Jasmine's face, these were her parents. Maisy had known Billy since grade school. He had spent most of his formative years in detention, so he was certainly on some slippery moral high ground if he got too upset about his own kid making a bad choice.

"Settle down, Billy," Travis said. "My kid is here, too. All right, let's be calm and go have a seat and hear what the kids have to say."

He gestured for the parents and teens to follow him and they entered a small conference room at the end of the hall. They shuffled into seats, but Maisy paused at the doorway. As fond as she was of Perry, she wasn't really sure she was a part of this. Ryder glanced at her and grabbed her hand, pulling her into the room with him. Okay, then.

"All right," Travis said. "Let's hear it."

Perry and Cooper exchanged a glance while the other two teens stared at them. It was pretty clear whose idea the painting of the barn had been.

Cooper stood and said, "It's my fault. I thought we were doing a good thing, but it was dark and I didn't realize that I had the wrong paint."

Perry shot to her feet next to him and said, "No, it's my fault. The whole thing was my idea. I got the paint and the rollers and I talked everyone into helping me, because I thought we were doing something nice for Mr. Hargraves, you know, trying to pay it forward because he, well, he's kind of mean and he doesn't have anyone else, and if anybody ever needed a helping hand, it's him, but—"

"Perry, no! You have more at stake here than I do," Cooper said. He turned to his father. "The blame is all mine, Dad. I screwed up and I'm really sorry. I'll make it right. I swear."

"No, it isn't," Perry said. She looked at Chief Wainwright. "It wasn't Cooper, it was me."

Travis pinched the bridge of his nose as if warding off a headache. "You kids realize that in North Carolina vandalism is a class-one misdemeanor punishable by a minimum fine of five hundred dollars and at least twenty-four hours of community service?"

"But, Dad, we weren't vandalizing the property—" Cooper protested.

"Wainright! What the hell is going on?" Mr. Hargraves, who was eighty if he was a day, stomped into the room, wearing his usual overalls and flannel shirt. His skin was deeply tanned from years in the sun, and his white hair was tufted on his head, probably from removing the John Deere cap he held in his hand.

"I'm sorry to call you down here so late, Mr. Hargraves," Travis said. "We have a bit of a situation."

"So I reckoned when I got home and found one of your lackeys in my driveway," he said. He glanced around the room. "Who are all of you people?"

"Mr. Hargraves, I am so sorry," Perry said. "The paint was supposed to be red, like, barn red, but instead it turned out pink. We thought maybe it would dry red, but it didn't and we finished a whole side before we realized it. I don't know how the mix-up happened. I am so sorry."

"I'm sure you are," Mr. Hargraves said. His voice was thick with sarcasm as his bushy white eyebrows met in the middle, making one severe line across his forehead. "It must have been a real hoot to play a joke on an old man. I bet you thought it would be hilarious for every person driving in and out of town on route twenty-seven to have a big old laugh at old man Hargraves and his pink barn."

"No, sir, we didn't. I swear," Cooper said. He reached

down and took Perry's hand in his. "We really were trying to do something good."

"Liar," Mr. Hargraves snapped. "You rotten kids were up to no good and you got caught. Don't try to turn it into something else now."

"We're not," Perry protested. "We really were trying to do a good deed."

"Why?" Mr. Hargraves stared at her. It was a look full of disbelief and distrust and Maisy was impressed that Perry didn't buckle under the hard stare. "Why would anyone want to help me?"

Perry's voice was soft when she answered, "Because you need it."

Hargraves was the first one to look away.

"Here's what I don't understand," Ryder said. His voice was tight and Maisy could tell he was equal parts furious and bewildered. "How did the idea to paint someone else's barn even pop into your head?"

"We thought doing an anonymous good deed would make us feel better about ourselves," Perry said. "But it didn't really work out that way." *Sorry.* She mouthed the words to her friends.

"Oh, dear," Maisy said. She had a feeling this was one of Perry's random good deeds for the Royal Order of George, but it had clearly gone horribly awry.

Ryder turned and gave her a questioning glance.

"This is going to go on our permanent record, isn't it?" the other boy asked. He looked at Billy and turned a sickly shade of green. Maisy feared he might throw up. "If this keeps me out of college, I'll just die."

"A misdemeanor stays on your record," Chief Wainwright said. He looked at Cooper as if he couldn't believe he was having this conversation with his son. "Even if you don't do jail time there are collateral consequences that will follow you for the rest of your life. I believe that you were trying to do something good, but this is serious. Every background check run for school admission, a line of credit, a job, is going to see that you have this in your file and it will take you out of the running automatically with no chance to explain your good intentions."

All four teens paled, looking shaken and scared.

Ryder looked at Perry and shook his head. "What were you thinking? You realize this could keep you out of Saint Mary's Prep? You've put everything you've worked so hard for at risk and for what?"

They stared at each other for several seconds and Maisy wanted desperately to jump in but she knew it wasn't her place. This was between father and daughter.

"I'm sorry," Perry said. "I don't know what else I can say."

The air between them practically vibrated with anger, frustration, and hurt.

Perry turned away from her father and faced Mr. Hargraves and Travis. "It was my idea, all mine. If you're looking to file charges against someone, please just file them against me. The others don't deserve to be punished for this."

"No, I—" Cooper protested but Perry shushed him.

Mr. Hargraves rocked back and forth on the heels of his well-worn work boots. He studied Perry as if sizing her up.

"You're a feisty one, aren't you?" Mr. Hargraves asked Perry. She looked uncertain as to whether to agree with him or not. Then she gave him a slow nod. He nodded back as if they understood each other. "I suppose it's a good thing that I'm kind of partial to the color pink."

The entire room went still. Was Hargraves going to let the kids off the hook? Maisy wanted to kiss the old duff right on his downy head. He was clearly rethinking his position but, honestly, how could he live with a bright-pink barn? Unless . . .

"Mr. Hargraves, have you ever considered using the side of that barn as, say, a billboard?" Maisy asked. The entire room turned toward her and Maisy felt her face get warm. She had an amazing *Idea!* but it would only work if she could convince Mr. Hargraves that it was a good one.

"I'm not following," he said. Then he squinted at her. "Well, shoot, is that you, Maisy Kelly? You look more like your aunt Eloise every day."

"Thank you." Maisy smiled at what she considered a high compliment. Then she explained, "I just opened a bookstore in town, and I would love to pay you a monthly stipend to let me advertise my shop on the side of your barn."

She felt Ryder straighten up beside her. She didn't look at him, because if he didn't approve she didn't want to know.

Mr. Hargraves scratched his head, "You did hear the part about the barn being pink, didn't you?"

Maisy grinned at him. "Pink is actually perfect. How about seventy-five dollars per month?"

"I say you just bought yourself the side of a barn," Mr. Hargraves said. Then he turned to Travis and snapped, "What are you doing? You need to let these kids go. It's a school night."

With that, Mr. Hargraves left, and everyone else followed in varying states of surprise and relief. Travis paused by Maisy and patted her on the shoulder. "That was genius."

"Thanks," she said.

She glanced back at Ryder, but he wasn't looking anywhere near as pleased. In fact, he was glowering. As everyone left the room, he motioned for Perry and Maisy to stay.

Ryder ran a hand over his face. Maisy recognized it as his *calm down* gesture. She glanced at Perry. There was no calming happening there. Her chin jutted out and she looked ready for a fight. That should have been her first clue.

"Would you care to explain to me this 'good deed' that you led all of your friends into?" Ryder asked.

"What's to explain?" Perry asked. Maisy wanted to jump in and wave her hand across her throat to signify that she should can the 'tude but she doubted it would do any good. "I belong to a group, a secret society, in fact, and we do good deeds anonymously to help anyone who might need it."

"'Secret society'?" Ryder asked. "Like a cult? What crackpot talked you into that?"

Maisy raised her hand. "That would be me."

"You?" He looked at her as if he didn't recognize her. "You're having my child keep secrets from me?"

"Not secrets, just anonymous good deeds," Maisy said.

She glanced at his face. He was not impressed. "That probably doesn't sound much better."

"My kid got hauled into jail for vandalism, so no, not better," he said.

Maisy couldn't argue the point.

"Explain, please," Ryder said to Perry.

"Okay, so when I broke up with Cooper, I was feeling really bad, and we had a girls' night." She glanced at Maisy for confirmation and Maisy nodded. "While we were talking, we discussed how doing good deeds, like saving King George, made us feel better when we were low and so we decided to form a secret society that did anonymous good deeds. We've all done a whole bunch of stuff, but I wanted to do something big before I leave for school. You know, something Cooper and I could share, so I thought painting Mr. Hargraves's barn, which desperately needs it, would be something special."

"Let me get this straight," Ryder said. "You formed a secret good deed club and you've been doing stuff for people all over town and not letting them know what you've done?"

"Yes," Perry said. "Like Je—one of our members helped her neighbor's son come home for a visit, and another is helping a certain person with his website, stuff like that. It's supercool. I plan to write my college essay about it."

"Oh, good idea," Maisy said.

"Yeah, great idea," Ryder said. "Try to leave out the part where you got hauled into the police station and almost arrested."

Perry glowered at him in an expression so similar to his that Maisy was taken aback. They really did have the same jutting chin and bright-blue eyes and donkey stubborn disposition.

"Are we good now?" Perry asked.

"Not even close," Ryder said. He glanced at Maisy, looking at her as if he couldn't believe she was involved in all of this. "You know this could have ruined Perry's chance of going to Saint Mary's." He looked back at Perry. "It's the best school in the country and you've worked so hard to be accepted. How could you jeopardize it like this? This was so incredibly thoughtless of you."

"Thoughtless?" Perry spat the word at him. "How can you say that when it was exactly the opposite? We were trying to do something nice. Mr. Hargraves isn't pressing charges, there isn't going to be a fine to pay or community service, and it won't be on my permanent record. So, what is the big deal?"

"The big deal is that you're keeping secrets, and it could have cost you everything," Ryder said. He said it as if it was all suddenly making sense. "You know how I feel about lies and secrets. How could you, Perry?"

She shrugged. It was full of teenage attitude and Maisy cringed, knowing that it was only going to piss Ryder off, which it did.

"That's not an answer," he said. Perry crossed her arms over her chest and looked away. Ryder stared at her as if he didn't even recognize her. The tension in the room was clearly at a breaking point. Still, Maisy said nothing.

"Oh, my God, you did it on purpose, didn't you?" he asked, looking as if he'd just figured it all out.

"What? No," Perry said. She didn't meet his gaze.

"You painted the barn pink so that you *would* be caught," he said. "You probably hoped you'd get into so much trouble you'd get kicked out of Saint Mary's so you could stay here with Cooper. Is that it, Perry? Was that your plan?"

Maisy knew she should stay out of it, but she felt like she needed to try to defend Perry. "Ryder, no, you know Perry's not like that. She was just trying to do something nice. Only it just didn't work out as planned."

"I'm not really sure you should be defending her, given the bad influence you've been on her with your 'secret society,' " Ryder said. His tone was high snark and he even used the finger quotes. Maisy felt her own temper begin to heat. Before she could say anything, he turned to Perry and said, "If you didn't do this on purpose, answer me this—how do you mix up bright pink and dark red? They aren't exactly next to each other on the color wheel."

"Fine. I did do it on purpose."

Maisy sucked in a breath. She hadn't seen that coming.

"I did it. I hoped I'd get caught and I hoped it would keep me from having to go away. I don't want to go to Saint Mary's and you can't make me."

"Oh, can't I?" Ryder said. "This isn't negotiable, Perry. It's been the plan since before you were born."

"Plans change," Perry said softly. Her lip quivered and Maisy could see she was about to cry.

"Not this one," Ryder said.

They stared at each other, and Maisy felt her heart pound in her chest. Should she step in? What could she say? It was clear Ryder was blaming her in part for this, and he might have a point. Oh, man, she wasn't a big conflict person and she'd already had her quota for the day.

"You're going to Saint Mary's and that's final," he said.

Perry glared at her father and cried, "Are you that desperate to get rid of me?"

"You know that isn't true," he said.

"Then why are you sending me away? Why?"

"Perry, we've talked about this. You know why. I want you to have the best of everything and all of the advantages I never had," he said.

"Why?" Perry plopped her hands on her hips. Gone was the threat of tears. She looked fierce.

Maisy glanced between Perry and Ryder. Perry was pushing him for something. Each word was like a fist punching a pane of glass, trying to make it crack. Ryder's face was stiff, his expression frozen as if he knew what she was looking for and he just couldn't deliver the goods. Maisy's chest hurt because she sensed beneath his stoic facade, he was hurting mightily.

"You can't say it, can you?" Perry asked. "Even when you're about to send me away from everyone I love and care about, you still can't say it."

"Ladybug, don't do this," Ryder said. "You know how I feel about you."

"Do I?" Tears coursed down her cheeks. She looked angry and miserable and then she turned away as if she couldn't take it anymore. "How could I? I'm fourteen years old and you've never, not once, told me that you love me, so how could I possibly know how you feel?"

Maisy felt all of the air whoosh out of her lungs. Perry
stormed from the room. Maisy glanced at Ryder, who wore
an anguished expression as if Perry had ripped his heart right
out of his chest. She reached out and squeezed his arm.

"I'll go after her," she said. "She can stay with me tonight.
I think that's for the best."

Ryder nodded. He looked like a man who had just lost
everything.

Chapter Thirty-one

"AND then what happened?" Savy asked. She was sitting on the edge of her bed, shoving cookie dough ice cream into her mouth as if Maisy were recounting the latest episode of *This Is Us*.

"Travis gave us a ride home," Maisy said.

"Just like that? Ryder didn't say anything? He didn't come after you?"

"Nope," she said. "Perry is down in the hidden room with George and she's going to crash on our couch tonight."

"Wow," Savy said with wide eyes she stared at Maisy. "What do you think is going to happen?"

"I have no idea," Maisy said. She stared at the melted puddle of ice cream in her bowl and felt a sob hiccup in her throat. She was not going to cry. She refused. She was not going to shed one tear over that man. She had promised herself when this started—no crying.

"Oh, sweetie, I'm sorry," Savy said. She put her bowl down and put an arm around Maisy. "I was hoping Ryder was different. I was hoping he was the one guy you fell for that didn't have something wrong with him."

"There's nothing wrong with him," Maisy said. "Maybe he isn't great with verbal expressions of his feelings, but that's pretty common with adult children of alcoholics. His actions speak so much louder than words. I know how he feels about Perry and she does, too."

"What about you?" Savy asked. "Do you know how he feels about you?"

"I thought I did, but it might have changed," Maisy said. As much as it hurt, she knew it was important to be brutally honest, mostly to herself, about the very real possibility that her and Ryder's relationship was over. "He's very unhappy with me right now. I'm pretty sure he blames the Royal Order of George and me in particular for tonight's debacle."

"He'll get over it," Savy said. "He's just not used to life changing the direction of the wind in his sails."

"Wind in his sails?" Maisy asked. "You're awfully poetic tonight."

"I've been reading scholarly romances," Savy said. "You know, *Time Traveler's Wife* and *Possession*."

"Oh, those are good ones. You must be feeling the pressure of living in the shadow of our alma mater," Maisy said. She was quiet for a moment and then she looked at Savannah and said, "You know, I'm wondering if I should have named the shop the Happily Ever After Bookshop, because for the first time I can remember, I'm not certain that HEAs are the sure thing I've always believed them to be."

"No, the name is perfect," Savy said. "Because the books are what inspire us to keep trying to find that elusive happily ever after for ourselves. I mean, really, why should we settle for anything less? Ryder will come around and things will be better in the morning. You'll see."

It wasn't better.

THE next morning, Maisy saw Perry off to school just before Ryder came in the front door. Maisy was working the front counter of the bookstore, which wasn't open yet, and he didn't slow down or stop to chat. He just tipped his head at her and started up the stairs. So that's how it was going to be. The silent treatment. Oh, joy.

Luckily, Maisy was busy. There was a readers' group coming in for their first Regency Tea that afternoon, which Jeri was hosting, and they had decided to hold it in the front room and deck it out with Auntie El's old Haviland china with the pretty yellow roses on it. Maisy'd had Seth retrieve a steamer trunk full of Auntie El's old hats out of the attic. She thought the ladies might enjoy donning hats during their tea.

Not that she was trying to catch Ryder's eye—she totally was—but she was wearing the teal dress Perry had pointed to in her closet as being Ryder's favorite color, and while arranging the hats in the old trunk she found a fantastic hat that looked like a big powder puff in the same teal color. She plunked it on her head, stuffing her curls up underneath it.

She then went back to the counter, where she continued working on her laptop. Maybe it was the hat, but she felt empowered and at least four inches taller. When the workmen trickled out through the shop to go to lunch, she perched on the counter, pulling on a pair of Auntie El's old elbow-length gloves as she waved them out. Ryder did a stagger step at the sight of her and Maisy met his gaze with a wicked one of her own, right over the top edge of her glasses.

Ryder didn't take the bait, however, and after he took a second to collect himself, he followed the men out the door. Maisy tossed a sour look in his direction and settled herself behind the counter and back to work. She was writing the bookshop's first newsletter and she felt extreme pressure to get it exactly right. Ryder had killed her mojo, however, and she propped her chin in a gloved hand and stared up at the newly repainted ceiling, seeking inspiration.

"Don't move!" Savannah cried when she came out of the office. "That is so great!"

She had her phone with her and she began to snap pictures of Maisy. She knelt down and shot from below and then dragged over a chair and shot the pics from above. She fussed with the lighting and the items on the counter. She had Maisy smile, pout, look bored, then friendly, until Maisy put her head down on the cool wood and said, "No more, I beg of you, no more."

"All right," Savannah said. "But these are going to be fantastic on the website and in our social media feed. So retro! Yay!"

With a twirl of her knee-length skirt, Savy disappeared back into the office. Maisy glanced out the door to see if Ryder was on his way back yet. He wasn't. But there was Jeri, dressed in retro chic for her first run at hosting the tea. She was in a high-waisted, bright-pink dress with tiny blue polka dots on the poufy skirt and matching pink high heels. She looked very retro, especially with her pink pillbox hat and clutch purse. Adorable.

A flurry of ladies arrived at the top of the hour. Maisy helped served the tea. Since this was Jeri's show, she had chosen to start the high tea with a discussion of Georgette Heyer. Maisy was more of a glorified waitress, who also happened to be in charge of a cart full of classic Regency romances. When the call came for more petit fours, Maisy dutifully trotted to the kitchen.

She pushed through the swinging door and came to a stop. There he was, right where they'd made love a few weeks ago, and he was standing in front of the counter, looking forlorn.

"Oh, sorry," she said. "I didn't know you were in here."

He didn't say anything. He just looked at her as if he was battling a whole host of emotions and he was trying to figure out which one should win. He walked toward her, and Maisy knew he was going to leave again. Damn it.

"So, is this how it's going to be?" she asked. "We're just not speaking to each other or is it just you not speaking to me, because clearly I'm talk—"

Ryder cut her off by putting his mouth on hers. He looped one arm around her back and hauled her up close while the other hand dug into her hair, knocking her hat off, allowing her curls to spring free and twine themselves about his fingers as if they could hold him prisoner. If only. He kissed her with a single-mindedness, his lips capturing hers while his tongue made a thorough sweep as if trying to taste the essence of her. It left Maisy breathless and clinging to his shoulders.

"Maisy, do you need help in there?" Savy called. "Jeri said you were bringing out more food. I need some pics of the petit fours."

The door started to swing open and Maisy shot out an arm and a foot. She heard a thump and a grunt as Savannah walked into the door.

"Sorry," she yelled. "I'll be right out."

She didn't let go of the door until she heard Savy mutter a confused, "Okay," and walk away.

Ryder let Maisy go and she bent down and snatched up her hat, shoving her curls into it. She must have been making a mess of it, because he brushed her fingers out of the way and took over the task. Neither of them spoke. For Maisy's part, she absolutely didn't know what to say and apparently, he didn't, either.

When Maisy was set to rights, she turned around and grabbed the box of petit fours. Ryder stalled her by catching her around the waist. He leaned close and whispered, "Meet me in the turret after the shop closes tonight."

"All right," she agreed, and hurried from the kitchen. If Jeri or Savy noticed that she was flustered and flushed, they didn't remark upon it. Maisy was grateful because even while she couldn't deny how eager she was to be with Ryder, she also couldn't help fearing that this was the beginning of the end.

THAT evening while Maisy closed the shop, Ryder waited for her in the turret room. The crew had finished it that day, and they were all pretty stoked with how it had come out. A fancy crystal chandelier Ryder had found at an estate sale hung overhead, sending splinters of light all around the room. The turret was mostly large windows with built-in bench seats. The ceiling was high, with exposed beams. The scent of sawdust and plaster lingered, which made him feel as if he was leaving a part of himself behind. When Maisy entered the room, she gasped.

"Oh, wow. It's perfect," she said. She clasped her hands over her heart. "I love it."

I love *it*, not you. He knew he had no right to expect her to say words to him that he couldn't bring himself to say to her, but it didn't change the fact that he treasured those words from her and he desperately wanted to hear them again.

Watching her stand in the room he had built for her, in her pretty dress with her dark eyes sparkling behind her glasses, made his heart swell and ache at the same time. In two weeks, he'd be gone and he wouldn't see her every day anymore. He wouldn't hear her say *I love you*. Despite their being at odds last night, the thought was almost unbearable.

How had she come to mean so much to him? He'd been involved before. Heck, he'd been married and had a child with Whitney, but he'd never felt this way about his ex. The thought made him feel as if he'd done a disservice to them both by insisting on marriage. They had tried for Perry's sake, but there was no question that they had never suited each other.

But this tiny woman, who had made him laugh the very first moment he met her, she had managed to capture his heart. Ryder didn't share his feelings; he didn't talk about emotions. But during their time together, he'd told her about his father, about his brother, about becoming a dad. He'd let her in and Maisy had made it feel okay, like his feelings were safe in her delicate hands.

Ryder watched her examine every bit of the room. The hardwood floor, the window seats, the built-in bookshelves around the doorway. She spun around with her arms spread wide in the circular room, as if it had been made for spinning. The joy on her face made every single detail he had sweated totally worth it.

"Oh, Ryder." She stopped spinning, dizzy on her feet, and lunged toward him. She went a little off course because of the spinning but that was okay because he got to pull her into his arms to steady her. She looped her arms around his neck and pulled him down so she could rest her forehead against his. "I know things are weird between us, because of Perry and the Royal Order of George, but I have to tell you, you've made my dream come true. Thank you."

Ryder reached behind him and snapped out the light so that they weren't illuminated to the outside world. Then he kissed her and held her and rocked her in a slow dance to music he hummed. He just wanted to hold her in his arms and make the moments where she was his last as long as he could.

Maisy seemed to understand. And when she let go of him and stepped back to slide out of her pretty dress, Ryder thought his heart would hammer right out of his chest. The full moon shining through the big windows gave him enough light to see her beautiful skin revealed inch by inch. When his gaze met hers, the sexy glitter in her eyes about undid him.

He shrugged out of his shirt and tossed it onto the ground. Then he scooped her close and swept her down on top of it. If this thing between them was ending, then he had two goals. One was to savor every inch of her and the other was to make replacing him with any other man as challenging as humanly possible. Perhaps it was selfish, but he'd rather have Maisy be a cat lady with King George while running a bookstore than have her hook up with a substitute guy. The mere thought gave him heartburn. If he could make this good enough, maybe he could convince her of how he felt and that distance didn't matter. That what they had was worth crossing the miles between them.

He trailed his mouth down the curve of her neck. He felt her fingers bury themselves in his hair. He placed the softest kisses along her collarbone and down across the top of a breast where he paused to tease the nipple. Maisy let out a sigh that turned into a moan and he smiled against her skin. He moved to the other breast and was rewarded by her response as she arched against him. She wrapped her legs around his hips and drew him against her, cradling his arousal in her soft feminine hold. Ryder's blood ran hot and thick. He wasn't going to let her distract him from his purpose.

He put one hand in between them and spread his fingers across her midriff. He held her still with that one hand, pinned to his shirt on the floor, while he hooked her underwear with his other hand and drew it down her legs. Then he pushed her thighs apart and settled in.

"Ryder, I don't—" she began but he interrupted by blowing softly on the curls between her legs. She gasped and he smiled. Then he kissed her there.

It was a bit of a tussle. She resisted the intimacy at first and he could feel her get tense and self-conscious.

"Shh," he whispered against her skin. "Trust me."

He felt her take a deep breath and force herself to relax. Excellent. He took his time, he savored, he tasted, he nipped, he licked, he suckled, he loved. When Maisy thrashed, lifted her hips, arched her back, and cried out his name on a moan of wonder, he felt a satisfaction he had never known before. He did that. He made her feel that. The only thing that was even close to this feeling was being inside of her.

He kneeled before her and unfastened his pants. Maisy reached up to help him, pushing his jeans down his thighs with her feet, but she was impatient and pulled him back down, guiding him with her hands right where she wanted him to be.

"Oh, sweetheart, the floor is hard—" he began but she interrupted him. She wrapped her legs around his waist and put her hands on his hips, then she pulled him in hard and tight. It was Ryder's turn to moan. Then she pushed him out and he hissed a breath. She was hot and wet and felt so damn good. A couple more times and he had to grab her hands and hold them or he wasn't going to last.

The laughter in her eyes when he kissed her told him that had been her plan all along. But Ryder wasn't going to rush this. Oh, no, if he couldn't convince her that what they had was special and worth keeping then he was going to savor every single second with her.

He rolled so that they were on their sides facing each other. He liked this. He liked the way she fit against him. Then he turned onto his back, so that she straddled him. The mere sight of Maisy, bare breasted and moving up and down on him, almost killed him. He clenched his teeth. He wanted to watch her—every expression that flitted across her face, every bounce of her perky breasts, he wanted etched on his memory forever. When he couldn't stand it any longer, and he felt her begin to tighten about him, he rolled again so that she was under him, and he thrust into her so deeply he was sure they were joined for life.

It was too much. His poor body couldn't help but respond. He felt the electricity coil out from his spine as he hit his peak, forcing Maisy into another one of her own. When their bodies relaxed after the passionate onslaught, Ryder rolled onto his back and brought her with him, so they were nestled together, staring up at the domed ceiling above them, breathing as if they'd just run for their lives.

There was so much Ryder wanted to ask, so much he wanted to say, but he didn't know how. Judging by Maisy's silence, she didn't, either. Perhaps they weren't able to find the words right now, but this, this loving that they shared, was the purest communication Ryder could manage. This woman had him heart, soul, mind, and body, and leaving her was going to kill him.

Chapter Thirty-two

IT was the meeting of the Royal Order of George that made all of the feelings Maisy had been pushing down deep inside of her roar up to the surface like a tsunami after an oceanic plate shift. The group was sitting inside the hidden room, and it was the last meeting that Perry would be attending as she was leaving for school in a few days.

Maisy and Ryder hadn't spoken about Perry, Mr. Hargraves's barn, or anything else, opting to spend each evening in each other's arms working on their nonverbal communication instead. Maisy noticed there was a desperation to their lovemaking, as if they were trying to savor every second together to make it last in their memories when they parted, or maybe it was an attempt to satiate their longing for each other to purge the desire for each other once and for all. Either way, it wasn't working. She knew that it would take a lifetime and forever for her to get enough of Ryder.

The group took turns, sharing their latest good deeds, while they ate chocolate cake, because it was Perry's favorite. When it was Perry's turn, she glanced up from George, who was stretched out in her lap. At a little over two months old, he was so much bigger than when they had found him and yet he was still small enough to be picked up with one hand. His ears stood up now and his face had more angles, which were accentuated by the dark stripes on his forehead and around his eyes. His fur was the softest Maisy had ever felt and even his paws, which, like the tip of his tail, were black, were soft to the touch. He was an amazingly gentle kitten, rarely using his claws. She wondered if they had failed him there. What if he got outside by accident? How would he defend himself if he didn't know how to use his claws? She made a mental note to ask Hannah about that.

"I got up extra early one morning and cleaned out the stables for Uncle Quino," Perry said. Her voice wavered a bit, and Maisy felt her throat get tight. "I haven't had much time to do anything else because I've been packing."

A sob halted whatever she'd been about to say, and Savannah reached over and patted her back. "It's okay, hon. I think you're pretty amazing to have cleaned those stables. I've seen what Daisy can do when she puts her mind to it."

This caused Perry to snort-laugh, and Maisy was grateful to her friend because, honestly, she was going to miss this kid so much, she was having a hard time forming the words to tell her without bawling her eyes out.

"Anyway, I made these for everyone," Perry said. She reached into her pocket and pulled out several string bracelets. "You have all meant so much to me this summer, I wanted to give you something to remember me by."

Jeri examined the colorful friendship band with a tiny silver charm in the shape of a cat's silhouette dangling from it. Then she slipped it on and adjusted the length. She turned it in the light and said, "It's lovely. I am honored to wear it."

Perry's tears were flowing freely now and she scrubbed at her face with one hand. Her voice was tight when she said, "I thought they could signify membership in the Royal Order of George."

Perry held up her own wrist and Maisy saw she was wearing a matching bracelet. She slipped hers on as did

Savannah. They stacked their hands together in the middle of the circle so that they could see all of their bracelets. Maisy looked across at Perry, who was holding George in one arm, and said, "No matter where you go, you're one of us, and we'll be here for you when you need us."

"Without question," Jeri added.

"Always," Savannah said.

"Thank you," Perry said. Then she burst into great big hiccupping sobs. She held George up to her face and sobbed into his fur. The kitten looked alarmed for a moment, but then settled into Perry's hands as if he knew she just needed to get it out. "I don't know how I'm going to leave George. I love him so much. And then there's Cooper, and all of you, and my best friend, Jasmine. I don't want to leave. I feel like I'm going to die."

The last of her words ended in a wail and this time George did leap from her arms. He strutted over to his bed and climbed in, where he began to preen the tears off his fur. Perry buried her face in her hands and cried in earnest. The other women looked at her and Maisy nodded. She knew it was up to her to talk to Perry, since she was seeing her dad and all. Savy and Jeri hugged Perry and then slipped upstairs to leave them alone to talk.

Maisy grabbed a tissue out of a nearby box and handed it to Perry. She used it to dry her face and blow her nose. When she looked at Maisy, she said, "Well, I sure know how to end a party, don't I? Be sure to call me if ever your guests stay too long."

Maisy laughed and then put one arm around the teen and hugged her close. "Aw, kid, I'm going to miss you."

"I'll miss you, too," Perry said. "I feel like my life is this runaway train and I can't do anything to slow it down or stop it."

"Your dad isn't budging about Saint Mary's, huh?" Maisy asked. She had suspected as much, but given that she and Ryder hadn't been talking, it needed confirmation.

"No," Perry said. "You saw him that night at the police station. He is immovable about this. He will do anything, sacrifice everything, even you, if it means I get the opportunities he thinks are so important. How can I fight that?"

"Can your mom talk to him for you?" Maisy asked.

"She tried," Perry said. She shook her head. "No luck."

"I'm sorry, Perry," Maisy said. "I wish I could do something."

"Me, too," Perry said. "But I don't think anyone can help me. It'll break my dad's heart if I refuse to go to Saint Mary's and I love him so much, I just can't do that."

Perry started to cry again. As if sensing he was needed, George came out of his fish shaped bed and climbed into her lap. He started to knead her sweatshirt, making kitty biscuits, trying to soothe his pal.

Maisy sat with the two of them for a while. It was a wrenching moment to listen to Perry say good-bye to the kitten she had helped save. As long as she lived, Maisy knew she'd never forget hearing Perry tell George all the things she felt he needed to know to grow up to be a good cat.

"Don't go off into the woods or you'll be bear food," she said. She rubbed the tears off her face with her sleeve. "Always try to keep the litter in the box. It's rude if you don't. Don't chew the books. While it's lovely of you to catch any rodents or bugs, they do not need to be presented to anyone in the middle of the night, just leave them by the back door to be found in the morning."

Maisy was laughing and crying as Perry went through her list. When she was finished, Maisy asked her if she wanted to have some alone time with George, and Perry nodded. Walking away from the girl with their rescue kitten made Maisy's heart hurt in ways she didn't expect, because she had never felt this sort of loss before. In fact, other than losing Auntie El, she'd never experienced *any* sort of loss before.

It was then that it hit her. What a life of loss did to a person. It made them not trust in the good and the happy. It made them suspicious and ever watchful that it could all be yanked away at any moment. Ryder had lived a life like that. First the death of his mother, then the absentee alcoholism of his father, then his brother took off for parts unknown when Ryder found himself with a wife and baby, and then the wife, who wanted to have a chance to pursue her own dreams, left, too.

And now he was sending his daughter away to the fanciest school in the world. He didn't have to. It was clearly not Perry's choice. So why was he doing it? The answer was so obvious, Maisy thought she would literally stub her toe when she tripped over it. Anticipating the greatest loss of his life, Ryder was maintaining control of his pain by orchestrating the loss himself. If he sent Perry away to the best school, he could make a preemptive strike against the hurt of having his girl grow up and leave.

Well, to hell with that noise, Maisy thought. She stomped through the house, her temper gathering steam like storm clouds on the horizon. By the time she made it out the door to the front porch, where she knew Ryder would be waiting for her, she was practically frothing at the mouth.

She banged out of the house like she was the FBI on the trail of one of their most wanted. Ryder turned at the noise and she had one second to appreciate the beauty that was her man, sitting on the porch rail with this hat tipped over his brow, the moonlight above casting shadows over the sculpted shape of his body. He was breathtaking and for one second she soaked it in. Then she let him have it.

"You!" she said. "I want to have a word with you."

"Maisy? Are you all right?" he asked. He stood up as if he was going to hug her. "You sound upset."

"You bet I'm upset," she said. She held up a hand to ward him off. "I just had an epiphany about you, this, us, and I've got some things to say."

Ryder sat back down on the rail, taking off his hat and tossing it onto a nearby chair. If Maisy could have described his expression, it would have been "shocked with a dash of admiration and a pinch of humor."

"This whole thing is a mess," she said.

"Which thing are we talking about?" he asked.

"Us," she said.

"Phew, for a second I thought you were talking about the renovation," he said.

"No, the house is amazing," she said. "Especially the turret." She didn't look at him when she said it, because she didn't want to remember their nights there together right now. "But we're not okay, not even close."

"Agreed," he said. His voice was so soft she barely heard him and this made her even angrier.

"Why?" she asked. She put her hands on her hips and jutted out her chin. "You show me in a million little ways that you love me, but you can't say it. Why?" His eyebrows went up and she knew exactly what he was thinking. "No, you can't escape this conversation. We're having it and we're having it right now."

"You seem a bit irate," he said. He rose to his feet again. "Maybe if you take a few deep breaths, you'll—"

"I'm not irate!" Maisy snapped. She rolled into her professor persona, making her voice frosty enough to grow icicles. "I'm pitching a hissy fit and it's my first real one, so kindly do not interrupt me."

Ryder sat back down—again.

"You arrived in my life, wearing a cowboy hat, looking like every woman's fantasy of the perfect guy, and then you were kind, funny, smart, and loving. And I realized you were *the one* and that I actually want to be with you today, tomorrow, always."

"Maisy, I think—"

"Hush." Maisy held up her hand. "Here's the thing. I love you. You know this. How do you know this? Because I've told you I'm in love with you. But you've never said it to me, not once, and *you're leaving*." She began to pace the porch, waving her arms while she worked through her ire. "So, here, I finally think I've found one of the good ones, my soul mate, but he's beating feet to git. What am I supposed to do with that? Buck up and have the long-distance relationship I don't want, when he can't even tell me how he feels about me?"

Ryder opened his mouth to speak, but she held up one finger and said, "No!"

"And that's just the part about you and me," she said. "We haven't even gotten to the part about how much I love Perry, and I don't want her to leave, either. Just look at what she made me."

She held up her bracelet but kept pacing, because if she didn't she was afraid she'd do something desperate like throw herself in his arms and beg him to stay or slug him. It was a toss-up at the moment.

"Now, I get that you're the child of an alcoholic and that you lost your mother young. I understand that your entire life has been one loss after another and that by shoving Perry into boarding school, you're preempting the pain you will feel when she eventually leaves, but guess what? You don't get to escape the pain. It will come whether it's in a few days or a few years.

"And here's the really important part. This isn't just about you. You're wrecking lives here, lots of lives. If you're determined to send your daughter to the best school—if you ignore what her heart, my heart, your heart, and even George's heart, want—just because you think this proves you're the best dad, well, then, you've got it all wrong. Being the dad she needs, being here to raise her in a place she loves, with people she loves, that's being the best dad. And if you're doing it to avoid the heartbreak you'll feel when she does leave, well, that's just a chickenshit move and I thought you were braver than that."

Tears were coursing down her cheeks and the sobs had built up in her throat, making any more words impossible. Ryder was staring at her as if he didn't recognize her. He rose as if he wanted to take her in his arms, but she held him off by putting both of her hands up. She couldn't bear it if he touched her now.

"Maisy, I'm sorry. I'm just doing what I believe is best for Perry," he said. His bright-blue eyes implored her to understand. But she didn't. She couldn't.

"If it's what's best, then why are we all so miserable?" she asked. With that, she crossed the porch and went back into the shop. She locked the door behind her and dashed up the stairs to her apartment.

There was nothing left now. It was over. Done. Finished. Kaput. She couldn't stay in a relationship with Ryder anymore. It was just too painful.

* * *

"Y OU wanted to see me, Dad?" Perry asked. She appeared at Ryder's elbow, where he stood looking at the horses in the corral. Quino had a night class going on and light poured out of the barn and across the stable yard. Ryder was standing by the horses that were not being used tonight.

One of his favorites, an old gray nag named Esther, was nudging him with her nose, trying to shake him down for more carrots. Too old to ride, Quino kept Esther around because she had been his mother's favorite horse. Funny, the things people hung on to when they'd suffered a tragic loss. Quino held on to Esther after losing his mom, Maisy held on to her auntie El's house, and what did Ryder hang on to? The pain. That was all he had.

After a childhood spent constantly broke and on the move, he hadn't wanted anything from his father and there hadn't been anything left to hang on to from his mother. Or so he had thought. In the mail that afternoon a very small package had arrived. It was for Perry from his brother, Sawyer, all the way from Texas.

Of all the losses he'd sustained over the years, losing his brother had been one of the hardest. Oh, Sawyer wasn't gone from his life. They talked every now and then, but the closeness they'd shared as boys, surviving dire poverty and an unreliable father, had faded as they both went on with their lives. Ryder's world had become Perry, and Sawyer had left Austin to go find his own way. And yet, today a package had arrived, as if Sawyer knew that Perry leaving for school was a very big deal for Ryder.

"Your uncle Sawyer sent me something to give to you, ladybug," he said. He took the small box that had been in the package and handed it to Perry.

"Uncle Sawyer?" Perry asked. Her eyes went wide as she took the box. She glanced around, looking hopeful. Uncle Sawyer had always been one of her favorite people. "Is he here?"

"No, he's still in Texas, but he knew you were leaving for school and he thought you'd like to have this."

Perry gave him a confused look. She opened the box and her eyes went wide. Nestled inside the dark blue velvet was a pendant. It was a delicate gold chain with a blue sapphire in the shape of a teardrop hanging from it.

"Wow."

"Here," he said. He gently lifted the necklace out of the box and when Perry turned around, he fastened the tiny clasp. She turned back around. The pendant hung just below her collarbone, like it always had when his mother wore it. Ryder smiled past the lump in his throat.

"It's beautiful," Perry said. "But I don't understand. Why did Uncle Sawyer send it to me? Did he break up with another 'special lady friend'?"

Ryder laughed and then cleared his throat. "Uh, no. He sent it to you, Perry, because it used to belong to our mother."

Perry gasped and glanced down at the pendant. "Really? This was my grandmother's?"

Ryder nodded. "I thought it was lost forever, but your uncle apparently got it back from the pawnshop where our father had taken it. I'm pretty sure I don't want to know how, but he did, and he's kept it all these years just for you."

Perry looked awed, which was exactly how Ryder felt. Sawyer. No matter the time or miles between them, they were always connected. Brothers.

"Seeing that necklace reminds me of something my mom always said. When she would tuck us in, she would kiss our foreheads and say, 'You know, I loved you before I even knew you, and I'll love you forevermore.'"

Perry looked down at the necklace and then back up at Ryder. She gave him a small smile and her eyes were watery when she said, "I wish I could have known her."

"Me, too. You have her spark. She would have loved you so much." His throat got tight and he gave her braid a gentle tug. "You know that I feel that way about you, ladybug, don't you?"

She nodded. A tear spilled down over her cheek and she wiped it away.

"I know I never say it, but the truth is I loved you before I even knew you, and I'll love you forevermore."

"Aw, Dad," Perry cried, and she threw herself at him. "I love you, too."

Ryder hugged his daughter tight. He kissed the top of her head and said, "I love you, ladybug. I always have and I always will."

Perry sobbed and Ryder held her. He ran his hand over her back, trying to soothe her just like he had when she was little. When the tears eased and the sobs stopped, he leaned back and studied her swollen eyes and red nose.

"So, about this good deed club of yours," he said. "I know you're supposed to keep it anonymous, but do you think maybe the group could help a guy out?"

"Why?" she asked

"Because there's been a change of plans," he said.

Perry blinked. She studied his face, trying to determine what he meant and then her eyes went wide and she grinned and said, "Yeah, I think they'll be happy to help. So, what's the plan?"

Chapter Thirty-three

MAISY didn't see either Ryder or Perry after her dramatic tirade. A week had passed since her epic hissy fit, and she was sure they were already in Connecticut getting Perry set up at her new school. The thought gutted Maisy.

Ryder was probably over her for calling him out, and she knew she had disregarded Perry's request not to say anything to her father, so she was probably unhappy with Maisy, too. Ugh, the whole messy ending made Maisy's stomach hurt, or maybe that was the half gallon of cherry chocolate chip vanilla ice cream she had eaten with a side of an entire package of Oreos.

She put her spoon in the cardboard container and pushed it away. She was sitting in the middle of the empty turret, wishing she could take back all of the harsh things she'd said while also wishing she had doubled down and said even more until Ryder saw sense.

She'd picked up her phone a thousand times to text Ryder, but she didn't know what to say. King George stuck his face into the ice cream container and came out with a spot of vanilla on his black nose. Despite her misery and her stomachache, Maisy chuckled.

"Oh, George," she said. "You're the one man I can count on, aren't you?"

"Okay, your pity party is getting to be over the top," Savy said. She was standing in the doorway with her arms crossed over her chest. "I ignored the no showering, the midnight-eating benders, and the sound of Carmen Miranda movies coming from your room in the middle of the night, but enough. You have to get back in the game, Maisy. The shop needs you. I need you."

Maisy didn't respond. Savannah wasn't easily ignored, however. She marched across the room and stood over Maisy and said, "You have two choices. You can either get up and go take a shower or I will haul the garden hose into the house and wash you down myself with the sprayer on high."

"You're being awfully aggressive," Maisy said. "I'm brokenhearted—you're supposed to be nice to me."

"I have been nice, but you're starting to smell," Savy said. She grabbed Maisy's hands and pulled her to her feet. "Upsy-daisy."

"Why the rush?" Maisy asked. "Can't I wallow for a few more days?"

"No, the new neighbors have invited us over and we're going," Savannah said.

"Ugh, I don't want to meet anyone," Maisy said. "I'm not up for chitchat."

"Listen, we have a lot of traffic coming and going," Savannah said. She took Maisy's hand and dragged her to their apartment. "No pressure, but you need to go over and be charming so that they love you and don't get annoyed about living next door to a busy bookshop."

"I'll bring them a pie next week," Maisy said.

"No." Savannah opened the bathroom door and shoved her inside.

Maisy thought about lying down on the bathroom floor, but she knew Savannah. She would just plow her way in and bodily toss Maisy into the shower. This was one of the disadvantages of living with an Amazon who thought running and working out were fun. Savy was ridiculously fit and besting her in a show of strength was virtually impossible.

Maisy took her shower, putting in minimal effort. When she got out, a pair of clean clothes were waiting for her, a dress and strappy sandals. Fine. Maisy put them on but she refused to fuss with her hair or put on makeup. Yes, her rebellion was strong! She towel-dried her hair and let her curls do their thing.

When she stepped out, Savannah was waiting for her. She glanced at her phone and then at Maisy. "About time," she said. "I thought you were trying to drain the hot water heater."

"Several days of crud required me to chisel the dirt off," Maisy said.

A small smile played on Savannah's mouth. "Come on. It'll be painless, I promise. We'll just do a pop-in, meet our new neighbors, and ghost out of there."

"Fine," Maisy said. "Where's George?"

"I put him to bed in his room," Savannah said.

Maisy wanted to go visit George. Who was she kidding? She wanted to go hang out with him in the hidden room until the world went away. Savannah kept a grip on Maisy's hand, clearly sensing she was a flight risk.

The late-August evening was cool, a nice break from the humidity of the day. The house next door was another Victorian, but it was square in shape, with a mansard roof and lots of windows.

It had been empty since last year when the elderly owner, Aurelia Ortiz, had passed away. Her children had opted to sell it, since one lived in Charlotte and the other in Raleigh.

Maisy wondered who they'd sold it to and hoped they were friendly. There were lights on in the house and she could hear the sound of music and low voices. Savannah went right up to the door and rang the bell. Maisy looked over her shoulder, longing to be back in her turret, wallowing. She really could have an advanced degree in wallowing, she was just that good.

The sound of someone moving behind the door brought her attention back to the house. She forced a smile onto her face and stood beside Savy, ready to greet the people who would be her neighbors. If they didn't read, that was going to be problematic, but if they dissed romance novels, that was going to be catastrophic. It could lead to a spat, which would escalate, and they might even find themselves on a crime show about bad neighbors.

The door was pulled open, and Maisy opened her mouth to say hi, but the word stuck in her throat. Framed in the doorway was Ryder.

"What the . . . ?" Maisy stared stupidly.

"Maisy!" Perry dashed around her father and hugged Maisy tight. "Surprise!"

Maisy hugged her back and then pulled back to look at her. "You're here."

"Yes!" Perry bounced on her feet. "Dad changed his mind. I'm not going away to school. I'm staying. Are you surprised?"

"Stunned," Maisy said.

She glanced past Perry at Ryder. He was studiously staring at the floor, clearly avoiding her gaze.

"Come on, kiddo, let's give these two a moment," Savy said.

She hooked her arm through Perry's and dragged her toward the open kitchen at the back of the house, where Maisy saw all of their friends gathered. Most of them were watching her and Ryder, and she was suddenly irritated that she hadn't put more effort into her appearance.

"Well," she said. She crossed her arms over her chest. She was flummoxed, good and truly flummoxed.

As if sensing this, Ryder unhooked her arms, took her hand in his and led her into what would have been the front parlor back in its heyday. It was empty of everything but a few boxes and there was a window seat underneath the big bay window. Maisy pulled her hand out of his and sat down, waiting for an explanation.

"I was going to tell you about the change of plans the other night, but I wanted to tell Perry first, plus you were too busy yelling at me," he said.

"You were already planning this?" she asked.

"Partially. I'd already bought the house, figuring if we were going to have a long-distance relationship, I should have a place to come back to," he said. "But then you made me see everything differently, and I knew I had to rethink. But things were in play, so I had to fly down to Charleston and see if I could get out of the contract I'd signed. That required some finagling. And Perry and I had some stuff, a lot of stuff, to sort out, too."

"So, you've been busy," Maisy said.

"Yep, but the biggest challenge was trying to figure out what to say to you," he said. "*I'm sorry* seemed lame, and *You're right* was just so obvious."

"It's always nice to hear, though," Maisy said. She was struggling to catch her breath. He was here! She wanted to hug him, she wanted to hit him, she wanted to hear him say what he was feeling. She stayed still and quiet, hoping.

"So, after our talk, I figured a few things out," he said. "You know, they say actions speak louder than words, but it turns out some people need to hear the words, as they should."

"Do they?" Maisy asked. Her heart started hammering in her chest. She had said that to him. Did that mean he'd heard her, really heard her? "I don't know. Buying a house is a pretty loud action."

"You think?" he asked. "I thought it would seem strange that I bought the house next door since I've never owned a house, but I figured if we want to start a family we'll need more space than the apartment above a bookstore."

"Start a what?"

"A family." He took her hand in his and knelt down in front of her. His gaze met hers and held it, and he cleared his throat and said, "Maisy Kelly, I love you more than I've ever loved anyone before, and I don't want to live one single day of my life without you in it. Will you marry me?"

He opened his right hand and a fantastic sparkler of a ring winked at her from his palm. Maisy was unsure of what to do. Should she kneel also? Should she snatch the ring, so he didn't change his mind? Or should she—

"Say it again!" she demanded.

"Will you—"

"No, not that part, the other."

"I love you," he said. His bright-blue eyes met and held hers. "I love you, I love you, I love you."

The sob that came out of Maisy felt as if it had been ripped from inside of her. Her throat was so tight it burned and she couldn't speak, she couldn't breathe, and she was a little afraid she might pass out.

"How?" she asked. It was all she could get out, but he understood.

"I had to do some soul-searching," he said. "I had to deal with some ghosts."

She looked at him, studying his face, trying to figure out what could have happened that her man had finally found his voice. She wanted to believe him, she wanted to jump all in, but she needed to know the whole story. He seemed to understand.

"The last person I ever said *I love you* to was my mom," he said. "I was seven. I stood by her bedside, holding her hand, it was shrunken and withered, not the hand of the mom who used to pick me up and swing me in circles over her head.

"She had no hair, gone was the long mane of thick black hair that always covered me like a sweet-smelling blanket when she would lean down and kiss me good night. She had become a shadow of herself, this little fragile shell, and I loved her. I loved her so much."

His voice was gruff, tears shone in his eyes, and Maisy felt her heart clench tight like a fist. She could feel his pain. It was raw like an undressed wound and she desperately wanted to help him heal with a hug or kiss. Instead, she forced herself to be still and listen.

"My mom was pure joy, with sparkling eyes and a laugh that was music. When she smiled it was like getting hit with a blast of sunshine. You remind me of her in that way," Ryder said. "As I stood there, by her bedside, I thought if I just loved her enough, if I told her how much I loved her, she would get better. She would come back to me. I clung to her hand, and I whispered to her over and over and over, 'I love you, Mama, please don't leave me.' She died a few hours later, with me still clutching her hand."

"Oh, Ryder," Maisy sobbed. She opened her arms and hugged him close. "I'm so sorry, so very sorry."

He clutched her close and buried his face in her hair.

Maisy could feel the tremble in his arms and she held on tighter. She wanted him to know he could be sure of her. That she loved him and she wasn't going to leave him. Not now. Not ever.

"I've never told anyone that story before," he said when he drew back. "I thought if we were going to build a life together, you deserved to hear it first."

"Thank you," Maisy said. It reminded her of the night he had thanked her after she told him she loved him, and she laughed as she wiped the tears from her face. He must have remembered, too, because he smiled at her. Just to be clear, she cupped his face with her hands and met his gaze and said, "I love you, too, totally and completely."

"Then . . . ?" He let go of her and held up his hand again. The ring sparkled at her. "Will you marry me?"

"Yes!" It came to her then with no hesitation or second-guessing. "Yes, yes, yes, I'll marry you." Then she dropped to her knees to be level with him and looped her arms about his neck so she could kiss him.

Her assault took Ryder out and he sprawled onto the floor, clutching her close and laughing. Maisy lay across him and stared down into his eyes.

"That was a *yes* in case you missed it," she said.

"Say it again," he said, and kissed her.

"Yes."

"Again," he said, kissing her longer this time.

"Yes."

This time he took her hand in his and slid the ring onto her finger. Then he kissed her, not letting her go, even when the door opened and light spilled across the floor onto them.

"Uh-oh," Quino said. "I'm not sure but it looks like she decked him."

"With her lips?" Savy asked, sounding as if she thought he was too stupid to live.

"You can deck me with your lips anytime you want," Quino said.

"Get over yourself," she said. "That is never going to happen."

"People, we're kind of having a moment here," Maisy said

as she wrenched her mouth from Ryder's and squinted into the light at them.

"Ah!" Savy gasped and then she dashed across the room and hauled Maisy to her feet. "Is that an engagement ring? Are you engaged?"

"Yes," Maisy said. Then she jumped up and down. "Yes!"

Savy hugged her and then jumped back to look at the ring. "Nice work, cowboy-architect guy."

"Thank you," Ryder said. Quino held out his hand and helped him to his feet. Ryder looked at Maisy and asked, "Should we tell the others?"

Maisy nodded. He slid his arm around her and they made their way to the kitchen, where Perry and Cooper and his parents, and Jeri and Davis and their boys were gathered.

Quino stepped forward and said, "Everyone, grab a glass."

The group, already smiling at Maisy because they knew that the love of her life was staying in town, complied. And then Ryder took over.

"I'm happy to officially announce that Perry and I will be staying in Fairdale," he said. Everyone cheered. "But I'm even happier to say that I am in love with the beautiful Maisy Kelly and have asked her to marry me. She has, in a singular lack of good judgment, said yes."

Maisy touched her glass to his and they both drank, while the room erupted into cheers, hugs, claps on the back, and joyful congratulations. It was lovely and perfect and Maisy was smiling so much she was sure her face would cramp.

When Perry rushed her and hugged her tight, Maisy held her close for an extra second and when they broke apart, Maisy asked, "Are you okay with this? Did your dad warn you?"

"He did," Perry said. "But I told him it was too late."

"What do you mean?" Maisy asked.

"I already knew you were *the one*," Perry said.

"Oh." Maisy smiled. "How did you know?"

"Because whenever he catches sight of you, he gets that look on his face. It's the one he usually has when he's looking at a house he wants desperately to restore," Perry said. "It's his *She's the one* look. I've never seen him look at a person the way he looks at a house—until you."

When Maisy turned around, she saw Ryder looking at her. It was there in his eyes just as Perry said. She was his and he was hers. Maisy slid her arm around his waist and he pulled her in, wrapping one arm around her shoulders. She melted against his side, realizing that this was the start of something amazing.

"Happy?" he asked her.

"Happily," she corrected him. "Ever. After."

Keep reading for an excerpt from
Jenn McKinlay's next Happily Ever After Romance . . .

THE CHRISTMAS KEEPER

Coming soon from Jove!

She had never believed in love. Maybe for others but not for her. Then he smiled at her, and it was as if she'd found a piece of herself that she didn't know was missing. When he took her in his arms and held her close, she knew that for the first time in her life, she was home.

SAVANNAH Wilson closed the book and sighed. No one, but no one, wrote a love story that hit her in all the feels like Destiny Swann. The woman plucked her heartstrings like a virtuoso playing a sonata.

"Savy, come on," Maisy Kelly said as she entered the room. She slapped Savannah's feet off of the coffee table. She grabbed her arm and hauled her up to her feet, which was no small feat given that Maisy was the short side of petite and Savannah was more Amazonian in height and build.

"I'm reading," Savannah said. She held up her book. "Isn't that sacred time? You own a bookstore; I would think you of all people would respect that."

Maisy glanced at the book. Then she crossed her hands

over her heart and said, "Oh, *Her One and Only*, that's one of my favorite Destiny Swann books. I totally get it, I do, but you're my sous chef, and I need you in the kitchen. Besides you shouldn't be hiding in the parlor when we have a house full of people coming for Thanksgiving dinner."

"I'm not hiding. I'm just not very good company right now," Savannah said. She tossed the book onto the coffee table.

"Work stuff?" Maisy asked. She tipped her head to the side and studied Savy through the black framed rectangular glasses that she always wore.

"Yes, but it's not about the bookstore. It's stuff about my old job in New York, and I don't want to talk about," Savy said. "Thus, the book."

"Escapism 101?"

"I'm getting an A," she said. "Although, Swann does set the bar pretty high in the hero department. I mean what man could possibly live up to Tag McAllister? He's smart, kind, devoted to his grandmother, and completely swoon worthy."

"Maisy, where do you want me to put my famous smashed potatoes with green chilies?" Joaquin Solis called from the doorway.

Maisy glanced at him and then turned toward Savannah with her eyebrows raised above the frames of her glasses as if to say *Him*. Savannah shook her head. It made her long wavy red hair, which she'd twisted into a sloppy knot on the top of her head, unravel and fall down around her shoulders. She glanced at the man in the door.

He was watching her as if he could happily do so for the rest of the day, never mind the Crock-Pot of mashed potatoes he held in his hands. This little bit of domesticity only added to the package of hotness that was Joaquin Solis, but Savannah was immune to him. Mostly.

She could, in a completely objective way, acknowledge that he had a certain something, sort of like acknowledging that diamonds were sparkly and chocolate was yummy. It didn't mean she was going to partake of either and break her bank account or add some squish to her middle. She had greater will power than that. Still, Joaquin, Quino to his friends, was the sort of man who made girls with good intentions do naughty things and not regret it one little bit.

Tall with broad shoulders, he sported a thick thatch of dark hair, chiseled features, and eyes so dark they appeared bottomless. Joaquin was the sort of man women noticed. If it wasn't his rugged good looks and honed physique, it was his wicked sense of humor and flirty ways that made women fan themselves when he walked by with a casual wink and his charmer's grin. It worked on every woman who crossed his path, Savannah had noticed—every woman except Savannah.

While she could admit that he was a fine specimen of a man, she had less than no interest in getting tangled up with Quino Solis. He was as entrenched in Fairdale as the old maple trees on the town green. Their trunks were the size of small cars, and they'd been there since the founding fathers had declared Fairdale a town and planted them in an attempt to tame this wild patch of earth in the Smoky Mountains of North Carolina. Quino was like those trees.

He owned the Shadow Pines stables on the outskirts of Fairdale, where he offered trail rides, riding lessons, and worked with special needs kids using equine therapy. He was never going to leave this town he loved, and Savannah had no intention of staying. Anything that happened between them was just flirting with heartbreak, most likely hers, and she'd had enough of that lately to last a lifetime.

She was leaving Fairdale as soon as she got her old job in Manhattan back and no ridonkulously hot stable boy was going to change her career trajectory. She was one hundred percent immune to him, okay, more like ninety-five percent. But she figured if she stayed out of his gravitational pull, she'd be fine.

"You don't know what you're missing," Maisy said under her breath. She tossed her short dark curls and turned away but not before Savannah retorted, "Neither do you. The fact that you're marrying his best friend does not mean you are an expert on all things Quino."

"I don't need to be," Maisy said. "He is legendary in Fairdale."

Savy rolled her eyes. Like she cared if Quino had dated every woman in their quaint college town of seventy-five thousand. She paused to do the math. If half of the population was women, that was over thirty-seven thousand, and assuming one tenth of them were available, that meant he had dated over thirty-seven hundred women. Was that even possible? She frowned.

"I'll take those, Quino," Maisy said. She scooped the Crock-Pot out of his hands and swept from the room, leaving Savannah and Joaquin alone. Subtle, Maisy was not.

Savannah would have cursed her friend, but Maisy had been doing this for months, pushing the two of them together, clearly hoping to start a romance between them that would prevent Savy from returning to New York. Not gonna happen.

An awkward silence filled the room. At least for Savannah it was awkward. Joaquin just shoved his hands in the back pockets of his jeans and studied her in a way that made her feel like he really saw her and that he liked what he saw. It was too much. He was too much.

She twisted her hair back up into its sloppy knot, and he tipped his head to the side as he watched her, as if fascinated. It made Savy self-conscious, which never happened. Being taller than average with fiery red hair, freckles, and broad features, she was used to being overlooked as unfeminine, more handsome than pretty. She was fine with it, as she liked getting by on her brains more than her looks, but Joaquin never overlooked her. She faced him, crossed her arms over her chest, and tried to stare him down. This was a mistake.

He looked amused as he met her gaze. As if she was issuing him a challenge and he was eager to accept it.

"Quit looking at me like that," he said. The twinkle in his eye let her know he was teasing, but she took the bait anyway.

"Like what?"

"You know."

"I assure you, I don't."

"Like you want me to kiss you," he said. His gaze moved to her mouth and then back up to her eyes. It made her heart beat a little faster. She ignored it.

"What?" she scoffed. "Did you fall off your horse and hit your head? I do *not* want you to kiss me."

"No?" he asked.

He was the picture of innocence, meanwhile Savy could feel her face heat up, because in fact she had thought about him kissing her before. Not right now, but the idea might have flashed through her mind once, okay, twice, all right, probably five or more times since she'd met him but that was only because she hadn't been on a date in months and her hormones were wreaking havoc with her common sense.

"No." The word fired out of her like a bullet shot from a gun.

"Huh," he said. His gaze dropped back to her mouth. "My mistake."

"I'll say it is," she said. She tried to sound indignant but it was shaky at best.

She marched stiffly past him, not giving him a chance to back up as she brushed by his muscle hardened shoulder. A quick glance up and her gaze met his. His dark eyes were amused but they were also full of desire.

It occurred to Savy that all she had to do was rise up on her toes and twine her arms about his neck and she could kiss him and finally put to rest the curiosity she had about the feel of those full lips against hers. Would his kiss be soft or firm, gentle or rough? Would he hold her low and tight or high and loose? Would he bury his fingers in her hair while his mouth plundered hers, making it bruised from the impact of his kiss?

Her thoughts must have been reflected upon her face, because the teasing glint left his eyes and he let out an unsteady breath. His voice when he spoke dropped an entire octave and was little more than a growl when he said, "You really need to stop looking at me like that."

Savy felt a pull in her lower belly as strongly as if he had hooked a finger in her waistband and was drawing her in close. From the overheated look in his eyes, she knew he'd most definitely been thinking about kissing her. The attraction between them had its own sizzle and zip, and she knew if she gave into it, she was going to get burned. She quickly stepped away.

"I don't know what you're talking about," she said. She made an exaggerated shrug. "I was just thinking about how badly my toilet needs a good scrubbing."

Joaquin blinked at her and then he tipped his head back and laughed. Full lips parting over white teeth in a deep masculine chuckle that made her want to laugh in return. Whatever he'd been expecting that clearly wasn't it.

Savy took some satisfaction there, but the grin he sent her was full of admiration with a nice dose of heat, making it nearly irresistible. She fought the urge to fan herself as she hurried to the kitchen to help Maisy with dinner, and maybe while there, she'd just crawl into the freezer until her body temperature went down.

"THE countdown has begun," Ryder Copeland said as he handed Quino a beer. They were standing outside Ryder's half-restored Victorian house in the chilly midday air, because Ryder thought deep-frying a fourteen-pound turkey was the coolest thing ever.

"What are you counting down?" Quino asked. "How long until Maisy kicks your butt for drying out her bird?"

"Ha ha," Ryder said. He gestured to the bird that was sitting in a tub on the wrought iron table beside them. "This poultry is going to be amazing. Just look at him."

"He looks like Dead Weight Dougie," Quino said. "Same male pattern baldness and beer gut."

Ryder looked at the bird, then he picked it up under the wings and made it dance across the plate. "He's got about the same sense of rhythm, too."

Quino snorted. "Worst foreman ever."

"And how," Ryder agreed. "I wonder what ever happened to that guy." He put the bird down with a pat on its rump.

Ryder and Quino had become fast friends, while working construction over a decade ago in Texas, under the dubious supervision of Dead Weight Dougie, so named because he was usually drunk and when he passed out he had to be rolled because he was dead weight and too heavy to pick up and carry. The man spent more time sleeping it off in the bed of his pickup truck than he did supervising his crew.

"No idea, but I'd bet dollars to donuts, he's snoring on someone's couch today." Quino glanced at the stone patio that was covered in a heavy tarp to catch all of the oil splatter. "So what are we counting down, the time until kick off?"

"Nope. The tick tock is for you," Ryder said. "I'm calling you out. You said in July that Savannah would be your wife by Christmas, we are one month out and unless I am misinformed, you haven't even had a date with her."

Quino took a long pull on his beer. "Details."

"Yeah, kind of important details," Ryder said. He squinted at his friend. "She may be the first woman who has not succumbed to the Joaquin Solis magic."

Quino lifted one eyebrow. He knew Ryder was teasing him, and he was cool with that, but his friend was also speaking the truth. Quino had never felt the sting of rejection from a woman before. Savannah was the first woman in memory who seemed indifferent to him. She was a challenge, which he had to admit made her sexy as hell.

"That's how I know she's the one," he said.

"Or *not* the one," Ryder countered. "You've been playing it pretty chill with her, keeping your distance, working the banter angle without being a pain in her ass."

"Is that what she said?" Quino asked.

"No, that's what Maisy said she said."

"I love having spies." Quino grinned. "So, what's the intel. Think she's ready for me to go full court press in the charm and disarm department?"

"Not unless you want to be dropped by a sharp knee to your junk," Ryder said. "Last I heard, Savannah was still planning to get back to Manhattan by the end of the year. She wants her old life back. She's a city girl through and through and living here in the Smoky Mountains is not her bag."

Ryder checked the temperature on the oil in the deep fryer. Then he hefted up the naked bird and gently lowered it into the boiling oil. Quino felt for the bird. Whenever the subject of Savannah moving back to New York came up, he felt exactly like that, a dead bird, hanging by a metal handle from his innards while being dipped in boiling oil. He clearly needed to step up his game.

"Why the face, bro?" Desiree asked as she stepped through the French doors and paused beside him. "You look like someone ate the last piece of pumpkin pie."

Quino glanced down at his sister. She was twenty-five but to him she would always be fifteen. That was the day he stepped up and became her guardian. It hadn't just been legalese so he could take care of her. Quino felt the need to protect his sister, the only member of his family to survive a horrible car crash, all the way down to the soul. He'd lay down his life for her without hesitation.

"Ryder's going to burn the bird," he said.

"I am not," Ryder protested. "You're such a doubter."

"Oh," Desi said. She tossed her long black hair over her shoulder and gave him side-eye. "I thought you were frowning because Savannah is ignoring you."

"She is not ignoring me," he protested.

"Yes, she is," Desi said. Then she grinned at him and hit him with a one two punch of deep dimples and twinkling eyes.

"Snot," he said. He tapped her nose with his finger, the same way he had when she was five and dragging her pink blanket behind her as she tried to follow him on all of his twelve-year-old boy adventures.

Desi smacked his hand away. "Quit it. I'm not five. I'm twenty-five in case you haven't noticed."

"Sorry, you'll always be five to me," he said.

And she would. Not just because she'd been so stinking cute at that age but also because when it came to life skills and common sense that's about where Desi would always be. Her insides didn't match her outsides. The brain injury she had sustained in the accident that had killed their parents had left her as trusting as a child, and Quino was on constant alert to keep her safe from people who would use that to take advantage of her.

Desi blew out a breath and it stirred the bangs that were cut in a blunt line across her forehead. She looked like their mother. The same round eyes with thick curly lashes, the same button for a nose and full mouth that was usually curved into a smile, as if Desi found the world to be a happy friendly place of which she was pleased to be a part. He never wanted that to change.

"One of these days, big brother," Desi said. She looked at him in exasperation, as if she was about to put up more of a fuss, but then the door to the kitchen opened and Maisy popped her head out.

"How's the bird coming?"

"We're calling him Dead Weight Dougie, or Dougie for short," Ryder said.

"Why?" Maisy asked.

"Because he reminds me and Quino of our first boss," he said. "He even looks like him in a bald and paunchy way."

"I am not calling my turkey Dougie," Maisy said. "Perry, back me up here."

Ryder's teen daughter popped her head out beside Maisy's. "Yeah, naming the turkey is weird, and I say this as a teenager well versed in all things strange."

"She's got us there," Quino said. "How about we call him Dougie Fresh?"

"No." Savannah appeared beside the other two. "Focus, people. We're at critical on timing if we want everything served hot. Cornbread and green beans are cooking, while the sweet potato casserole and mashed potatoes are warming up. Get cracking!"

"Time for wine!" Maisy said. She disappeared into the house and Savannah followed with Perry and Desi right behind them.

Quino wistfully watched the redhead, who'd been making him crazy for months, vanish from sight. When the door closed with a decisive bang, he turned back around to find Ryder watching him.

"You got it bad, my friend."

Quino looked at him and said, "To quote your teenage daughter, 'Duh'."

Ryder laughed and then turned away to tend his bird. Quino moved into position to help him hoist Dougie out of the fryer and onto a fresh platter on the table. When they pulled the bird from the oil, letting it drip for a bit, he had to acknowledge that his friend had done an amazing job. Dougie looked perfectly seared on the outside while the juices from the inside ran clear when Ryder stabbed him with a fork. Quino had a feeling this was exactly how his poor heart was going to look if Savannah left Fairdale without giving them a shot.

It was in that moment of turkey clarity that Quino decided he did not want to look or feel like Dougie. It was time to work his magic. The question was how. How did a guy get a gal—who seemed to be attracted to him but was doing her level best to keep it on lockdown—to take a chance?

Flowers? Nah, too cliché. Candy? Same. Plus, he needed to approach her in a way that made her want to spend time with him. She was a publicist. She had come to Fairdale to help Maisy open up her romance bookstore. He happened to know that she was trying to make Maisy's bookstore a massive success not only to help her friend, but also to show the publisher from which she'd been let go, that she still had game. And that, in fact, hers was the best game in town.

Once she succeeded and a job offer came from the Big Apple, she'd be gone, baby, gone. There was no help for it, Quino was going to have to make his move and soon.

Ready to find
your next great read?

Let us help.

Visit prh.com/nextread